dominion

Also by Calvin Baker

Naming the New World
Once Two Heroes

dominion

Calvin Baker

Grove Press
New York

Published simultaneously in Canada
Printed in the United States of America

FIRST EDITION

Library of Congress Cataloging-in-Publication Data

Baker, Calvin, 1972-
    Dominion / by Calvin Baker.
      p. cm.
    ISBN-10: 0-8021-1829-1
    ISBN-13: 978-0-8021-1829-5
    1. Freedmen—United States—Fiction.   2. African American men—
Fiction.   3. African American families—Fiction.   4. African American
farmers—Fiction.   5. Frontier and pioneer life—Fiction.   6. United
States—History—Colonial period, ca. 1600–1775—Fiction.   I. Title.

PS3552.A3997D66 2006
813'.54—dc22   2006041055

Grove Press
an imprint of Grove/Atlantic, Inc.
841 Broadway
New York, NY 10003

Distributed by Publishers Group West

www.groveatlantic.com

06 07 08 09 10   10 9 8 7 6 5 4 3 2 1

For Ariane,
Gift of Paper

dominion

I

chronos

o n e

~~~

They ate the dead that first winter on the land, such was their possession by vile hunger, mean desperation, and who can say what else, other than it was unnatural. Any decent history will vouch for the truth of that. And, according to lore, the majority of the graveless sacrificed were uneasy souls, who walked certain nights on top of the earth—haunting not just the ground of their defilement but all the contiguous lands— until they possessed the entire continent as surely as if they had been more fortunate in life.

Ould Lowe, one from that legion of unblessed, had prowled the wilderness since anyone could remember. Each Sunday he could be seen standing atop the hill on the southern side of the lake, ululating as any wild beast, or grief-stricken man, from the first moments of creation.

It was why the land was sold to him at all, because to put up a proper house there he would have to begin construction on the very spot of the ghost's weekly sojourn. Surveying east and west; north and south—to the edges of the horizon in each earthly direction—Jasper Merian sought a better place, or some compromise that would give him access to his lands without disturbing the unburied. He could see no other way, though, so started digging where he was forced, out there on the very boundary of civilization and silent oblivion. He was not generally a man to go against common sense or community, but this was all any would give him to purchase or settle when he finished his term of servitude.

Nights he went back to the outpost to sleep, until a half-proper roof had been put up out in the forest, over the little shack he had managed. The villagers all stayed away from him once they learned what he was doing out there, but he did not mind. Or rather he learned to show no sign, having concluded in earliest youth certain things about the inner levers and measures of assembled man. There was besides nothing else he might do about it but continue his building.

As for the ghost, he had not yet seen him. Nor was he bothered in the way other men might have presumed to be when he finally did catch sight of the fiend. For when his own forebears arrived on the land, not many years after the first settlement, God had already been brought in to tame the heathen new country—so that superstition and minor deities, along with pestilence and death, dwelled only in shadow and certain corners too mean to allow Him entrance. Over time, so say the writings, other gods would be imported as well, and all stand atop the aboriginal like a totem with none except true God at its sylvanite apex. This was He to whom Merian principally paid the respect of prayer when he paid it to any at all. Owing in large part to this, he saw no need for fear. For another thing he had borne the spirit no insult and looked on his presence not as divergent but an extended part of the numinous world.

When the roof was sound enough from the elements he slept out there his first night, still unafraid. It was Saturday and, if there was anything to lore and ancient saws, Ould Lowe was said certain to be visible in his full horror and abomination that next day. Merian stared out at the stars through his unfinished roof and despaired of other things, but banished them from his waking mind lest he thwart his own enterprise before it was properly begun. As for ghosts, he gave no more thought at all.

Morning was his first on the land, and he rose in the still darkness to make his way to the ceaseless work of clearing away timber for fields and digging rocks from the soil to increase its fertility. They were onerous tasks that on a proper farm would have been distributed among many. He toiled in solitude and did not swear oaths or otherwise complain.

In the small clearing he had already claimed, Merian raised ax to tree and listened to the sound echoing around the forest. He smiled, knowing it was his own woods and, as far as that sound could be heard, more than likely his own trees and property as well. Merian's ground. After this ceremonial first blow, he rolled his sleeves and heaved the ax again, relishing the sound of his effort each time as it rang through the woods, like a shot from a musket, until the energy of his labor was so great that it deflated even this small pridefulness. He was mute as the wood creaked against itself, before crashing to the earthen floor of the forest, exhausted amid a thick storm of dead leaves and debris.

When the great oak finally gave way to his hand, Merian could not contain his vanity and surveyed the increasing space he was creating in the woods, beaming broadly as he imagined with preening care where each field would lie, and each barn, after the main building was finished. None could stop him from dreaming then, as he looked upon his lands and shone like a newborn constellation in the early evening sky. He was twenty-nine years on earth and three months a free man.

It was as he walked over to the downed giant, to clear away its limbs and prepare it to be made into rough boards, that he saw Ould Lowe the first time. Rather, it was then that he heard Ould, for the fury and passion of the creature's wailing caused his heart to stop still in his chest and his blood to run backward through him. When he had recovered enough from his first shock, and gathered courage to raise his head and look upon the beast, it was just as the writings claimed. The specter stood not five paces from the future doorway of the settlement, and held in one hand a great polished walking stick that he leaned upon, having otherwise but one leg to support his immense frame. From his face a pair of deep-set and ill-matching eyes stared out from their withered sockets, each a color and disposition of its frightening own. Merian faced him full, holding the ax still in his hand, and the ghost in turn gazed on the man, holding the staff that supported him in his wandering to and fro between this world and the one not fully known. Neither the living nor the dead moved from the spot where he had staked himself, as Lowe stared the interloper over in appraisal before letting his great bellow curdle the woods again, so that all in town below who heard it knew exactly what strange new sound it was and swore that the fool who bought those cursed acres had met his fitting and proper end out in the Indian wilderness.

"What do you want?" Merian asked, carefully leading the ghost, as he had been instructed, toward a plate of offering he had set out the night before as providence against the creature's coming. The fiend, when he heard Merian speak, began to laugh at his ignorance, as the last to dare address him so boldly was well versed in the left-handed arts, and what even he received for his courage was a fate worse than that of Ould Lowe himself.

When Merian repeated his question, even at once with the ghoul's laughter, Lowe walked to within inches of him, then leaned in closer still and began to swear a string of obscenities that burned in the man's ear. Merian did not move from his spot as the creature spoke but, when it had finished, motioned toward the offering he had set out before. The ghost eyed what was on the plate, made his way toward it—as rapidly as his condition would allow—then seized the platter and flung the thing away into the trees. As it spun through the air he pronounced again his curse over the land and the things that would befall whomsoever should settle there. Merian heard the curse and again approached the creature with calmness, but when Lowe again made one of his violent gestures it sent the man back on his heels in terror and cold blood. The ghost gave pursuit with a quick arm, which Merian neatly dodged and countered with his own fist. The two then locked in the most unsavory embrace and began a fearsome struggle that ended only at the shores of the lake, where their embattled forms seemed as one violent mass. Both were so disheveled, drenched, and unsteady from the effort of trying to master his foe that none looking, had there been witnesses to that epic, would have been able to tell flesh from spirit, body from soul, past from future, or Merian from Lowe, so tangled were they limb against limb in a single coil of mortal and immortal.

When the fight finally reached the banks of the lake, Merian jumped into the water, fleeing from the beast, and Ould came after him in quick dangerous pursuit. This, though, was the man's wish, having heard that any spirit who finds himself in water will soon become disoriented and lose his way there. He hoped it was true, as the Gospels claimed, for themselves, as he dove under the surface of the lake.

Out upon the water Ould Lowe did lose track of his prey and fast found himself unable to distinguish north from south or east from west. Neither could he tell confidently between the natural world of his haunting and the unnatural world that was his proper abode. In this confusion of watery enchantment Merian resurfaced to cast a stone attached to an old chain he had brought with him, around the spirit's neck, and

Ould Lowe sank to the bottom of the lake bed. There his profane songs could long be heard, trapped between Earth and the Palaces of Death, especially each spring when the thaw came, as he tried to find his way to either one world or the other.

In this way did Merian rid his land of the spirit that had haunted it since the ill-starred first settlement, in ages untold. When he arrived back at the shore, he took the ghoul's stick and his own knife and began to carve a leg for the drowned ghost.

When he finished he was shivering and graycold, as he buried it under an outcropping rock on the shore of the lake, hoping this was the reason of Ould Lowe's wandering and that its cenotaphic restoration might bring him peace.

Years later, when his sons wanted to take a certain stone and put it to use as a boundary marker, Jasper Merian would tell them it was no mere rock but a gravestone for the spirit he had battled in order to win their place of home. They would look at each other then, silently, and though both knew better than to say so out loud, in his heart each refused to believe his father but that he was telling stories.

When he had finished his tasks on the side of the lake, Merian went back into the forest and began readying the fallen timber, as if nothing strange or unearthly had happened on his farm that morning. The forest brightened with birdsong, and he worked serenely to hasten the day when he would no longer be forced to sleep half out-of-doors, under the naked canopy of heaven, as he had done so many twilights since leaving Virginia.

Over the course of the summer Merian's house continued to rise from the floor of the virgin woodlands, and he planted crops in the ground, both foodstuff and tobacco to trade for cash. That summer in the clearing he was master of both masculine and feminine tasks, as there was not yet a mistress of the place to give him comfort in his toil. It was then, in those first days, a sad house even after the roof was completed.

In his private heart, however, he was not without companionship but thought often of the saltwater woman he had left behind in Virginia. He dreamed of her often as he worked outside in the hot months, and he dreamed of her when he lay down at night in the cold first hours of winter. The force of these nostalgic passions took him unguarded, as he had never before known the occult powers of memory so fully but only seen them in others, seized and bound by its invisible teeth and shackles. He himself had never before been separated from kin and home, or had any one thing or place to miss.

He was far away as the other shore of the ocean but swore to himself he would someday return.

He had left behind—more than just the woman, Ruth was her name— a small child as well, whom he could not take with him, as he belonged properly to his mother and her master.

He knew it would be at least a year before he would see either of them again, if indeed he ever did. He planned, though, in his brain and bosom to recross the trail that had brought him out to this forest in time for next holiday season. It was a hard and solitary home in those early days as the roof went up in the clearing, and Jasper Merian was alone in the ancient forest with nary a beast for company.

Jealous neighbors swore that his success, when it came in time, grew from a compact he had made with the same devil who once frightened travelers on the southern and western roads. But he wrestled the wilderness as he did Ould Lowe and the rattling forces of fear, those first days, trying to gain permanence and soundness for his roof and the empty room beneath it. Over years and generations the path crossing westward grew broader, and smaller paths cut back across it in every which direction, so that no place was ever again uncharted or alone. However, Merian then lived pressed against the very boundary of the known, and the two roads were barely new-blazed trails that took the nearby settlement the last provisioning stop before the unknown.

Populations looking over that place in distant years would not know how fearful and wild the woods were, or the bright beauty of light when it reached into the provinces that darkness alone had known when beasts still fought and foraged the ground, before the man claimed it for himself. These, the wind, the shadows, and the light, were his companions as he pitted his wits against the forest to draw out partridge for dinner or else outmaneuver the straggling bear who ventured sometimes uncomfortably close to his door.

When the woodlands went barren and his own provisions also failed, it was the same old bear who supplied him with its sweet meat the last weeks of that first winter, without which he would not have made the spring. The bear was felled with a single ball from the musket, it being old and unwilling to cling too fervently to life, or surely it would have claimed victory over the man in that contest, and lined its own hungry early-waking stomach with human flesh.

After the first of his meals of bear meat, venturing over the property he had purchased, Merian stopped to measure again what was his, arguing with himself the finer points of possession and trying to fathom certain secrets from the webbed, foggy circle of his experience. He asked himself whether that which was half divine on the place belonged to him in equal measure as things like the partridge and cypress. He also counted his own freedom and the depraved fiend Ould Lowe in that same lordly grouping of things and saw how much all of them struggled and bargained against one another, so that his life or another's, his freedom or his failure, were things that circled about—like-shaped and taloned as eagle's claws—looking for a place to grab and rip at their natural or made prey, as had always been and would always be on that place. His supremacy on his lands increased something great that morning, and he knew he would not die of starvation or ever allow himself to get so close to hunger out in the forest again. Other monstrosities he knew not the names of, but was certain that they would come as inevitable as hardship. However, having staked so much already to achieve the trove of freedom, he would do anything to preserve and keep it with him. He muttered the name of the fiend to himself and swore that, as he had vanished it, so would he everything else that stood in the way of his well-being and prosperity.

Spring, he set his sights to improvements upon the bare hut and fields he sowed by hand. In order to make the most of what was his, though, he knew two things were indispensable: the first being a good mule, the other a woman. Nor would he let a shortage of funds keep him from either.

To get the mule he saw no other way than to steal it, so woke early one morning and made his way out to those stretches of the trail in the mountains where no law ruled but only strong arms. When night came he made his way toward a camp and untied one of only two pack animals that belonged to the party traveling away.

In the darkness he led the mule over the ridge of earth back to his lands. Morning found the beast learning to bear the yoke instead of other burdens.

In this way he would clear twice as many acres that second spring as he had the first and increase vastly that year his purchase over the wilderness—where he had gone, when none other would go there, to make a home in the world where none existed before him and all said none could be made, to exist and hold him.

For the woman he turned in other directions. At the settlement's center was a tavern where one of three rooms could be rented by those with no other place to stay the night or, if so happened, the month. This is the same outpost where he had spent the spring before his own roof was yet ready to cover him. The proprietors of the inn were free-thinking people and had been the only ones who did not shy from him when they learned where he had bought and was building. They had even nodded on it as the scientific thing for one in his position who wished to improve it. As he did not see a way to steal a woman as you would a mule, he turned to these friends for advice as to where he might find one who was eligible.

"I am looking for a woman. Do you know where I might find one?" he asked Content, the husband.

The two looked at each other when he put this question out, and at first made no reply.

"Well, you might do as I did," said Content, "which is to search in the church."

"No," Merian answered his friend.

"What do you mean no?"

"That I will not look there. I cannot go."

"Of course you can. If they are not set up for it, they are certain to make arrangements."

"That is not what I mean."

"What is it you do mean, Merian?"

"That I have no faith in that course."

"Still, you should go there if your aim is a wife."

t w o

The man rises half clothed in darkness and dresses himself fully. At his fire he heats yesterday's porridge for his breakfast, then sets out on his journey. A cold spring rain belts the landscape, and he pulls himself tight trying to keep warm. He is solitary and on his way.

His cold form plows the gray empty roads of Sabbath morning, but he is happy to walk out here without encountering anyone. He holds his thoughts close to himself as the goose bumps on the underside of either arm, which are wrapped around his coldness. He does not consider himself to be making a sacrifice, or ask for special favor or forgiveness from Providence for this great effort in getting to the meetinghouse, but wants only to sit as a parishioner among parishioners and a believer among the devout. He will do this to gain their human company and does not think any more or less of himself for it; certainly he does not think it a thing to speak to God about in the silent talking back and forth that Protestants and Deists do with their Lord, or pagans and hypocrites with their idols.

He wishes for and, in his mind, talks to the mule—whom he could not resist naming after his former companion, his wife, even if there were some who would not agree to that term, as they had not been wed in church or made any other formal arrangement with authority.

He curses himself for not saddling the beast and wishes for its presence. If you were here, Ruth, he whispers against the morning wind, this road would not be half as hard on a body. He wonders now whether he should not turn back and spend his Sunday improving the hut or sorting his grain for the first planting. He frets over these constant worries, as well as the minor ones that have occurred to him only this morning. What if the congregation judges him in an unkind light and is not willing to have him among them? Or what if there should be no eligible women? He knows he is foolish to have taken Content's advice. As the rain pounds down on his shivering body, still before daybreak, he thinks again of turning back. It is dishonest, Jasper, he argues with himself. You going to take another woman, and already Ruth back there in Virginia with the little one.

He stops this talk as a terrible creaking sound reaches him from somewhere on the road above, whence he has just passed. It takes him near a minute before he recognizes the timbre of its complaint and realizes it is Lowe, cursing or else singing, from the bottom of the lake where he was fastened the year before. Something has disturbed him there. Merian starts and hurries on his way, lest he have to repeat again a history already settled and past. Who should like to repeat his own story? Merian asks himself. What man can be certain that victories once his would be so again? He hastens on from the sound of Lowe's voice, picking his steps with less care and greater speed, over the muddy roadway in the first light of Sabbath day.

He reaches the outpost without further incidence and finds his way to the meeting place, opposite the unkempt square. Outside, he stands for a long moment and looks to the eaves and joints of the building, admiring the workmanship, before removing his rain-soaked hat from the top of his head and entering. In the back of the church he finds a seat and takes his place, but does not make eye contact with anyone. Some smile on him, even those who in other rooms would shoot him for his boldness with no further question over the matter than that. He waits for his friends, then begins to grow angry at Content for not coming, feeling even greater betrayal when a hand seizes his shoulder, making him startle.

"Welcome." A voice greets him. It is the preacher, and Merian nods his head in an idiosyncratic bow of acknowledgment that moves three fourths the way down his neck before quickly accelerating the last quarter bit, and snapping back to forward attention. He does not remove his gaze from the room the entire time, nor, when the preacher goes off, does he feel any more at ease, but regards it nevertheless as an opportunity to take in the compass of the assembly.

The gathered parishioners try to avoid seeming rudeness and avert their eyes when he looks at them, but try as well to seem open to all who would come and worship there. He sees the mason to whom he had occasion to sell some of his unused boards, and the merchant who sold him grain, as well as the smith and some few others he had come to recognize from his winter there in the village center.

Other than those few the faces were entirely strange to him, and more numerous than he seemed to remember the population as being. Their collective impression on him was not unlike the meetinghouse he visited from time to time with Ruth back before leaving, except, if anything, those here were even more hardscrabble and wanting. He surveyed them again and counted his chances for success very small indeed, as it seemed unlikely that any among them might spare even a heel of bread, let alone a grown daughter. And if they should chance upon some generosity, he counted himself near the last who might receive it. His mission already a failure in his mind, he kept his eye open for his friend so he might abuse him openly for sending him so out of his way.

When the sermon finally started he could only figure that the preaching had something to do with the intersection of wilderness and temptation, but then every sermon he had ever heard seemed to have in it something to do with wilderness and something to do with temptation, unless it was the one about kingdom and wickedness.

"We are congregating with wickedness right here among us," a man from the congregation testified, when the preacher had finished the formal sermon, staring hard at Jasper, as each parishioner spoke in the voice of his guiding genius. "It seems hypocritical to tolerate in the flesh what you would not in words or in the spirit."

His words went unremarked upon, but all knew they were a reference to their outland neighbor. Merian himself sat rigid and did not need to look at the parishioners to know that their eyes were on him, in either judgment or sympathy. His own emotions, though, clenched up as he tried to contain them. When the service was over, he bundled himself again, made his way back into the unrelenting rain, and started out to his own lands, wondering where else now to find a woman.

On the unpaved road he spied Content and tucked his head into his coat, trying to go on unrecognized.

"I am sorry we were not there, but Dorthea has come down sick. I spent the morning at her bedside," Content said, after catching up to him.

As Merian listened to these words he could barely look at the man without anger. For the sake of former friendship, he held back from saying that it was an outright lie he was hearing and had walked seven miles through the rain to suffer. He felt a great anger at his circumstances. If he were more prosperous, he explained to himself, there would be no need to resort to desperate works to achieve his ends and desires in the world.

"Let me make it up to you," his friend offered. "Next week we are celebrating Easter and would be much pleased if you came."

"It is a fairly long way, especially in weather," Merian reflected, letting his accusation hang there as Content looked at him. "I will see how it is next week."

"Well, we would be much pleased," Content said again. "And I am sure there is bound to be a woman there or two. I know at least Dorthea's cousin is coming from the coast."

"I will see what the weather is, " Merian replied. "It is not so short a way for someone walking in foul elements." At that he took his leave, bundling himself back into a knot of angry shivers and tension that warmed his muscles briefly against the springtime cold.

The next week brought nothing but more weather, and Sunday was the wettest day among them. Under his roof, Merian pattered about, preparing his porridge and trying to decide whether he would go into town or not. He listened to the spikes of rain hammering the boards and, in his own self, felt emotions hard and bitter that the growing season had still not arrived and his fields remained untilled. Beyond this, he felt a deep sense of gnawing discomfort that was not so sharp or hateful as hunger but reminded him of an abiding sickness. He knew it was loneliness that roiled within him, for he had been out on the land over a year and a half with scarce any human company. Still, he was surprised to find it so sharp within himself, for he seldom felt need for association of any kind. He remembered then the celebrations of springtime they had had back in Virginia, and how he felt among them like part of the company, even if he could not always share fully in their belief. If only for the sake of this remembered fellowship, he resuscitated his expectations, allowing that he might join in the Easter Day services and the festivals that followed.

He dressed himself diligently before the low flames, taking from a stool beside the fire his pants, which he had washed by hand the night before and hung to dry. From a box beneath the bed he removed his other shirt and wrapped it around his body. At the flame again he took a piece of glass and a sharpened knife, which he lifted to his throat and began scraping until his neck and face were passable smooth. Outside, he saddled the mule with the harness it wore when he first liberated it from its former captivity and climbed on top of the animal. Man and beast then were prepared and headed down the road combined in a single quixotic form.

At the bottom of the hill he listened again to the ghost, singing with even greater strength than before. The creature's tortured sound caused him to stopper his ears in fear, with the base of his palms pressed against his minor lobes, as he knew everything that lives, or else half lives, does so on the constant edge of annihilation. There were those who saw this edge and got on with it—that is to say past it, smartly—and those others who looked on it and passed through the rest of life in paralysis of fear. The beast sang its dirge. Merian adjusted himself in the saddle astride the mule and coaxed it into a faster and faster trot. The animal would never reach anything even approximating a proper gallop, but it gained speed enough to hurry him beyond the sound of singing and on his chosen way.

The mule moved over the muddied pathways toward civilization, sure-footed even without the man's hand guiding its journey, until they neared the settlement's center. Half a mile from the burgeoning square, the animal came to a flat stop and refused to budge, regardless of goading or the eventual outright violence. The spot where it stood was the railing next to a stone-built house with a plot just inside the fence. Instead of keeping to the road, the animal shoved its head between the slats of wood and began rooting in the garden for whatever might reveal itself.

From the side of the house a man, who had watched and saw this, stepped forth and called to the two of them. "We just planted that ground."

"I don't know what her interest is in it," Merian replied, whipping at the animal's hide. "You know how mules are."

15

"I know that mule," the man said, walking closer toward them. "It belonged to Mr. Potter, who took his family west last spring."

"Wrong mule," Merian answered.

"Well, I would swear."

"You would be lying." Merian looked the man in the face, and the man looked away, past him at the animal, then back toward the house.

"I didn't mean nothing by it. It's just I had a neighbor with a mule that was the image of that one, liked to root in the same spot."

"Must be something there that attracts them all," Merian said.

"Must be," the man returned, then took a half eaten and moldy apple from his pocket and offered it to the animal.

The mule lifted its head from the soil and nuzzled the man's hand, taking the fruit from his grasp.

"Mule's name was Potter too, just like the man. It liked apples nearly as much as yours here."

"Well, we thank you for it, friend," Merian answered, as he coaxed the animal back onto the road and they finally turned toward the square. The animal finished the apple in two great bites and began to trot again. In its mouth the taste of fruit was ancient and sweet.

three

The spring when he was released into the company of manumitted men, all were told by court and legislators they could not remain in the colony but had to leave under penalty of death. Those who did not hide and ransom their lives to chance in order to stay near loved ones and old ways joined the lines on the roads heading north and west at the beginning of the year. The month when he set out had been marked by pox, but it was very mild that year and put in check before too long, so that only twenty thousand souls died in the season. It was this fever and dying that he would associate with springtime for the rest of his days. On the square that morning it was brought to mind as bile welled in his throat and he tried to turn it back down, to force himself into better spirits before the Sunday service.

He dismounted outside the tavern and tied Ruth Potter to a railing, then straightened his shirt and went across the square to the little building that served as a church. He was met at the door by the sound of communion and found Content and Dorthea among the milling crowd, enthusiastic to see him as they attempted to banish any possible ill feelings from the previous Sunday. Merian nodded warmly, acknowledging that their fight was now behind them, and followed the couple into church, where they took a pew in back. Some who noticed him there a second week tried to be more generous in their gestures toward their outland neighbor. There were of course also those who did not. He took both sentiments in stride as he sat on the bench and listened to the Easter service.

That week was a different preacher than the one before, and his talk was all of schisms and something he kept calling Utopia, which they would build right there in the newbornland. The sermon was a towering success, and everyone brimmed afterward with talk of this grand enterprise the preacher kept calling by that name all the rest of them seemed to know. The idea, at least in its rough form, was not unknown to Merian, but the word itself was new, and when he asked about its exact meaning later he was told it was a vision for the perfection of place. He smiled with pleasure, savoring its optimism. It was years before he found it also meant nowhere.

"I am building a utopia in the woods," he said, later that afternoon, when he was introduced to Dorthea's cousin, Sanne.

"Are you now," she asked, with bemusement. "And how far have you gotten with it?"

"Oh, I'd say about as far as that preacher," Merian answered, his face atwinkle.

Sanne cast her eyes downward, then looked across the room, where Dorthea was busy attending to her other guests. "I had better see if my cousin needs any help," she said, and with that slipped out of the range of his admiration.

"I see you met Sanne," Content remarked, when he found Merian in a corner off to himself, appraising the room.

"I did."

"What did you think of her?"

"She is lovely," Merian answered, holding in check anything that might appear overeager. "Is she married?"

"Widowed," his friend answered. "Since a year ago."

"How many children did he leave her?"

"They had none."

"That must be very hard for her," Merian said, looking out into the crowded room and trying to make sight of her. He said nothing else but felt a growing wave of empathy for the woman who had suffered what everyone he knew seemed forced to bear: to be widow or widower or else orphan—as he himself was—or in some other manner bereft of kin and mooring to fellow beings. It is simply how things go, he thought, and no use complaining over it.

18

When Sanne gathered the courage to look over at him again, a sadness sat on his face that made her want to reach toward him but also to draw away, for she could not read what was behind it and distrusted any emotion in people so close to the surface.

What if he is in his nature just a sad man? she wondered. She could imagine few worse things than to be perpetually phlegmatic. It would be worse than a curse, she surmised. Not that she herself was all light humors, but she believed in governing what was willful or overstrong in Nature.

When he caught sight of her staring at him, Merian flashed her a smile of such easy warmth she could not help but beam brightly in return. Why do the sad ones always have such lovely smiles? she thought to herself, starting to smile about the corners of her mouth almost involuntarily, though there was nothing insincere in her gesture.

Before he left that afternoon, Merian made his way purposefully toward her. "We did not talk as much as I would have liked," he said, "but I hope I might happen to see you again."

"I will be back for Whitsunday," she volunteered.

"What is that?" he asked, knowing neither what it meant nor, more important, how far away it was.

"It is also called Pinkster. Seven Sundays from today."

"We never had that where I grew up," he told her.

"It will be a grand carnival."

"I think I would enjoy that," he answered, and took his leave, much better pleased than the Sunday before.

As he made his way home on the western road he watched the sun beginning to set over the countryside and its final plunge of red intensity over his own land. I am building a utopia in the wilderness, he said to himself, quite satisfied, as he egged Ruth Potter up the hill to his front door. And his spirits were so lifted that it did not seem so much like a joke to him as a thing he might actually achieve.

His first year he had approached the farm with all the enthusiasm of a new transaction, but he went to work on the fields that spring with a new confidence and even greater energies than the one before. As the

19

first shoots of his crops poked forth from the black soil, his diligence toward them was unflagging. He was not grumpy when he rose in the morning to go out, but eager, and he worked through the day sustained by this same feeling. He found himself hopeful in ways he had not dared express before, even in the final days of his servitude. He thought often of the woman he would meet again at the new holiday and imagined her within his rooms. It was greatly relaxing to his mind, and he would fall asleep with romantic notions he had not entertained since his separation from Ruth.

When Whitsunday came, he dressed in his clean shirt again and saddled the mule, then climbed astride, carefully guarding a bouquet of wildflowers in one hand. Outside of the settlement, the mule slowed down in front of the house where it had paused before, but he was able to keep control of it this time and persuade it to continue on. The animal obeyed and carried him on into town, where they stopped outside the inn and rested.

Merian dusted his shirt, rearranged the flowers in his hand, and went inside. The first person he saw when he opened the door was Dorthea, and he found his courage leave him, not knowing what was proper behavior under the circumstances.

"Merian, what pretty flowers," she commented when she saw them.

"I am glad you like them. I thought they might look nice on the table," he answered, thrusting them at her.

"Sanne, look at the lovely flowers Merian brought from his place," Dorthea said, drawing out her cousin.

The other woman came over slowly, cautious both of him and of seeming too bold. "They look wonderful," she offered stiffly. "What are they?"

"Why, they are utopia flowers," Merian answered. "You must see the place I picked them someday."

Dorthea looked at her cousin with a sidelong glance from a corner of her eye, but Sanne cast her look away in shyness at Merian's offer—although she did not fail to smile.

"If you keep asking, perhaps I will," Sanne replied at last, before hurrying away across the room on an invented errand.

Throughout the afternoon the two of them went on to trade nervous and youthful looks when they thought no one else might notice them. During songs they gazed at each other more brazenly, staring directly across the room as they sang. It was a joy for him to hear songs sung he had not heard since his childhood, as well as those altogether strange to him, which Sanne said she learned as a young girl.

At the end of the evening he bid her good-bye and asked again when they might next meet.

"I am staying here for a few weeks," she answered. "You can stop by when it pleases you."

Merian promised to visit, and even though he thought they had gotten on well, he was careful not to presume that the invitation meant anything more than that.

That evening, after their guests had departed, Dorthea and her husband questioned their houseguest good-naturedly but reminded her all the same how little they still knew about Merian and advised her to proceed with what care she thought due.

"How much do we ever truly know about anyone, other then the way they strike us ourselves?" she asked, but said no more.

Husband and wife looked at each other across the table. Both, however, allowed she was a grown woman and said there was nothing more to be argued. Still, they reminded her again it was her own self at stake.

Two days after the celebration, Merian found himself in town again for reasons scattered and varied, and after buying supplies he stopped off at the inn to call on his friends. As it grew late they invited him to stay on for dinner, out of politeness, and were genuinely surprised when he accepted.

"You don't have to be in the fields in the morning?" Content wanted to know.

"I suppose things there can get on a bit without me," Merian answered.

"Why, Merian," Content said. "I've never known you to be slack about work before."

"A man can't just work and nothing else," Merian replied, looking at Sanne. "There are other things."

The four of them, each with their own ideas, then went out into the kitchen, where the men sat down at table as the women served.

At the end of dinner the entire company found themselves in quite good spirits, and even a bit drunk as the evening ended. "Well, I must get back," Merian said, bidding good-bye to his hosts.

"It is too dark to be out on the road now, even for you," Content warned. "Stay in one of the empty rooms and get a good start in the morning."

"I cannot impose further," he answered, looking again to Sanne. The widow woman cast down her eyes but smiled softly from the side of her mouth. It decided for him his action and he was shown to the small room he had stayed in many times before.

He had never, however, heard the night there open up with singing, as he recognized through the wall one of the hymns Sanne had sung to him that previous Sunday.

He listened to her voice in long measures of closed-eyed well-being, then sang back softly from his small room the refrain as he remembered it. When their singing stopped, the entire house was quiet and drawn in darkness.

See the man in darkness. He rises and goes to the woman in her quarters, where he gets in bed next to her and bundles in the warmth she gives off under the covers. The woman is stone still and tries to slow her breathing so he will not hear how it catches in her throat or the thump her heartbeat makes under her bed gown. The man hears only this, and his own breath adds to it, coming harder the closer he moves toward her. She is generous fleshed. He is greedy of it but tries to restrain himself. Man and woman lie with each other in the dark chamber and fill it with a muffled paean of wanting that nonetheless does not disguise the expression of what is tender in their thoughts for each other.

It is morning soon.

four

Devotion to Sanne was natural as desire for almost everyone who knew her long. For Merian, though, it did not come so easily and, in fact, did not arrive fully for many years. It was not that he found her wanting for any of the good attributes of her sex, but simply that attachment for him was slow to come always, even to his first wife and own boy.

Devotion to him came slowly to Sanne as well, because they had come together in haste and also possibly that she was no longer a girl but a full-grown woman, with one husband already in the ground. Perhaps this one would also die in her arms.

In fact, not until well after the time that their child was born did she find in her bosom a deep wellspring of loyalty and love for the father as well, and it was said this emotion came then not because of domestic need and convention but because they had donated each from their own personal treasure to the crucible of common creation.

When they first arrived at the farm, after concluding their contract, he showed her those acres he had bragged about before with self-consciousness.

Well it is no utopia, she thought to herself but, when asked her opinion, answered instead, "In time it just might grow to be something."

She began in those early days, as he had two springtimes before, with the very basic tools of sacrifice and a task before her so overwhelming she found it best not to think of its completion—but rather that each chore was a step whole in itself—so that she might live in small victories instead of constant setback or failure. She was alone then as Merian himself had been in his first days, even as he toiled in the fields beyond the house, which seemed to her like leagues away.

Besides the great mass of dust she found caking every exposed surface in the room there was the matter of the measly fireplace, which was little more than a circle of stones under a too-small hole in the roof, and that circle hardly big enough for cooking with more than one pot. The vegetables he grew in the garden were not enough for proper sustenance, and of household hardware there was nothing but a knife worn down to the thinnest strip of metal and a spoon that looked like it had been used for digging in the dirt. These were merely the things that caught her eye upon entering her new abode. She knew there was likely to be much worse when she started looking, and great labor indeed if the place was ever to be made a home. She set about this self-assigned task with iron resolve, mistressing those things he had failed to master even in his other victories, great and small, in the wilderness miles from the end of the road—and quite a ways farther from the seashore, which was her natural home.

She tried never to feel self-pity or doubt as she contemplated the works in front of her, but simply labored at improving her lot, so that when she finished they could no more properly be called Merian's acres. That is still how they were known for a time, but from her first day there it was a misnomer.

Inevitably, as she went about rearranging things, the time came when the place also began to show its secrets to her, and she learned what was on the bottom of the lake bed. It was as she did the washing on the shore, at the end of their newlywed weeks, and counted the small victories she had already achieved, that she learned what was the matter with the land that her husband struggled so hard against. She wrung the washing, feeling pleased with her accomplishments, and began pinning it in the trees, when she suddenly heard the sound of Ould Lowe's canny voice calling filthily to her. She knew immediately what it was she heard, though she had no name for the specific fiend.

When she broke free of the fearful spell the beast was trying to enchant her with, she marched directly back to the house to await her husband's arrival. Shortly Merian came round from the fields for the midday meal, and she asked him what kind of land it was they lived on again.

"It is our utopia," he said, filled with the sweetness of their young union.

"It is devil's ground," she retorted. "Now, what is the thing out in the lake?"

"It is vanquished," he insisted, giving her its name. "At least it was till you come."

"It is half done, like everything else around here," she replied, beginning the first fight of their marriage.

They rowed all afternoon, and when he finally considered the argument finished and done Merian went back to the fields. When he left, she went to the corner where her wedding trunks were still stacked and removed the chain that had fastened them together, then went back to the lake, where she found her laundry no longer pinned to the trees but floating out on the water.

After removing her boots, Sanne waded into the lake, calling to the ghost as she went, "I don't know what you are, but you'll not haunt this house."

When Lowe heard his prey and himself spoken to, he reached out blindly to the woman and dragged her by the feet until she was submerged. Beneath the surface of the lake, he pulled her toward him in a ghoulish embrace with his heavy arms, where he might make her his favorite new plaything. Terrified, Sanne struggled to free herself of the monster's grasp but could not break his hold until she was near enough to smell his skin. When she was, she needed no dark arts but gouged at his strange multicolored eyes until he let go of her.

The beast relinquished the woman only with hesitation, even in his great duress of pain, and churned at the water in anguish. Once he had relinquished her, Sanne took the chain she had brought with her and bound him, arm and leg, then shut tight a lock around its links so he could no more harass her household. When she had finished, Lowe sat alone on the bottom of the lake, restful as a monument of one in heaven.

She returned home that evening, satisfied with her work, to find her husband waiting for her to make his dinner. "And who cooked for you before?" she wanted to know.

"I did it myself," he answered.

"Then it is not so long that you have forgotten how."

"You're not going to feed me?"

"Isn't it enough I left my home for you?"

"I gave you a new one."

"It is filled with bad omen."

"It is virgin and must be tamed as all land like it, if we are to have a place."

"I once had a home."

"You are free to go back to it."

"And what waits for you to return to it?"

So continued their fight until she barely had voice to speak. "I left my home for you," she said again, before falling asleep, not knowing what future her union to him held or what future of any kind she might expect anymore.

The land, though, was finally free then of the tyrant Ould Lowe, for he had finally been toppled and no more would he be heard singing in springtime.

The monster himself, who had roamed those forests since time out of mind, rested then in silt, among the weeds at the bottom of the lake, twice slain and no longer a force to haunt human habitation. His titanic head curls against his chest and his spine folds to meet his feet as a child in the womb of the world. He will rest near silent almost a hundred years.

In the days after their fight, Sanne rose in the dark hours while her husband still slept, prepared breakfast for herself, then cleaned the dishes and went off onto the land to dig stones for her oven.

When he found a decent one, Merian was always certain to bring it back for her, but by this labor alone it would take all year before she tasted bread again, and she was determined to have it sooner.

Before midday she ceased and headed back to the house to prepare his supper. When both had eaten she went back to her work, hauling the stones she had dug up to the back of the house. There were nearly enough for the belly of the stove by midsummer, and all she needed was another stack for a chimney. She still could not believe he had lived in his little room for so long without a proper stove for cooking. She knew from her last marriage, though, that the natural state of man with woman, or woman with man, was turbulence and strife. Perhaps not always loud and bursting forth from the seams, but it was ever-present nonetheless, as a deep inner spring that stored tension in its center belly and released it, either slowly over time or else all of a sudden, as in the eruptive fights that had begun to curse their young house. Nor was there time enough between their less significant scrapes for things to return all to normal. If she asked him about the stove, there would be no end to the argument it might plunge them into, so she left him instead to his fields and fried bits of pone, but no bread, and did not mention it. She would have bread for herself before the end of the season and began looking for stone for her chimney. If there was bread for him as well, so be it.

In the forests at the edge of their land she found another lode of rocks and figured it would be enough to finish her task. She considered her fortune as she broke up a stone too big to carry with a pickax, and put the pieces into the wheelbarrow. She was a powerful sight as she guided the apparatus through the woods, and there was little doubt that she had in her the will to defeat any other thing that stood in her way.

On the old farm they had said it of her as well, though she could not defeat the death that came and snatched the first one she married, neither with her skills as a nurse nor in sheer combat with the demon god once he came. For Death, she knew by then, is indeed something none can defeat but that Other in Heaven; God is most certainly other, and sometimes the two of Them in cahoots for the same end. She thought of this as she made her way home with the evening load, and how her fortunes had always been mixed in their blessings. But she knew, if fortune had marked her for it, she would master this charterless province as well as she had mastered all the unbalanced ascents and descents before it.

Nor were these her only contributions to the husbandry of the place once she decided to stay. She also wove textiles so that there was new cloth to protect their naked skin from the elements of the season, and then increased the plot of vegtables outside their little room, so there would be enough not only for summer meals but for canning and drying as well, to nourish them properly through the winter months, when all was desolate except for foraging beasts, which seemed to her too hard a way for a person to have to come by their daily meals.

When he happened upon her at midday and saw all the progress she was making, Merian thought himself lucky and wise to have made the choice he did of brides, impetuous as it might have seemed to some onlookers, who did not know them or how their house was beginning to prosper there at the edge of the world.

When he and Ruth Potter went to the settlement on one of their monthly provisioning trips, he thought of all the changes that had taken place since the previous year there, as he nudged the animal on. "Come on, Ruth Potter," he cajoled, "we got to get home before this time tomorrow." The animal looked around at the man with its deep willful eyes, then turned its head back to the ground, stopping now and again to take whatever it found curious, before grudgingly moving on under his prodding.

Instead of having to visit here and there for the things he needed, as he did those first years, though, he was now able to acquire all his basic needs from the chandler who had set up in the town center. Although there was no ship to be outfitted for miles around, it was how the owner insisted on styling himself, though he was just a plain dry-goods merchant such as might be found anywhere in the colony. At the inn, Merian saw they had put up shutters to the window, giving the place an air of respectability, so that the streets were in every way becoming not unlike a town still inside of human habitation instead of the end of that rough and desolate road. He began to wonder what else he might see as he sat at the bar of the inn having a pint with Content.

"There is talk that the road might be graded and boards put down."

"And who will do this?"

"They will hire a man."

"Who will pay him?"

"The merchants."

"Business is good on the square?"

"It hasn't been bad."

Returning that night he wondered whether his own gains were as much as the merchants' on the square and whether the little farm would keep up. He had paid that year for his goods one quarter more in hard cash than the year before.

At home he climbed into bed next to Sanne but did not mention these things.

"How is the oven coming along?" he asked her.

"It should be finished before summer's end."

"And everything else?"

"That's a fair amount. Hard to say when all of it might be done."

"And with you yourself? How are you getting on here?"

It was the first time he had ever inquired about her general well-being since they were wed and he had brought her out there. The small tenderness moved her to forgive him certain other things, so that the coil which had been tensing day by day found release in the open atmosphere that night, where it was able to let loose of its stored energy without harm. On the contrary, it was energy that manifested itself in the same tenderness with which they sang to each other that first night, so that the early days of their marriage were not all full of strife and turbulence but also of the bliss that marks happier houses, when their inhabitants are so wise as to give it free reign. No, they were not Merian's acres alone at all anymore. Nor did he see them as such.

five

⤙

The house grew and the farm grew and Ruth Potter bore the yoke and the burden of domesticity—both in the field and on the road—and Sanne and Merian began to thrive and feel at ease in the clearing that was the boundary line of creation. In the corner of the room nearest the door the belly of the stove grew; and in the fields maize, which would fill it with meal in the winter months, reached ever skyward.

At trading that year Merian acquired a cow that was not too badly used, a pig for the slaughter, and several chickens, which would give them eggs. He also bought sundry items for the house and farm, including a large tin tub, shoes for both husband and wife, a dress for Sanne and a peck of apples for Ruth Potter. When the accounts were said and figured, he owed no one, and still had monies left for the first time and did not want for anything.

From their private garden, Sanne pulled tomatoes, peppers, potatoes, okra, yam, pear, various berries, greens, onions, and other herbs. Merian saved from the harvest a separate lot of America corn for seeding in the spring, tobacco for his own personal consumption, and the hay he had planted in anticipation of acquiring livestock. Sanne prepared preserves of the berries and pears and helped her husband in digging a root cellar at the side of their house to store their other surplus.

As the harvest came to a close, Merian and Ruth Potter went to the mill with the maize they would need for the year to have it ground into flour. When they returned, Merian noticed the house had grown hotter than any day before, even during the height of the southern summer, and he could not determine what the reason was until he saw the little stove his wife had built was fully fired and glowed, waiting only for something to give its heat and warmth to. She provided it with a pan of bread dough made from the new flour, and a pie made of berries she had set aside. The house filled with the smell of baking bread and sweets, and Merian thought he had never in his life had it as good, though his back ached as much as he could remember.

Still, he knew this was his own farm and labor given for his sustenance and his new wife's, a thing which none but the most rotten man could begrudge. They basked that night in comfort from their toil, and neither thought of any of the other rooms, in times recent or far distant, in the houses and halls of their memories, they had inhabited before.

By the time the caravans that headed west each year started out that season, the Merians were already well ensconced in their winter home, which was a full three weeks earlier than he had been able to ready it in the past. The snows arrived earlier that year as well, and when a knock came to their door one morning, during a sudden storm, Merian left bed reluctantly to open it for the stranded traveler who greeted him.

"I have lost a wheel," the man said, as snow blew over the threshold and into the house.

While in the past he would barely have opened the door, let alone offered his assistance, his sense of peace made Merian eager to help, and he went off with the stranger in the snow to see if they could repair the carriage before the storm grew too foul.

It was as he walked home with the stranger and his team, after helping to right the overturned coach but not repair the wheel, which needed the attention of a smith, that he saw smoke from a fire not his own, which looked as if it rose from a built-up chimney instead of the bare ground of the forest. He thought then that he no longer lived at the edge of oblivion but had pushed its claim from his doorstep. He also envisioned how much easier the road would be to travel than when he walked it the first time, as parts of it were now graded. He thought then for the first time he might be able to keep his vow of the first year and return to Virginia someday soon for a visit.

He gave these things reign over his imagination as the dual aches of nostalgia and guilt seized him. One for the first family he had known and now missed, and the other for the wife to whom he owed his presence and loyalty.

As they waited out the storm in his house, he asked the stranger where he was headed and where he was coming from. The man answered only in half riddles but told him the trip had gone well so far, as the roads had been without hostility. When the storm let up several hours later, Merian continued to question the traveler, as they went into the village and even still as the smith turned the wheel on his lathe to realign the warped rim. When he finally escorted the man back to his carriage, he still had only a dim notion of who he was but reasoned that was the way it would remain.

Riding home in the snow-shadowed forest he looked around himself to ensure that no one else was on the road who might see his tortured thought. Instead of going into the house directly when he arrived even with his door, he went on a bit farther into the night, as if testing the road's disposition toward him.

The stranger on their ride through the dark woods had inspired in him a feeling of great dread, as well as hope, that manifested itself now in the brooding trip he took back and forth along the road, thinking of his previous existence. "There is a great change coming to these precincts," the man had preached, as they searched for the carriage in the darkness. "It will not make itself visible for years yet, but prepare thyself, for when it does it will be as if a hood has been lifted off the eyes of the world."

"What hood is that?" asked Merian.

"It is the great darkness that prevents men from seeing the natural state of us all is in eclipse and shadow, and we had better not ask too much how such a life came to exist, but why any did. That is the hood that the preachers and politicians use to fool us ordinary folk. They tell you they have the postal address to Providence, but I tell you that you and I have a channel to the same divinity as the Bishop of Canterbury or the baby Christ, and you do not need permission for access. What they want is to assume your agency in this, the progress of your own salvation, and add it to the number of other souls they have hoodwinked, until they have amassed an authority to rival that of Lord John himself. No, brother, we must all be self-governed on this journey and keep any who wants it from getting control of this vessel, like some popish Argonaut, which he would then steer only toward his own destination and neither yours nor mine nor God's."

Merian went silent to hear this blasphemy and struggled to get the iron fastened around the stranger's wheel. "What kind of preacher are you?" Merian asked at last, standing up. "Every other one of you I ever heard said the only plan for any of us is already mapped out by God."

"No preacher at all but a poor pilgrim."

He asked nothing else to be explained that night.

When he turned to leave, the man pressed a small coin of solid gold into his hand, which had embossed upon it a seal he had never seen before. "Now, there—there is something with materiality," the man said in a conspiratorial whisper, though there was no one else on the road. "Remember our conversation, brother, and mark it when it comes around to you again."

In his heart, which was superstitious and had not thrown off all the old tales he had learned in his boyhood, Merian began to tremble and look around himself as he paced the greedy road.

If it is oblivion that is our state, what indeed keeps anything from disappearing just as easily? he asked himself. This in its turn caused a great sadness to visit him that night, as he thought on things he had not visited in a very long time, and that indeed he thought perhaps best now forgotten.

When he returned to the house, Sanne sat up in bed waiting and asked why it had taken him so long.

"The wheel was worse off than I suspected," he said.

"I see. And the traveler?"

"He is back on his way, but he was a strange one."

"How so?"

"He was all talk of signs and claimed he had found a new way of measuring time's progress."

"You know what kind of talk all that is, don't you?"

Merian was not pious, as his wife was, but thought he knew what she made of it all. He was happy, though, to have the talk turn in a different direction than the pathways of his worries. "Now Sanne, he was just somebody who was stranded and needed help."

"This road is tarnished by all sorts," she said sternly. "Who knows what all we're likely to see out here before the end of it all?"

When he went out for wood that winter he found he had fallen into the habit of staring down the road whenever he happened to cross it, appraising its straightness and thinking how it went all the way back to Virginia in one form or other. He could not help but daydream of the other terminus. It was his current end, though, that always found and reclaimed him before he ever gathered the nerve to set back out toward the other.

As the spring came, and the ice thawed from the lake, he began to prepare his fields. On one of those mornings when thrush song was loud enough to cover the horrendous creak of melting ice, he looked out to the road and saw a new figure headed directly toward him. He kept at his work until the stranger stood in front of him. When he looked up from the shadow that covered the ground, he saw it was one he knew from long years before.

The two men clasped like kinsmen, and Merian invited the new arrival into the house, where his wife prepared for them a meal. When they had finished eating the two old friends began to reminisce and tell each other of former times and still other friends not forgotten.

As they grew comfortable, Merian had his friend, Chiron, wait while he went out of the house and into the root cellar. He returned with a jar of corn whiskey, which he had made in the tin tub he bought at the end of the previous season, and handed the jar to his guest.

"A drink," was all the new arrival said as the hot liquid burned its way down his throat.

"It is the first batch," Merian said, "but I could not imagine a better occasion for it. Tell me, what has brought you all this way?"

"Same as what brought you," replied Chiron, who had a reputation as a seer back where they came from.

"How far you going?"

"I do not know."

"You could stay on awhile."

It was settled as simply as that, even after so long a separation, as each of them knew it was what he owed to the other man as a tithe to their shared past and common fate.

When Sanne asked about their relationship, Merian answered that they were cousins and did not elaborate on how.

They did not speak, however, about everyone they knew from the past, being content to enjoy each other's company, and silence, and the occasional jar of corn whiskey. When Merian did ask once after one of their mutual acquaintances who had gone unmentioned, Chiron invoked the unspoken rule that had governed all of their discussions about the past until then. "Things always getting separated from their roots," he said. "When a man grows up in one place and leaves, he goes off part of the original and part of something new. The original don't always acknowledge the little offshoots, and all of them don't always acknowledge the master copy, because they need to get on with being separate and new and sometimes so different it don't make sense to talk about them at all anymore, other than gossip."

In the mornings the two men went out into the fields and worked until midday, then returned home together, where they shared supper. The new man acknowledged this abundance of hospitality by working as hard in the sowing of Merian's fields as he would have if they were his own. One morning, though, late in his visit, when the crows were in full commotion, he paused to read his friend's fortune in their pattern, for he was learned and well-practiced in auspicating from the flight of birds. "You will profit twice more," was all he said, as he stood from the place where he had sat to concentrate. Merian took the words as a mysterious gift to ponder and hope for, but he did not ask for further explanation, as he knew that was not how such things operated.

The arrangement continued well between them until late in the spring, when Chiron began to show signs of restlessness. As they worked outside one day, Merian asked him whether he wouldn't consider staying on longer.

"There is a nice spot over that way where you could put up a house of your own."

"I appreciate it, but I think it best to keep to the road a little longer," Chiron replied, without looking up from his work.

"Well, it is there if you decide you want it," Merian said, returning to his own work, as he was not one to argue with a grown man what his own best interest was.

With Chiron that year he had already planted twice as many acres as the season before and hoped to improve on that by yet a few lots more.

Without his friend, Merian knew when harvest came there would only be him and Sanne to work the land, so he stopped his ambitions there where his hand might reach by its own power alone.

His mind, though, did not stop dreaming of increasing his till, and he began to experiment with a small batch of rice seed he bought from the dry-goods merchant, who claimed it had made men rich throughout the Caribbean. Chiron nodded when he saw them, and helped Merian to set up the patch, as he had some memory of the way the stuff was cultivated.

By early July, however, the plants were dry and yellow with no hope of growing further, even with Chiron's nursing. Merian knew then the seeds were bad, and cursed the merchant for selling him them, swearing that would be the last time he did business with the so-called chandler.

"He has robbed me of my time and labor from two seasons," he cursed, when he realized the plants were hopeless. "The first I spent saving to buy his rubbish and the second I spent trying to get them to grow."

Sanne tried to console him. "It is no guarantee that a thing will grow only because it was planted."

"There's no chance of it at all if the thing is infernal," Merian countered gloomily. He spent then long hours that night thinking of ways to recoup from the unreliable merchant, if not to cheat him of something as precious.

By morning his anger had departed and he could admit to himself that if nothing else was lost it would still be a better year than the one before. He devoted more time toward convincing Chiron to stay on, though, telling him that there was little to nothing in the country beyond them.

"Good," he was answered, "because that's what I aim to find. I've spent about enough days working and getting nowhere to know that nothing is a fine place for a man with a certain kind of head to be."

"What kind is that?"

Chiron did not answer the question, saying only, "I'm going to go over there and think about all me and you and the Virginia folk been through and see if it doesn't mean something more than that, like bird patterns against the sky."

"What good can it mean to be bonded or else a hermit, with nothing but rags keeping him from the harm of cold and heat?" Merian asked.

"All of that is just passing," Chiron said, in the old country way, and it was not his own way of reasoning but Merian could not argue against it.

When the crop was weeded, Chiron came and told him he was leaving, and did not care to be reminded that the caravans westward did not depart for several weeks still.

"Where I am headed I can't imagine much caravanning."

Merian paid him his wages with silver and added to it the coin that had been pressed on him many months earlier by the stranger he met that winter. He found all again beside the hearthstone next morning and nothing else gone from the storeroom but a little food and the bearskin.

So he had two visits that year and both of them religious in their own way. Nor would they be the last visits either, from seers, strangers, or holy men on the property. Nor were such the only ones to come to the house in those early years.

six

In the round heat of the summer months Sanne found herself beginning to grow heavy, and Merian realized there would be another mouth,
and in time other hands, on the land. In optimism he began to expand
the house, which he had first built in the old African style with a square
foundation of twelve on either side. To this initial square he added a
second, first placing in the foundation certain herbs said to be propitious
and other provisions.

After laying the groundwork himself, he saddled Ruth Potter for
the trip into town, intent on hiring someone to help with raising
the walls. On the trip that year he noticed the village center seemed
to be growing steadily outward. Where stands of wild trees stood before were now farms and storehouses, some of which, though newer
and still modest, were already larger than his own. In all, things had
changed so much over the previous year that Ruth Potter barely recognized her way, either to the general store or to Content's inn, and
offered up resistance as being in a strange land when they entered the
town center.

"Still riding that mule?" Content asked, when Merian stopped by the
tavern for his customary drink.

"She ain't no worse off for it."

"Seems like you're doing well enough to get yourself a horse."

"Next you'll be trying to sell me on a carriage and livery."

"It would be an improvement over that mule."

"We can't all be such country dandies as you, Content."

"Can't all get about on mules, either."

"Do you know where I can find a man to hire? I need to make some improvements to the farm."

"What is it you need?"

"Add a room."

"Now that is fancy."

"I can't help it."

When Merian told his friend the reason for the addition, Content nodded and refilled his glass, then called to Dorthea to share in the good news.

They drank a toast to Sanne, after which Merian followed his friend's directions to a new tavern on the other side of the square, where the small road crew was said to take lunch.

When he walked in, he found the crew was nothing more than two brothers who had hired themselves out for the summer, being without land of their own.

"Would you like another job?" he asked them.

They answered that they were disinclined to work at all after their present job, work not being their preferred vocation.

"What is it you would rather be doing?" he asked.

"Just about anything," the elder brother answered. "Work is not for us."

"Then why did you take this job?"

"To eat," the younger brother replied.

"You will still have to eat when you're done."

"But this one will feed us until the end of summer."

He did not press beyond this, and when he left he did not berate them as hostile, for he could see they were short of wits. He but hoped his own children would not turn out so.

With Sanne growing heavier each day, he spent the rest of the summer as he had his first on the property, in grueling solitary work that lasted from first until final light. Mornings he woke and tended his fields; then, in the evening, began construction on the new building and cellar. As the warm days grew shorter, he began to despair he would not finish the task before the weather came down from the mountains.

By the first days of September it was nearly time to harvest his crops as well. The maize was as high as the archer's bow over Old Cape, and the tobacco leaves were two full hand spans across. Sanne's garden was also prospering, and they looked forward to reaping as much as in the last three years combined. He went to sleep nights that month thinking of his cellars bursting with the year's increase, and his pockets overladen with money from the produce he would sell at market. How he would enjoy these rewards from his labors and reinvest the surplus well back in his fields.

The land, being free and fickle, though, conspired with the weather in mid-month against him, when a violent storm began to lash the house as they slept in the coolness of the old building. Merian awoke to the full force of the gale whipping the boards and joints of his house and the violent rains already under his door.

When Sanne woke she found her husband standing in the doorway cradling his head in his hands. "Are you going to stand and hide while it takes the whole season away from us?" she asked, as he stared out at the storm.

With an enormous effort he gathered himself and marched out into the rain to begin harvesting maize from the soggy plants, trailing a muddy sack behind his bent form as he went. In the house Sanne lit her oven, and when each sack was filled he would haul it to the house and unload it near the door. She then took and arranged the ears in stacks for drying in the heat of the kitchen, as he went back into the storm for the rest of their production.

They worked at it through the darkness, but in the morning the rains still slashed down in an onslaught that flooded the fields. Merian, exhausted, threw himself onto the earthen floor in defeat at about ten that morning, unable to work at all anymore.

"Are you quitting?" Sanne asked, as his weight oozed agreeably into the mud in front of the door.

"Let the devil have it," he said, refusing to rise again.

"I did not know I had married a lazy man," she told him, taking the sack up where he had left it, and going off into the rain to save what was left of their harvest. Seeing her go to fulfill the contract that he himself could not caused him an abiding sense of shame. He nursed this emotion but did not move from the floor.

It was only when he saw her pregnant form struggle to bring the first full sack to the door that he rose and went off to help.

"I am just a man, Sanne," he said, taking the sack over his raw shoulders and setting out again. She looked at him then and was filled with pity. Her children, she swore, as he dragged the sack behind them in the feeble morning light and she looked at his mud-streaked face and the tatters of his shirt clinging to his frame, would be greater than this.

When they reached the door of the hut, she stopped short at the threshold, sensing disaster. "You don't smell that?" she shrieked when she figured out what it was.

He did then, but he had not before. The maize that was outermost in the pile had taken on too much fire and was charred down half its length. Both looked at the burnt husk of their efforts, not speaking either to the other.

"We'll have to throw it all out," she lamented finally.

"It might still be good for feed," he told her.

"Not even the pigs," she answered.

"We will try and see."

Nor was that the end of the disaster. The rains went on another five days, and when they were done, he was left with little else besides his despair. When he took what remained to market, he was paid a third for his labors that year of what he had the one before, and the merchant told him to be happy he was having that. "The markets are depressed for even prime crops," he said, "and your own is nearly rotten." Merian took what he was given and boiled with rage that he should have so little for his work and so little to say over his fate. But he had no other recourse.

He went on to the dry-goods shop, where he bought that year almost the same inventory as the one before, adding to it the nails he would need to finish work on his building, but there would be no new tub for liquor and no new shoes for himself.

He returned to his farm at the end of that day so woebegone he did not bother to unhitch Ruth Potter from the crude wagon she hauled. Sanne went out to the back of the house and performed this task for him, unloading the wagon as well, feeling the same pity for her husband she had the night he lost his crop but not afraid as she had been.

41

When he started the next day, however, Merian showed no sign of his defeat as he went to work finishing the outer part of the new building. As he sat on a beam, nailing roofing shingles to the top of the structure, he looked out over his property and possession and called to Sanne inside the house.

"Sanne, what is it I used to tell you I was building out here?'

"Utopia," she said, heavily making her way to him to see exactly what it was he wanted.

"Well, I am still building it," he said defiantly, "and no one is going to break me in that."

"Stop your foolish talk," she reprimanded him. "You'll tempt God or else worse."

He hammered away and said nothing more to his wife that day, but in his heart he was as intent as he had been that first day on the land. He nodded to her in the muggy summer light and drove another nail into the crossbeam.

The roof went up on the new building just before the first snows fell that year, but the structure itself sat empty as the root cellar beneath it. There were no extras that year and no need of the additional space. For the interior of the building he had run out of funds to continue construction. When Sanne's waters broke, just after the turn of the new year, she left their shared bed nonetheless and went into the other house, where she had instructed Merian to build her a set of furniture of her own design. When she disappeared into the other dwelling, he was not permitted to go in, and neither could he go for help, there being no midwife and him being afraid to leave her alone for the time it would take to go to town for Dorthea.

Merian paced in the old house, opening the door from time to time to go roam around out-of-doors. From the other room he could hear an occasional groan that caused him to stand still wherever he was at the time. A great shock of fear would pass through him during those moments, heavy with the wailing agony that emanated from the other room. As the night wore on, the frequency and severity of her groans increased, until he found himself pressed with his back against the wall

between the two rooms in paralysis. After another of these noises he
knew he would not be able to bear it any longer and called in to her.
"I'm going to go fetch Dorthea."

From the other room Sanne screamed back at him. "Don't you dare
leave me out here in the middle of creation"—she added, "just because
you're scared of a birthing."

Merian walked out of the house and all the way to the road with
worry, before turning back to the house, trying to figure out what he
was supposed to do, either leave her for help or stay there helplessly while
she cried out in pain. Finally he made his way back to the other house
and pushed at the door. It was fastened from the inside, and he was
forced to shove his shoulder into it with his entire might until it budged
but only the smallest bit. Through the crack he could barely make out
her form but saw that she stood in the middle of the room, holding on
to the halfborn violently.

He thought then, that this was how she escaped her prior marriage
childless, by killing them off as they came into the world. He yelled at
her to stop as he rammed his frame into the door again.

The rough-hewn door was swollen with dampness and cleaved to its
position. Merian threw himself into it again with greater and greater
force, until the wood began to creak and splinter. Still Sanne said nothing to him nor made any motion to let him into the room; rather, she
continued on in her task and the sounds of pain she had emitted before.

Finally he rammed the door with his foot and succeeded in making
it give way. He entered the dark room and rushed toward his wife, as
his eyes adjusted to the lack of light. When he was upon her he saw that
she held the newborn creature with all the gore of birth still attached.
She looked up at him with an implacable face.

"He came first by the feet," she said, telling him to get her a towel.
"What is all the commotion you are keeping up?"

He said nothing, ashamed of his former suspicions.

She took the child then and moved sorely to her side, where she
reached a basin of water and began to clean it. When she had finished,
and he could distinguish the baby's human shape, she held it out to him.
He, for his own reasons, looked on the creature but did not move to
receive it.

* * *

For days after the birth she stayed in the other room with the newly repaired door still barred and forbade him entrance. She sat then with her child and talked to him and sang to him the songs that had been sung to her when she was small, but for the father she gave little thought except when he came around to bring or retrieve something at the door.

In all the two of them, mother and son, were sequestered nearly a fortnight in the other house, and Merian began growing used to their absence. When they finally did emerge, he was at work mending the chicken coop and did not see them until he returned to the house later in the day, when he entered the room to find it hot as the oven could make instead of cool as he liked to keep it. Sanne sat in her chair by the little window cradling the boy and, when she saw her husband, held his son out to him. Merian looked at the child a second time but did not take him in his hands.

"Don't you want to hold your boy, Jasper?" she asked. "What is the matter?"

He said nothing but went over to the fire to get his lunch, his hands trembling as he poured the soup he had prepared days earlier into a bowl.

"Well, have you thought about what you want to call him?" Sanne asked, as Merian took a bit of the watery broth and looked over at the child's hovering eyes.

"I thought you might of named him already," he answered her.

Sanne did not respond, as he sopped at the bowl with a piece of hard bread and stared straight ahead of himself. When he finished he stood up and went back to his work outside, leaving the two of them alone as they were used to being.

When he returned at dusk Sanne had baked new bread and prepared their dinner. Merian, still sulking, did not take his accustomed seat but avoided the common table.

Seeing that he was committed to his act, Sanne sat down and ate alone. Merian left her to the table and entertained himself with a pack of playing cards he had acquired. When the boy started to cry Merian cut his eyes between mother and infant, seemingly annoyed with both of them for disturbing his peace.

Sanne went to the baby and began to feed him. Merian watched for a while without comment as everything in his house satisfied its belly except him. Nor did he speak the remainder of that evening, but went to bed sometime after Sanne and the baby, giving both a wide berth.

They continued in this way for several days, neither admitting they had given offense to the other or doing anything to change his behavior. They shared the bed together with the child but did not touch, until Sanne began to think of moving back into the other house permanently.

It was another week before she offered the baby to her husband for holding again, and days even after that before Merian could bring himself to take him, who still had yet to receive a name of his own.

Merian had borne his exile as repentance for his behavior on the night of the birth, but when he looked at her curled up with the wrinkled form, although he knew it to be his own issue, he could not help but think a tiny new master had come upon his lands.

It was the baby who finally broke the tension in the house. Sanne woke in the middle of one night, disturbed by something in her sleep, to find Merian holding the child on his chest and speaking to him in the same abracadabra he sometimes used with Ruth Potter.

"He must of crawled on top of me in the middle of the night," Merian said, when Sanne sat up and looked at the two of them. "When I opened my eyes, he was here on my chest."

"He probably had a nightmare about utopia," she said.

Merian ignored her barb and continued to play with the boy. "Did you dream of utopia, Mr. Purchase?" he asked.

"Who is Purchase?" Sanne wanted to know.

"It seemed like it fit him."

Sanne did not answer but let the man hold his child and continue to speak to it in his gibberish meant to make the uncomprehending understand.

As Merian played with the tiny new baby, it was the first time he could remember ever holding anything so small. Nor could he remember being held by either mother or father when he himself was little. He knew this, of course, to be only a likely trick of the mind, one of the false floors or hidden rooms of memory deceiving him. There was, however, no way to verify either the one thing or the other.

seven

An orange liquid sun clung low over the white landscape most of that winter like a shield, cast and left as welcome gift for whichever strange new god slept and dreamed in the western lands.

Merian spent the darkened months beneath the burning sky learning to dote over his new son, Purchase, until the two of them started to became as inseparable as the boy was from Sanne, who considered him a miracle brought to her barren womb by unseen Providence. In the evenings, after finishing work on the buildings and grounds, Merian would go home, where instead of turning directly to food, corn whiskey, or wife, he would go to the boy and check on him, asking about his day. "Purchase Merian, what did you do while me and Ruth Potter were out cording firewood?"

Sanne regarded the child with protective affection as his father tickled him or else tossed him into the air. "That's enough, Jasper," she would say then, when she felt he was roughhousing the baby. "He's still just a little one."

Sometimes Merian argued the toughness of the child. More often he gave in to her demands and placed Purchase back on the mattress or else withdrew his hand and stopped trying to make the baby laugh. He found himself pleased that the building was still unfinished, as it gave him a project and excuse to be indoors and near them.

After Sanne finally vacated the other building, which had been taken over by their few livestock, Merian began tearing down the interior wall between the two rooms, to combine the whole into a single structure. Although he worked frequently in the empty room, he constantly invented reasons to be in the part of the house where they were.

It was during this season that proper warmth began to flow between husband and wife as well, when Sanne saw how her husband went through no end of invention to be near the newborn, and Merian saw how well she guarded his boy from harm.

That was also the winter Sanne began to take over management of the stores, beginning at first with her helping Merian count how many bales of hay were left until the time the cow would be able to graze outdoors again. It was then that she saw how precarious their own survival was as well, and dependent on an early spring. In fear she began to make suggestions about how the land was allocated to the different crops.

"We'll have to feed the cow from our own food," she said, "and unless you give another field to hay this year we might be in the same position next winter as well."

"We might have to slaughter it," Merian replied stoically, going to count the preserves in the half-empty room. "Now, how long will the cow last if you divide it by two people and the rest of the winter?"

Sanne thought it was a joke, even though she found herself involuntarily performing the math in her head. When she realized he was serious, though, she grew incensed. On her last place they would rather get down to the nub of their stores than kill an animal that wasn't marked for slaughter, and a cow was almost a living relative. As the weeks progressed, though, the hay continued to thin, and Merian was forced into giving the animals smaller and smaller portions. To save the cow, Sanne would sneak some of her own meal to it when her husband was not looking. Still, the animals all grew thinner, until the cow's warm morning milk had given out well before there was yet any sign of thaw in the fields. In desperation Merian went out and dug up turf from the ground beneath the snow, and took to feeding the animals that, but it was not enough to sustain them properly. They continued to weaken.

"Do you want to wait until your own milk has given out too?" he asked, arguing his course of action with her. "The little one can't eat turf."

Sanne did not answer him, and indeed began to withdraw some of the affection she had previously restored. He is just barely an animal himself, she thought. If he managed his stores right we would not be in this situation.

Their misfortune, he told her, was not his doing. "I am as beholden to the climate and the mercy of God as anything out there," Merian said, as if reading her thoughts. "I do not make it rain or hail or snow or drought, or else descend on a poor fellow like the locusts, or bring fire, or make crops die from disease that can't nobody see till the corn is withered all to ruin."

He got up from the table, leaving half his dinner for the woman and child, or rather the animals, as he knew what she did with the scraps from her own plate, even with her husband's head aching and light from hunger.

"If you kill the animals we'll never have anything more for ourselves than season to season," she said, as he stormed across the room and made a pallet for himself on the floor.

"If I don't we won't make this one, Sanne," he said, with increasing frustration.

He woke up early the next morning and left the house before she knew he was gone. By the time she did find him missing she was already at the stove, making the thinnest ashcake ever measured out and set over a bed of coals. She looked around presently and counted the animals, as was her usual habit. The cow and the mule were both missing, and she went to the door in great agitation to see if she could find sign of either her man or their beasts.

Out in the wet melting snow she could still fathom the marks of hooves and the man's feet next to them, leading off into the dark woods. "He has gone into the forest so I would not hear when he slaughtered her," she said to the baby Purchase. "Next he will kill Ruth Potter for meat." She looked back out across the fields, following the tracks in the snow until they faded at the entrance to the forest, and wondered which direction out there they had gone off into, so that she might listen for the animals' scream.

She sat and listened all day, cursing both the man and herself for marrying him. I left my home for this she reminded herself again, daydreaming about her former house, which was always well stocked with both food and good company, as the rooms and halls of memory inevitably are.

Near dusk he reappeared, and just as she feared he had meat with him and was covered in blood.

"I'll not cook the proceeds of your murdering," she said, when he put the flesh on the table. "Take it out of here."

"You have to eat too, Sanne," he said. "It is good meat."

When she heard him say this, the core inside her gave way and her eyes turned into hate-filled saucers. "Get it out of here," she said again, taking up a knife from near the stove.

"What are you planning to do with that?" he demanded cautiously.

"Get it off my table," was all she said.

"Calm yourself," Merian told her. "It's not your cow."

"Where is she then?"

"I left her in the woods to feed. I took her out there this morning, down the valley, where the snow is melted enough that we found forage."

"What is that then?" Sanne asked, motioning to the flank on the table. "Did you spare Ruth Potter too or assassinate her?"

"Yes, I spared Ruth Potter," Merian said, but she still held the knife. "You'd rather die or kill your husband than eat those two beasts? You are a stranger one than I thought."

"You cannot bring an animal to you with one promise and then abuse it another way. What is on my table?" she asked again, not yet putting down the knife.

"It is bear, Sanne. The rest of it is hung up out back if you want to see for yourself."

She took him at his word, though, and cooked the meat as he prescribed, cutting it into thick steaks, which she grilled in a skillet with its own fat and onions from the otherwise empty cellar.

He sat down to the table and bade her eat as well. She sat and sliced a portion of the tender flesh and took it into her mouth, where its savoriness and nourishment nearly made her tear. She realized how thin she had become, and that the child was put in jeopardy because of it. She felt absurd in her relief, as disaster had been avoided, for the way she defended the cow and the mule and even the hog for a time, guarding what was dear almost to the expense of losing what was most precious. She sliced the steak again and let out a low sensuous moan of pleasure, as she began to enjoy the taste of the meat itself, which was denser and unlike anything else she could remember eating.

At his side of the table Merian took the hot meat with his bare hands and lifted it to his mouth, then tore off a great chunk from it and began to chew. He did not savor the flavor, but ingested the mass of flesh into his own dwindled stomach. The juices from the meat and fat rolled down one side of his face unchecked, as he finished the steak in three or four great bites. When he was done, he attacked the onions and only then remembered the first time he had eaten a wild bear and the awfulness of that winter.

We will make it through this one as well, he told himself, and looked over to Sanne to see how she enjoyed her dinner. He was glad of it, and to know they would not die of starvation, even if the cause of this salvation was desperate luck.

As his parents sated themselves on meat, from the corner of the room Purchase Merian began to cry. His mother went over to him to offer her breast, not feeling any of the angriness she had on some nights when his little screams would not cease. For all ate in the house that evening and no more mention was made of hunger or murder.

There was fresh meat the next meal as well, and then smoked and pickled meats in the days that followed, until they had feasted from the animal for the better part of six weeks.

When spring did finally come at the end of that interminable winter, it came vengefully, with a hot blast of heat that made going out of doors feel like punishment for some unspeakable crime.

Merian bore it gladly, though, as the animals could graze again, and he went about clearing a new field for their provisions, having learned a hard lesson from the previous months. However, when he began digging out the new plot he remembered just how rocky much of his property actually was. He worked from the first finger of light until sundown, plowing the land already under cultivation or removing stones from the soil. As he dug under the primitive sun he was never as thankful for its warmth, even as it burned and parched him to exhaustion.

From the heat it grew green quickly in the other fields and his crops began to soar again, as they had seasons before, when he dared dream he was getting ahead of that vast wilderness and all the things set against him. That year he dreamed only that he might reduce the debt he had amassed. Either because of this or to spite it, he tried again with rice, using a different seed but the same method Chiron had taught. As he irrigated the little plants, he thought of his old friend and wondered where he had disappeared to under the summit on the other side of the mountains. He remembered then what he had said about things always separating out from their source.

He looked again that summer down the long road back to where he had come from and tried to banish the other end from his mind, once and for all, to concentrate on the pleasures of home, uppermost of which was watching Purchase grow.

"If you keep growing like that you'll end up a giant," he said to the boy.

He meant it as well. The child was growing so remarkably that he worried there was something the matter with him. "Why don't you and Purchase go see that new doctor in town, just to make sure everything is all right," he offered to Sanne.

His wife laughed at him, the idea was so ridiculous. "With what money and what reason?" she asked. "Don't you think a doctor has better things to tend to than just a child growing?"

Merian let it rest there for the time being, but he watched the boy's growth with awe and fear together.

This was the same summer that his satisfaction and optimism also grew to such prodigious heights as to prompt him to give the place a name of its own.

When he finished his daily chores in the fields, both the ones that grew food for humans and the ones that supported their animals, he would bring old Ruth Potter around to the acres he had just cleared, load her cart with the stones he had dug up, then bid her haul it. Ruth Potter strained under those loads as she had under few others since coming into his possession, both because of the weight of rock in her wagon and because she was getting on in years. Merian tried to make the loads light as possible, often finding himself walking beside her, hauling nearly as much as the beast. When they finished their work for the day, he would share with her his water and give to her one of the apples from the cellar.

Still, the labors were a drain on her, and Sanne suggested it might be time to retire the mule. "Ruth Potter got as many years left as I do, don't you, old girl?" he asked convivially. A sadness would creep into his voice, though, for his first helpmate on the place was reaching a stage that no one could deny or change. "This is the only work she has to do this year, besides the harvest," he said, and went back to his own chores.

With the fieldstone that they hauled up from the slope stacked in loads out back, Merian began to face the two conjoined structures until it was one solid formation without crack for wind or cold to penetrate. It was when he finally finished that he began to call the place Stonehouses.

In the beginning Sanne could scarcely stand to hear the name come from his mouth.

"You'll get your comeuppance yet, man," she warned.

"I bet the little lord likes it, don't you, Purchase?"

"The what?" she asked him, stupefied.

"Tiny lord."

"So, man, I have married an honest heathen?"

"No, but you live on a true farm now," he said, standing near the front door. It was a fitting assessment. He had made the rock-infested acres in the forest into a proper freehold that had at last begun to show signs of prosperity, even after the winter that brought them near full ruin.

The year, however, still held suffering in its maw, which it did offer up in due course of time. As he worked the fields with Sanne and Ruth Potter, reaping a harvest he hoped would be rich enough to unhitch him from debt, the mule tripped one day and lost her footing on a rock, then went tumbling loudly to the ground in a heap of sagging skin and snapping inner mass.

When Merian went to help her up, the mule brayed at him and kicked out with one leg to drive him off. Merian, hunched over her, finally succeeded in jamming the dislocated bone back into place, and coaxing the mule to stand and test it. It was no use. When she took to her legs Ruth Potter looked at him shakily and took one pained step before beginning a hopping walk on her three sound limbs.

Merian led her gently back to the house, where he sat up, cursing her clumsiness and feeding her apples late into the night. For a week he let her convalesce, until it became apparent the leg was not getting better. It was beginning to rot, in fact, right on the bone.

Flies hovered around inside the house, and her wispy tail flailed halfheartedly at them, causing the creatures to scatter briefly before re-settling right where they had been, until they no longer even made the pretense of scattering but only an increase in buzzing before resuming their banquet on the festering meat. Merian soothed her mottled head and scattered the flies with his hat, while proclaiming to Sanne that the leg looked to be healing.

Sanne did not say anything when he went on like this, but nodded her head and brought him a fresh bucket of water, which man and mule alike used to quench their thirst in the sweltering heat. "Might be," she said at last, trying to give him comfort.

By the second week it was apparent that the mule had no chance, and even his affection and loyalty could no longer hide this from him. Early one morning before Sanne and Purchase awoke, Merian lifted Ruth Potter up from the floor and led her out deep into the woods, beyond the trails that anyone knew but him, and into the same valley field that had served him as an emergency pasture in winter. There he untied the animal, and bade her luck with her own devices, turned, and went back to the house.

When he arrived, Sanne saw his weariness, and the mule missing, and did not ask what he had done that morning. He for his part was silent much of the rest of the day. As they bedded down for the night, though, Sanne told Merian that she heard a noise outside of the house. "It is only your imagining, or else the wind," Merian told her, turning back to sleep. When she would not desist he went out, where he was greeted by the old speckled beast.

He led her limping inside and gave her feed and an apple, then a blanket, before returning to his wife in bed.

Sanne did not say anything as he wormed his way back under the covers, but let him try to sleep.

In the morning Merian repeated his routine of the day before, un-certain how she had made her way back on just three legs but deter-mined she would not do so again. This time he led her even farther away, by back roads he was confident she had never trod. That night the mule was at the house again, same as any other day in the last four years. Sanne helped her husband feed the animal, and stroked the back of the poor man's head when he lay down to sleep. The next day he tried once more but to no avail.

"I know," was all she said, when he led the mule in the third night.

Despite the pretension of taking a name for the house, he knew it was senseless to keep and feed a used-up animal. That morning he faced the task as it was laid out for him, taking Ruth Potter by a long tether—as she was used to having when she had any—into the same field, where he leveled the musket against her temple. His anger, though, flashed and welled up as he saw how innocent she looked at him and munched dumbly on the summer's sweet grass. "Goddammit, Ruth Potter, what good is it letting you loose if you don't know what to do with yourself?" he growled at her. "If you don't know that, what sense is there in living?" He fired the musket into the animal's head. She fell where she stood, in a tumult of limbs, and he dug for her a grave, which he did cover back up with dirt and sweet grass.

As he made his way home late that morning his heart blazed with emotion, as the sun itself fires false things true.

eight

~

A train of princely coaches thundered over the road the first passable day of spring that year. A herald out front proclaimed its origin, and the king's standard flew high overhead, guarding it against inhospitable actions. Its presence so far out was a confounding mystery to Merian and Sanne, and it was continuing on even farther—to an outpost that had cropped up more than two days' journey from them, for it was a long time since they were the final dwelling on the road.

The mystery of the coach remained unsolved until Merian's provisioning trip a few weeks later, when he stopped for his usual draught, and Content mentioned the self-important travelers who had stayed over at the inn about three weeks earlier.

"Who were they?" Merian asked. "What was their business?"

"I guess you didn't hear"—Content nodded, offering him another pint—"but we're going to be a colony of our own."

"Don't you think Dorthea and Sanne might be a little upset by that?"

"It's no jest," Content countered. "The colony is dividing in two."

"On what grounds?" Merian asked, though he didn't see how it could make a difference to them out there, whatever the case.

"Rulers and ruled upon. Anglicans and Presbyterians. Plantation and freeholder. Crown and colony," a man sitting in shadow at the end of the bar interjected. "Past and future. However you want to square it. There's not a whole lot of grounds where things aim to stay the same."

"That's all dukes' and governors' business," Content said. "It won't matter any to us out here."

"You are an optimist, my friend," the man at the bar argued, standing and coming over to join the other two, "as well you should be, all the way out here with no arrow in yer skull. But it will have everything to do with what goes on. Mark that, both of ye." The stranger looked intently between them, and when he said, "Mark that," Merian recognized his costume as one and the same with the fellow whose carriage he had fixed out on the empty road a few years past.

"You're one of those wandering preachers, aren't you?" Merian asked him. "One of your kind passed this way before."

"I am no such thing," the man answered. "If I were, though, I would tell you great fortune has smiled on both of ye in the sundering of these lands. The other side is no place even for a dog, or else a king's created harlot." With that he downed his drink and stood to depart. "They want inventory of things that should not be in their cupboards to count," he said. "Give them those stores and you'll not run a free house anymore than you will the Holy Roman Empire."

When he had gone, Content went to collect the monies left on the bar and held up a silver coin of the same marking that Merian had seen once before. The two then drank silently for a spell, wondering whether there was anything in the preacher's forecast to concern them.

They decided in the end there was nothing for them to do about it and switched the conversation over to local gossip and general speculation about the future. Merian arrived home that night in a good mood, although there was nothing to account for it other than a feeling of being near to great events, even if those unfolded happenings concerned more the great landowners and estates of religion and did not weigh on him directly.

"There are going to be two colonies from here on," he told Sanne. "One for the religious planters and another for everybody else."

"I don't see what religion has to do with it," she asserted, as always on guard against his blasphemies. "In any case, they're both for the big planters."

"Well, one of them wants everything for Crown and landed, and the other claims looser confederation."

"Will you still be able to go between them or will you need special permission?"

"They're both still the king's lands," her husband answered. "I imagine for somebody with the idea, it will be just like going from here to Virginia or from there to London." As he finished his sentence Merian grew suddenly less jocular, and he stood up to go out-of-doors where he could walk a spell by himself.

Outside the sky teemed low with stars and he charted the figures as he had known them in his childhood, trying to remember their names as he learned them then. He found, however, that he could not name them all as he used to and eventually went back indoors still burning with thought.

Sanne, after seeing him seized by one of his unpredictable moods, tried to ignore it, and when he reentered the house he found her already closing everything down for the night. He helped silently, then got into bed alongside her, where he attempted to mask his earlier moodiness with talk of how good the harvest was going to be again this year, if the weather should hold.

It was a mask but a true one; his yield from the ground had improved steadily as he invested it with fertilizers and good care each year, so that he expected nearly twice again what he achieved the year before. All the result of steady work and getting to keep his benefits for himself. This season, he reckoned, when his accounts were settled, he would leave with more ready cash than he had ever seen in his life, and no debt to any man.

When the harvest came he took his produce to market and received payment, more than a little amazed at the amount—for it was a sum that would have been unthinkable to him only recently.

He splurged then at the merchants' shops and even spent a few pence at his sworn enemy the chandler's, after seeing a handkerchief in the window he thought Sanne might fancy.

When he went home that evening he was loaded down with the winter goods in a new cart, which was pulled by the gelding he had bought to replace Ruth Potter, though he considered that particular creature irreplaceable and without peer in all the annals of animal husbandry.

He arrived back at Stonehouses at nightfall, and Sanne came out to help him unpack the cart and put things away in their cellar. He was proud then that, while before he had barely been able to fill a single basement with his labors from the season, this year two storerooms were scarcely enough to hold all his goods. He celebrated with a little of the bought whiskey he had picked up in his splurging, then presented his wife with her gift.

"Oh, it's just foolish," she protested, as she looked at the spun lace cloth. "What do I need with such a thing around here?" She could not, however, disguise her merriment at being presented with something so precious, or, for that matter, at receiving anything besides another pair of sturdy boots.

Nor was it his only gift to her. As he unpacked the crates there were all kinds of sweets and delicacies, such as had barely been available for sale in the place before but which were now well within their means. He drank in celebration of his growing wealth as well as the commerce that made it possible. He had amassed a sum of capital that was tremendous to his mind, and he knew exactly what it was worth and what purpose to put it to.

"I have another family I left back in Virginia," he said to Sanne that night, as they lay in bed.

"What do you mean another family?" she asked, even as she had always suspected he kept secrets from her. "You have another wife?"

"Not legal like you and me, at least, but yes, you can say another wife."

When she heard this she began to cry and berate him. "I always knew you hid things from me," she said, sobbing. "What else is there? Do you have other children? Why, I bet you have them all the way up to Massachusetts!"

"Just one, Sanne," he answered. "I had to leave both of them when they changed the law about where freed men could settle. I never made it a secret that's how I ended up here. Or did you think I had lived all that time before you just by myself?"

"You never told me about another family," she said, still tearing.

"That's because I couldn't do anything about it," he answered. "I can now and intend to."

"Intend to what?" she asked, sitting up. "What are you going to do?"

"Buy them out," he answered her. "It don't affect you and me, but it is what I promised them and still intend." It had been his heart's truth for longer than he could bear, although when he made the promise it had seemed like an earthly impossibility.

"You can't bring another woman here; I won't stand for that!" Sanne screamed at him. "I don't care what you promised. If you try to bring your slave woman here you'll both pay in hell."

Merian chewed the inside of his mouth and said nothing else. He tried eventually to embosom and comfort his wife, whom he did love, until she could sleep. But in his pocket that money from the harvest lit him with singular purpose.

He rises the next day, before the sun has gained the rim of the horizon, while his wife still sleeps soundly, and saddles the gelding. Sanne wakes and listens to him outside, leaving, but does not stir from their shared mattress. By the time she realizes to herself where he has gone the sun will be at noonday and he will be unredeemable to her except by his own will.

He stopped for lunch at his customary time and ate in the saddle, to save an hour before taking back to the road again. The last time he was on this path he had been pressed to it by the legal inability to earn a wage and the misery that ensued. Still, he did not consider this ride back triumphant, for he did not know what to expect. He only knew he was in better condition than before—when he was beyond whipped and defeated and damn near dead. He tried not to think about it any longer or ever again, but if he did speculate in isolated moments he surely did not dwell on it, and certainly not on the last night before his manumission was a legal fact. Ebsen, the overseer, had visited him then at the party they were having in one of the cabins and, unprovoked, smashed him full in the mouth with a leather-wrapped fist.

Everyone in the room stared between the two, waiting for a response as the blood welled in Merian's lip and Ruth clutched their boy toward her bosom.

Merian looked at the other man quizzically, determined not to be hedged. "I thought you and me were friends, Ebsen," he said. "We never had discord before."

"Well, we got it now," Ebsen answered, smacking him again with his sheathed fist. "You think you're better than everybody else here."

The other men in the room made a cordon of bodies around the two combatants, though they knew it would take much more provocation for Merian to box.

"I'm not better than anybody," Merian said, as the other man drew up to strike him again. "But I'm no less than anybody either."

Ebsen beat his mute hand against Merian again, as if he wanted to teach him a lesson, though he himself did not know what lesson that was. He knew only that the other man's lot had changed and his own had not; not for six years had it changed at all. He beat him in accordance with no known law but only because men do not like to know defeat, and he felt, with Merian's advancement, something was lost to him, so tortured whatever he might to rectify that feeling.

He struck him again and Merian withstood the blows with his hands raised in defense and an equanimity that bordered on indulgence.

I bet he won't try to hit me again, Merian thought now, as he drew himself up in the saddle and spurred the horse. I bet won't nobody ever lay another living finger on me. The memory, though, of what had passed before filled him with a shame he could not speak. I hope Ebsen is the first person I see when I get to Sorel's Hundred.

He rode for three days, barely stopping to sleep, as he stoked in his imagination the narrative of how the journey would play out and all the flattering variations of his original imagining. They were almost as fanciful as those of his last night on the old place, when he dreamed himself larger than his natural size, which was very mighty, striding a great mountain and holding a balled gavel in his hand. To the east the skies parted and he saw an antelope's head rear and stare after him, as if to give chase. He responded by running, still clutching the gavel, until the eyes of the animal bore into him with such intensity he felt himself beginning to melt. To escape he flung the hammer directly at the stars and the sky, and only then saw that it was fashioned of horn, as it split in two along an enormous chasm that began to fill immediately with a great inrush of water, the eastern half receding, as if falling into the abyss of a well, and the western sky pushing up toward him slowly as if he were sinking to the bottom of a river. He woke before he touched bottom and reached out to Ruth. He knew there were those who could interpret it rightly, but he had never revealed this vision for fear, even while waking, of what it might mean.

A mile from the main gate he stopped the horse and went into the bushes, where he changed into a new set of clothes, like war paint or a lover's talisman, which he hoped would render him stronger to stand and face the combined forces of time's elapse before proceeding. He sat high in the saddle, marking the things he knew from those he did not recognize as he headed to the stable. In front of the red brick building, a crowd of children formed around him, all from curiosity but none in recognition. He dismounted and walked the horse to a fence post, stopping to shine a small one without hair on top of the head, and asked if they knew whether Ruth was round back.

The children giggled at him and ran off as he went on ahead, back to one of the old cabins, where he paused at the door to remove his hat before knocking on the weathered gray wood—as he realized that to let himself in was no longer his right. When he lowered his hand he heard movement from inside, causing him to hold his breath as the wooden slats gave way, and he laid eyes upon Ruth for the first time in over five years.

When she looked up and saw him standing in the doorway, he could plainly see she did not immediately trust it was him, as she looked on him as you might a phantom, or else something half-dream in origin. When he called her name, though, she responded by coming nearer, and they were both torn by a series of complex emotions as he entered the room.

He had built this structure himself, even if it was long ago, and though he could barely remember its bricks and beams when he entered, he knew its deep inner blueprint as he did his own hands and hide.

Ruth pointed out a low bench next to the table for him to sit at and asked evenly—as though his presence made sense to her—"What brings you this way?" There was such determination and so little revealed in her voice that it pointed to a knot of the spirit cord that held her and would not unravel even for this man who was once hers and stood here again after more than half a decade away.

"Ah, Ruth," Merian said, standing and moving toward her, "is that the only welcome you got for me?"

"More than I had from you all these years," she rebuked him. "You got nerve, man. I will give you that."

He tried to explain to her that he could not just pick up and travel when he wanted, then began to tell how he had been hounded but found respite in Carolina. He stopped and settled on saying simply that everything got beyond him.

"Yes, it is," she said. "Even if all you telling me is true, I know. . . ." Her voice trailed and her mind lit on to something that had been stoking there ever since he started talking. "Who is she?"

She halted as soon as the words tumbled from her mouth, when she sensed her betrayal and anger were revealed for him to appraise, and she didn't want to give him anything more in that moment.

Merian did not answer for a while. He had not thought jealously of her in years, but her accusation planted its own counterweight in his mind, which pressed upon him. "What about you?" he asked.

And even after she had replied in the negative, "No one," he would not believe it, because the curve of desire he found to be permanent and sturdy as lignum vitae.

"Stay and see who else comes here then," she said, but he still would not let it go.

Just like that they found themselves embroiled in domesticity again. While the pair sat staring each other down, the door flew open and a child burst in, running to clutch Ruth around her legs. "Mama!" he screamed with delight, as if having waited for her all day.

"What are you running from?" she asked sternly.

"Nothing," he swore.

"Hm," she said, unbelieving. "Look who's here," Ruth instructed then, turning him toward his father. "Look who came all this way just to see you."

It was a leap of faith that the boy made when he ventured— "Papa?"—waiting anxiously after that as his voice passed through the room.

Merian picked the boy up and hugged him. "That's right," he said, holding the child in his arms. "That's right, Ware. Your papa has come to fetch you." He looked over the boy's head at Ruth as he spoke.

Ruth turned away to the cooking fire. "Don't fill him with fool's talk," she reprimanded coldly.

"Here you go, Ware."

Jasper gave the boy a hard candy he had thought to bring and put him back down on the floor.

"I mean it." He turned to Ruth. "I promised it when I left here, and I came back to do it."

"Magnus, go outside for a little while." She shooed the child, calling him by his other name. The boy left grudgingly and went to sit in the dirt in front of the cabin as the two of them began at it again inside.

"What are we going to do, go back and live with you and your new woman?" Ruth asked indignantly.

As they argued there vigorously, someone knocked at the door, and Ruth opened it to a small crowd gathered out front of the cabin. "We heard Jasper come back," one of the men asked. "Is he really?"

"There he is." Ruth opened the door the rest of the way to show Merian, still seated on the low bench by the table. He rose as he looked out on all those faces he had not seen for so long, which filled him with a warmth of familiarity he had lived in the wilderness without. This is who he belonged to, he thought.

What his wife would not give to him by way of praise the neighbors did, telling him how well he looked.

A simple feast was produced then, with everybody contributing something, and he ate thankfully, thinking how long it had been since he had eaten the foods of his youth. He sat with the boy balanced on his knee. The child devoured glass after glass of milk, which had been brought out for the whole room, and pressed hard against his father's chest. He was enthralled and said excitedly, to anyone who would listen, "My papa came back for me and Mama." Those close enough to hear smiled at him with warm uncertainty.

Ruth commanded the boy to be quiet, shooting Merian an accusatory look. Merian for his part lifted his hand to his mouth and filled it again with food, as a couple of men began singing a bawdy song he loved and the party spilled over into the night. It is what he promised and intended, he told her beneath the din.

When the neighbors had gone Ruth took up their argument again. "I told you not to go filling his head with all of that."

Merian did not want to argue with her, but neither would he be deterred. "You'll set up somewhere near me," he said. "It will work out fine."

Ruth told him in her turn that she was going nowhere with him, even as he went on, trying to inveigle his way into their old bed. "Don't be so stubborn," he said at last. "You know, you're so stubborn, woman, I named a mule after you."

"No you didn't give my name to a mule, man," she cursed. "If you did, I'll skin you and your mule alive."

She turned her back on him, as he laughed, then started in with more of his beguiling talk.

She listened to him skeptically, trying to resist his advance, even as she half wished for all he said to be true. More than that. She wanted all of it to be all true, all of her wanted that, but she knew she only had less than half a man and wondered what that was worth if you followed it somewhere. "This is what you leaving cost the two of us."

"It's not me going, it's being bonded to begin with," he answered.

She did not respond but allowed him to draw in closer as they negotiated whether it would be a night of greater or lesser rest.

In the morning, before Ruth set out, there came a knock at the door. When she opened it a small child blurted that Mrs. Sorel said Merian should come by the house and say hello.

Ruth looked at Merian and asked whether he had heard.

"Tell her I'll be there directly," he answered. He had thought fitfully about how he would encounter the Sorels on his ride from Stonehouses, but the scenarios always pushed against, then overflowed, the boundaries of his imagining. Now, once it was put to him, he tried to assume the best possible mood. He finished dressing and went up to the house as commanded, mindful of his original purpose in coming.

In the kitchen he greeted the new cook cordially and sat down familiarly to wait for his audience with Mrs. Sorel. Sitting there he felt like a younger version of himself and tried to remind himself of all that had changed for him since he lived here.

Nothing proved changed, though, when Hannah Sorel entered the kitchen. He found himself standing promptly then as on any day in the past to greet her.

"Jasper, Mr. Sorel is at Richmond," she said, sweeping into the room. "He will be upset to have missed you."

Merian's breath stopped in his chest but he was quick to mask the fact, asking how she had been and admiring how much the place seemed to be prospering.

"It is not the same since you left," she answered. "I'm almost sorry we let you go."

"Well, I'm almost sorry I left," he replied, playing in this game with her.

She asked him again how he was getting on and then whether he had been keeping up with church. "You haven't joined with those Congregationalists or any nonesuch out there, have you?"

"I hardly know what that is," he said, assuring her he kept much to his own company as he had always done. He asked again when she said Mr. Sorel would be getting back. "Because I actually wanted to speak to him, if I could, about Ruth and Magnus."

"I see," Mrs. Sorel answered, smoothing the top of her salt-and-pepper head and looking out the window, as his intention became clear to her. "Jasper, I don't think he will go along with it. You must know that already. Peter doesn't run things as Father did, and he doesn't believe in selling slaves, let alone freeing them." She said her words all at the same time, not at all certain how she should answer her former slave. "In any case, he is away until the middle of next month."

Merian looked around the kitchen, which unlike the rest of the house had barely changed since it was first put up. He had been there with them since the beginning, when they were newlyweds, and counted this room among the ones he had joined in building.

"Mrs. Sorel, fair is fair," he protested.

"I wish I could believe that as true, Jasper," she replied.

He knew she was being honest with him, and that there was little in her power to do. His own manumission had been on terms set by the original estate, not her husband's. The old man dictated his fate, as he did everything else when he lived, allowing him to leave either because of caprice of will or because he had served them so well from the beginning, as he had stated—when she was setting up house with the strange planter from Barbados and Jasper was her only reminder of home. Her father had made her promise as much when he presented her with him.

65

"How much do you think he might want?" Merian asked, returning to business.

"I don't know, Jasper." She could barely look at him as she said this. "I am glad to see how well you're doing for yourself in the new colony, though. You must come back to visit them again."

Their congress concluded, she left the kitchen, telling the cook to fix him something for his belly. "He's getting thin down there so far from home."

Her last words stuck in his ear, as he thought how he had lived over half his life here and grown all the way from child to manhood. He even allowed that he felt more a part of Sorel's Hundred than he did his own place in many ways, but he did not want it to be his own family's home. He thought then of Hannah Sorel's father, who had always called both him and Hannah little Columbians. He wondered at the time what had been meant by this, but it was a bond to the place and the daughter through the father, not the strange island man she married or his British friends, who hung about the house scheming adventures that should never be allowed to transpire.

When he left there that evening, his trip a failure, he pressed on Ruth the money he had brought to purchase them out with.

"What do you want me to do with this?" she asked.

"When he comes back see whether you can still do it. Go to her first, though, not him."

"Is that it?" she asked. "Is that all?"

"Ruth, what else do you want me to do?" he demanded of her sharply. "I am just a man and have done all I have it in me to do. I need to get back to my own place now."

"Yessir, my own place," she taunted him. "Go say good-bye to your boy now. Make sure you tell him you did all you had it in you to do."

Her cruelty stung at him, but as he hugged Ware good-bye he told her again, "Do like I said."

Ruth began to weep as he went to his horse, leaving them a second time trapped in captivity with little chance of ever seeing him again. Less than little, she thought, realizing his new woman was unlikely to let him get away a second time. She tried the word *never* in her mouth and knew immediately that is what it would be.

dominion

* * *

He spurs the horse and looks out on the gray horizon, heavy with a black storm cloud that darkens and gathers everything around itself, like spilt ink on a blotter. It is the Columbian sky. He hurries on beneath it back to Stonehouses.

n i n e

$\sim$

As he traveled the road home Merian found himself muttering various half-remembered recitations, though he did not know who or what he was invoking when he spoke them. They came to his lips all the same with the persistent force of ingrained habit: *Amama amachaghi amacha.* He would say the words from memory, then look down at his hands, desirous of glimpsing some part of his destiny or journey that had not been revealed before, or else praying that the fate of Ruth and Ware, called Magnus, would be gentle. He prayed because he knew their future was no longer in his power to affect. He recited his prayer again, then opened his hands again unconsciously, to release them, hoping that God, such as He was, would catch both.

How many people would have ever gone back there at all? he asked himself, trying to absolve any stain of felt guilt that might rest upon him. *Amama amachaghi amacha.* He chanted the strange words like a talisman of battle, yet he still could not remember what they meant or how he knew them in the first place. He rode the horse harder and followed a slope of his knowing southward through the forest toward his home.

Nor did he sleep the first night of his journey, but only got down from the horse and built a lean-to in the woods, while the animal watered and recuperated for the night. For him there was no rest; he cursed himself again for his failure and eventually for going back there at all.

He rose at the first shading of light and took to the southward trail again. For the first time since the week before, he began to wonder what had happened at Stonehouses during the days he was away. It was not concern, he told himself, but only curiosity. He did not even ask himself how Sanne and Purchase might have gotten on in his unannounced absence. He was headed back to them, so saw no harm done for anyone to complain about.

When he stopped the second night it was in Huguenot country, and he decided to try an inn he had not seen on his earlier trip. He tied the horse up and knocked at the door, then went inside, where he was greeted by two small round people—one a man, the other a woman. Whether they were husband and wife or brother and sister he could not say, but that they were related was unarguably clear, as both had the same set to their face and a general shared air about them. When he tried to order pork they responded to him in a language he thought might be Frankish but could not understand. They brought him out what he had asked for without further complaint, though, and he was satisfied until the little one, the woman, spoke to him sharply and pointed at a picture of the Accepted Son of God that had been pinned to the wall. He nodded his head at it, turned back to his plate, and began eating. At that point the larger one of the two came and took the spoon from his hand.

"As I haven't paid, I guess it is your spoon. So you are lucky today," Merian said, standing and towering over the man. The hotelier then pointed at the picture drawing and folded his hands together with bowed head. Merian understood that they expected him to pray before he had his meal, or else they thought he was not Christian and were trying to convert him. It was not his understanding, though, of how such things were done. He took his coat and continued out the door.

Outside he sat his horse again and pulled a piece of hardtack from the saddlebag, which he ate, half wishing he had not left in such haste. He appreciated, however, that he would now get home that much sooner, so long as the gelding's legs should hold.

He rode half possessed into the evening, when the sun became a thin yellow line at the horizon, silhouetting the heavy tarnished-gray sky that descended from the heavens as a breeze from the east began to tremble and scatter the clouds. When he finally stopped that night it was to sleep under the stars, as he had not done since he was still a young man. Half his natural life, he thought, bending slowly to avoid aggravating an ache in his knees, was passed now and over. He lay down on his pallet and tried then, as he watched the night, to draw out all the lines that had led to him, and all that led away—parsing events and faces, trying to remember the different iterations of his character and seeming fate. One had gone to Ruth and Ware, and another to Sanne and Purchase. One to Virginia and Sorel's Hundred, another to Stonehouses, or else one led to Virginia and then away, breaking again across the schism of that place into two. Only one line, though, continuing through each station, both itself and its own tangent, bending before the objects in its path and reuniting on the other side of them to continue its passing march. And one of those boys to grow up fathered and the other abandoned; one left with a knowable inheritance; the other a patrimony of questions. There is no sense to be made of it all but a pretend one, he told himself, pulling his saddle blanket up under his chin and staring up mutely before falling asleep, as he used to in times past, under the blanketing stars, the cold and naked canopy, systemic and random, of heaven.

When he finally reached Stonehouses first frost had already set in, and the crystalline glow from the fields danced in the red sunrise as he approached, making the whole place look as if it were on fire. Around the lake district all was quiet, and he reached the house without disturbance or indication that anything was the matter on his farm.

He stabled the horse at a small outbuilding he had put up, which served as a barn, then walked the worn path to his door. Inside nothing stirred when he entered, and he touched the oven to see how long it might have been since Sanne went out. It was stone cold, and a fine dust covered its surface, but he cast about briefly for her anyway, before admitting she was nowhere on the place. He did not know what he would do about it, but knew whatever it was would have to wait until later in the day. He fired the stove then and made himself some porridge and a handful of okra, as he was used to from his days alone there.

He had never considered his and Sanne's rows a thing to be worried about, but as an elemental part of the working conflict of creation. He was concerned, though, as he went out to the barn and fed the wan-looking animals, that he might have disturbed the very base of relations between the two of them. He returned and finished boiling water for a wash, savoring the hot cloth across his dirty, tired face, then bedded down for a spell—collapsing from the demands of the journey just passed. He had returned a full day quicker than it took him to go there, but when he added the time he was away, almost two weeks, he realized he had been far and gone indeed.

* * *

When he woke from his rest, he checked on the horse and decided to let the creature continue sleeping as he went on his errands. "You're no Potter," he said, slapping the gelding's shank. "Potter would've—well, never mind what Potter would have done."

He gave the beasts new hay, bundled himself in warm clothing, and set out on foot for the town center. When he reached Content's place, exhausted from the trek, he hollered around back before going inside, where he found his friend at the bar.

"Sanne here?"

"Mad at you a bit."

"But here?"

"Since three days. Scary out there by herself."

Content did not say anything else to accuse him, and Merian did not feel the need to explain himself. All the same, he told his friend, "I came from somewhere too, Content. Just like you and Dorthea and Sanne and that little boy. I came from somewhere that didn't just dry up and disappear when I left."

"Still, scary out there at night by herself," Content said, pulling a pint and placing it before Merian.

"I appreciate your looking after them."

"Nothing of it."

"Will she see me?"

"We can try and find out."

Content went out back and upstairs to the main living quarters, returning after fifteen minutes and nodding to Merian from the doorway. Merian rose and removed his hat, going the way his friend had just come from, as Content went back to the bar.

When he entered the room Dorthea said hello cordially before withdrawing to help Content in the tavern.

"I had business to attend," he said preemptively. "I had put it off already, and put it off, but it was getting older and older until it couldn't wait anymore."

"Did you bring her back with you?" Sanne asked, staring directly at him. "Is she out there at my home right now?"

"No, Sanne," he answered her. "There is no one else there, nor will there ever be."

Still, she would not return with him that evening, and it took almost a week of negotiations before she would go back to Stonehouses at all. When she finally did, she reminded him at every opportunity what it was like to sit waiting for him those first two days after he disappeared, after she had put two and one together to figure what he had done.

He bore the recrimination silently, knowing it would eventually die down and be replaced by some other passion. In due course this proved correct, when she turned her attention back to Purchase, gathering him up in her arms. "Why, I bet he hardly recognizes you anymore," she said, without looking at her husband.

Merian's face deflated, and she witnessed then the same look she had noticed when he was courting her, and wondered again whether he was not a man cursed with sadness. But Merian simply began playing with Purchase, speaking to him softly, until they were all at ease. His only remark to Sanne then was to ask whether the boy had grown in the brief time he was away. "Didn't anybody comment on his size when you were staying in the town?" he asked.

"Just that it proves country air beats all else for raising little ones," she said. "There's nothing wrong with him, Merian, he just aims to be tall, as you should know."

All the same, Merian took to measuring Purchase with a ruler to mark how much was adding on from month to month that winter, and then from season to season and year to year after that, until it was generally acknowledged that he was the tallest person, man or boy, in the colony.

The strife that had befallen husband and wife that winter, though, was not the last discord in their house, or even the last over that particular subject, but it was the end of serious conflicts. They settled in again as a unit that winter that would survive whatever was given them, understanding that they might disagree at times but would not divorce their union.

Deprived of one, his dedication to the other child continued to strengthen and served increasingly as the bond between them—so that when he added a second-floor attic to the house, he did not say to Sanne, I think this will be good for us, but rather, "Purchase might someday appreciate it if the house had a second story."

For his part Purchase continued the business of growing up, now infant, now crawling, now toddler pulling the bread down from the table, until one of his parents would take him up. As he matured and began to express interests of his own, less tolerant of whatever Merian and Sanne put before him for amusement.

Wooden blocks he found satisfying, but only when he banged them together with all the force of his fat arms. Shapes made against the wall were dull, no matter what form or what noise was made to accompany them. Birds, however, he thought intriguing and would lie in waiting when they flew into the yard around the house, before pouncing, making them scatter briefly just beyond his reach.

Near his eighth birthday, when he was old enough to go about independently, Merian began to take him on the rounds of the farm, but the boy showed no interest in any creature save the chickens and the geese, who swam out on the lake in summer. After his father released him from his chores, he would go lie in the meadow where Ruth Potter was buried to stare at the falcons as they circled the sky in search of an evening meal.

When he returned home at night, Merian would invariably chide him for his laziness, warning what tribulations that particular path held.

To break him of bad habits and daydreaming, Merian tried to instill respect for laboring in the fields, taking him at his side and pointing out how each crop was grown and what they received for each thing there. At harvesttime, he took the boy to market with him, to learn from his bartering; he would produce then a crude tally sheet of the hours Purchase had helped him, and count out two coins, which he gave to him before they entered Content's free house. "A man should always be paid for his work," Merian said, giving the boy his monies. "There is no exception ever to be made to that."

Purchase's eyes lit when he received his pay, and he pocketed it, promising to save and add to it until he could use it for something worthy. Merian rubbed the boy's shoulder and pulled up to the bar, where Content greeted them both.

"You'll be bigger than your own father soon, if you don't stop it," he said, giving the kid a watery punch.

"Uncle Content, look," Purchase said, showing off his wages.

"Yes, well, this one's on the house," Content told him, adding a penny to his bounty.

"Don't go giving him charity," Merian complained. "He's already half spoiled."

Purchase eyed the penny still on the bar, unwilling to let it go but certain Merian would make Content take it back if he didn't do something clever. "I'll sweep for it," he volunteered, thinking what useful task he could perform.

"You can't go hiring yourself out," Merian said. "We need you at Stonehouses." When he went and got the broom and began sweeping from the front of the store, though, Merian was proud to see the boy busy with honest work.

As the adults talked at the bar, complaining of the harvest and the way the outpost had grown beyond all recognition, Purchase worked diligently moving the dust around the ankles of the drinkers and other guests of the inn, until he had amassed a respectable pile of dirt at the back of the store. As he swept this into the alley, finishing with his work, he heard a man calling to him.

"Ever seen a baby falcon?" he asked, opening his coat to reveal a blind hatchling.

The creature was still covered in down, but as he stared at it in amazement, Purchase thought he saw the rippled under muscles of flight and capture.

"Where did it come from?"

"He fell from the nest," the stranger said. "But for a shilling he'll make you a right hunter."

"I don't have a shilling," Purchase complained, going into his pocket to retrieve his wages. "All I have is this much."

"Well, I suppose I can make you a deal this once," the man said, lifting the coins before Purchase had even finished the sentence and bestowing the bird on the boy with a courtly motion before disappearing down the narrow alley.

Purchase held the bird in his hands, trembling from palm to sole as he ran back into the bar to show his father what he had acquired.

"You did what?" was all Merian said, hanging his head in dismay. "Look, Content, my boy here has bartered a whole season's labor for a sickly vulture."

"It's a falcon," Purchase argued. "That's what the man who sold it to me said."

"What man was that, son?" Content asked, looking at the poor miserable bird.

Purchase looked around and admitted the seller had already left. "He was sitting right there." He pointed to the stool where the bird vendor had been sitting as he swept.

Content looked at him. "No one ever sits at the stool," he said. "It's just there to block access."

Still, the boy swore the man had sat just where he said, and also that the bird he held was a falcon.

"I would never tell you other than the truth," his father told him, before deriding the bird as "carrion vulture," and "rotten buzzard." Purchase knew, though, it was a raptor of prey, and he need only wait for it to fly.

First he held it in his hands and gave it small tosses that he hoped might make it lift off, but which his mother claimed only frightened the animal. "It is a wonder he eats," she told him. "Anything that young away from its mother should be rightfully dead." When she saw the anger in his eyes, though, she desisted and told him how the great brick oven in the kitchen came to be built over many years.

He did not want to take many years, though, and installed the hatchling falcon among the chickens, hoping he might learn from their efforts of remembered flight, or else that the instinct of the hunt would seize it and he would turn on the weaker animals to devour them.

To his surprise, one day while they were in the chicken coop, his falcon did find wing, jumping a few wide feet when a chick ventured too near. From these flichtering beginnings he soon took the entire room with a few easy beats of his wings.

At dinner, Purchase was excited by the new development. "Well, what are you going to do when you take him from the coop?" Merian asked. When Purchase inquired what he meant, he was told that the bird could no longer stay in the pen, or it would eat the chickens, and that it would not ever return once it had gone free.

"It will," Purchase argued, looking to his mother for support. At night, though, he was seized by the fear that he would lose his bird and decided to keep it in the chicken pen forever.

He was stubborn about it, but his father more so, and he left the house one morning to find the bird tied to a post in the yard. "Now untie it," Merian commanded.

Purchase did as he was told and walked over to his bird, noticing that it did not look like the falcons that he had seen over the pasture, but neither was it a vulture. He undid the hitch in the twine and smoothed the bird's feathers.

The animal released a low thrill of approval, then climbed onto Purchase's shoulder and down his arm. The boy looked at his pet in this pose and his heart beat with pleasure, because it was so like a true raptor responding to its master. His joy, however, was short-lived when the bird lifted off his arm, with a motion that generated a deep pressure on his flesh, as it leaped into a tree.

The boy called, and the animal would not come, but it also did not go off on its own. It stayed perched there, receiving table scraps until the first of spring. He thought it might stay on indefinitely, but when he went to feed it one day it had disappeared.

Merian tried to explain to him how everything separated out from its source eventually but also had to stay near to it. That's what the bird was doing, he said. But to his son the words sounded victorious, and he searched the sky for his bird, until far off he saw a speck high up over the rolling hills. It was his, and he knew it would return. His father looked at the boy and said nothing. His mother came to him in the yard to offer her sympathy, but he was getting too old in years to accept her comfort so easily.

He looked between his father and mother again, and again to the sky as the speck wheeled and turned on high, before making a blunted attempt at its first dive. The father took the son's shoulder under his hand and began to talk to him of that year's planting. The son listened dispassionately. He would forge his own way.

t e n

As Purchase grew older, and his own health began to grow less dependable, Merian looked more and more to his son for help with Stonehouses. Without his eventual aid, Merian knew, he would be forced to turn to the market for hired labor or else scale back what he had worked so hard to increase over the years.

He tried to interest the boy in caring for the herd of cattle he had bred each from the other over the long winter months. But Purchase, true to his nature, became lost in the pasture himself, given over to reverie and daydreams or simple inattentiveness. When Merian employed him in the fields, he found the boy less productive with each new day, as if playing slow. There were also many tasks he simply could not master. The only interest he ever showed in farmwork seemed to be when Merian went to the barn to fix something that had broken. Then the boy would watch the tools in motion, as he had once watched the birds over Potter's Field, until the repair was complete. Merian was always careful to explain what he did and allow Purchase a hand in the repair. Try as he might, though, he could not convert this interest into general enthusiasm for the land.

Come harvest that year, Merian hired three hands and relegated his boy to the house with his mother, trying hard not to complain or display the bitterness he felt.

Finally he could not take it and took the lash to the boy, but even the welts on his hide could not make Purchase pretend to love labor and exertion. When the harvest was done, Merian had Purchase accompany him to town. This year instead of going to Content's immediately after the market closed he stopped the cart in front of the smith's. After some time inside he called for Purchase, who came sheepishly to the door. The man looked at the boy and nodded. "He'll do just fine."

In all of this Purchase did not speak but did as his father bade him, taking a sack that was already packed for his stay.

When Merian returned home Sanne wanted to know where Purchase was.

"He is apprenticed to the smith," Merian answered.

Sanne was stunned when she heard this. "You cannot apprentice the boy," she said. "He is hardly ten years old."

"He looks fourteen to the smith."

She yelled at him to hitch the cart and go retrieve her son. Reluctantly Merian did as she bade, and when she joined him for the ride into town he fully expected to be upbraided the entire way.

"What were you thinking, man?" Sanne asked. "How could you do such a thing?"

"I was thinking he is old enough to learn to work."

When they arrived at the smith's shop she pushed her husband from the cart to go reclaim her son from the harm in which Merian had left him. Inside, where she had expected to find him crying and miserable, waiting for his rescue, she instead found him studying all the action without complaint and performing his chores with such diligence he did not notice their arrival. All around them the heat from the smith's oven baked the room, and the hiss of hot metal placed by another assistant to cool in water nearly drove her to distraction, as she told Purchase to get his things so that he could come home.

The smith complained to Merian that they had a deal and that any boy in the county would be happy to apprentice there. "What can I do?" Merian replied to the man. "His mother says he isn't old enough yet."

"Fourteen is old enough to work at the devil's own hearth," the smith argued.

"Yes, but the problem is he's only barely ten. He's just a bit large for his age."

"I'll be," the smith swore, slapping Purchase on the back. "You can come back in a few years, or any other time you like, son. I promise to make you a place."

Purchase was happy for this, for he had found in the furnace of the shop and the working of the element of fire an excitement he knew would never be present on the farm. "If my papa says so."

Merian was pleased to be deferred to by the boy and thought his brief stint at work was already beginning to pay dividends. He assured him it would be all right to rejoin the smith as a proper apprentice when he was older. "As long as you do your chores at Stonehouses in the meanwhile," he said exactly.

Sanne looked from her husband to the smith, trying to decide if they had arranged some pact between themselves that she was not privy to.

"Jasper, you'll tell me what this is about yet."

"Say what you want about his age, it's never too young to teach him good habits and honest work."

In subsequent years Purchase would recall his day at the smith's as among the most memorable of his early years. Although he did not speak much about the experience later, the primacy of heat and water and force was nearer to him than the slow plantings his father dragged him around to witness and help with every spring, or the wheat that was harvested when the seedlings had matured. "Eating seems to interest you plenty, though," Merian, in lighter moods, would always joke when Purchase was older.

Still, Merian worried deeply for all he had sacrificed to create at Stonehouses. Feeding a family is enough satisfaction for your labor, he always tried to console himself, but with a second story added and very nearly the entire land under cultivation or pasture, he thought it would be a shame and a waste if the boy never developed an interest in it. "I wish my father had given me an interest in something," he reproved whenever the youngster rebelled against his work or teachings. "Or that I had been anything other than an orphan. You don't know yet how difficult it all is."

To Purchase's young ears, his father's words sounded like little more than scolding. He wished to be a falconer and hunt his birds, or else a governor with the king's business on his hands, or a knight defeating great dangers. He did not want to be a farmer ruled by weather and caprice. Despite this, he respected his father and tried to obey him. Still, he never did know whether he would be able to please him.

Sanne watched the two of them and hoped they might fulfill the hopes and expectations each had for the other, which she knew to be different from her own for either of them, which were only that each should find contentment.

Merian watched the land, taking satisfaction in what he had done but aware that someday all would be dismantled, and that he should plant on a scale small enough to sustain alone in his old age. He no longer remembered what he made that first year at market, but it was still the season he was proudest of, when he had no company and battled nature without a reserve of food or safety. Having survived that he could not fret for the future. His natural optimism, though, no longer had a place to expand to and express itself.

"He is young still," Sanne counseled. "You'll be proud of him yet."

Merian hoped she was prescient in the way mothers often are—and fathers too seldom—but he spent the fall months after the harvest going on long walks, inspecting both his lands and the new buildings that had gone up in the intervening years. A new road, north and south, now crossed the original westward line ten miles farther on. It moved goods and peoples all in a tumultuous rush, to settle the areas of the even farther-outlying counties, making him wonder how long before everything had been seized and a man either had gotten in with the original parceling or would be left without, until some new land and new parceling of it, fair and first-come, came about. And what about the last one there at the great partitioning? He could not answer but thought he should like to see Chiron again one day and ask him what would happen to him who had no direction, physical or otherwise, to move in away from his original source. Would he be satisfied, never knowing the tear of separation or else pained by the constriction of his movement?

He thought only that the boy better make up his mind on one thing or the other before too long, and that the other lines he had crossed, and been custodian of, must take custody of themselves soon.

He thought again then for the first time in years of Ruth and Ware, called Magnus. In his mind they were locked on the Sorel place, as he knew they always would be, either because she had lost courage to ask what was even in the rights of a bondswoman or because he had been too impatient to wait. He forced this last thing away from himself. He had done what was his responsibility and knew you could no more make someone free than you could keep that same thing away from one determined to have it.

On his walk home from the edge of his lands, he stared out over the rolling hills and valley, which were now under cultivation as far as he could see, and decided then he would continue in any case with the land and no more wait for the boy, Purchase, to show an interest.

He took this new optimism and set out on a project of improvement, so that when he finished it would be the equal of any farm in the colony and his fortune beyond any he might have imagined for himself when first beginning. Jasper Merian set his mind to growing rich.

Sanne, who was well into her middle years now as well, watched her husband in his new ambition for fortune. It reminded her of their early years together and also instilled in her a new hope for the future. She took it that he was decided on being less demanding and more forgiving of the boy, but also that he would rest less of his own ambition upon him. She was more tender in turn with her husband, cooking and teasing as she did all those years ago when he was clearing the second field and she was building her stove.

Purchase that winter often sought his father's approval for his various pursuits, telling him, "I'm going to build an army camp in the barn" or "I am off in search of pirate's treasure in the woods just there," so his father would take it that he was engaged in constructive activity.

Merian then, looking at the boy, thought he might not be such a disappointment, and, when he took him into his latest scheme for the improvement of the place, was much pleased with the boy's contributions, finding him quite natural with measuring tools and also able to imagine things before they were cast in hard reality, and—while perhaps still lazy—not at all slow.

The project, which was to be the last of the improvements for the year, was something Merian had long dreamed of but thought too presumptuous for the modest scale of Stonehouses, especially given the fact that he had already thought to give it a name. Now that he had decided on improving the place once more, he also decided his new creation was the first thing he needed for the new phase in his life, as it marked a man who took his affairs seriously and would let him better manage them.

He went into town for various small pieces and to check his designs against other examples of its kind, but found he could mostly make it himself, and with Purchase's offers of help with the measuring and cutting he was certain of its accuracy.

When he finished, a great seal marked the center of the garden where Sanne still planted vegetables and herbs for the house. Now the movement of hours and seasons would be marked there as well, no longer a crude thing measured out in plantings and the metronome of the harvest, or the length of his shadow as the sun rode the back of his labors. For he had installed a sundial at Stonehouses, and it was more than mere decoration; he had brought time and chronology onto his property and into his possession.

What he measured that night, though, was less time than the sum of his dealings in his early days, which he did to appraise how much he had been gaining or losing. What he counted was zero parents, equal siblings, two masters and one mistress (depending on the count), an untold number of voyages, three houses built, two languages learned (though only one remembered), a solid handful of dependable friends, two male children, and two wives.

Of the future he knew not, and tried not to give much care, knowing only that he could not foresee it, but that things would pass in their time and work either for good or ill, depending on other devices.

These were the reckonings of Jasper Merian, after a half score of seasons had passed at Stonehouses, in the ancient days of Columbia, in one of those districts named for Carol Rex, before the nameless Indian battles, in the beginning, second immemorial age, in America.

II
age of fire

o n e

~◞

He is a forger of metal with no interest in the ground except its hidden ores and nothing of the plow except the strength and sharpness of its blade. He stands bare-chested from the waist up and, you can see, he is black as pig iron, or molten just after it is quenched. All except his eyes, which are light as wheatcorn. They belong to no one anybody around here has ever seen except he himself, and it comes down that he was not born with them but that they turned so from the intensity of his gaze into the furnace. He seems blind standing there—mute. Preachers will come one day to lay their hands on him, to release whatever has taken possession of those orbs, and women as well, who hope to know what lies behind them.

He keeps his stare fixed to heaven just now, as a cluster of white comets passes over the sky like angels, before turning fiery bright and speeding toward the lower reaches of the divine universe, right to the illuminated edge of this world, where they become blue-lined and red centered as God's own heart worked in a blast furnace, before burning out and disappearing somewhere in the forestlands below.

He marks the spot well, etching in his mind the exact position in the mountains where the specks of light were last seen, then saddles his horse and sets off in discovery of the fallen bit of sky.

* * *

He journeyed three days and two hundred miles through the woods, without food or water for either man or horse. The trip, so says the lore of that country, would have taken a mere two days at the clip he rode and the animal flesh he made it upon, but the horse did fall of thirst in the last thirty miles and the man would not abandon it but carried him the rest of the way. This much was not true. The people of that country are well-known liars, though, especially as regards their history—making everything reflect well on themselves and region, but castigating all that might betray any secret weakness or want.

He arrived at the place he had marked, deep in an uncharted desolation of black pines and walked through their shadow nearly blinded, so little light penetrated those branches to reach the earthen floor. For what he searched, though, he did not need light but could find it even in the bosom of the darkest cave with his eyes bound. He sought as much by his nose as his eyes. When he smelled the odor of iron he knew his hunt was nearly complete, and he kept on until he saw the first dark rock, two fists in size, with a blue scrim from Heaven all around it. He touched the grooved surface and found it still cool as the roof of Heaven itself. He picked it up, placed it in his bag, and went on, until he had collected them all like a goose hen shepherding her flock. The bag weighed near a hundred pounds when he finished, as he lifted it up like a hay bale over his head. He went back then to the exhausted horse, whom he led at a gingerly pace, no matter how much he desired to be back home with his newfound treasure.

He knew the value of the rocks from the first, but not yet what he would make with them. That night as he rested it was revealed to him in a dream, and he rose and woke the horse, and the two of them began to fly toward home.

When he arrived back in town it was morning on the clock but not yet in the world, and he went on to his workshop, where he barred tight the door. The oven was still warm from the day before, but not hot as he needed it, and he spent hours stoking it back up to its maximum hotness. By the time he judged the furnace to be ready it was dawn, and one of the apprentices knocked at the door. He warned him off, to be left alone with his labor. The others came soon after, but he no longer bothered responding to their knocks and whistles, because he had started the rocks and watched them steadily without moving. When they were melted down he separated out the impurities, which were miraculous few, then fired the metal again. It was pure steel, like nothing the earth produces. When it was ready to be molded, he took it to his anvil and began working it into form with all the passion of force he possessed, raising and lowering the hammer onto the fired rock until it began to have shape and meaning beyond heat and mere metal. The sweat on his brow poured from his concentrated thought as much as from the furnace, but both commingled forms of perspiration evaporated almost instantaneously. He felt dry there in his cocoon of work, but to an outsider looking on he seemed to be covered in a cloud of steam.

After he had beaten a rough shape, he added to it a thin strip from another of the treated rocks, then hammered them until they were fused as hand and arm. The sound of his hammering, a familiar noise in the town, rang out that morning with a clarity and intensity that made passersby stop on the sidewalk to listen as he worked. Each time he drew the steel from the fire the metal screeched as it was being taken away, as two solids or else two similar elements crossing each other. Indeed, men who were later cut by it invariably described both the blade and the resultant sensation as a deep, mineral scalding.

Satisfied, he quenched it all in oil and left it to cool. In time he removed the blade and studied his effort, then fired portions of it again at various temperatures, hammering away the minuscule flaws and imperfections but also strengthening the metal a thousandfold more. He repeated the cooling, this time slackening the heat in water that had been mixed with certain liquids from his workbench.

He finished it on the second morning and quenched the whole thing in the vast vat of rainwater at the center of the room. He then took a stone to file and sharpen the edge, but found it was already dangerous to touch. He tested the edge and the tensile strength and was deeply satisfied. When one of the assistants knocked at the door this time he unbarred it and allowed the other man to enter.

He had worked until daylight pulled his head up to the horizon, just as the morning star, Venus, disappeared under the summit of the mountains, and he held the sword by its hilt up to the sun to see clearly what had been created in his furnace. It was perfect. Or nearly so.

When Charlton, the young assistant who was in charge of keeping the fires going, entered that morning, the first thing he noticed was the motif radiating out from the center of the sword, like patterns on Damascus steel, as it rested there on Purchase's bench. These were not ordinary etched formations, though. People lucky enough to view it over the years all claimed they saw different things there, but even the wisest men and women could only see what they already knew. The majority saw nothing at all. What Purchase and his assistant both saw in the metal, as it cooled from its own creation, neither would confess to the other, for it was the entire world and future of the not-yet-conquered continent.

First was Auriga, called the Charioteer, who was the son of Hephaestus. There were then the instruments: Caelum, known as the Sculptor's Chisel; Pyxis, the Compass; Sextens and Octans; and Norma as well. Great Fornax adorned an edge, as did Scutum and Horologium. Andromeda did burn brightly, and Ara, that most ancient altar, was there like a jeweled inlay in the metal itself. The celestial birds were present in pairs, Tucana and Aquila, the Eagle; Corvus and great Phoenix, though this was the only thing that might be called a blemish on the blade, as it was the same purple color of that creature in life, and was in fact the strongest metal, standing hard at the tip.

Delphinus played with other lighthearted beasts. Ophiuchus was present with his snakes, and Draco, the Dragon, appeared to turn, as it does in the night sky. Old Boötes drove the Bears as e'er he will—until the polestar turns away.

He saw Adam and Eve and their children, whom he did recognize, but hundreds of other people he did not. He saw in fact whole peoples who seemed strange to him and so could not make out their actions, only the ones he had already heard tell of. But everywhere on it he saw hope.

Down, not far from the base of the sword, Purchase Merian saw a man who was undoubtedly his father, Jasper; then himself. There were other figures as well near to them, but when these two appeared he nearly dropped the metal, for while the others were all strangers or only distantly known, these two stood so forcefully and lifelike he recognized that it was work even beyond what he could create and knew he held what had been blessed by God.

Besides his own hidden history he also saw a face that was clear and knew it was another close to him, though he did not recognize the man. He next saw the history of the country, from the explorers Cabot, Columbus, Balboa, Magellan, and Raleigh in their armadas first sailing, and the king's chartering each of the colonies one by one. He saw as well fantastic inventions that he could not decipher from the more mythic things that adorned the blade. Had he an interest, he could have counted and named the great artists and scientists of the land and even its immortal bards. Of the philosophers there were not a great many, but its generals were numerous and mighty.

He also saw wars. He saw them first in what he recognized as the African and European lands, and he saw the Indian conflicts, ending with that race sent on a great trek out of their countries. Nearer he saw a war between Englishmen and another people who seemed much like them. Deeper down the blade he saw war again in Europe, that conflict then spilling off and onto all known parts of the globe. He also saw wars with the strange races he did not recognize and could not name, but that his countrymen did fight with them.

Next he counted men he did not know but could tell were to be the great leaders of the colonies, and of them were every race of men, including some he had not seen before and could not recognize. His eye did stop and go back, though, when he realized how close was the first of the mighty wars imprinted on the sword, and this he surmised was the reason for it being called into being.

When he could see no more, as the motif faded at a point and would not reveal its mysteries, he bade Charlton to hold it and feel its faultlessness, but the instrument was too heavy for the boy. One by one the rest of the workers entered the shop that day and marveled at what Purchase had created in his sequestered fever, but none could lift it, nor could any decipher the legend that ran down the center of the blade.

The sharpness, though, was evident to all. One man touched a solid iron bar to it, which was split evenly in two. The same was true for paper, hair, and even rock. Nor did the blade dull. When he asked that they try to break it, they all balked, not wanting to harm anything so lovingly crafted. In fact none would approach until Purchase offered a reward for whoever could break that steel. Each man tried it then, but none of them could succeed. For Purchase had made a perfect sword, which he told all who would listen was the only need it had for existence, though he knew by then it would eventually be part of an altogether different and very sad business.

Defeated in their efforts to break the blade, the other men retired, each speaking in awe of it—most of all the master smith who had been first to teach Purchase about fallen metals. He then spent the rest of that day creating a scabbard for the weapon. Although the scabbard was itself a fine item of worthy craftsmanship, and even beauty, it was quite plain compared to the sword. Nor did Purchase see any reason it should be any other way. He wrapped the entire bundle in a piece of handsome fabric, then swaddled it again in coarse burlap to protect it. When he had finished, he bade an assistant bring his horse around.

When the boy appeared with the animal it was already nearing darkness, and Purchase boarded it in one graceful motion, holding the package in his hands. He set out briskly for Stonehouses, where he was expected.

He arrived just as the shadow across the sundial out front spread into general communion with the shadows around it, and the thumbnail of a sun, which had held up just long enough for him to say he was there before sundown, vanished.

He stabled his horse, rubbing it down a little before entering the house through the kitchen, where Sanne's great oven was filled with foods. Before he even opened the door, he could feel the warmth from the other side of the wood and smell that his mother had been cooking all day. Inside he found Adelia, the girl who helped Sanne with the house chores, stirring a large pot as he greeted her.

"They were waiting for you to eat," she said, as he made his way to the dining room. There he found his parents, as well as Content and Dorthea, several of his father's friends, and their immediate neighbors— except Rudolph Stanton, who never mingled—all gathered to celebrate Merian's birthday.

Purchase first greeted his mother, then all their guests, as his father watched from the chair where he sat. Finally he went to his elder.

"Since when is sundown half past eight?" Jasper asked, looking at a watch he had bought some years before. "You know how we appreciate punctuality."

"You have my profuse apologies, Papa."

Purchase knew his father's moods by now, as well as how best to avoid them, but tonight he found occasion for good cheer, seeing that he was not intent on punishing him for his tardiness. The two men clasped and he bid his father a happy birthday and good health. Adelia then came out and Sanne announced dinner to be ready.

The guests sat down at a table of warm cherry wood, which worked on a scheme of folding and expanding sections that, when let out to its full length, was big enough to accommodate all the guests comfortably.

The table was expanded that evening the entire length of the room and laid with hot dishes of venison, beef roast, ham, turkey, duck, partridge, potatoes, yams, green peas, and warm bread. For dessert there was pudding, apple pie, and cobbler.

Afterward the cider and wine continued to flow at the table, with everyone drinking and enjoying themselves tremendously. Tea and coffee were served at the end, after they sang in that most comfortable hall to Merian's health and grand hospitality.

When everyone had satisfied himself with food and drink, and they had cheered their host sufficient enough for a king, they began to bestow gifts upon Merian to commemorate this day of joy and feasting, for he had been on the land then some twenty-odd years, and could say he was a man in old age. The exact number he knew not, but that it was around fifty. Stonehouses was known by then across the county, and his years and prosperity there had surpassed even his own expectations. True, he was frustrated in the desire to keep expanding his lands, but he had done well, bringing wealth enough to his house, and counted his time now in blocks and cycles of years instead of a single calendar turn. He was happy with what he had wrought and been blessed with.

His only living sorrow was in his son Purchase, who went steadily in his own direction, and that never closer to Stonehouses and the hearth but farther away.

First Content and Dorthea presented him with a cask of the best brandy sold in the colonies, and Merian was much pleased. Then there came a French hunting pistol from the chandler, who over the years he had grown, if not fond of, at least able to bear on friendly terms. "It'll not backfire on me, will it, Pete?" he asked, to gales of laughter from all present who had ever had dealings with the man. He was then given a hat by Sanne, that was very dear, and he was a man at ease and good comfort.

When he thought he had received all his presents, he smiled and lifted his glass to the assembly. He did not begrudge his son not giving him anything, as such notions are not held in spite among members of the same family. No he was not sorrowed.

Purchase, however, came forth then with his present and placed it before Merian, who smiled with abundance and gratitude even before opening it.

91

When everyone saw the size of the package from Purchase, they all pressed near to watch as Merian undid the wrapping. After the cloth flew away the entire room held its breath as they looked on the scabbard, for it was beautiful in itself. Merian closed his hand around the sword's hilt and drew it forth. Purchase himself was apprehensive, remembering that no man in the workshop could lift it, but Merian pulled it forth quite handsomely, as if he had been handling swords his entire life.

Everyone in the room looked at the metal when it came forth among them, and the wondrous flash that danced in the light, and each of them let out the breaths they had been holding, as if pining for something or someone. Jasper himself looked at it and saw his entire history written on the blade: first were two people he could not make out fully but knew instinctively to be his mother and father. He saw next the Sorels, and he saw Ruth, and he saw Ware, called Magnus, though both of them were, to his mind, abstractions. Even Ruth was not as he would have her be but much receded from his mind's eye—so that he saw very little of her when he tried to look there, though he did try sometimes. On the sword she was bright and perfect, and he began thinking again of those lines that had nearly tied him down all those years ago on the road out from Virginia.

He saw the gods of a strange people, as well as the same Adam and Eve that Purchase had viewed. There was so much there that, as he read it all, he allowed himself a rare moment and wept, bedazzled both by the sword and that his son had thought so lovingly of him.

His chiefest pride was in knowing that Purchase had made it, for everyone could see it was of a craftsmanship hardly seen, either in the colonies or, said one present who had been there, in Europe. For the sword itself, he was a farmer and sometime carpenter and housewright, with no pretensions to anything else in the world, besides that he was lord of Stonehouses. He was a man of peace with no need of the blade. Nonetheless, this one did take on a place of utmost honor in his home, and he embraced Purchase again. For he was so happy his son could do such things and that it might mean he intended to do all right as a man in general.

All the men present then tried one by one to lift the sword and found they could but only stare at it, resting there on Merian's table. This was well and good, for if anyone could have moved that magnificent gift, even the most honest among them would not have hesitated to steal it.

Sanne kissed Purchase for doing so grand a thing for his father, and she too beamed with pride at her son's ability to turn rock into something so wondrous with nothing but his skill and the furnace.

After the gifts had been bestowed, they drank another toast as night grew real, and it was soon time for the guests to depart. When their friends had bidden good-bye and were safely on the road again, only the three Merians and Adelia were left in the house. There was then a knock at the door. As Adelia was in the kitchen, Purchase went to answer, to see whether it was one of the guests returning for some forgotten trifle, a latecomer, or one come for another reason entirely.

When he opened the door he saw there a very tall man who seemed vaguely familiar—for he had seen him in the sword—although he had never met him before in life.

"I'm looking for Jasper Merian," the man said, holding his road-beaten hat down over his hands.

"Who should I tell him is calling?" Purchase asked, wondering that one who looked as lowly as the fellow at their door should have come to the front and not gone around to the rear of the house. "What is thy name?"

"Tell him it is someone from Sorel's Hundred."

Purchase nodded and went back inside to his father.

"There is someone at the door who says he's from somewhere called Sorel's Hundred and claims to have business with you," Purchase announced to his father, after reentering the dining hall. "Didn't seem to mind that it's well past normal visiting time."

Merian excused himself and stood to go to the door, as his wife and son milled there waiting to see who this late arrival could be. When Merian returned, he held the other man with great affection and introduced him to the two in the room. "I'd like both of you to meet someone very dear to me, who I have not seen in a great many years," the old man said, presenting the stranger to his family. "His name is Ware, though he is also called Magnus, and he is my son. You can see that, because he is punctual."

"Purchase," he said, leading Ware over, "this is your brother, even if you never knew you had one."

This was not entirely true. Sanne had told him on a couple of occasions, late at night when the two happened to meet up in the kitchen or else were otherwise awake when the rest of the house was quiet, that his father had whole secret lives she knew but little of, and one of them included another wife and child. This, though, was first proof to Purchase of his father's life before them. Still, he went to Magnus and embraced him as bidden, and the affection between them was very natural.

Ware, called Magnus, stood there in the center of the great room and received his brother's embrace. He would have returned it but could not hug him back, because his hands they were still shackled.

t w o

~

The two men sat across from each other with the fire burning low behind them, looking at one another only tentatively. Although they touched often, it was by accident and caused them both some small embarrassment at first, until they grew used to it. Breaking the center chain was very simple. Purchase did this with a strong chisel and a good sharp whack from one of the hammers on a workbench in the barn. The bracelets, though, were another matter, and he was forced to work at them a long time with the smallest tools in his possession.

It was an admirable lock, and when he finally deciphered its clenching mechanism he would feel some small sympathy for his defeated adversary, for its maker had designed that lock with great care and deep insight and intended it to hold until whosoever had mastery of the key released it, but not before.

"How is that?" Purchase asked, pausing in his work to get a better hold on one of the shackles.

Ware massaged his raw flesh beneath the iron and answered, "Not bad. But I have lived with them awhile and am not the best judge."

"Do you want me to wait so you can catch your breath?" Purchase asked, for he could see how the skin under the handcuff had been almost completely removed and what pain Ware must be in, despite shrugging it off.

"No. Better to go ahead and have done with it."

Purchase resumed work, trying not to aggravate the skin under the irons, which was orange with rust around the wounds where the metal had contacted his blood. As he watched the stoicism with which Ware bore this pain and intrusion, Purchase felt a tremendous respect for the other man and his private travails.

Ware, for his part, looked at Purchase, and how deliberate he was with what was undeniably an unpleasant and rough business, and his affection for the younger man took hold as for a brother raised under the same roof, and even if they were very different men, they were bound together then nonetheless.

They went on like this, with unspoken tenderness for each other, as they shared a singular understanding until the lock finally revealed itself and opened. Nor when it was done did they thank or comfort each other, but took it each in stride as roles that might easily be reversed.

When the irons were finally off, Ware plunged his hands up to the elbow in a vat of water, washing the filth and dried blood from them. As he did this, Merian and Sanne came into the barn. Sanne carried with her a parcel of clean rags, which she had cut into bandages. When Ware took his hands from the water, she dried them and began to dress his raw wrists in the cotton.

Merian surveyed this scene and did not speak, but he was exceedingly proud of all his family. This, he thought, far surpassed any birthday he had ever celebrated before, even that original year of freedom when he was still in Virginia and first gave himself one, knowing not when he was actually born. He went carousing that year with friends until the celebration turned some unmarked corner and he was left very sore off from celebrating. He figured then it was because he had not done it before and so was not used to it, but soon learned that that was the nature of joy—a flying that could also turn full around if you took it out of sensible range.

He thought this year he had achieved perfect balance.

When Sanne finished dressing Ware's wounds, they all returned to the main house, where Sanne had Adelia bring out food from the kitchen for Ware, which he devoured at first in a rush, but soon slowed down, seemingly full. When he had his fill of meats he took a very little bit of pudding and a half glass of cider to wash it all down.

"Are you feeling better?" Purchase asked.

"Do you want anything else?" Sanne wanted to know.

"I'm fine, I'm fine," he answered them. "A whole heap better than before."

"What else—" Sanne began, but Merian intervened.

"There's plenty of time for getting acquainted. I think Ware might like to rest right now."

Merian led him to an empty room above the kitchen and asked whether there was anything else he needed to pass the night in peace. The new arrival replied there was not, and very soon after Merian left the room.

Magnus, as he himself preferred to be called, looked around in the dark, staring into the edges and corners of the unfamiliar chamber, trying to grow used to the climate indoors again and to figure what sort of course he had charted—not knowing whether he would be received here or not, or why exactly he chose to come to this place rather than great Philadelphia, or even as far off as Boston, anyplace where he might blend in with the general population instead of stopping where he had. He wondered still whether the law might catch up with him—and if they had been pursuing him at that very moment they surely would have, for he scarcely finished the thought before falling asleep from tiredness.

After showing Ware the room Merian went to his own bed, where Sanne lay awake waiting for him. "How is he?" she asked when he entered.

"Fine as might be expected," Merian answered.

"And you?"

"It's a great day for me, Sanne. I never on earth thought I would live to see it. Thank you."

"Well, what happens now? He just shows up a grown man, very likely wanted by the authorities, and you take him in?"

"We will see, Sanne."

"What about her? Where is she?"

"He didn't say, and I haven't asked him yet," Merian said. In truth, though, he knew what had most likely happened. The boy would have never left Ruth if she was still alive, not if he had suffered everything long enough to become a full-grown man and hadn't left before that. "There will be plenty of time for questions."

"Don't you want to know?"

"Good night, Sanne."

"And I'm supposed to just stand back, whatever happens."

"Good night, wife."

"Good night, husband."

Merian woke the next day before the rest of the house stirred and went first thing to town, where he met with Content but did not tell him straightaway of the new arrival.

"If a man needed to get papers, Content," he asked, "where would he go?"

"Depends on what he needed them to say."

"That he was legitimate."

"Legitimate what?"

"Legitimate free before the law."

"Are they for you?"

"In a way."

"Everybody knows you and knows who you are."

Seeing no other avenue Merian confessed to the new situation on his place and slid a guinea across the table. "Can you take care of it for me?"

Content nodded that he could but asked Merian why he hadn't come out and told him the thing to begin with. "It would be a lot simpler that way, Merian."

"Don't give me your lectures, Content," Merian said. "I don't see that it's all so complicated now."

"It isn't," Content answered. "It just would have been simpler the other way." Content went to the door, locked the tavern, and had Merian come with him to his office in back. There, he took out a sheet of very fine writing paper, an ink pot, and his quill. He asked Merian again for the name of his son and began to write a letter stating that the bearer was a free man. When he finished, Merian asked him to read what he had written and, satisfied, expressed to Content his deep gratitude.

"You would do the same for me," his friend answered him, pushing the coin back at him.

"Well, you and Dorthea ought to come out and meet him soon. Maybe this Sunday," Merian said, as he stood to leave.

"We just might. But why not give everything awhile to get to normal out there first," Content replied.

Merian tipped his hat to his friend and took his leave. No longer able to sit a horse as he used to, he climbed into his carriage and rode the seven miles back out to the farm, remembering his own first days of freedom, and his own fresh beginning in this strange new country, though he was not a fugitive as his boy was.

Sanne had given Adelia instructions to let Magnus sleep as long as he wanted and to see that he had whatever he required as soon as he stirred. When he finally did awaken, she went immediately to see to him. Being unaccustomed to service, he could not even think what a person might need brought to him first thing in the morning other than another parcel of sleep. "No," he said, rubbing his eyes, "but I might like a spot of breakfast if that's no trouble."

When he went downstairs, she directed him to the dining room where the family ate, not knowing what his position in the house was and deciding to err on the side of generosity, as Sanne had always told her to do with their guests.

When he sat down she asked what he would like, and he responded that he wouldn't mind some milk and biscuits. She then brought out to the table a breakfast of eggs and bacon, as well as what he had asked her for. He ate everything and seemed satisfied, but when still more biscuits and milk were put before him he ate the biscuits in a flurry of surprisingly tidy activity, then drained his glass of milk with one turn up to his mouth. The girl asked whether he would like more and he said yes. She filled his glass again and watched as the milk disappeared, and another glass after it, until he had drained nearly an entire pailful.

When it was reported to Sanne later how he had consumed an entire cow's morning offering, she said that the girl should find out whether he required any special preparation for it, or if it was fine as brought to the table. Magnus told her any way he could get it was fine with him, and proceeded that first week to consume milk at a more prodigious rate than anyone would have thought possible.

Merian entered the dining room, just as Ware—as he would always insist on calling him—was finishing his breakfast, and asked after his sleep.

"It was very good, sir," Ware answered, but did not tell him either on that occasion or any other that he preferred to be called Magnus and, in fact, did not remember ever being called Ware to begin with. None of this mattered to Merian, who had given him the name in the first place.

"Is it great yet, though?" Merian asked. "I want you to let me know when it gets to be great."

Magnus looked at him but did not know what he meant. "I'm sorry?"

"I want to know when your sleep start to feel different. After you wake before first light and realize you can sleep all the day and won't nobody say nothing. Then again when you realize you still got to get up around first light if you want anything from the day. The first time you sleep a night knowing the day before you and every one after that is yours. I want you to tell me when it starts to feel great to you."

Magnus smiled ruefully, unable to imagine that such a moment might ever come or that such an idea was anything but an old man's fanciful remembering of his own past. "Well, they might still come after me."

"No, they won't," Merian said. "Nobody is after you. And if they were they surely won't look this far from where you started."

"I don't put it past them," Magnus said. "Sorel hate to see anything get out from his control. That's why he wouldn't let my mama buy us out in the first place, on account of that would be one more thing in the world, besides the sun and what-all, that he didn't have say-so over."

Merian nodded and said nothing, not wanting to interrupt the other once he had started talking—for fear he might never tell what it was he had to say. He did allow himself a question, though. "How is your mama?"

Magnus looked at Merian, and it was hard to tell just then whether there was not hatred in his eyes for the man who had given him life and was providing him shelter. Whatever it was passed quickly, and his face sloped toward sadness when he replied, "She passed on."

Merian was sadder than he had thought he would be when he first suspected it to be the case, and sadder than anyone would have ever been able to tell him he would be to hear the tragedy of a woman he had known so long ago. He withheld his emotion from Magnus, for it was something he found he did not understand entirely, and that was not a pleasant sensation or knowledge for a man his age to discover about his own inner life: that his heart it was still very cunning.

He was pleased, though, at the way Ware had put it, thinking that is exactly what Ruth would have done, as if she planned it out long ago.

"When?" he asked.

"This November past."

"I see. How did she go?"

"Her blood. It turned sweet."

Merian knew this to mean she had sugar in the blood, which was common in older people, so that they could never satisfy the craving for sweets but were pitched into distemper immediately upon having them. He also knew it was said to be caused by a love that had been thwarted or never satisfied in youth. But he was happy to know she had died in old age, for she would have been nearly fifty years old, which he reckoned was as much time as was allotted most. His own days he had grown greedy and less sensible about, counting them as his getting-back time. When he first found freedom he had not been that way, but he was not always a stranger and foe to bitterness in his later years. He figured if he could get back another twenty or so, he would be just even.

"She go peaceful?"

"Peaceful enough."

"You know, your mother, she was something else," Merian said, for he had not marked her death and wished to remember her now that she was present before his memory's eye.

"I know what she was like," Magnus said sharply, with the same flash of intensity about the mouth and eyes that had appeared there before.

"I remember when I first laid eyes on her," Merian continued. "Both her and her mother came home with Hannah Sorel's father one day, and he installed the mother as cook. Ruth was just a little girl who didn't even speak English yet—no more than *hello,* and besides that nothing but pure Congo, or whatever it was in the port she was first from. You could tell she was quick, though, because she picked up better English than most people born to it by the end of her first year. That's just what it seemed. It was even more striking because her mother never learned it at all, beyond the few words she needed to do her job. Then the old man come to find out she spoke schoolmaster's Dutch on top of that.

"The original house there was called Colonus and was fairly small, so the two of them shared a room just across the hall from me, and I would see both of them all the time. At first Ruth was so little that didn't nobody pay her any mind aside from, Well, she sure is one fast study with English speaking.

"I had never given her any more mind than anybody else anyway, but one day, after I came in from working, she was in the hall playing with a puppet she had found to amuse herself with, and she looked up at me as I was going into my room and asked, 'Where Jasper mama?'

"That was the first thing she said to me, and the first time I even knew she knew my name. I just smiled at her—she couldn't have been no more than eight or nine—and went on to my room. But I was aware of her from then on and, like I said, she was something far out of the usual."

The two men were silent then, thinking about Ruth. Magnus also thought of Merian as real flesh and bone for the first time since arriving, after nothing but having heard of him for so long. Merian's open affection for his mother made the younger man more trusting as well.

For Merian it was the first time he had talked about Ruth since the last time he saw her, and it did him good to speak about her. He would have taken Magnus into his home even if he wasn't his son but only as Ruth's boy, which, in truth, is how he saw him.

"You don't remember me, do you?"

"No more than you do something out of a dream," Magnus admitted, then worried he might have sounded too hard, "In my mind, yes, but I know or think I know it's just something I been told. The same way you and Mama say they used to call me Ware."

"Wasn't used to call, it was named," Merian said. "Tell me how you came to get away?"

"No different than anybody else," Magnus said.

Merian nodded. "Here," he said, holding out to him the papers Content had written up, which testified that their bearer was his own proprietor. "If somebody aim to do something anyway, they won't be much good, I imagine," Merian said. "Then again, if somebody aim to do something, you deal with that the way you must. Things haven't turned out as bad here as they are in Virginia and down the coast. It ain't what it is in some other places," he allowed himself optimistically. "There's a few free African families around here, so it ain't so strange a sight for people, and they let you go about your business same as any other man. So what you can expect, if this is where you decide you want to be, is that everybody will act toward you the way you act toward yourself. I can't tell you what way that should be. I don't know, but the way I would think about it for myself, if I was in your shoes, is: I started in one place and now I'm in another and aim to be all right there. Simple as that. No different from anybody else in these parts."

"Is that simple?" Magnus asked

"Anyway, it says you're free, and if you ever need it there it is."

Magnus took the papers without comment and looked at them. He was touched by the gesture, but it was holding the paper that made it all real to him, and he did not care if they were legitimate or only fakes worked up to fool constables and sheriffs. What they said was the truth and very real—he was a man free of any other's hold, and the sole fore-man of his soul and being besides the Almighty. That was real as sun-shine, and it would never be different. Even if he acted before Merian as if he had carried the papers himself the whole while and only dropped them in the road, he was very much affected.

Merian stood to leave and give Ware the day for himself to do what-ever he thought fit. He moved by then like a man who was at ease with himself and who he was in the world. It would be a great many years before Magnus, as he was called, gained the same assurance, but once he did he moved with much the same bearing as his father.

Merian, as he left the room, knew Sanne would raise the devil about it, but for him there was no choice but that the young man, if he wanted, was welcome to stay on at Stonehouses.

three

His terror that second night, when he realized his condition, was abject and complete. He was not normally a sensitive man, but his teeth chattered against each other and his legs locked at the knees as he thought about what challenges lay before him. His manufactured freedom papers were clutched to his breast, making real all that had changed since he arrived there, still he was unmoored by this new status, not knowing whether he would prove master of the thousand strange contests it would pose for his every fiber.

After he had stayed there six days, Merian suggested that work might be the best thing to set his mind and body right again. Magnus agreed to try it, and as he worked out in the fields the next morning, alongside Merian, the older man asked again how he was faring.

"Everyone here treats me fine," Magnus answered.

"That's not what I mean," Merian said. "You will know it when it happens." He walked away then, leaving Magnus to puzzle just what he did mean.

That night, when he tried to find sleep, Magnus instead found himself disoriented and dizzy to the point of losing his dinner in the chamber pot. As he told Merian the next day, all he felt was that he was in a different place, and he could not stop thinking about Sorel's Hundred and all he had known there.

"Do you know the story of that place?" Merian asked him then, sitting down to the midday meal.

"Just what I witnessed," Magnus replied. "I didn't know there was any story about it to know."

"You never knew about the old man?"

"He never affected me."

"Well, he came over here from England—it must have been a full hundred years ago now—and when he bought that land there was nothing at all around there, or anywhere else in all of Virginia. Even so, he thought to name his new property, and the name he thought to call it by, as you well know, was Colonus.

"He would stand out on the porch, after the house grew to a certain size, and stare at all that virgin country around him, with no idea what lay beyond the other side of the river, and get the most forlorn look on his face. He would turn then and say, to anyone who happened to be in hearing distance, 'See how Edenic it all is.' That was his word. 'We are in exile, but only to be purified. If we let ourselves be cleansed without despoiling it, we will be allowed home again.'

"Then, not too long after the time Ruth and her mother came on the place, he started one day to call the old woman Antigone for no good reason. 'What are we having for dinner this fine evening, Antigone?' Or, 'How does the weather agree with you this afternoon, Antigone?' He claimed that if his wife had agreed to it that is what he would have named Hannah. 'I can't think of any better name for a daughter than that,' he said.

"Nobody paid it much mind at first. Some men rename a slave at the drop of a hat, like a name is nothing more than a plaything. We just thought it a little peculiar, because he was not that way. When time came for Hannah to marry that Sorel fellow, he gave them some land out on his property to build a house and sent me off with them.

"It must have been the night before we were set to leave, and I was going into the house when he called me out there and told me to sit with him. Now that wasn't very strange either, as he always had somebody to sit out with him after his wife died. What was strange was when he started talking that night, and wanted to tell me it seemed like everything he knew, starting with where the name of his house came from.

"'Once, long ago, there lived a great king, and those are precious few, who committed two gross and unforgivable crimes, and when they had made him poor as a beggar for it, his people's gods let it be known that Colonus was the place that would receive him in his old age.'

105

"When he finished telling me that I could see how very old he had grown, and I thought perhaps he was trying to remember the rest of his story, but he just looked at me and said, 'It is terrible to be loved by God. Most cannot endure it, Jasper. But name all thy houses Colonus and all thy daughters Antigone, and thou shall never know sorrow.'

"That nearly brought tears to my eyes, to see how scared he was out there on his place; and that it would always be strange to him, even though it was his house. His advice, though, seemed sound as any I ever had. 'Name all your houses Colonus and all your daughters Antigone, and you will never know sorrow.'"

That night when he went to bed, Magnus lay awake for the same long time as before, staring at the beams of the ceiling in his room and thinking of the last months. But instead of fearing what trial could possibly come next, he saw the good fortune he had had and the strength of the way he had acquitted himself. It felt then as if a great pressure was lifted up from him. He began to see that strength was as much a part of him as the fear he had been carrying since he ran from Virginia and had nearly been consumed by on the journey to Stonehouses, when he spent every day in hiding, waiting for nightfall so he could move on again. He began then to laugh, not altogether maniacally, but he had a good roar at all of it, and when he finished he was in tears. He fell asleep quite peaceful, and the next morning before Merian asked him he could say for himself, "It is good now."

Merian was pleased when Magnus announced that he had finally put his fear aside. "It is a special day when that happens," he told his sons, as Purchase left for his shop and he and Magnus went on to the fields. "It is like becoming a man all over again, when you come to know you're alive but will eventually die and so start to celebrate that. Everything changes. You start winning the struggle, because it is your own."

Magnus did not feel anything so profound as all that had happened to him, but he told Merian he would take him at his word, as they went to work the fields with the hired men.

The previous days Magnus had worked lethargically, barely keeping up with the slowest man out there, but that afternoon when he worked he produced handsomely, thinking he owed Merian something for all he had given to him, and the only way he could repay him was with good labor. He was not invested in that land, but he worked as though it meant something to him, and as the days passed he found he was beginning to grow attached to the people of Stonehouses.

Still, he did not sleep as well as he was accustomed to. At the end of his first week, when he was finally able to drift off for more than an hour or two, he had a strange dream that was very haunting and disturbing to him. In it he pursued a woman continuously but never caught up with her. He would run faster and faster, but she would always manage to elude him, until he grew frustrated and could not remember why he chased her in the first place. "Go on, you old witch," he called out in the dream. "I don't want you no way."

She laughed at him when he said this and began taunting him. "Even if you did catch me, you still couldn't get what you want."

"I don't want nothing from you," he yelled at her again, then added, as if she were an animal he could command, "Pass on."

"Oh, yes, you do," she countered, raising her skirts up so that he could see all her private parts.

"Man give the meat,
Man give the gravy,
But woman give the milk
And woman give the babies."

She laughed and dropped her skirt.

"Get away from me, you evil thing," he called out. She continued laughing at him and ran off again. Despite himself he started to chase after her, even though he understood by then he would never catch up.

He awoke frustrated and understood from the dream that he was meant never to have children. This in itself did not play at his emotions, because he had never been overly drawn to children in the first place and so could not see any shame in not having them. As for women, he had known several at Sorel's Hundred and the surrounding plantations, but never one whom he would have thought to call a wife. For to tell the truth he could not see the great pleasure in being so intimate with anyone and sharing all your thoughts and time. When he did take a woman, it was because nature could not be suppressed, or when he found one pleasant and thought to spend a season or so in her company—but not longer than that, for it began to weary him. He had no need for children and marriage but preferred his own solitude and thought, when there was the luxury for it, which was but very seldom for family men. That was why the dream disturbed him even more, because he did not think it revealed anything true but was only a deep taunting, and he worried someone had put a root spell on him to make him want what he did not.

After dinner the following day, Magnus was still trying to puzzle out the dream when Purchase asked him whether he would not like to go for some amusement.

"What is there at this hour?"

"I thought you might fancy a game of cards."

"I don't have money, but I'll join you for company if you don't mind."

Magnus was not generally one for drinking and the concomitant sins, but he appreciated the offer from Purchase, and thought it might do him well to go out in the air. The two brothers went to the stable then, where they saddled horses and went off in search of entertainment.

The town where Purchase took Magnus was not Berkeley, though. Rather, they rode some five miles in the opposite direction to a small building set off in the woods with nothing else around it. Inside men and women of all stripes and countries milled around, and it was easy for Magnus to see what kind of place he had been brought to, even if he had never been to one before. It was also immediately plain that Purchase spent a great deal of time here, for the proprietor seemed to know him well.

The two brothers ordered drinks from the bar and sat alone with each other, not speaking very much but watching the room in silence. When two men sitting at a card table went off with a pair of the harlots, who had procured their attention beyond what the cards could, a place at the gaming table was free for the first time.

"Would you care to play?" Purchase asked.

"I don't have money."

"It is my invitation."

They sat down with the four already present: a Creole and an Indian, who didn't seem to know either each other or anyone else there. In addition there was an Englishman and an African woman, who seemed to be partners of some sort or other. When they sat, the woman began the deal, but neither the Creole nor the Indian had very good cards and soon put down their hands. Purchase proceeded to bet with abandon, studying the African woman very carefully, as the Englishman made friendly talk with Magnus. When there were as many coins stacked on the table as he had ever seen, Magnus had sense to put down his cards and watch the other players, knowing that the monies he had already lost were not his but Purchase's.

Purchase, though, did not seem to care about the coins and continued to put more into the stack in the center of the table, until the Englishman also withdrew and there was only Purchase and the woman left in the game.

By now the men who had sat there earlier were finished with their business and took seats at the bar to watch the card game unfold. "She'll have his very skin before long," one of the men said, looking at the cards on the table. At this Purchase cut his eyes menacingly and pulled a pistol from his belt. "Not before I've had yours if you keep flapping," he answered, leaving the gun on the table pointed at the other man. The man who had been threatened was quiet after that, as much from fear of Purchase as the fact that the gun was made of unmixed gold. "It will put a golden bullet in you too," Purchase said, looking steadily at his cards.

Magnus could tell very little about who had the better hand from the cards that showed on the table, but when the next one was revealed, he saw Purchase's face slump and the woman begin to glitter. "It's all right, Sugarloaf," she said to him. "If you lose I'll let you stay the night with me in my room." The Englishman who had been her partner was not pleased to hear her talk so saucily, but he held his tongue, waiting for the last card to be turned over.

Before it could be revealed, though, there was a ruckus outside that spilled immediately through the door of the tavern. Three highwaymen stood back-to-back-to-back, holding guns, and began moving through the room, taking purses from the patrons at the bar. When one of them saw the money stacked in front of the cards, and the golden pistol, he broke away from the others and went to take the bounty from the gaming table. As he held his hand over the pile of money, though, a shot rang out and he fell where he had stood.

Contrary to what Purchase had claimed, the bullet from the gun was made of lead. He and the woman then jumped from the table and rushed toward the door, as the other robbers fired randomly into the bar. In the melee Magnus searched for a way out, before finally discovering a back door and sneaking out into the hushed night air. The scene he left behind was of bloody carnage, and when he found his horse he whipped it into a frenzied gallop, not caring which direction he was going as long as it was away from that place, before he was shot or the authorities descended upon them.

The horse half obeyed and half did as it pleased, until Purchase rode up from the other direction and took the reins, as Magnus drooped in the saddle full of liquor. The jostling of the ride was awful on his head, and when they reached the road before Stonehouses, he climbed down and began walking the horse to the stable, unable to ride any longer.

"Who would have won?" Magnus asked, as Purchase helped him into the house.

"Hard to say," Purchase replied. "But for the offer she made I would have gladly lost."

"Not me," Magnus told him. "Not for all the money that was piled on that table."

"It wasn't so much," Purchase said.

"More than I've seen."

"I would have given even more for her offer."

"What about her white man?"

"I suppose that's who would have lost."

"Not with you paying through the nose for what you could have upstairs for a lot less."

"I'll have it later tonight for nothing," he claimed.

"How so?"

"I left her where I can meet up with her."

"You'll stay in gunfights at this rate of living."

"And you for stealing horses."

"What horse did I ever steal?"

"The one you rode home on."

"It was a mistake. I'll return it first thing in the morning," Magnus said, falling quiet. But he thought the woman from the bar reminded him of the wicked one in his dream. "I don't think drinking is much for me."

"Do you need help getting inside?"

"I'll manage."

Purchase watched as Magnus made his way inside, before turning and riding back to the room behind his workshop, where he had left the woman.

When he arrived he found she had gone without leaving any sign. He returned home alone not very long afterward, and in the days that followed he asked everyone what they knew of her. Try as he might, though, he could only gather bits and pieces of stories, each new one contradicting the last, so that all he knew for certain was that she had not waited and was gone from him.

four

❦

He is a tiller of the soil with little interest in the affairs of other people, save the family that has taken him in, and no real bonds but to the air and the land that gives them sustenance. After his initial buffeting by the newness of the place around him he settles back into himself, keeping his own company and never complaining, but only occasionally imagining to himself other ways certain things might be done. At Sorel's Hundred he engaged in the same idle wondering until it became a permanent ache and then a murderous craving he would have acted on, but for his mother. For her sake he held his hand patiently. After her he can be patient no longer.

* * *

At Stonehouses the days were more flexible and he worked as he saw fit, discounting, of course, the things Merian himself was rigid about and would broker no dissent or discussion over. He allowed Magnus a free hand with everything else, letting him, for example, experiment with the crops, if he pleased, but not on too large a scale, and even with his time—so long as all the work was done and no complaints from the men. Where he was rigid, though, he was hard as any overseer on the coast.

That second week he was on the land, after wages were paid out, Merian saw Magnus turn his money over to Purchase to cover his gaming loss from the week before.

"I told you it was for fun and my invitation," Purchase said, refusing the money.

"You go ahead and take it," Merian said sharply, startling the two of them, who had not seen him approach.

Under Merian's watchful eye, Magnus paid from his wages the same number and kind of coins Purchase had given to him at the roadhouse.

"Now, how much do you have left out of what you just gave Purchase?" Merian asked, after the debt had been paid.

Magnus looked at the specie in his hand for a long time before answering. "Five shillings."

"If I told you I was going to give you another five shillings, how would that figure up?"

Magnus thought hard, carefully imagining the coins in his palm before answering. "Ten shillings."

"Now tell me the number of pence in that."

Magnus was silent.

"What about parts of a pound?" Merian continued, as Magnus began to grow hot with embarrassment.

"You don't have to make a fool of me," he said finally, glaring at Merian.

"I'm not trying to embarrass you," Merian answered. "I'm trying to help you get on better than you got on before. For that you need to know proper ciphering. A man can always trust somebody else to read something out for him, without too much worry over it, because what's important here ain't written down, unless you count the Bible—and there's whole legions of preachers tripping over each other to do that for you—but if a man can't cipher he can't trust nobody to make up the balance or tell him what it is. Purchase is your brother, so he won't cheat you out of your shillings. Then again he might. Do you trust him not to?"

Magnus thought about it, before answering, "I don't think he would."

"Well," Merian said, "I've known him a bit longer than you, and he is dear as life to me, but I'll count my own silver."

Every day after that, when he left the fields, Magnus had to sit with either Merian or Sanne and practice arithmetic for hours on end, until he went to sleep at night with his brain aching from pondering figures and symbols. Still, he stuck with it every night that entire season and all the way into the next, until eventually he could count as well as a Dutchman.

When he found arrows out in one of the far fields, though, it did not take arithmetic to figure out there were three of them, all deadly.

At first Merian thought they were only old arrows that had been held in the ground for a long time, since the last hostilities with the Catawba, but he soon saw they were new and still bore the markings of being cut from their source. There had not been Indian troubles around Berkeley since before Merian settled there, but he knew immediately that the caravans pressing westward must have gone far enough out that the Indian was beginning to press back the other way.

He did not say anything else but gave Magnus an old musket to carry with him from then on, when working in the more distant fields.

"Can you shoot?"

"I can," Magnus said, taking the gun.

"Good. If you see anything that looks like it needs to be shot, you do it."

The next day as he worked out there again, with the gun slung over his shoulder, Magnus saw something approaching from the westward country and stood up to investigate. It looked to him like a wild animal of unusually large proportions, but as it grew closer he saw it was a man carrying pelts and skins for the market. It wasn't until the man was almost right up on him that he saw that the pelts were human scalps, strung together and wrapped around his shoulders like sashes.

In addition to the scalps he also wore a double necklace of fingers, ears, and what Magnus finally figured out were noses. Other than that gruesome vesture he was stone naked.

In his arms he carried a large unadorned box, which he protected very carefully as he made his way up the road

When the man saw Magnus staring, he stopped at a distance and pointed at the articles on his person. "Any one of them will make you a good medicine," he said.

When Magnus failed to reply, the man set down the box and opened it. "I have the vitals too, if that's your aim: red, negro, white, whichever you want."

Magnus looked into the box and saw a collection of grisly organ parts, and in the middle of it an intact human head. He turned away his face and looked back up the road.

"Well, I thought neggers liked such things for their doctoring. The one in the box was very powerful. Very good medicine." The man closed his parcel of death and took it back up in his arms.

"Who is he?" asked Magnus, who had not spoken since seeing what the man was.

"I thought you could hear and talk," the Indian agent replied. "I said to myself as I stopped here, Lacey, you done seen many things ye never thought ye would, and it's fair you'll see one or two more, but a mute Ethiop with a rifle, that you will never witness."

The man seemed almost sad that this should be the case, making Magnus wonder briefly what else he had seen out there gathering scalps. "Him, his name was Kasatensera. You would rather fight any six other men. With his enemies he and the Negro sorcerer he worked with liked to have splinters of wood inserted in every little pore of their skin, until they stood out like frightful wooden hairs, and then set them all afire. Nasty stuff. Very powerful. If you were the type for it, very good medicine, I imagine." He lingered over the word *medicine,* waiting to see whether Magnus would not change his mind. "Well, no matter. The governor is said to be paying thirty shillings a scalp, and more for this one, I wager. What would you reckon?"

Magnus, in the time he stood there, had counted fifty-two scalps on the man's sash and quickly figured that he had 1,560 shillings, or 78 pounds sterling, worth of human flesh and profit wrapped around him, but he did not say anything.

"If you're not interested, I better be moving on," the agent said to him, taking up his awful box as if they had been carrying on any normal conversation.

When Magnus told Merian later what had happened, Merian told him to prepare for the worst of it. "No one takes a scalp but a war party," he said. Sure enough, word began to come to them in the days that followed of settlers farther out on the frontier being attacked and one settlement being razed entirely. The governor had sent a dispatch of soldiers out to hunt down the offenders, but it disappeared without ever reporting back.

The rest of the spring and summer the road was filled with regular troops going out, and after that a party of allied Cherokee from the tidewater, who had licensed on to fight their sworn enemies. When that particular conflict was over, the flow of people across the road would be much larger, but its increase brought death down its whole length.

They were working the August harvest as usual at Stonehouses when one of the hired men yelled out "Fire!" at the top of his voice. Magnus looked into the western distance, where he saw thick oily smoke rising up. He climbed a tree and saw that a farm down in the far country of the valley was all ablaze.

He ordered two of the men to go over to investigate. When they returned both of them shook with fright, as they reported that their neighbors were well beyond helping.

That night the sky was still lit with the smoldering embers from the farm that had burned down, when another one, even closer to them, went up in flames. No one had to climb anything to see the resulting inferno, as it reflected ethereally off the clouds and stars, it was so bright and near to them.

Merian himself went over this time to see what help could be offered, and on the way a boy climbed out of an embankment of weeds and stood in the middle of the road when he heard the sound of wheels. Merian stopped the carriage and lifted the child up. When he had had a drink from Merian's flask, he told of being attacked by a band of Catawba warriors. "They killed everybody where they slept," he said. "The only reason they missed me is cause I climbed into the well and hid." The bottom of his feet were bloody and raw from where he had pressed them against the rock, scrambling out.

When he heard this story, Merian turned the carriage around and went back to his own place, where he gave the child to Sanne to look after until more permanent shelter could be found for him. He then assembled all the men working there for the harvest and handed out what weapons there were to the most trusted among them. One group he sent on patrol to keep lookout, others he posted as watchmen from the edge of the land to the front porch. Everyone else he barricaded inside, where they passed the night in vigil and fear of death.

Merian, Purchase, and Magnus each kept watch on horseback at a different corner of the yard out front of the house, coming together every once in a while to report anything they had seen. This went on until morning was well advanced and they finally decided they were safe for the time being, as the Indians were known to attack only at night. They then went to take breakfast.

As they sat and ate they suddenly heard a great thundering of horses' hooves off in the distance. Purchase jumped up and led Magnus and two other men up a rise to see what it was. What they saw was yet another detachment of soldiers marching out toward the valley.

That night another farm was put to the torch, and from his porch Merian could see just how much of the county had been brought under cultivation since the time he moved there, so that one would hardly know it for the same land. "This used to be a peaceful spot," he told his two sons. "Not so, now that the governor aims to have full war with the natives and drive them right off of it."

In the morning, Magnus and Purchase went to see what damage had been done during the night. Three farms lay in complete ruin and all their inhabitants dead. Neither of them said anything about what they saw at the time, but as they rode back to Stonehouses they came upon a long spike that had been driven into the ground. At the top of it was a half-rotten human head.

"His name was Lacey," Magnus said, examining the work that had been done to it. "He had made almost enough money to go back to Scotland."

Purchase asked how he knew this, and Magnus told him of meeting the man almost a week before. "He tried to reach for too much," was Purchase's only reply. "He might have made it to where he was headed instead of back down this road if he hadn't tried to go for so much."

They were quiet then, from the thickness of tobacco smoke that clung in the valley air, sweet and oily, like the inside of a colossal pipe bowl. Smoking was a luxury Magnus had scarcely been able to afford in his previous existence, and the few times he tried it he coughed violently upon inhaling the smoke and never found any pleasure in the experience. Purchase, though, closed his eyes and breathed deeply of the fragrant air, relishing the taste, now of old tobacco carefully cured; now of bitter green leaves just off the stalk, both of them suffused with the headiness of that plant's hypnotic powers. He inhaled again, savoring the taste and sensation of the smoke in his lungs, then exhaled and eased back into the gentle ride they were on. He laughed, however, when he turned and saw how sickly Magnus looked. "You're not a big one for pleasure, are you?" Purchase asked him.

"Not this kind. Not especially," Magnus answered, quelling the nausea that was sweeping over him and yoicking his horse toward the high ground above the smell of smoke.

When they arrived at Stonehouses, Content and the chandler, Pete Griffith, were there on the front porch with Merian, as Merian told what had been happening out where they were. At first Magnus was greatly concerned to see the two strangers there, as he had made it his business to avoid contact with anyone outside of Stonehouses, and thought at first to run, but, when Merian bid him, he entered in the circle with the other men.

Content was friendly and relaxed with him, and warm in the way he was well known for, but he also studied the new man intently, trying to see exactly what sort of character he had. He was tall and well made—only a half head shorter than Purchase—and seemed to keep his mind to himself. On the whole, Content was reminded not unfavorably of Merian when he had first met him all those years ago, but the younger man was not so bold as Merian himself had been. This last thing, though, was not necessarily negative. He sensed the man was capable enough but thought in general that men, especially those born in the colonies, were becoming less hardy than those who had traveled the ocean to get here, whether from England or from Africa. He did not attribute any of this to the fault of Merian's grown sons, both of whose strength and vigor was obvious, but simply notched it as the sign of his own years.

"The governor has sent a party to sue the Indians for peace," he said, going back to his conversation with Merian and giving the news he knew they would be most anxious to hear. "Some of the frontier people pushed deeper than the treaty permitted, and the Indians grew irate at it. But everyone thinks they'll take new terms, so things should get back to normal soon enough."

They all looked at Merian, waiting for his reply, but he made none, and Content could see then how the last several days had made his friend's age show in the lines of his face, especially about the eyes. "It will never get back to what it was," he said finally, moving to the window. "This used to be a quiet country, Content."

"I know," Content answered. "No one can argue there."

He also knew, however, it was possible the two of them had merely been fortunate enough to be born in a time that had not known the full pressures and deprivation of war.

Merian was so shaken by the last week, wherein he had nearly lost everything, that he told them all he no longer wanted to speak about it but instead began to relate the story of a heroic ancient king who blinded himself and went into exile because of crimes he had unknowingly committed. They were crimes he could not help, he explained, because they were in the design of his people's gods. "In ancient times was a king who the gods marked for greatness," he said. "It was a terrible thing."

When he had finished the story, Magnus and Purchase were both very still and pensive. Content, meanwhile, had grown cold at his fingertips and looked through the window with a grievous expression on his face.

"I would have named my own house Colonus," Merian said, as he stood and went to the window that Content peered through. "But I thought by now they surely must have heard of that place. I called it Stonehouses instead, in hopes it might keep them off us awhile."

five

It was several weeks after the Aborigines' siege that Magnus was in town on an errand and met Purchase afterward to go to Content's. As the two of them sat there looking out onto the square, an uncovered wagon drove up to the door and stopped directly in front of it. Two men then climbed out from the front and came into the bar. In the bed of the wagon was a cage, where another man was tied and bound.

When the men entered the bar they made it loudly known that they were out on official business: one of them a bailiff for the court in Edenton, the other his assistant. "We'll take two whiskeys," the bailiff commanded, as they sat down and began to talk about how unruly that part of the world was, and the dangers of their work.

"Why, the one out there is wanted for murder, sorcery, and a whole host of other crimes. There is a bounty for him big as a king's ransom."

Purchase and Magnus said nothing to either of the newcomers, but continued to drink. When Purchase later turned and looked out at the man in the wagon, he found the other man also looking at him steadily, as though he had been awaiting his attention. What passed between them then was the recognition of kindredness, if not necessarily kinship. There was no witness to anything that happened after that, but the man was gone from his jail before midday and the cage left untouched as if the key holder had let him out himself, which was not possible since the bailiff had the only key and he carried it in a pouch around his neck. Both, the key and his neck, were still upon him as he went about cursing that afternoon.

Late that evening, the one who had been released from the cage showed up at Stonehouses. Merian was very happy to see him, but Sanne, when she saw what state he was in, was alarmed almost to the point of despair.

"You don't have to live your life like this, Chiron," she said. "Merian, tell him he doesn't have to live like this."

Merian agreed with what his wife was saying but knew his old acquaintance was on some path that none could sway him from. Still, he offered him the same spot for a house he had offered once before.

"I would accept if I could," Chiron told his friend, as the men drank from the cask Content had given Merian on his birthday, which seemed never to reduce in the amount that was present. "Tell me anyway how everything has been with you here, besides that the liquor has gotten better."

Merian talked of the hostilities with the Indians, boasted on how Purchase was the best smith in the colonies, how Magnus came upon the land, and how he himself had once set out to grow rich but settled for more modest expansion when he learned the cost of labor. He also showed Chiron the sword Purchase had forged, and Chiron alone among men who were not in that family was able to lift it up. He was also the only one, even among those who were its owners in the future, who could see everything that the legend on the blade contained. It was marvelous to him, as he held it aloft and examined the finely balanced steel.

"Aye, it is the right one," he said to Purchase, who had not known who he was when he saw him earlier that day, but only that he was a man who was being held as no man ought to be. Then he put the sword down and said to Magnus, "You don't remember me, but I knew you when they called you Ware and you lived with your mother in a room at Sorel's Hundred."

He looked at the marks on his wrists and bid Magnus follow him outside, where they went a short way into the woods. There the older man pulled a spiky weed from the ground and broke the stem open until it oozed white with nectar. He rubbed this onto the scars on Magnus's arms, and took a rock to slough away the dead skin, then added another anointing of the nectar. "It will heal the scarification," he said, "so you will not be so vulnerable." When he finished they went back to the house, where everyone talked until late into the night, because, other than perhaps Content and Dorthea, he was the most welcome visitor Stonehouses ever knew.

In the morning he was gone again when the house awoke, and Merian did not look to see what he had left or taken from the storerooms. He only hoped his friend would not be hunted down out there in the frigid wilderness but would make it to wherever he was headed on that path only he knew.

Nor were these the only disturbances that autumn on the land. The other, Magnus was first to see, as they sat in Content's the day after Chiron had gone. It was then that the woman from the gambling house in the woods, and her partner, entered and took seats at a table. Instead of drinks, though, they asked only that supper be brought out to them immediately.

Jannetje, one of the lasses who worked for Content and Dorthea, brought the pair plates of stew and mugs of cider, and they began eating and talking together calmly, though it was strange to see a woman in the bar. When they had finished eating, the two stood and left to go back out, never once having acknowledged Purchase or Magnus. At the door, however, the woman turned to them and brazenly winked at the two men. When they asked Content later who the two were who had just left, he replied that they were traveling preachers, unattached to any kind of formal congregation. "It is scandalous to have a woman preaching, and even more than that for what the two of them have to say," he opined, which was unlike him, because he usually tolerated or suffered all equally.

That night Magnus and Purchase went again to the roadhouse in the outlying country, Magnus only to keep Purchase company, Purchase because he was intent on finding the woman.

When they entered the room it was unchanged from how they had last seen it. The card players were arranged around the tables, and those there for other pleasure lined up against the bar as the women came in and went out in their costumes. There was a subterranean quality to the light that made it seem later in the night than it actually was, and the din from the crowd when someone either won a large amount of money or when a familiar customer came in, gave the room a depressed feeling that made Magnus uncomfortable. Purchase, on the other hand, enjoyed this about the place, finding that it built up whatever sensation he was already feeling.

He wished for the woman who had run away from him, after they were there last, and tried to channel that desire into a game of tarok, but the cards were unable to siphon his mood and he eyed the door expectantly whenever someone entered.

Magnus, surveying the crowd, began to think Purchase had only gotten himself wound up over something he was not to have. Still, as the night wore on he sat there in order to watch over his brother if he could.

When he had lost as much at the cards as he could stand, Purchase rose from the table, walked around the room, picked up one of the girls' hand, and let her lead him to the back. She was not an attractive woman, and he had looked past her a hundred nights without seeing her. Tonight he wanted her in the ambiguous manner of wanting everything and nothing specific at all.

In the back room a lantern burned very low at the wick and he pulled his pants down, and pushed the woman to the mattress. He mounted on top of her without ceremony, letting her guide him inside, then began thrusting until he had finished.

The woman she lay there neither damning nor redeeming him but simply giving off a few moans for surprise and pleasure and doing what she had been paid for, which was to bear his weight in the darkness for a spell.

It was very quick satisfaction, and when he finished he pulled his pants back up and left the room with the feeling of having done a low thing. His sex and wanting, though, were sated, no longer gnawing at the inside of his brain like a untamed animal.

For the first time he noticed just how dingy the entire establishment was, and wondered how many hours of his life had passed there without finding the satisfaction he came in search of. What he also asked himself, and did not know, was whether it was more satisfaction than he would otherwise have known.

As they rode back home he felt a whistling emptiness and did not know whether it was caused by missing the one he sought or lying down with one he ought not have had. He was surprised that this last thing should occur to him, for it was something he had gotten away with a hundred times in the past.

Magnus rode alongside Purchase with a half smile on his face but tried hard to suppress it when he saw how the other was feeling. "If she is a preacher now, you'll be hard pressed to find her in a place like that," he said finally.

"You might be right, but I wish you had said something before," Purchase replied.

"Don't throw salt on me," Magnus returned. "It was your notion."

"Do you think I'm mean for what I did?"

"It is a funny sort of reckoning that takes one woman to get over another. It might work, but no one will ever explain how."

"Well, it seemed like the natural place to look."

"To look for a preacher?"

"That is where they were before. Where else do you think we should have gone?"

"You might have tried the church."

In the end they did find her in church, though not the one in town but rather in an outdoor tent that had been set up in a field outside of Berkeley, on the road that ran past Stonehouses. It was Sanne who suggested they go, saying it would do them all good to hear some new voices mixed in with the old ones they had been hearing their whole lives. As she grew older she had become increasingly concerned with the keep of her family's salvation, and she liked to believe that praying for people made up part of the way for them who did not pray enough themselves. Still, she knew this only made a small difference, so if she could get Merian and Purchase to pray any kind of way she would be happy. As for Magnus, she had no idea what condition his soul was in but would bet it needed upkeep as well.

On top of these other reasons she had never heard of a woman preacher before and was keen to know what she would have to say that might be different from what the other preachers promised and claimed about the state of the world.

Merian had never had much use for any of them and told her it would be the same as the rest, only set in a woman's mouth instead of a man's. "You might think its something different on account of the novelty, but I wager there won't be anything new in it."

"Since when have you been listening to so many preachers as to be an expert?" Sanne challenged. "Anyway, what's different is that it is a woman. That itself is something new, in my mouth anyhow."

In the end it was this that compelled all of them to get out of bed before the sun that Sunday, to get good seats under the tent, which had been pitched in the middle of a muddy field for what had been promoted in the area as a Revival and Awakening.

As the four Merians looked around, they were surprised both by the number of people who had come out for the event and the general number that lived within walking or riding distance of Stonehouses. It was perhaps a hundred fifty souls, but all gathered together they seemed legion. Their own seats were midway back, and they could see very clearly when the first preacher, the Englishman Magnus and Purchase had played cards with at the roadhouse, came onstage. He was dressed smartly in a purple robe, with golden thread at the sleeves and a red sash he wore over his neck, along with a great golden cross.

"I want to talk to all of you today about the Knowledge and Love of God," he said, "and how it belongs to all of us in equal measure. It is a message that will not be popular with some, so let me first give you my background and how I came to be here today."

The tent was silent as they listened, for he spoke with intense care for his words, but also with a strange accent.

"I am what is known as an Episcopi Vagantes, which means I have been fully invested with the sacraments of the one original church. I received my ordination first as a priest, while still in my youth, and was raised still young to bishop—I was twenty-six at the time—by no less a vassal of God than the Pope of Antioch.

"None can undo what a Pope has done without undoing the ancient communion of the church itself, so I remain now a high bishop but have had an argument with the other churches on your behalf.

"I can see some of you are saying, He is still the Pope's man, and what do you mean with this lowercase and uppercase pope business? Isn't there only one? The truth is there are five popes, all equally entitled to the claim, and the Roman pope is little more than a bishop who has gotten pretensions to be master of the world. The more haughty he has got, the more he has separated all of us from the works of Jesus and His apostles.

"Why he does this is because there are things in the Gospels that the Church in Rome would rather bar all of us from knowing. But all of it belongs ever to the flock of the faithful.

"'Now what is this Knowledge he keeps talking about?' I can see you asking. 'Isn't Jesus the perfection of Love and all of Love?' Yes, He is, but also other things besides.

"You see, the seventh seal has long been breeched, and it is silent in Heaven as They watch."

The residents of the town were baffled by much that the preacher was saying, but he put up such a show with that great purple robe billowing out on the wind under the perfect cerulean autumn sky, along with the red coronation stole, that they decided to let him finish his sermon before making up their minds.

"Today I wish to read to you from one of the Hidden Books of Christ, which the popes and high bishops have all conspired among themselves to keep out of your knowing, certain Knowledge they would like to keep hidden in order to elevate their own earthly kingdom. I am here to tell you that you can know the True Heart of Christ, as intimately as those apostles who sat down with Him in Communion, and not go supplicating to any interdicting authority other than your own hearts."

He opened a gigantic old tome, turned to a well-marked page, and began reading.

"Mary Magdalene said to Him, 'Lord, then how will we know that?'

"The perfect Savior said, 'Come you from invisible things to the end of those that are visible, and the very emanation of Thought will reveal to you how faith in those things that are not visible was found in those that are visible, that belong to the unbegotten Father. Whoever has ears to hear, let him hear!'"

"What Jesus means by this," the preacher went on, "is that God's bounty is available to us all without interference. He will create each of you a prince of your own Destiny, but you must first sabbitise your belief, and the joy that comes from knowing, and the sharing of Bread with the College of the Faithful. You must be born and weep in the jubilation that is Christ and, through Him, receive the Hidden Knowledge that will sanctify all your works. For only then will He reveal to you the Truth.

"As proof of this I offer my assistant minister, Mary Josepha, who has been ordained by God with the power of healing, even though she was nothing but a common maid before He sought her out as His servant."

The woman whom Purchase had met earlier that summer then took the podium, and she was as beautiful as he remembered her, even a in her vestments of office, which were a purple robe like the other preacher's and, in place of the stole, a garter of different-colored glass beads, which caught the light as she moved to the lectern.

"When I first met her she prayed to strange gods and spoke of an oracle called the Aro Chukwu and places with untamed names, where the weaker of her people took shelter from the stronger because they did not have God's knowledge to protect them. But since she found Christ she hides from no one and needs no other strength. As proof I invite any of you with an ailment, any seeking relief, to come up here and let Sister Mary Josepha put her hands on you so that you might be healed. You must hurry, though, because there is, as John teaches, but half an hour left."

There was a great clamoring among the audience and many people stood to receive her blessing, even some who were devout in the normal church. The Merians sitting there all felt something stir in them as well, as the Englishman began a chanting behind the woman.

When the preacher spoke, Merian thought he could remember things he did not remember and closed his eyes, seeking to pin down those elusive flickerings. He was also reminded of the stranger he had met that dark winter day years ago, who prophesied the end of unions when it was still barren woodlands around him.

Magnus remembered then how he was once called something else, and that there was a truth about him he could no longer possess but had died with his African mother.

Sanne, when she saw the woman standing there in the office of preacher and healer, felt a great pride that all but the church fathers were going to get blessed by her, and that she had in her the power to make them defer, and that she very obviously did not wear the yoke of the household. It was an affirmation for her that was not religious but was powerful all the same.

Purchase, when he saw her standing before the crowd with the girdle, which accentuated her shape and the length of her limbs to an effect of great beauty, was moved mysteriously into standing from his seat and walking forth to get a better look at her. He soon found that he kept moving closer, as though hypnotized by the glass beads.

"You see," the preacher said, as people streamed forth in a great throng under the tent to receive blessings, "there is but one original of each thing: one slave and one master; one church and one believer; one convert and one righteous heathen; one husband and one wife; one king, one subject; one father, one son; one Wisdom and one great Lie.

"All marched forth from the Original Element in the Beginning in pairs, to either stay with their original other or else get lost from it; either remembering their purpose or forgetting it. The farther they get from the Beginning the less they know, unless those binds are renewed, and if they are not, eventually they will lose all their original way and purpose. Such was the fate of Sophia, and of preacher and believer. We are here today to remember and to redeem that mission.

"I want the Seeker to come forth now to rejoin with the Sought After; and the Pursued and Persecuted to come forth and know again Original Freedom."

"They will have you all burning in hell," a man from the crowd called as the preacher went on. "He is a charlatan and preaches original heresy. If you ask him how he found himself among you he will tell you a fantastic story about being waylaid by pirates off the coast. It is not true, and his deaconess is no religious woman but his common married wife, though what kind of marriage it is only the devil can tell. Probe about Antioch and you will find it is a pub in central London, and he was ordained there, all right. My Jesus, how he was ordained!"

The Englishman defended himself. "He is an agent of the pope."

"It does not take an agent of the pope to know God would never hide His wisdom from us," the other countered. "And if not for theology then for the sake of philosophy, but he is illiterate and ignorant as dirt. If he were not, he would not so disregard the doctrine of Telos, as described by Aristotle in his thesis of metaphysics. Sophia is no more lost than a bird in winter, but fulfilling her function according to divine plan, which is mysterious. Anyone who claims to know it is a bigger blasphemer than Satan himself."

In all this the crowd began taking sides, arguing either from religious, superstitious, or philosophical views about who was right and who was wrong, as others ignored both men and kept moving toward the woman, some shouting as she touched them, others falling down in the aisle and weeping. The most profound feeling among all of them that morning belonged to Purchase Merian.

After the last congregant had finished wailing he walked up to the healing chair and sat down. Somewhere inside himself he knew what he did amounted to bad faith where God Himself might have been concerned, but the religiousness of his feelings was undeniable. He had made his way to that chair with a palpitating heart that quickened when Mary Josepha put her hands on him. As he sat there under her hand, every desire within him was to join with her. If she were truly a vessel for the spirit, he would accept conversion and serve her God. If she were vessel for some other concern that stood unseen behind her, he would serve that instead, so long as he could keep her hands on him. He held his eyes closed and allowed what she offered to course through him. He knew there were unknown forces in the world that he had felt, unbidden or else in deep moments of contemplation. When she touched him he did not know what it was that she offered, and it reminded him not of the energy of creation, as he had known it before, but something just as white hot in his breast. When he opened his eyes he thought he knew what it was and shivered. To his surprise he also felt her hand trembling as she held it there on his forehead. He knew not only what it was then, but that it was also experiencing out of the ordinary for either her church or any other. In that instant he almost pulled her down into his lap, but he stayed still and rigid in the chair, receiving her touch.

The other preacher looked at them with a fiery stare that spoke not of spiritual disapproval but erotic jealousy. Whether she herself struggled with religious notions or the more earthly ones that sometimes pulled on them, he did not know, but Purchase was certain he would win her over for his own.

As he sat, there was a shot fired in the audience, and people began climbing over each other to leave the tent, which was quickly brought to lean on one side. Magnus reached for Sanne and Merian, and they began making their way toward the exit. Someone pushed against their back, and Sanne was knocked down to her knees, and her purse disappeared. While the two men made a cordon around her with their bodies to give her room to stand, they were manhandled by the crowd and nearly toppled over, as the other side of the tent came down and full pandemonium erupted. Finally they were able to get Sanne to her feet and, with brute strength, force their way out of the commotion.

When the tent finally cleared, it was collapsed everywhere but under its main pole. There Purchase still sat in the healing seat, with Mary Josepha's hands still on him.

s i x

⤙

Their congress when it was finished had lasted a full ten minutes, through all the bedlam, and if Mary Josepha had possessed healing power Purchase would have been cleansed and fixed of all that ever disturbed him. Instead, he was possessed by a great wanting, and when she removed her hands from him he was afraid such as he had never been before—of being without her touch.

She looked slightly wild about the eyes, and her girdle was misaligned. After she took her hands down she did not know what to think of the man who had sat so calmly through all the commotion without flinching, as if he were afraid of nothing in the world. When he finally stood and took her arm to find them a pathway out of the fallen tent, she felt hot beneath his hand and realized she had been wanting for him to return her touch the entire time he was seated there.

Outside, Purchase placed her on his horse, mounted the animal behind her, and rode off. Mary Josepha had a prearranged meeting on the edge of town with her husband, Oswin Palmer. When Purchase rode in the other direction, however, she did not protest.

Purchase took her to the same room in back of his workshop where he had asked her to wait for him the last time they met. This time, instead of going off, he went inside with her and bolted the door. There they spent the entire rest of the day in the thrall of each other's embrace.

They were still there the next day, when Magnus came round from Stonehouses looking for him. Sanne had been very distraught that he had not come home after the chaos at the prayer meeting and worried

131

he was hurt in the mayhem. Magnus, though, who had observed him as he sat in the chair, suspected he had finally conspired a way to be alone with the preacher woman.

When Magnus knocked at the door there was no response from inside at first. He knocked louder, finally calling out, until Purchase responded. "What do you want?"

"Open the door," Magnus said.

It was silent inside, but after a while the worn wooden door creaked open and Purchase stood there, looking as though he had not slept for many days.

"Sanne wants to know what happened to you."

"Tell her I'll be around for dinner."

"Will you?"

When Magnus came back without Purchase, but told them he had found him in his workshop, Sanne was quieted. Merian, however, grew suspicious.

"What was he doing there?"

"Repairing a wheel," Magnus answered.

"Likely," Merian returned. "Any sign of those two preachers around town?"

"None that I have seen," Magnus said.

"You're a remarkable poor liar," Merian said. "That's a marvel for a slave, but it's a sign of your mother's character, not your own. You would lie if you could; you just can't. You are trying your mighty best, though."

"He says he will be here at dinner."

That afternoon, as Sanne and Adelia put food out for the family, Purchase came through the door, and Magnus was relieved to see his brother had not gone mad enough to bring the woman with him.

During the meal he answered all their questions glancingly, hiding his secret thoughts, and departed as soon as the table was cleared. Merian watched him go with a heavy heart, for he could see the beginning of unhappiness in his son, who until then had seldom known the evil of tears. At least that is what Merian imagined. Purchase to all the world looked elated that afternoon, and, when he took his horse and galloped off in a frenzy, anyone watching would have thought it was a youthful hunger for speed and experience rather than eagerness to find heartbreak.

When he returned to the shop that evening, Mary Josepha was gone again, as were all of her things, and the room was carefully straightened. Next to the place where they had made their bed, he found a coin with a strange marking on it he had not seen before. When he realized she had abandoned the place, he felt as if he had just walked through a sheet of glass and was only waiting for the noise to reach him. He knew then he could not hear the noise because he was inside it and its sound was pain itself.

He sat there awhile, still hoping her departure was only momentary and that she might come back through the door with all her things proclaiming the desire to stay with him, until he could no longer bear the atmosphere of the room and soon went out and mounted his horse, intending to ride a spell so that he might gather himself. His feelings were still tender in his breast three hours later when he stopped the horse in front of the roadhouse.

He entered and there was very little activity, as it was still the middle of the day and midweek at that. Soon the proprietress came out to oblige his needs, sending him into one of the rooms.

When he was done if he had to describe her he would have failed in all detail except her sex, which was female, and so all that mattered to his end of the trade.

As he rode home, he agreed with what Magnus had said, that taking one woman to forget another was indeed a peculiar sort of arithmetic. But, like some clever trick of calculus, it worked a shortcut to forgetting for him, and he was balanced enough so long as he was able to stay in the anonymous arms of the other woman. Seated on his horse, taking the trail back to Stonehouses, he felt a compounding of the shame that had seized him from the time he was there before and sensed how he was neglecting himself to behave in such a way. He knew nothing but the devil could work such low misery on a man.

"I must get this out of myself," he said aloud, as he turned onto his father's property. As he thought how he might be falling into Satan's grasp, he resolved to himself never to go to that place in the woods again or do what he had done out there with anyone else.

When he came on his father's land, he composed himself before riding to the house, but both his parents were still able to tell he was brought fairly far down by something. Sanne, not yet sensing its seriousness, did not try to comfort him. Merian, though, asked slyly whether he did not think it was time for him to begin thinking of taking a wife. "Of your own," he added, as if in afterthought.

Purchase, when he heard this, looked severely at Magnus, thinking he had betrayed him.

"What puts that into your mind?" he asked Merian coolly.

"Only that it's getting to be time. But you seem to have your own notions. What about you, Magnus?"

"What, sir?" Magnus replied.

"Have you given thought to a wife? Worse things can happen to a man at your age in life."

"I'm still getting used to all that has changed in the last two years," he said. "I don't think a wife would help any but to confuse things."

"Is there a drink to be had anywhere?" Purchase asked, when they had finished dinner.

Sanne, hearing this, grew worried. "There's no need of drinking with every meal," she said.

"No need for it, just asking," Purchase said.

"Nay, have a drink," Merian told him. "You too, Magnus. Let's all sit down, since it is so rare we seem to be all together of late."

Sanne went out into the kitchen, muttering that it was not temperate to drink in the middle of the week for no reason other than want of drink. "Salvation is in resisting urges, not giving in to whatever we want just for desire of it," she said. Out in the kitchen she sent Adelia away and sat herself down at the low table, where she began praying for all of them in the house.

When she was younger all her prayers had seemed very abstract to her, and merely the habit of ritual and good behavior. As she prayed now, in the later part of her life, she was stricken with a great terror, and even the things she worried might happen in the afterlife seemed very real, nor did they seem far off. She prayed with an anxiety that she might pass at any moment and did not want any of her thoughts for her family to go unheard. She did not know what influence anyone on earth could have, either up there or in the other place, if people down there had sympathy for those still up here, but she knew that, without her, Merian would go to church very seldom, and Purchase and Magnus, whom she had taken in as an orphan even though he was well grown when he came into their lives, would not go at all unless it was for needs that had little to do with salvation. She did not think they were unscrupulous, any of them, simply that they did not pay enough heed to the care of their religion, in the same way some people would sit down to table without paying mind to the cleanliness of their hands.

In his own way, Merian was much concerned with the same thing, as he uncorked a cordial in the parlor and poured the spirits into glasses for each of them. "Temperance is the best way to go with this stuff," he said, giving out the glasses. "But I tend to think that of most things."

Magnus sipped at the spirits carefully, being still distrustful of their effect in any amount. Purchase, when he received his glass, emptied it in two great swallows and set it on the table beside himself without self-consciousness.

"Are you sure you haven't had a drink already today?" Merian asked him. "That's no way to act in your mother's house."

"I'm sorry," Purchase said. "I forgot myself."

"Well, why don't you tell me what has been going on with you lately that has you forgetting yourself. How is your trade?"

"The same as always," he answered laconically, without offering any elaboration.

"It is never the same. Magnus, why is Purchase acting so possessed?"

When Purchase heard that word it set off in him the worry that he actually was under an unnatural influence. He glowered at Magnus to see if he would betray him.

Magnus was not one to trust authority with any information they did not already have in their keep, but his concern for Purchase was strong enough that he thought about giving him away right then and there.

"I don't know," he answered at last, deciding that lying to Merian might give him more influence to help Purchase right his own course instead of the old man trying to fix it.

"Whatever it is, you had better get it under control," Merian said, taking away the bottle. "Otherwise I fear you might lose your way. You always have been one to wander, but as you get older the danger from that is worse and worse," he concluded. "You'll tell me if you need help getting it back under control?" he asked, to let him know it was all right to do so. "The thing for both of you," he went on, "is to start thinking of marrying someone to help hold you upright in all of this, because sometimes I fear it is too difficult for any one of us to do alone."

Purchase and Magnus both nodded, and it pleased Merian a great deal that they listened to him so thoughtfully. As if to prove the effect of his advice, very soon after this speech in the parlor Magnus did become involved with a woman—even if it did not lead straightaway to respectable marriage. Purchase, though, he was bent on the dangerous course he had fallen onto and was soon lost to it entirely.

He slept very poorly that night, tossing under his blanket as he tried to put the woman out of his mind. He knew well that no welcome end would follow from his desires if he did not master them. In the middle of the night, still unable to sleep, he got up and went to the front porch for air. It was late October and already the frost came in at night, making everything before him sharp in the moonlight from the shards of crystal that clung to the grass and foliage. His own breath rose on the blue darkness in front of his face, and he placed his hand in front of it to feel the fleeting warmth, then rubbed both hands together. He was happy for this moment alone. He found, however, he could not concentrate on any one thought, but everything went scattering before his focus and examination until there was nothing but the diffuse desire for what he knew he should not want or, if wanting were no crime in itself, what he should not do.

He stayed sitting in a corner of the porch until he was everywhere numb from the air and his brain had stopped its overactivity. When he stood and went back to his bed, he lay down and found there was no thought of anything else except the woman. This time, though, when he tried to sleep the thought of her was warming to him and he drifted off with a mirthful smile on his face.

He woke the next morning unhappy again and soon after breakfast went to his workshop, where he was in the foulest of moods all day. The other smiths and assistants avoided him as he worked with his tools irritably. After supper he was unable to bear his anguish anymore and saddled his horse to go off in search of her.

Five days later he found her back with her husband, leading a meeting in Columbus County. It was much like the one that had taken place near Stonehouses, with the tent pitched in a field and congregants come from all around to hear what they had to say. When the healing chair was put out, Purchase could not control himself and went and stood in front of it, but he did not sit down this time. He only looked at Mary Josepha as she went through the pantomime of releasing people from their aches and demons.

Oswin, the Englishman, smoldered at him from the pulpit, but when Purchase moved away it was of his own accord, as nothing in the world would have been able to move him otherwise. All his strength had gone over to the thing that afflicted him. He was sick with love.

After the meeting she was gone very quickly with the Englishman, but Purchase pursued them and showed up at every one of their revivals until he could have given Palmer's sermon himself. Once the Englishman even fired a shot at him, telling him he knew how to handle his sort. This was in Bladen County, when he saw him on the road behind their carriage, but Purchase escaped unharmed. Nor did he see it as his business to argue further with the husband, as the only talking he wished for was with the wife.

It was in Georgia that he finally persuaded her to come off with him again. She and her husband had done their preaching that day to a crowd that was mostly slaves but receptive to the message they were sharing. When she looked out and saw Purchase standing at the back of the tent she nodded to him, as if it had been her intention all along to wait five weeks then come to him again.

He did not know what her nod meant, for she had refused to speak to him the entire time of his pursuit, and, as the crowd dispersed after the sermon he was still half surprised when he turned and saw her standing there behind him.

"Are you ready?" she asked.

He nodded and led her to where his horse was and put her upon it. Once he had her he galloped off, with a quick pacing heart, and all want pressed against him from the inside out.

They stopped in a pine stand and slept that night out-of-doors. It was late November and the days still held a little of their autumn warmth, but at night there was nothing deceptive about which time of year it was, and the two of them bundled tight as a single coil of hair all the night long.

When he woke in the morning it was because he no longer felt her under his outstretched arm. He opened his eyes in the half gray of a clouded dawn and found no sign of her, but for another of the little keepsake coins she had left before.

They had been so rapt in each other's arms he had not even asked her why she changed her mind and came to him, but he thought it must have been his steadfast presence that persuaded her. There on the cold damp ground, with pine needles prickling the side of his face, Purchase felt like a born idiot. She must have had a falling out with her Englishman and only taken him for revenge on the other.

For his own part he could not answer why he behaved as he did, but that it had gotten beyond his ability to govern his own actions. When he realized this he felt a deep penetrating shame that, more than her drumming his emotions and hoaxing him, brought him close to tears. This in its turn increased his shame and he grew angry with himself, as something hard and dark turned over inside of him—showing a burning underbelly that shone in his eyes as he rose that morning and went off again in search of her.

That he should get back to his people he had no doubt, but he was lost to them as he was to himself, thinking only how he would keep the woman from leaving once he had her back.

The night with her had been tender, and the one before that endearing, but after this there would only be the power of his will and her will when they were with each other, locked in contest.

seven

～

When Purchase disappeared from Stonehouses everyone thought he had simply slipped off for a few days, as he was wont to do when one thing or other had caught his attention. After three days of not seeing him, though, Merian knew something must have happened and tried to keep Sanne calm while he discovered what it was.

He went first to Magnus to ask whether he knew what had happened to his brother. Magnus, looking at his father, knew he had to confess what little he knew. "He sure had it for that preacher woman," he offered, leaving Merian to ponder aloud whether Purchase could be foolish and unsensible enough to run off after a married woman. Sanne, when she heard this, was filled with woe, worrying that his emotions had led him somewhere irredeemable.

Magnus, for his part, could not understand his brother at all in this instance and, try as he might, could not relate to him. Not long after Purchase disappeared he had the dream again about the woman who lifted her skirts and taunted him. When he awoke, instead of the malaise the dream usually left him with, he found himself thinking about the nights he had spent at the roadhouse with Purchase. He tried then to recall the women he had done his best to avoid looking at before, as he satisfied himself on these pictures drawn from memory. His nature had gotten up, though, and he knew he would eventually have to do something about it.

When he saw Adelia in the kitchen that next morning his eye lingered on her longer than usual, until the girl grew uncomfortable under his staring. It was the first time since the month he arrived that he had paid any more attention to her than he had the dining room table. This morning, though she was entirely present to him. "What a pretty girl you are," he said, sounding full of sorrow, as he left the kitchen with his cup of coffee that was mostly milk.

As he walked past her she tried to shrink out of his way, not wanting an involvement that could jeopardize her position.

She thought momentarily about confessing her uneasiness to Sanne later that morning, after the older woman had come into the kitchen, but was not certain Sanne wouldn't reprimand her as having done something to invite Magnus's attention, or else of being the kind of servant who was just a certain way, no matter who the man was or how imprudent the idea would strike a reasonable person. In the end she kept her misgivings to herself, deciding out of hand it was all inappropriate to her station and employment.

As the weeks wore on into winter that year, Magnus did not leave her alone but grew more and more forward with his interest and intentions. In the face of such attention, Adelia found herself growing increasingly ambivalent in her refusals, until she was no longer certain about her position in the matter at all.

Sanne was the first to suspect there was something between them, seeing how Adelia became silent whenever Magnus entered a room, always hurrying herself away or else lingering over him, if she thought no one was paying attention.

When she mentioned Adelia to Merian as a possibility for Magnus, though, he was set against the idea and said he would speak to Magnus about his behavior.

"He can't help if she is who he's drawn to," Sanne argued.

"Yes, he can," Merian answered. "Everything can always be helped, and what can't be helped belongs to the devil."

"Who are you to be so high-and-mighty all of a sudden?" Sanne asked. "Their coming together, if that's what they want to do, can't hurt anything."

"It just isn't proper," Merian argued. "And what isn't proper, if it is allowed to happen in a house, begins to break down the very roof."

"It wouldn't be the first time such a thing has happened," she answered. "Besides, there's nothing improper about it."

"He should think about himself in a different way," Merian countered. "She's not the kind of wife who will make him a good helpmate and partner."

"And what do you know of that?" Sanne wanted to know. "She's perfectly capable."

"That's just it," Merian said. "He needs someone more than just perfectly capable, or else he'll start heading backward."

"Is that how you chose your wife?"

"It did not hurt," he answered.

Sanne was angry at him then for assuming airs and growing so far out of his own station that he looked unkindly on another.

"A station isn't a given thing," he countered, "but something a man makes for himself if he can, and if he doesn't like it he changes it or not—loses or gains what he should in the great marketplace—so that by a certain age he should end up in the correct one.

"I came out here without a station. I was not even a slave. A slave is something that belongs to the system of organization of courts and law. But if I had been taken up on charges, what would the law have called me? It would not have properly known. That is why I came to where there was no law and no station, so I might answer the question myself."

"Well, you are certainly in one by yourself now," she said, turning her back and giving him her coldness. "Just what do you think he has done?"

At this Merian was silent, but there was still something in the arrangement that did not sit right with him. Nonetheless, he said to Sanne, "Let them do as they please back there, then, but don't come to me if it turns out poorly."

Whenever Sanne saw Magnus around Adelia after that she would smile beatifically at both young people, in such a way that put Magnus at ease but made Adelia feel very lonely in the house, for now she knew Sanne would not be her champion against Magnus if it came to that.

She was only twenty-two years old at the time, but she sensed something odd about Magnus's interest in her. She also knew she had to be very careful in the business of love and husbanding, not having anything else in this world. As he continued in his pursuit, though, she eventually could not bear it any longer and took control of the situation one evening, when they were alone, when she gave him a little kiss.

The kiss fired his imagination and he persuaded her to lie with him in an upstairs room after the house had all gone to sleep. By the time she came to him that night his head ached from needing her. It was very intense and passionate then, and even though she felt she had done something she should not have, she came to him again the following night. They burned through with need again that night as well, but when she visited him again the next day he did not want her as much and, in fact, sent her away at the end of the week.

He could hear her crying through the floor when she went back downstairs, but he was helpless to do anything for her. The day afterward she seemed very tired out as she went about her chores, and Magnus tried to avoid her. She continued on in her theater of sadness for the rest of the week, though, until Merian himself had to intervene.

"That is no way to treat a person," he said, as the two of them worked at repairing a broken door on the barn. "If you didn't want her you should have stayed off."

"It's not that I didn't want her, but that I wanted her very badly and don't anymore," Magnus answered. "There are no guarantees in things."

"You should be shamed to talk to your father that way," Merian said. "Do you think I'm Purchase to just go support you in whatever you want, instead of what is rightful? They have places where you can treat a woman that way, but my wife's kitchen is not one of them."

After such a strong rebuke, Magnus did feel ashamed of the way he had behaved and apologized to Merian for it. "I couldn't help it, " he said. "I just couldn't."

Merian started to tell him that everything we do can be helped but, seeing he was already cast low, decided to leave him to his thoughts. "Well, it is her you should apologize to. You led her to one set of expectations and dashed them. That is no way to live."

"It is not what I meant," Magnus said. "I will say something to her."

Merian wondered why his sons acted as if their wants were so important they could not deny themselves anything for the sake of other people. He did not understand it and counted it as a way people were becoming when they were not before. He felt a fear for Magnus, just as he did for Purchase, that he could not abide by the sacrifices of life but only its bounty.

Marriage is like that too, he thought. Some days you want to be with each other and other days you do not, but you determine how to balance

them so they are fair. You cannot just pursue her one day and send her
away the next.

Magnus did not want a wife. He wanted to remain untethered to
anything outside of himself, especially anything with so many different
kinds of need as a woman. Nevertheless, he did go to Adelia some few
days later to try to set things aright.

His heart was by now remarkable heavy with the notion that he had
used her wrongly, when his only intention was to be rid of the disturbance that thundered in his own head. It was the same as it had always
been for him. Where other men, like Purchase, were constantly thinking of women or their own pleasure, with him it simply all built up then
burst forth and went away for a while.

When he saw Adelia she was stooped over the fire trying to coax a
bit more heat from the embers. She looked up from her task and backed
away a little upon seeing him.

"What are you doing here?" she asked, when she saw he was not
moving on. "I thought you didn't want me."

"I was hoping for a little part of your time," he answered her.

"You did not seem so interested in it a few days ago," she managed,
looking around the room with pulsating nervousness.

"That is what I wanted to talk to you about. I did not mean to treat
you low. It's just—well, I am different from other men."

"I thought you were exactly the image of a certain kind of man."

"I do like you, Adelia," he pleaded. "I like you as much as anybody
in the world."

She turned away from him. He had had these scenes before when he
had brought someone else into his situation. Some of the women would
be very easy about it, as if nothing had happened, while others set to
remonstrating and wailing until they had their fill of self-suffering. He
only hoped she was not like the latter.

"When I saw you standing here Monday morning you seemed to me like
the whole world that was worth having, and it took all the self-governance
I had to keep from reaching out to you. Then, after I finally got you to me,
I felt cast down because I knew I could not offer what you wanted."

"You did not have a problem taking," was her only reply.

"Adelia, I could not make you happy," he finished. "I thought it
would be better to cut it off before we got too far wrapped up."

"You didn't even ask what I wanted. You couldn't even treat me with that decency but just turned me away from you." She did start crying then, and Magnus was very moved by her tears.

"What is it you want, Adelia? Tell me that now and I will try to hear it." He walked closer to her and looked down at the top of her head as she wiped her face with her hand. She looked back up and he saw again that she was very pretty, and was sorry he could not maintain the steadiness of devotion that a good husband must have. He was, however, taken again with wanting for her and touched her very lightly, in case she should be shocked or offended by his gesture.

Instead she put her head upon his chest and cried there, until he lifted her chin and kissed her. It was not what he had meant to do, but he told her to visit him again that night. It was not what she intended either, but she found herself in his chambers when all the rest of the world was asleep and it was only the two of them awake in creation.

She began to spoil him after that, making little cakes and cookies every day or cooking his favorite meals for dinner. He was kind with her for a while as well, until it seemed they would be together. Inevitably, though, it turned off in him again. The ability to reciprocate her feeling toward him. When it did, he told himself he was wicked, but he did try his best to rekindle his former feeling. When this failed he simply withdrew into himself remorsefully.

For a time he still suffered her company on occasion, but gradually refused even that and spent all his time with work or, in the evening, sitting late with his aging father discussing matters of great outward import, so that she dare not interrupt.

As he removed himself from her she offered more of her best attention to him, leaving the little sweets outside his door or knitting him warm things to have on his body in the cold weather. He took her gifts but could not enjoy them.

When he came into the kitchen one night, after two weeks of this treatment, she sat waiting up for him and asked why he abused her affections. He replied that he did not mean to. He was merely bound to his own ways and could not be always spending so much time in idling with her.

She began then the same weeping that had worked on him before, but his heart was steel and would not bend to her words or tears. He went off and left her crying in the kitchen. "What have I done to be abused?" she sobbed loudly in the night, so the whole house was awake with pity for her until dawn.

The next night he had his dream of the naked woman again, and it set in him the determination to have nothing to do with Adelia but get on instead in his work. During the time he had been there, Stonehouses had grown in size, as he and Merian worked more and more as a team, and his influence grew steadily to the point that when their neighbor to the east died he was able to convince Merian to buy the dead man's land. Not that it was so difficult, as he was merely rekindling a dream Merian had in his own youth, so that when the properties were combined it was a sizable estate by any measure. There were also stores to be managed and disputes to settle and new tilling methods to try out, all of which suited him well, as he shared with his father a love for the land. He was in all other matters a quiet soul, and domestic life was too turbulent to him. He knew he must eventually either marry her or send her away, and he was not the one for marriage.

All that spring he stayed away from her, and eventually left her little gifts untouched by the door where she left them, until she stopped leaving things altogether. She determined in her heart then to leave that house and find work and a living elsewhere.

One day he came into the kitchen and found Sanne there with a girl he did not recognize. He did not think to say anything of it, but after a week of not seeing Adelia he did ask after her whereabouts. Sanne thought it was bold of him to mention her at all, but told him Merian had arranged for her to go work at Content's place.

For a week he did not go, satisfied with merely knowing she had not gone too far off. Eventually, though, he had one of his bouts, as he had begun to refer to them, since they had become so frequent that they were no longer a separate part of his life and seemed to need to be called something. When it came it was like truth to him, and he went bravely, as he saw it, to seek her out.

When he entered Content's the older man greeted him warmly, and they talked for a time about Merian, and then whether there had been word from Purchase—for his case was beginning to be known around the colonies and sometimes news or conjecture would reach them there in Berkeley. "What happened to him was a bewitching I would not wish on any man," Content said, as he moved away to another customer, "but for you, Magnus, you know it is not so bad being close to someone else. Nothing at all for a man to fear. Then again, I am often surprised by what people do and don't fear."

"Will she see me?" he asked, when Content finished lecturing him.

"Ought she to?" he asked. "If you don't know your own mind, you don't need to go stirring her up again."

"Well," Magnus said, "to be all the way honest, Content, I don't know if I know my mind or not. Some days I think about her and I am ready to be with her and all that means. Other days I think about it, and part of me doesn't know if I can be with anything else that stirs."

"Well, you are already with others that stir. What do you think Jasper thought when you showed up? It wasn't, Can I be with another thing that stirs?"

"We are not the same."

"It's a matter of what is right to do."

"Content, do you think it is more natural for a man to be with a woman all the time than for both of them to go about their business and come together when it suits them?"

"It might be or might not be," Content answered, "but I don't see what kind of coming together it can be, any more than beasts."

"You think I should see her?"

"I think you should see her if you can get clear in your own heart what it is you want of her," Content answered. "She is round back in the kitchen if you figure it out before closing."

He did not go immediately round back, but took his glass to a far table, where he sat staring out the window, nursing both pint and thought. When he finished his drink he called Jannetje to bring him another, which surprised her, as he seldom had more than a single drink and that one more for social custom than want of beer.

As he looked through the window and waited for his pint, it began to snow, lightly at first but then becoming very dense and beautiful. The thick flakes fell all in a pattern that to him looked like a very cold night in winter set deep with stars. He drank and stared up until he felt himself beginning to move through them all into the deep infinite darkness. It was then, as he was rising up into the firmament, that he thought of the water for the first time in a great many years.

He is very young and his mother calls him to come with her to see Mr. Sorel, their master. The man who is his father visited recently and there was a great upheaval in their lives for a few days before settling back to normal, but this he feels is somehow part of that upheaval. She has scrubbed his shirt and combed his hair, and he knows that before this meeting there were others with their mistress that kept his mother agitated and on continuous edge.

Now as they prepare to go to the house, she is nervous and fidgets with the buttons on his blouse repeatedly until she is ready to go. At the main house they are taken into Mr. Sorel's office, which he has never seen before and finds extremely frightening as they stand there. When Mr. Sorel greets them he is even more afraid, as the children on the place all try to avoid their master.

"My wife tells me you have something to request," their master says to his mother, making what seems to him a point of not using her name.

"Yes, sir, Mr. Sorel," his mother answered. "I was wanting to buy me and Magnus out."

"Out of what?" Sorel asked.

"Out so we can be free," she answered.

"Well, that is not generally my practice or view of business, Ruth," he said, "but I tell you what I will do. I'm going to take this little boy of yours here and put him to a test. If he passes the test you can pay for both of you and go free. If he fails, though, you will stay on here until the end of your days, and so will he, and so will his children and so on, as the law says should be."

"No, sir, Mr. Sorel," his mother answered, "he's just a boy and I don't reckon he's ready for tests."

"Well, you have tested me already tonight, Ruth, so it's my terms from here on."

When they left the meeting his mother was crying sharply, and he drew near trying to console her. "I'll pass whatever test he put me to," he said.

147

Instead of being consoled, though, his mother began to cry even more, until he was afraid indeed.

That next morning a man came to their room to take him away. She gave him a kiss before relinquishing him. "They want everything," she said. "If you ever make it back, just remember that. It is not human wanting that they have but something unmade and unnatural."

He did not know what she meant for a long time, but he thought over what she had said as he sat in the back of the cart being carried away from her. When they arrived at the river, Mr. Sorel was there with some of his men and watched as those who had been sent to fetch him placed him in a large sack. The boy did not struggle but could only succumb to the power of his master's men.

"Listen to me," Sorel said, before they closed up the sack. "If you drown in this water your mother will get to have what she wants and go live with your sire, but if you live you will both stay on here exactly as you have been."

He finished speaking and nodded for the men to close up the sack, crowding the child in dark fear. The boy breathed in quickly and deeply, hoping for air to be in him whenever the bag was tossed into the water. Finally, he felt himself up in the air; then a hard slap on the surface of the river and a frigid inrush of water as he hoarded his breath. The bag filled at first with a pocket of fresh air; then everything was water and he began to go very slowly to the bottom. He struggled against the sack, and struggled with it, until to his amazement it came open for him, and he began to swim up. As he swam he remembered his master's words and thought whether to allow what it was his mother wanted so badly or what his body told him he ought.

As he thought of this, he felt a tap at his shoulder and Jannetje standing over him. He stood up to leave and made his way toward the door unsteadily, for he had been drinking the entire while. When he found his horse out in the pen, he brushed it briefly to give it some warmth, then stood in the stirrup.

As he began to head to Stonehouses, he looked back at Content's place and saw Adelia in the kitchen through the snow. He stood there awhile, watching her in her movements against the yellow light from the warm room; then, when he thought he saw her turn to the window, spurred the horse for fear she might see him out there not knowing what to do.

e i g h t

⦿

Purchase ranged the countryside in desolation after Mary Josepha left him, sometimes earning his living by honest means and sometimes in more expeditious fashion. A month after she went back to her husband he knew he would not forget her but made it through the winter alone as best he could. Nor was his heart heavy with anything else that winter, except failing in his union with her.

He was almost in Maryland before he found her again and, after much persuading, convinced her to come off with him. It seemed to him it was either easier than before or else he no longer felt the pain of what he went through. This time, so say the stories that eventually sprang up around the two of them and reached Berkeley, he swore he would employ all his powers of strength and intelligence to keep her. When she came to him then, in a rented room, he put a potion in her drink that made her sleep very sound. She awoke in an impenetrable cage of his besotted construction.

He had dreamed of that enclosure all the way from the border of Florida to where they were now. At night small details would come to him, and he would get up then and there to jot down a diagram of what had been revealed to him.

The bars of the jail were stronger even than the blade of the sword he had made for his father, and the lock was of ingenious design. No one would ever break it or learn its secret mechanism. The entire contraption was exceedingly light as well, so that it could be taken up and put in the back of a wagon, suspended in air, or even floated on water. Inside he tried to make it as comfortable as possible for her, and when they were not on the move it had a mechanism that allowed him to expand it and give her more room. In all those hours without her he had figured out how to make the cage perfect for what it was and escape-proof. If it was cruel he did not see it, only that it accomplished his goal and kept her near him.

The only time he opened the door was to give her food, or when he wanted to be with her. For a month she suffered this fate, until one day she suddenly warmed to him again, calling out for him to come to her of her own accord. They were happy like this for many weeks. It was after one of these episodes, though, that he awoke to find himself imprisoned in his own trap and Mary Josepha gone back to the Englishman.

It took him twice as long to escape the dungeon as build it. When he finally was able to let himself free he was bitter with a disgrace that forbade him from returning home, as he should have, so he continued roaming northward until he could forget or else find a way to redeem who he had become. He swore this time he would not go after her again either but reflect upon what he had learned those months, until the suffering itself had become a kind of balm and solace. "Suffering has always been the price of God's love," Mary Josepha used to say to him, when he had convinced her to come off with him, just before she left. He did not feel loved, though. He felt hated, and he was all the way down bitter with himself over what he had done. For he was no longer Purchase of Stonehouses but someone far removed.

He was working in Rhode Island in a shipyard when she finally came to him of her own free choice. She was with a small child and said Oswin had put her out, claiming to know it was not his and no way would it ever be passed off as such.

He took her in, and they lived for a while in great harmony, each forgiving the other for the things they had done to cause one another misery. They lived above the smithy where he worked, and the rooms were always warm from the furnace, and she set about making a home for the three of them there. He had long ago melted the cage down, and from its remains crafted a great wrought-iron bed, which they slept on as husband and wife, for she claimed that a man and woman could marry themselves to each other with no more officiating than that. That it was the way it had always been done until the church thought to step in and charge a fee, but the institution was still built of just two people.

Whatever this state was called, it was blissful to him, and he went to work regular most mornings, except those he stayed home to be with her. On those holidays he always worked late into the evening the following day so that they always had dependable meals and warm clothes against the seaside winters. From this routine, life in the house took on the contours of regularity that did much to ease both their minds.

She had come over from Africa not ten years earlier and Oswin had originally been her master, until he had a vision one night and immediately upon waking repented of how he lived, saying now that it was not proper for one human to own another. When he set his slaves free he had thirty other souls he had been responsible for during the previous portion of his life. He told them they were all permitted to go, but he said to Mary Josepha that he would be much pleased if she stayed with him of her own volition. It surprised her, for he had never seemed to so much as look at her before. She agreed to stay with him, and they were happy awhile.

In time she found he was a very jealous husband and snuck off with Purchase, at first to punish him. The second time, however, it had been because she had found she preferred to be with Purchase and had no want of punishing anyone, if such were possible.

They wrestled with this for the years they were on the road together, him telling her she was his wife and her saying it was difficult to find a difference between that and being his slave. Shamed, he would be silent a bit, but when she abandoned him for Purchase he beat her to within an inch of her life. The next day, heavy of heart, he gave two very popular sermons: the first was about the rights of slaves to freedom, and the second was about the duty of the wife and the pain of marriage. "Both are among the truest penance to God," he claimed. That day they saved two dozen souls, more if one included the slaves one of the parishioners set free after the sermon.

Purchase was irresistible to her after that and she had come to him in Maryland intending to stay, until she found herself in the cage. When she returned to Oswin he at first took her in, and even kept her after he saw her condition, thinking perhaps it was his issue she bore. As soon as the child was born, though, he put them both out in the snow. He himself died very soon afterward, of an affliction either of the nervous system or of the blood. He had two different doctors and on this final diagnosis neither could agree.

That winter and spring husband, wife, and child were all content as could be in the warm little room above the shop, and when summer came they talked of visiting Stonehouses. It was put off because of Purchase's work, which picked up during the warm months, and on account of the child still being so small, but Mary Josepha gave every impression of being the most diligent of mothers. She seemed to be rid of the wandering that was in her blood before.

When Purchase came upstairs from the workshop she would have a meal waiting for him, and on Sundays they went to the Baptist church together for worship and praying on the things they could find no other answers for, or refuge from, in daily life.

It was here she first felt the need to minister again. Even though Rhode Island was the most liberal of the colonies, there was not yet a significant congregation of people who professed as they did, for Purchase had come to be an adherent of her unorthodox beliefs as well. She expressed her dissatisfaction at first by attending different churches to hear what their ministers had to preach. Usually she went for no more than a week, but sometimes she would maintain interest in a congregation for as long as eighteen months before moving on, until she had been to nearly every church in Providence. In the end she knew it was simply no use. They were none of them as liberal as they preached, all were beholden to an ordering she recognized as false, and none could explain these falsehoods away.

She began to give sermons in the square on her own, but what had been popular among the country people caused a great sensation in the town. There were two principal charges brought against her. The first was that she was uneducated and so could not interpret the Gospels; no one claimed her to be heretical, because heresy requires knowing and they denied her ability in this endeavor. The second was that she was a woman and, on those grounds alone, should stop and desist.

When they brought the complaint, they first spoke to Purchase, but he supported her steadfastly. "If she has it to preach, I don't see the harm. There's a thousand churches in Providence." The response did not endear him to anyone and soon his business began to decline, among both the whites and free Negroes.

Purchase told her it was nothing to cause them worry, and they would withstand the privations of opinion. For Mary Josepha, however, it was more than people talking against her, it was that she could not practice her chosen craft and belief. "It is my calling, and the price of God's love has always been and ever will be suffering," she repeated, and he knew this is what she truly believed and that he was in danger of her leaving. "Better a liar with true words than a false prophet and none of it worth telling."

He did not want to know anything more about that kind of love and told her they would leave the state and return the coming autumn to his people at Stonehouses, where there was always a place for them.

What she wanted foremost was to preach, and to know again the feeling of bringing souls to God on what she thought of as reasonable terms, even if there was theater out in front of that. "I will have the same problem there as here," she said. "The only way to keep going for me is to move and not rest still." He told her they should at least try his people first before settling into that kind of life, as he did not think it would be any great bargain for any of them.

He returned from work one day soon after that to find her gone again, as he had all those days in the past. This time, however, he was not frantic in his action but very deliberate. It was northern autumn and already beginning to freeze over during the nights.

He dressed the boy in heavy shoes and a thick warm sweater underneath a heavy coat. His head was covered in a woolen hat. Purchase affixed a bag containing some coins of silver in the pockets of his coat and another of gold inside his sweater. He also wrote two notes, one for the messenger and another for the receiver.

He then took the boy in his arms and carried him out into the night and to the other side of Providence, down near the quays. It was the home of one of his friends and customers, a half-caste sailor named Rennton who belonged to the Antinomian church with his wife and often did business in the farmost reaches of the Crown's possessions, including the southern colonies.

In his father's arms the boy felt safe when they left the house, but soon a sense of dizziness overtook him as they bounded over the small hills, which looked enormous from his perspective, and moved toward the fish smell of the docks. He knew something strange was afoot, but when his father set him down on the unfamiliar porch and told him to stay quiet, the child obeyed. He was still quiet an hour later when Rennton came home and found him there, and in fact would not speak for two full days afterward.

Purchase he could not help but go off again after Mary Josepha, as he had those days in the past when she still had another man and he chased after her. Both of them like the original Fools, or else original Lament and Heartache.

Rennton took the child inside his little house and asked his wife to feed him from their pot. While the child ate he unpinned the note from his coat and went out to his neighbor's place to have it read. He did not need anyone to tell him that something was amiss with the boy and that in likelihood he had been abandoned. It seemed too important a thing to guess at, though, and not be entirely certain. What if they only wanted to leave the child for a little while and then come back? But leaving him out there in the cold, Rennton knew, was the same as giving him away.

He apologized to his neighbor for coming at such an hour, but when he showed him the note the man marveled at the audacity of it. "Imagine them not just leaving the boy free and clear but leaving him with a lien they want you to pay off." Rennton thanked him for reading the note and went back to his own house, puzzling more how Purchase could do something like that than the inconvenience it would cause him.

When he returned he told his wife what Purchase and Mary Josepha had done, and she argued with him that it was Purchase who had done more wrong, because Mary Josepha only left the child with its father, as you would if going to the market or away for a visit to relatives.

Rennton did not argue with her—he never argued with her—but said he would take up the task Purchase had left to him—as it was good friendship, and someone had to take up responsibility for the little creature—and try, beginning the day after next, to deliver the boy safely to the place in the note. The boy, Caleum he was called, felt very safe in that house for the two days he was there and seldom cried for missing his parents. He was a manual of composure, and no one watching him would have known any of this, especially as he held his tongue and did not speak.

When they set out for Stonehouses, though, the boy was at first upset by the voyage and the life of the sea. He was almost as disturbed by the journey from Providence to Edenton as he had been when he finally realized for himself that his parents were gone away without him and what his condition was. Rennton, when he addressed him, always started out calling him Caleum, but in the end found himself saying *poor boy* or *pitiful orphan.*

It was on this voyage that Caleum began to speak again and ask his fate, as the sounds of the ship and its other passengers had unsettled him so he did not know what would become of him. Looking over the side of the vessel as they rounded Cape Lookout, the ink-dark water seemed lit from underneath by a strange, ominous light that would show itself if only the waves could part far enough. He looked at this mystery, hoping the water would leap higher and show the bottom of the ocean, but soon the waves began to toss the ship and make it creak with a horrible sound that seemed to him like an old person screaming. He ran back from the rail and sought out Rennton in the excitement of the sailors trying to fasten down the ship for the storm they had entered. When he found his caretaker, he could only think to ask him if they were going to hell. He asked this very calmly, as if he were prepared should that be their ultimate destination.

Rennton told the boy they were going to no such place but were only caught in a squall such is normal at sea in that season. Caleum went back to the rail of the ship and looked out again. This time he spied another boat on the horizon that was sailing under calm winds, and a young couple stood at the rail holding hands. The woman, seeing the boy, kissed her hand with great intensity then blew the kiss to him. Although she looked very different, and he had never seen her before, he felt when he received it that he had been kissed by his own mother. He waved back to the other ship, until they were nearly gone from sight, and the wind in the sails of his boat forced him to seek shelter below.

Rennton, when the boy came back, tried his best to console him, but he could not help worrying aloud what they were thinking to leave him in such a state of safety. He did not judge them though, and while not one man in a hundred thousand would have done what he did, he was good as the trust Purchase placed in him. When the boat docked in Carolina they disembarked, and the two continued overland together toward Stonehouses.

n i n e

In the end it was Sanne who made a way for Adelia in Magnus's affections, years after the start of the affair and even then under the most terrible of circumstances.

The night after she saw him riding away in the snow, Adelia knew Magnus was lost to her. While he sat in the tavern, she allowed her desire for him to seize and run rampant in her imagination. When he stood and, instead of coming to beg her forgiveness, went away, her heart clinched inside her chest and she lost her breath briefly. While he sat out on the horse in the snow, she was aware of him watching her and still thought it only a matter of time before he came back and they were together. When he rode off into the darkness, though, Content had to close the tavern, so distraught was she to see him ride away.

Nor would she come down from her room upstairs in the days that followed, and whenever Dorthea brought her food she sat at the edge of the bed and shoved it away, asking, "What have I done to be treated like this?"

All the sympathy and outrage shown to her, though, did nothing to move Magnus. Sanne, seeing how he behaved, knew it was not how he wished to be. Still, when she prayed at night, she began to wonder whether he was not hardening heaven against himself.

That was in the days immediately before illness took her, and life at Stonehouses changed forever.

When she first noticed it, one day in early spring, the crab on her chest was already livid, and extended out over her breast like a lover's jealous hand. When she gazed upon it she thought of her former husband, and how, when they were still a young couple, he would sometimes clutch her with maddening force as he swore his love. She guarded the crab as a secret for months then, as she had once guarded his affection for her.

When its limbs spread and began grasping for the other side of her body, though, she could no longer bear it. "This much will always be yours. All the rest belongs here to Jasper Merian and Stonehouses," she told her first man, unhappy to have him reaching for so much from where he was.

After breakfast she sent her new girl into town with a note, which the girl left at the doctor's place at lunchtime. He came round to Stone-houses before supper. After the examination he told her she could be happy that they now had hemlock, which was much better than previous medicines to treat such things, and that this procedure was not known even two years before in London, let alone in the colonies.

She thanked him and, in the months that followed, consumed a potion of hemlock twice a day, increasing the amount of the herb bit by bit, until what she ate in the third month would have been enough to murder a bull. There was no effect on her, but neither did her condition worsen. The doctor, when he came around, said recovery was only just around the corner.

When the crab began to grow again and turn scirrhous, he recommended to then a treatment of mercury and poultices. Sanne felt her strength beginning to depart around this time, and the afternoon walks she took to breathe of the deep pine air began to grow shorter, until she could barely make a full turn through her garden. This is when she sent to town to get Adelia back from Content's. The girl came to her immediately, not thinking of Magnus but only that Sanne, that soul of piety, needed her aid.

She nursed her for six months, giving her her medicines and applying a poultice twice a day, the first made from bark, the second from mercury. When the symptoms failed to go away the doctor began to let her blood with leeches, saying such diseases were caused by malign humors that needed only to be released. He prescribed a new poultice of nightshade and told Sanne she must have her daily walk no matter how short it was.

Each morning Adelia would wrap the old woman warmly and take her arm, and they would go out into the garden in front of the house. Both Merian and Sanne had been delighted by that garden when they

finally had the luxury one spring to plant flowers instead of simply vegetables. As she walked there now, though, she saw Samuel, her first
husband, walking beside her and looking continuously at the sundial
as if waiting on another appointment. "Do you have somewhere else to
be?" she asked him.

"No," he replied, "I'm here at your service, but if it would please you
I might finally take you back over the ocean and show you my home, as
we always talked about in our youth."

She was not frightened by this discourse as might be reasonably expected. On the contrary, it soothed her and took her mind from her pain
to have such steadfast company.

When the second treatment regime failed, and the ichor began to run,
the doctor advised both Sanne and Merian that the only recourse was
to try to cut away the diseased tissue. By then the hand that held Sanne
had become a claw, and they both knew neither poultices nor surgery
was very likely save her.

"You have been very good to me," Merian said to her that night after
the doctor had gone, holding her frail hand. "I could not have made half
of what I did without you."

"And I never thought you would build so great a property when I
married you," she answered him. "Or make me so happy."

"It has been better than we dared to hope," Merian said, giving her
hand a light, affectionate squeeze.

"What will happen to my orphans now?" she asked.

He did not answer her but smoothed her hair.

The next day she sent out on the farm to have Magnus come to her.
In the years he had been there Magnus had changed immensely to anyone regarding him. Gone was the hard, weary look he carried when he
first arrived, and his face, while still lean, had taken on a pleasing soft-
ness. Still, there was a hunger about him that was etched within and
had never gone away completely. As he stood at Sanne's bedside, she
tried to turn her head to get a better look at him but was weighed down
with drowsiness from the opium tablets she now consumed four times
a day.

Looking at her, Magnus could not but think how empty that house
would be when she was gone from it. "Ware," she said, unconsciously
using that name that no one but his parents called him by, "Come closer."

He sat at the edge of her bed and thought how he had once been frightened of her when he originally came. He thought then she might put Merian up to sending him away, but they had grown close enough over time.

He was completely quiet as she spoke softly, and he had to bend down over her to hear, until he found it easier to kneel at the side of the bed. He was very tense that she might require something he could not do, but whatever she asked he would strive in earnest to fulfill.

"I want you to promise me you will take care of your father," she said. "He is old and soon will no longer be able to care for himself properly."

"Of course I will do that," he answered. "You never have to worry about it."

"Do you still care for Adelia?" she asked next.

"I have not thought much about it," he replied, taken aback.

"I want you to marry her," Sanne said simply. "This has gone on long enough, and you will need someone."

"Sanne, I am not certain—" he began to protest, but she started coughing violently. When her cough had quit her she told him not to disagree. "Just do as I say," she went on. "If you ever loved my lost son or your own mother. If I ever made a home for you, I want you to obey me in this. It is hard enough to lose one son. I don't want to think the same kind of thing could happen to you, and you just get swept away by the first wind blowing."

"Sanne," Magnus answered, even as his thoughts weighed heavily upon him, "I would do it even if you had done none of those things for me but only because you ask."

"Good," she replied, smiling. "What a good man you are becoming." She wished nonetheless she could instruct him in those things about marriage and domestic life that only women can adequately tell, but she was overtaken by the opium and began to doze, happy for this last victory she had secured in the household.

The next morning, when the doctor came to perform surgery, Merian was by her side until the very last minute. She clasped his hand tightly as the surgeon gave her another dose of medicine to help her bear the pain, both that which she carried every day as well as that of the pending operation. As she looked at her husband, she thought about their courtship and how they used to sing to each other during their first days of marriage. She remembered as well their strife and how close to star-vation they were during those early winters. It had been at last a good marriage, and she wished to let him know how joyful he had made her, and all that is tender. The drug, though, had already begun to claim her consciousness—so that when she opened her mouth to speak, the words were all a murmuring flow. Undaunted she still held on to her husband and began to hum to him that song she learned from her grand-mother so long ago. The last thing she heard as her eyes fell closed was her husband singing back to her the refrain.

The operation went poorly. The doctor managed to remove the claw that gripped her, but it was so large by that point he had also to take away the majority of her chest muscle. When she awoke from the sur-gery it was only very briefly and what she felt was a lightness.

She was not so strong as to move her head, but she knew her first husband was trying to claim her with even greater force than before. Sure enough, when she was finally able to look around she saw him sitting by the side of her bed holding one hand as Merian held the other.

While Merian only clung to her in brief intervals, visiting four or five times a day, her first man never left her side. "I lost you once, girl," he said. "I have no aim of doing so a second time."

"Yes," she said, knowing what he wanted. "I will come away with you."

When Merian came into her room that evening, it was three days since her operation and the ichor still had not finished draining from her wounds. She was inflamed with it and he could she what pain she en-dured, lying there wrapped in the covers of their marriage bed.

"How are you this evening, Sanne?" he asked.

She no longer recognized him. She saw only a very old man at her side and wondered who it was who had found his way into her room. She looked around then, wondering where Merian was, because it was the time he usually came and he was always very punctual.

When the old man took up her hand, she grew increasingly fright-ened and began to scream out that he would have Jasper Merian to con-tend with if he treated her roughly. When Merian still did not come she screamed even louder, until her first husband appeared at her side and took her finally in both his hands.

Before, he had only held her by the fingers or else offered an arm as they strolled in the garden of Stonehouses, but this time he lifted her up as he had on their wedding night and promised no harm would befall her ever.

"I will take care of you," he pledged.

"Where we will live? Where are we going now?" she wanted to know.

"Back across the ocean, my love," he answered to her. "Remember?"

"Will I like it there?" she asked.

"You will. We will make a house for our love."

"What if I do not?"

"You mustn't leave me again," he said.

"You can't ask me this."

"I am your husband again."

"Yes," she said, recognizing the truth. "I will try to be a good wife and make a good home for us there across the ocean."

"You were always the best wife ever there was."

"That was on the coast," she answered. "I do not know how it will be for us across the sea."

"You know many people there," he assured her.

"Merian is not there," she said, "nor Purchase. Merian is still at Stonehouses, and my son Purchase is gone. Will they join us?"

"You must rest," he told her. "It is a long journey."

"Yes, we must start out."

The two of them left together then, as he took Sanne in his arms away from Stonehouses, back over the ocean. Once more across the sea.

At her wake Merian spoke very little, being both too lonesome to talk and upset at having the preacher in the house. Standing afterward in the meadowland he had long ago claimed for a graveyard he only listened as the preacher finished his sermon and Magnus and the other pallbearers began to fill in her grave. He was himself too old to shovel the soil back into place but could only watch until they were finished with the task. When they were done, and the grave was stilled over with earth, he issued to them one final instruction. "Dig mine just next to it."

"Yea, there will be time for that," Content said, standing beside his ancient friend.

"It was you and Dorthea who brought us together," Merian replied. "You did not tell me then it would be so short a while."

He walked over to the preacher and pushed a handful of coins into his hand, then turned and went back toward the house.

When the other mourners entered, Adelia had laid a table with foods and tried her best to make everyone comfortable, recalling from earlier times what the visitors and inhabitants of Stonehouses each required—so that when Content called for something they were able to offer him an eau de vie, and the doctor had his claret, and Magnus, when he went to the table, found a small pot of warm milk with his coffee.

He picked it up and smiled at her as he brought the cup to his lips. This was their first intimate interaction since she had come back to the house; he had done his best to avoid her the entire time, knowing she was there on Sanne's account and not his, and he did not want her to be reminded of their troubles before.

As he looked at her he remembered what he promised Sanne on her deathbed. He knew she would not have told Adelia what had been agreed upon between the two of them, and he struggled to decide whether he was bound to an old woman's delirious request. He had managed in the time he had been there to find appropriate means of dealing with those urges he could not control, but for the rest he felt as he had all his life. Seeing Adelia then made him curse himself for being so quick to give in to what Sanne had asked of him. He did not know if he could maintain his end of the deal, or even if she would still want him should he presume to try.

"You look very pretty today, Adelia," he said boldly, just as he had in the kitchen many years earlier.

He had not meant to invoke that memory and worried she would take offense, but Adelia only accepted the compliment with a bashful smile and withdrew into the kitchen.

Magnus realized he did not know where Merian was and searched for him throughout the house until he finally found him sitting in the parlor, where he had been counting what was lost to him and what was left. When he saw Magnus, the old man looked his son over and asked him what his plans for things were.

"No plans but what we have been doing," Magnus answered.

"That is not what I mean," Merian told him. "I mean what will you do with yourself when you are alone here?"

"There's always someone about," Magnus said to him.

"Ware," his father said, "that is not good enough. Out here by yourself, this is the loneliest place known to the world."

"Let me help you to your room," Magnus offered. Merian, however, continued looking out his window.

"We are exiled here. One day, when we are purified, we will be rejoined with what is beloved."

Magnus could see then the light had gone out from Merian's eyes. He thought he knew what had propelled him in his ambition there, but he could see it die that day, and with that it seemed revealed to him that this was never what the older man really wanted but was some elaborate substitution for something that could never be attained.

For Magnus, though, this was what *he* wanted, a place of safety and security. There was nothing more behind it. Merian loved what he could create and had created, but Magnus he loved that he was without any other's claim on him.

He helped Merian to bed, where he would sleep alone for the first time in thirty years.

When father and son awoke the next morning both were aware of how much emptier the house felt, a fact that each of them dealt with in quite his own way. After dressing Merian went into the kitchen and took a handful of meal from a cupboard, which he placed in a pot and mixed with water. When Adelia heard him, she came and offered to cook. Instead of accepting or relinquishing to her a place at the stove, he drove her off and continued preparing his own breakfast.

"If you don't like my cooking you could have told me long ago," she said. "I'll be going back to Content's first thing this afternoon."

"I cooked for myself for many years," he answered her, "until I had a wife; then I ate from my wife's table, and only once another woman's. You can cook for him."

Magnus had entered the kitchen and was surprised to see his old father over the cooking fire. He had always suspected that it was the one thing in the world Merian had no idea how to do. The sight worried him, and he thought to remove him and let Adelia make breakfast. In the end he thought better of it; if things got no worse than this they would all be lucky. Adelia looked at Merian and then to Magnus for instruction, and Magnus nodded to let her know she should simply leave him to his devices for the time being.

After Merian had finished cooking his porridge, he removed himself to the dining room to eat alone. When Magnus entered the room Merian gave him an aggrieved look that let him know he wished to be left in peace that morning. Magnus turned and went back to the kitchen, where Adelia was frying eggs for his breakfast. When she brought them to him at the table, he took the plate and then called to her as she was returning to her duties.

"Why don't you sit with me?" he asked.

Sanne was everywhere and on all of their minds that morning, including Adelia's. She thought then of what her patroness had said when she had found her looking out of the window one afternoon. "Are you watching him?" she had asked.

When the younger woman admitted she had been, Sanne had said, "He will come to you. You will see. He only needs a bit more time."

Adelia had not believed her, as she had already given him what she thought was all the time anyone could need, until she began to consider herself unwanted and ruined. When he asked her to sit with him that morning, though, she accepted his invitation so easily he thought she had been waiting for it, and that perhaps Sanne had said something to her after all.

Adelia sat down across from him, and the two of them had breakfast together that morning, and every morning in the future, from that day forward.

t e n

~

The inland roads of the southern colonies were as strange to Rennton
as the ice sheets of Greenland, and—knowing the business of their
ports—he picked his way across them with as much care. After inquir-
ing about until he found someone who knew the way to Berkeley, he
hired a coach to take them as far as Edenton, where they stayed the night.
In the morning, after presenting his papers, he secured passage to Bath.
Once they arrived he purchased a horse for not too much money, but
the dealer was unscrupulous and the beast only survived as far as the
Indian fort. From there, man and boy had no choice but walk the remainder of the way.

It was five days through the wilderness, with the trail sometimes becoming nothing more than a footpath in the woodlands. How coaches
came that way, if any ever ventured out there, one would be hard pressed
to say. When the boy grew too tired to continue, Rennton at first would
pick him up and carry him upon his shoulders, but the third time that
Caleum cried weariness and requested this treatment, his guardian
bid him to toughen up. "I'm not your mule," the man said to his charge.
"Now see if your legs aren't a little hardier." The boy responded dutifully after that, and even when his feet began to blister over and shred
he refrained from complaining for the rest of the trip.

Nights they made camp in the naked air, and in the morning both
were stiff from the cold and did not want to move from their pallet.
Rennton invariably ventured forth first and boiled water on the camp
embers for the few loose tea leaves he would throw into a pot. The two
then ate hard biscuits and charqui saved from the ship before setting
out on their campaign again. At midday they had the roasted carcass of
a hare Rennton had caught two days earlier, when they first started out.

"It isn't much," Rennton told him, "but safer than we would have been otherwise."

All the while the boy did not object, and when they finally entered Berkeley he did not mention his aching stomach that felt as if a timeless hunger had settled there, until Rennton noticed a tavern and said he figured it was all right for them to enter inside.

After ordering food, they asked the serving girl for directions to a place called Stonehouses and were happy to see it was well known. "Who are you?" Content asked him, coming over to their table after the girl had given them directions, for he still minded the bar himself some days.

"I am a stranger here and at your mercy," is all Rennton would answer, being as suspicious of Content as the other man was of him.

"You say you and your boy walked from the fort?"

"Aye."

"Well, no need of paying for the supper. I'll see if someone can take you on the rest of the way."

Content then sent for a young man who worked for him and told him to hitch a wagon and drive the strangers out to Merian's place.

The boy had been quiet since the ship docked, asking few questions, not even where they were going. He had hoped they were meeting his parents, but now he could not contain himself and asked Rennton where he was taking him. "Your father's house," the man answered the child, making the boy wonder that his father had a house he did not know about. "No, your father's father," Rennton explained. "I imagine it will be much the same."

It was not.

When they pulled up in the wagon, Jasper Merian sat in the cold air on the porch as if he had been waiting on a visitor, and Rennton could tell right away he was at Purchase's people's place because of his carriage. When he announced his business and told of their journey there, Merian was very aloof with him but invited them indoors nonetheless. He next gave Magnus the note Rennton had given him, and Magnus read it over. After he finished it he went in his pocket and retrieved a handful of coins. "This is for your trouble and expenses," he said handing Rennton the monies.

Rennton looked at the coins and they were a large sum indeed, far more than enough for his troubles. Why, if he wanted he could take the rest of the season off from the ocean. The house itself was more than he had ever known of any Negro to possess, save for the African kings, who everyone in his business knew were fatter with wealth than anyone else in the world.

"You are welcome to stay for dinner, but if you need to get back I can have a horse saddled for you that should serve better than the one you lost on the journey out," Merian told his guest.

"I would be happy to stay on for dinner, if it's no bother," Rennton answered, as he was tired deep within himself.

The boy was pleased to hear this response, for he did not understand yet that he was to stay there and was glad to have time in one place instead of moving on immediately.

"Hello, Caleum," Magnus said, going to greet the latest Merian to make his way onto the land. "I'm Magnus, your uncle, and this is your grandpa." The boy shook hands with his uncle very precisely, then did the same with his grandfather.

Adelia, who had come from the back by now, gave the boy a great hug when he came to greet her. He was comforted by this warmness but also confused by all the attention he was receiving. "You must be tired from your trip," she said. "You'll feel better after a rest."

Indeed, both Rennton and Caleum looked frightful from the voyage, and both were appreciative for the chance to restore themselves a bit. Magnus showed Rennton a room where he could sleep, and told him he could have a bath if he liked. Rennton declined, however, not being in the habit or wanting to imperil his health, even as he was tempted by the idea of such luxury.

Adelia had water raised from the well and heated in the kitchen, then poured into the laundry basin in the basement. When she took Caleum's shoes off, she was shocked to see the condition his feet were in and nearly went off in search of the man who had let him walk such a way. Instead, she put ointment on his wounds and commended Caleum for being so brave.

When Magnus returned from showing Rennton his room, Merian was still in the parlor. "I wonder how they made that trip out here on the trail they did without getting killed," Magnus wondered. "It was madness of him."

"No more madness than when you walked here," Merian reminded him. "Or when I did."

"Both of us grown men who knew our own ambition and limits," Magnus replied. "Not a six-year-old barely out of swaddling."

"Well, it pleased the Lord to bring both of you," Merian said, "just as it pleased Him to call Sanne home."

Magnus at first thought to argue with his father but checked himself, not wanting to excite Merian into one of his more unpredictable moods. He saw the good wisdom of this when he looked at Merian and realized clearly his advancing age, as if he had all of a sudden willed the years to hurry on their course with him.

"Sanne would have given anything to see that child," Merian said. "It broke her so to lose Purchase."

Magnus was again silent, now wondering how they would raise the boy that had shown up out of nowhere.

Adelia, who had not yet been blessed with children, had no such reservations but took to Caleum wholly and immediately, thinking not only that Providence had given them a child but that Caleum was there to replace the loss of Sanne in the house.

It was evident at dinner that evening, as she doted over the latest arrival to the point of inflaming Magnus's jealousy. "My father and I might like to eat as well," he said, when she lingered over Caleum's plate with the food for too long.

"No one is stopping you," Adelia replied.

Magnus did not say anything to her in reply but reached for the serving plate and helped himself, as Merian looked on with bemusement. "It must be harder when they show up already grown, instead of giving you a chance to see them grow and get used to them."

"You would know that better than me," Magnus said, his bad mood spreading across the table.

"I have things to teach you yet," Merian replied to his older son, as they finished dinner.

If they were tense with each other that evening, on account of what the new presence in the house meant to each of them, they were also very kind to Caleum when alone with him in the days immediately after his arrival. Merian especially liked to spend time with the boy, telling him of his father, Purchase.

"Your father used to sit out there by that tree and while away an entire afternoon, leaving the wood to stack itself," he recounted. But he would also call him to tell him things he dared not say to others.

"I came out here just as you did," Merian confided to him, "Magnus the same way. It was only Purchase who was born without ever running, but that he did later. You must remember to be pious in whatever way you can. Whatever covenant you make with them you must keep; only then will they ever consider to redeem you."

The child, when he heard these things, did not think they were overly strange. His abandonment and then the trip on the boat had already taught him beyond his years, and he understood somehow what his grandfather meant—that he was preparing to die.

It took Magnus and Adelia far longer to take up the evidence of this. Even after Merian informed them all he had written a new will—which they would find after his death in the drawer of a certain desk—they were still unwilling to accept it.

"You will live to be a hundred," Magnus told him.

"By God, not if I can help it," Merian replied. He took his food then and retired to the parlor, where he ate alone.

Magnus thought he was only being difficult or else eccentric, as he could sometimes be, but Adelia figured out his true intent. "Your father is starving himself to death," she told her husband one night in bed, after she discovered Merian's bowl in the room where he ate.

From then on they watched over him with extreme care at mealtimes, but he managed to begin wasting nonetheless. The cause was not, as they first suspected, grief at being deprived of his wife and son, but the exact opposite. He now no longer hungered for anything in the world and so was done with it.

"I have done everything I set out to," he answered them, unbidden, after making a final tally to himself. "All the rest is just waiting." High among the list of those things he was proud of was the fortune he had amassed. "I'm richer than I ever dreamed, and would have made even more money, but I never bought a man, nor sold one, nor tried to haggle anyone out of money for their labor. If I had been luckier at parenting it might have been the utopia I set out to create." He aimed his words at Magnus and Adelia, but he also made certain Caleum was around when he said them.

*　*　*

When the rest of the house retired for the evening, Magnus did not go immediately to bed but sat up worrying late into the night about the future of those at Stonehouses. When he finally did join her in their bed, Adelia was up waiting for him, but he was in no mood to share his thoughts.

"You will be good with the boy," she said, reassuring him, as though she knew his innermost thoughts. "Everything will keep moving forward, as it always has out here with your father."

It was not the first time he was glad to be married instead of carrying all the weight of his worries alone, but it was one of the most comforting moments for him to have a wife, being otherwise filled with the dread of his father's passing.

Merian, however, was not yet ready to leave them despite all his talk of death. He would live for some time to come yet—a fact that soon became apparent when he stopped losing weight, as if his body had reached some new equilibrium. Their worries then shifted back to Caleum and their frustration that he could tell them no more about what had happened to his parents than they already knew. This was still in those early days, when he was becoming accustomed to having lost one home and gained another. He thought Stonehouses the best place on earth but longed for his parents, and a remainder of the dread that had infested him during that trip from Providence made him quiet when left alone.

He spent his days exploring the property, especially the outbuildings and far meadows. It was the first time in his short life he was not confined under his parents' constant watch, and he delighted in it, even in the chores he was given to perform.

Seeing how well he liked work made Merian pleased as anything could make him, and he gave the boy his allowance at the end of every week gladly, telling him to be sure and keep a tally of how he spent it. There being little occasion to spend money, Caleum always accounted for last week's earnings by saying he had saved it all, which pleased Merian even more.

"Your father couldn't wait to spend it whenever he got a little money," Merian said. Then, not wanting to bias the boy against his father, "Not that there's anything the matter with spending. Saving, though, is what I always thought you should do with a shilling. But he wasn't one to care for money—only other things, I guess."

Thinking then to show him something of his father's, Merian led the boy into the living room, where the blade Purchase had crafted for him long ago still hung.

Caleum, when he saw it, was awed as any boy who ever beheld a sword. However, he was taken not only with the fantasy of war but also the pictures on the side of the blade. "I know them!" he said, pointing excitedly at the images. "And look, there I am!"

Merian, no longer able to see very much at all, indulged the boy a little while but reminded him that Purchase had made the sword well before he was born, and such talk did not figure.

Caleum did not argue with his grandfather but knew he had seen himself prominently displayed. In fact, in the image he saw, there he was holding the self-same blade as that of his reflection. Finally he asked whether he could hold the weapon.

Merian first told him no but then relented. When he tried to raise it up, however, it was far too heavy for him, and Merian took it back, promising one day he would be able to raise it.

"When?" Caleum wanted to know, but his grandfather told him he would know when. Merian put the sword back in its scabbard then, but not before noticing the blade had grown hot, as if just taken from the furnace.

Caleum looked at it so longingly on the nail over the mantel, Merian wondered whether it had been a good idea to put such a notion in the child's head.

He did not stop, though, confiding to his grandson all those things he had held to himself his entire life. Either because he felt he finally had a companion who was enough like him to understand or for some other reason, the two of them would sit out no matter the weather, and Merian would tell the boy tales and lore, until the only thing he had not properly recounted for him was the story of how the land was first settled, there being so much on the lifelong list of things Merian had done to relate that particular event did not make it, so that, as he had it, he came down from Virginia one year and after a little privation he was much the man he was at that moment.

When Adelia came upon the two of them, she would always reprimand Merian and take Caleum off to bed as he protested.

"Don't worry, I am not done for this world yet," Merian would tell the boy, somewhat morbidly, as he left.

After rising the next day and making himself a breakfast of porridge, he saddled a mule from the barn and made a tour of his lands. At the lake he stopped and heard the ice creak and, beneath that, the singing and distinct sound of a great passion. To anyone else listening, all in that area would have been silence, but Merian and the fiend had a catching up that did not displease either of them

That was the way Magnus found him, sitting on top of a mule on the edge of the thawing lake, muttering to himself, with a half smile. "I vanquished it, son," he said. "I conquered everything you see around you."

"You were very brave," Magnus replied, taking the reins and leading his father's mule back to the stable.

"I mastered the beast, and it was lonely, dangerous work," his father said.

"It was for the better."

"Everything I knew was behind me, and I did not know what lay ahead."

"Great men have bowed before lesser challenges."

"I kept the pact I made, and my sons should do likewise."

"We are intent on doing our best."

"No modesty in this, but life and death."

"You must rest now," Magnus said, leading man and beast into the barn.

"Bury me where I told you, and never let anything unsettle your peace here," Merian said, finally allowing himself to be lifted from the saddle.

Magnus was surprised both by how superstitious his father had become and by how little he weighed as he carried him to bed. There Adelia tended to him, as she would have her own father, and he was glad for her attention, but he never recovered his full senses, and eventually even his memory began to die within him. "I was bonded, now am free." What he clutched near himself then was his watch and an ugly carved doll he had kept all these years in the original cellar of the house and thought to retrieve that day. It was the face of the spirit he made all his pacts with, and as close as he ever cared to get to any god. No one commented on it but left it with him for comfort, though they were all of them Christian and would have no mandates with their father's god. None except the boy Caleum, who asked questions about it and, more than a decade on, when Merian eventually died, took it upon himself to protect the little idol as an heirloom, much as he would cherish the sword his own father had made: all of them in equal measures the patrimony of Stonehouses and not uncommon in that particular time on the continent, like the promise and prophecy of fire.

III
settlement

o n e

❧

The boy took quickly to Stonehouses, as certain plants transferred from one soil to another find their new environs equally conducive to growth—for example *Solanum tuberosum,* the common potato, which he ate for his lunch, or *Taraxacum officinale,* the dandelions they consumed as greens at dinner and which, when he was older, he and his friends would harvest late in the summer to produce a crude, heady wine—until it was impossible to tell it was not his original home. Though perhaps one might have called it his *urhome* or *great home,* as certainly it suited him as well as the first, which he never forgot. Being young at the time of his orphanage—once he determined it was a permanent situation—he also took to Magnus and Adelia's care with amazingly little rebellion and, in fact, great joy that this newfound warmth and security belonged now fully to him.

Nor was he without the normal assertiveness of boys his age, far from it; he often resented the scrutiny to which Magnus and Adelia, being new to parenting, subjected him. It was simply that, having lost one home, he was hesitant to do anything that might make the residents of Stonehouses angry at him or in any way jeopardize his station. Eventually, this habit of obeying became second nature to him, so that at the time when other young men felt the need to revolt against authority and claim independence he was calm and found the strictures placed on him quite bearable, if not always fair. In short, he was a model boy.

Adelia for her part never tired of spoiling him with attention, and Magnus, who could be so stern in everyday life, was made happy by the boy's ethic of work and good personal habits. This was especially vital, as there were some things they themselves could not help him with but had to rely on his own discipline to accomplish.

Although Magnus was able in mathematics, for example, after he enrolled Caleum in school there were many questions he could not answer for the boy but was still anxious for him to learn, so that certain skills and knowledge he deemed important might be restored to the household. Perhaps because of this expectation, Caleum soon became among the best pupils at Miss Boutencourt's, the woman who taught all the Negro children whose parents wanted them educated. It had originally been a white school, but as there were so few of either color interested in education she decided it prudent, and necessary to her income, not to discriminate between them. In the beginning, however, none of the Negro families sent their children to her, being uncertain of the arrangement, until Magnus inquired, through an intermediary, about teaching Caleum, and she affirmed a commitment to teach any child in the county who would learn. After that, Magnus told everyone he knew with school-age children what a brilliant teacher she was and that he was entrusting Caleum to her tutelage—this he did both to spread general knowledge and to ensure that his own ward would not be so isolated when classes resumed.

It always gave him pleasure, in the months and years that followed, to hear Miss Boutencourt report the boy's progress. He was as generous with praise then as Adelia was with sweets and gifts, telling his nephew how proud both he and his grandfather were, and that his mother and father would be as well if they knew of his achievements. For every subject mastered he would also add a pound to the boy's allowance, telling him to spend it freely. However, seized with worry about spoiling him, he then became careful not to let him slack at his other chores. In general, though, he thought he could not have asked for a better son if it had been given to him to choose.

This is not to say those early days were without incident. Whenever Caleum performed below satisfactory levels in schoolwork—else was lax with his chores or on rare occasions even unruly—Magnus was unrelenting in his punishment. Midsummer would find the boy out with the hired men under the unsparing sun, stomping water into clay and then molding rough bricks. When the brickmaker came and fired the kiln he was ordered to stay at the man's side as he supervised the fire, which could go on for days at a time without pause or rest.

When the firing was over, and the bricks were cooling in the kiln, Magnus would call Caleum—who had not slept properly for nearly a week by this time—and ask whether he had learned his lesson and now knew, for example, that it was offensive to fail at spelling or that drinking dandelion wine behind the church house was a disgrace. Magnus, even in these moods, would always attribute Caleum's bad behavior to the influence of his friends, but he knew the boy had to learn right from wrong whatever the case.

Caleum, however, being at least as prideful as honest, always pointed out that the activity in question had been his idea. He would do this even if it meant another week in the kilns. "I might be a bad speller," he would say, "but I'm not so much a fool as to be one because William Gibbs is." Or, "It was my idea to brew the wine. Who else of them do you think could have figured how it is made?"

It was true. Among the free boys of color he was the acknowledged leader, and if he had done poorly at his spelling exam there was as likely as not a rash of poor fourteen-year-old Negro spellers running around Berkeley that particular year.

The other parents, however, were all so happy to see their sons befriend the well-regarded young Merian that none ever suspected it was Caleum who hatched their more reckless adventures, believing rather that the slave Julius was behind it all.

During the three years he attended Miss Boutencourt's, Caleum's most steadfast and dependable companions as he began exploring the world around him were the two Darson boys, George and Eli, whose father ran a farm down the valley about half the size of Stonehouses; Bastian Johnson, whose father, also called Bastian Johnson, was the local gunmaker; and a boy named Cato, whose father was called Plato and had been born a slave but settled in Berkeley as a wheelwright after his mistress freed them, because he heard it was a place hospitable to people of his kind. Neither father nor son had a last name or, for that matter, saw the need of one. There was also the aforementioned Julius, whose master was too poor to care for the souls he owned and so hired out any with skill to support his meager holding. Although Julius did not attend school with the other boys, he was a most gifted apprentice to the cabinetmaker, who allowed him to come and go as he pleased, so that he often spent time with the free boys after their lessons.

Even if he was often scapegoated, Julius himself was hardly an innocent. Being aware, however, of his place, he would never have suggested
the boldest of their schemes, such as trying out their new dandelion wine
behind the church house; or, "the white church," as it was generally
known, as religion had not been integrated in the town since the days
Merian had attended service. In the time since the free Coloreds had
switched over mainly to the Baptist church, where there was a section
devoted to their exclusive use, and the slaves received their religious
instruction on the plantations.

When the six boys were found drinking behind what was nevertheless a house of God, Reverend Finch whipped Cato, the two Darson boys,
and Bastian Johnson. He sent word to the cabinetmaker about Julius's
behavior, not wanting to lay hands on another man's property. Nor did
he lay his hand on Caleum, although whether it was out of respect for
the Merians or for some other reason of his own no one ever knew.

When the preacher sent word around to Magnus about what had
happened, though, Magnus himself did beat Caleum, being very clear
that the lesson was not for drinking but for the position he had let himself into.

"You shamed us," he said to his nephew, with grave disappointment.

Caleum bore his punishment and was remorseful, never having
thought guilt for his actions might spread beyond himself. It was a
hard lesson, but he understood the truth of it when, later that summer, the two Darson boys began to tease him about the rumors they
had heard regarding his father, Purchase.

"We heard your papa once killed a man." George Darson taunted
one day.

"You're a liar," Caleum replied evenly.

"Are you calling my brother a liar?" Eli Darson asked, approaching
him.

"He is if he doesn't take that back."

"I will not!" George Darson shouted. "I heard it from my father, so
if you call me a liar you're calling my father one too."

"I'm calling the whole lot of you liars," Caleum said.

When he heard this, Eli Darson did not repeat his warning but, his
fists balled and angry, rushed in at Caleum. Eli was a full two years older,
but Caleum was big for his age and did not think twice about ramming

his fist into Eli's mouth when he came into range. The two were well matched, and fell to the ground wrestling, neither gaining advantage over the other, until George Darson joined in on his brother's side.

The other boys circled them, uncertain whether to intervene or let them continue until they reached their own conclusion. Being attacked by both of the Darsons threw Caleum into a rage, and he began to pummel the younger brother, George, violently as Eli clenched his throat. He struggled to escape, then bent and gathered a handful of dry dust in his palm, which he threw into Eli's face. When his opponent could no longer see he drove his fist into his gut, hobbling him, and squaring the fight again, as he momentarily faced only one assailant. Caleum continued to fight the brothers, angrier and angrier that the two of them should attack him together instead of choosing one to stand for both as fairness would have had it. Still, he proved their equal, beating both brothers badly, even though he took quite some blows himself.

When he arrived home later that evening, his eyes swollen, Magnus asked what had happened. Caleum said simply that the Darsons had told lies about his family, and he was no longer friends with them. He never once thought to ask his uncle whether there was any truth to their slander.

He ceased his studies soon thereafter, on the premise, as he argued it with Magnus and Adelia, that he had learned to read and calculate as well as he would ever need to know, and that he was due to be finished soon anyway. Miss Boutencourt, who was used to seeing the boys from the country cease their studies all of a sudden, was surprised when Caleum stopped, as he had been such a good pupil. If he was needed on his family's farm, though, as he told her, there was little she could do about it, as that was the rhythm of life in that region of the world. It was in moments like this that she herself longed to live in one of the great towns of the colonies or, in bolder moments of dreaming, even London. But even though she had started her own voyage in Devonshire, she knew she would never see London in her lifetime, and perhaps not even Philadelphia.

Under her tutelage Caleum had mastered his primer and could now read as well as any boy in the colony. Having full command of arithmetic, he could also keep a ledger, so when Magnus tested his knowledge he was not only satisfied but duly impressed.

He also had to admit he was happy for the extra hand, as a shortage of labor was thwarting any ambition he might have had to expand on what Jasper Merian had started. How Jasper had always acquired workers was simply to pay them a wage above what they would make in the first years of starting their own farm, so men who thought they were heading west might be easily persuaded to receive a salary for a time, before going on to face the privations of the frontier. When they amassed capital enough they pushed on, one way or another, or else stayed on. However, men had seemed to evaporate the last few seasons, being either greedier for the far country or, for reasons of their own, unwilling to stay. It had become increasingly clear to Magnus that, if Stonehouses was to last, there were only two hopes: the first was if Caleum someday produced many children, as he knew he and Adelia would never be so blessed; the other was to make an investment in permanent labor.

He found slavery too unsettling to contemplate and so contrived to think of it by other fashions, but the truth was still there before him. Despite this reluctance, he knew it to be a logical course of action. Even so, he dare not capitulate to it so long as his father was still alive. And so Jasper Merian's crippled existence in his upstairs room was all that kept Stonehouses from becoming like the places on the coast both father and son had worked so hard to escape.

That way of life was spreading, however, and Magnus did not think they would ever again do so well as when he and Merian had worked the land together and produced as much as any ten men between the two of them.

When Caleum finished his studies and began devoting himself to the farm, showing an interest in everything about the place, Magnus was relieved then from some of his anxieties and began to treat the boy from that point forth as more of an adult and partner.

Caleum still kept up his friendship with Bastian, Cato, and Julius, but now he was less prone to allow himself boyish pleasures and indulgences. When he would go to town on an errand for his uncle and happened to see one of his friends, he was just as likely to excuse himself as dawdle. Instead he would try to arrange some meeting for when he was not working. "I have to get back now," he might say, "but let's meet at Turner's Creek on Sunday and see if we can't catch a few fishes."

He would spend the Sunday as carelessly as any other youth in the piedmont, but Monday morning his newfound devotion was again upon his face. Like his uncle, he had also begun to sense the pressure upon their way of life and knew what was at stake if they failed in their way of doing things.

It was years since Berkeley had been the isolated place Merian settled, and the frontier was now moved far to the westward. In that time other ways had come steadily to their area, so that there were very few who remembered what life there had been like before it was all conquered and brought under cultivation.

Magnus, when he would go into the town of Berkeley, would stop by at Content's and Dorthea's, who had been as good friends to him as they had been to his father. He would drink a beer, and Content, who still came into the bar every day to see his customers, would look at the younger man absorbed in his private worries.

"You know it was never any easier," Content always said. "In fact, it was probably harder before."

At least then, Magnus thought, no one harassed them and their labor was their own.

"You are doing better than most," Content reminded him. "Better than Merian even, who braved so much uncertainty out there."

Magnus was an apprehensive soul, though, and when he left he would be just as worried as when he entered. These were the moments he thought most seriously about acquiring bought labor, and he would sink further into his anxieties.

Whether life in Berkeley had actually changed, or whether Magnus was simply bearing the burden of leading the family now, was a difficult thing to know. The area itself had changed undeniably, but he was also one of the better-off denizens and was a welcome guest of both his white and Negro neighbors. Still, no matter how well he managed the affairs of Stonehouses, he missed having Jasper to guide him.

Merian was still there among them in the house, but he was by then barely in command of his own faculties and certainly not in command of the same intellect he had before. He referred to Magnus, for instance, as Purchase, and to Caleum as Magnus. When he asked about Chiron he sometimes meant his old friend, who had once been a slave with him, and sometimes his second son. Adelia might be Sanne or Dorthea, and

Content—on the occasion of his last visit, was met at first with a blank stare, until Merian finally remembered him. What he called him then was not his Christian name, Content, but rather Governor of Utopia.

Content laughed, taking it that his friend was not so far dispossessed of his senses that he could not still make a joke. It heartened him, especially as he was losing power over his own body as surely as his friend was over his mind. "A fine pair we make," he said. But Content grew increasingly weak soon after that visit and could no longer travel. It was all he managed to make it down to his tavern in the afternoon, where he might still see an old friendly face.

When he died that winter it was a time of great disconsolation at Stonehouses, as it was throughout the valley and hill country. The entire reputable population, if not in fact everyone who owned shoes, came out for the funeral, including many who thought he had passed on long before. His death was seen by all as the endpoint of an era in that part of the world, and gripped all of them in sadness, for they feared the best days there might be ended.

Content had been among the first to settle the area and the very first to think it deserved a name, suggesting Berkeley after one of the Lords Proprietor. He had been first in all civic matters as well and had for a term represented them in the House of Burgesses. In matters familial he had proved fortunate and capable, leaving two sons and an equal number of daughters who survived into adulthood, and much goodwill and happiness. As a friend, his generosity and steadfastness were known to be among the best men may achieve. Even the old chandler, Pete Griffith, who could find an ill thing to say about every man in Berkeley, never found one syllable of bile for Content.

Jasper Merian, who recognized so little by then, remembered him who gave him shelter his first winter when he was without, and who introduced him to his wife, Sanne; Merian cried when he realized his old friend had died.

All his oldest acquaintances had seen him in life for the last time at the funeral of his wife, Dorthea. Her death had been cause for widespread mourning in its own right, as she had been friend and confidante to so many in the region. The two had been married since both were nineteen, and they had sailed from their home country before either was yet twenty-one. By all accounts, their marriage was a successful one.

She was near ninety when she died and, although her life had been other than what she would have expected, she was on the whole exceedingly pleased with it.

What is further, certain old wives' tales, and other fanciful sources, claim to measure the love between man and wife by the time between the death of each.

In cases of extremely strong love among young people, who have not yet learned to govern so violent an emotion, the death of one could cause the other to take his own life. Among the seasoned old it was thought more usual for those who had loved each other well and long to die within a decade of the other's passing. There were also a scattered few cases known in which the beloved departed within the year, oftentimes on the anniversary of the other's death or another meaningful occasion. But such cases were so rare that when they occurred they were immortalized in song, verse, and speechifying.

Content, when he lost Dorthea, lived on another three days, then took his leave with little else said about the matter but that he was also done here.

t w o

Not long after Content's death, a rash of outlanders appeared in the county. It began with the new tax assessor, a man named Paul Spector, who hailed from the neighboring town of Chase. He came originally out of Charleston and had set out that spring to do what he thought would be a favor for himself and the county alike. Instead, he finished by stirring up no end of mischief and bad blood.

The new tax code called for all members of free Negro households to be assessed thirty pounds sterling, and after Spector saw this provision he figured a way he could bring in even more revenue from his post. When he went to collect taxes from the Colored segment of the citizenry that year, he asked each head of household to show him proof of freedom for everyone in the house. For those who had been bonded, ready proof was easy enough. Those born in freedom seldom possessed documentation, though, as births were not yet recorded in that part of the world. Faced with this dilemma, nearly everyone he approached paid Spector ten additional pounds for a certificate attesting to the fact of their freedom. For those without the ten pounds, who were nonetheless willing to pay, he charged them whatever he could get for temporary clemency, warning them they had better have either their proof or his ten pounds the following year.

Such was his tack when he arrived at Stonehouses. As he stood in the doorway, telling of the two available courses of action, Magnus could only think of the harm he would like to do to the man. Instead of seeking to avoid trouble, as would have been prudent, he simply refused to pay this extortion. He knew, even as he did so, how foolhardy it was, but he hated what the man was doing so much he was unable to bear even the sight of him. He had lived with the fear of his legal status so long, he was bold then as anything attacked. "If I give you ten pounds this year, Mr. Spector, you will want twenty next. If I pay that, you will want more the following year, but if I were to treat you for the rascal you are and take a switch to your backside, that might just stop all of this before it gets going good."

The tax collector only stared at him in stunned disbelief before going away. He returned the next day with the county sheriff, Peter Wormsley, who knew all the Merians and knew them to be free people, and law abiding besides. He said as much to the tax assessor, but the other man ignored his witness and employed his higher rank to insist on Magnus's arrest.

"He will come round once he has a little time to consider it," Spector said, having grown up among Negroes and so claiming to know their ways.

"I just don't know," Wormsley argued. "Everybody around here has known the Merians a long time. You might start some stink with all this."

"I do not care for your opining," Spector answered, issuing Magnus a summons to appear before the county magistrate, who happened to be his cousin by marriage and whom he had sent for the previous day. He then ordered the sheriff to bring Magnus down to Chase to be held until his hearing.

Magnus, in irons, was quite fearful by now, but held himself in as dignified a posture as possible when they carted him off. Having provoked the law, however, he had no idea what would happen to him next.

They held him in the Chase jailhouse for two days, waiting for the magistrate to arrive from Edenton. During the time of his imprisonment, word of what had happened spread throughout Berkeley, until everyone was debating the fairness of the law or else arguing what they knew about the Merian family. There was no shortage then of invention to the stories people told, as they anticipated what would transpire and tried to fill the void of not knowing.

Some claimed Magnus deserved whatever treatment he got, as there were too many people settling in the area anyway. Others pointed out that the Merians were among the first to arrive. Still others claimed the

Merians weren't Negro at all but that Jasper was a Portuguese who once worked in the Crown's employ.

Adelia was unwilling to leave to her neighbors' imaginations what should become of her husband, and when the sheriff's wagon rolled away she did not despair but began to think what she might best do to help get Magnus released. At last it occurred to her, and she had Caleum hitch a team and drive her over to Rudolph Stanton's place.

Stanton was their neighbor to the north and one of the wealthiest landowners in the colony. Over the years, she knew, both Merian and Magnus had performed small favors for him, such as one neighbor inevitably does for another—returning a lost calf here, mending a broken fence there. He was also their representative in the Assembly and, although he kept slaves himself, was known to be otherwise fair and without general prejudice.

Despite these things she approached the house with trepidation, it being rare for anyone from Stonehouses to go outside of it for help in anything. She also knew Stanton to be greedy for land and feared, as she went up the driveway, he might try in some way to take advantage of their weakened situation. She fretted at last that she simply did not know the man and there was no reason for him to help her.

When she was let into the house it was early afternoon, and Stanton had obviously just woken. He received her nevertheless, and was outright angry when he heard what had happened. When she finished he promised to intervene on Magnus's behalf.

Having given his word in the matter he was true to it. Immediately after lunch he sent a message around to the sheriff stating that, among other things, Magnus Merian should immediately be released from prison and allowed to return to his home. Wormsley was only too happy to oblige with this, and sent word back to Stanton, as had been requested, promising to let him know when the magistrate arrived.

Magnus, as he awaited his trial at Stonehouses, thought how he would defend himself. He knew he was free, and none could prove otherwise without sending to Virginia, but he wondered what difference that would make to a court that let law be written by the whims and wants of the moment. As for his legal status, his only evidence was the paper from Content, and if anyone asked how he *came* to be free he would hardly have an explanation. He worried then those two nights—as he did his first out of captivity—about what would happen to him and his family if things proceeded poorly. If only, he thought, he had paid the tax assessor his toll. Never mind that he felt he had been paying tax since his first day on earth.

When the magistrate arrived in town, Rudolph Stanton sent round for Magnus to come to his house. Relieved that it would soon be over no matter what the outcome, Magnus left Stonehouses with a light heart that morning. The closer he drew to Acre, Stanton's place, the heavier the burden inside him seemed to grow, though, until he stood before the door almost unable to move. Mustering his resolve, he knocked at last at the towering mahogany door and was led to an upstairs room by the housemaid. When he entered, the judge was already seated, along with the sheriff and his nemesis the tax assessor. He looked at each in turn before sitting in a chair Stanton pointed out to him.

"I have called all of you here so that we might conclude this matter as expeditiously as possible," Stanton said flatly. "Now, it would appear that the tax assessor, Mr. Spector here, attempted to extort my neighbor, Mr. Merian there, and, when he failed to receive this *danegeld,* kidnapped him from his family's lawful lands and possessions."

The magistrate was taken aback when he heard such strong terms, because Stanton had not let him know his stake in the matter beforehand. Stanton then turned and addressed him directly. "John, you have sent here a man without scruples, who makes up law and spreads terror across the county without cause, other than his own need for profit and mischief. He has taken monies from its citizens and behaved in general like his very own private Parliament."

"He did not mean to, Rudolph," the magistrate said on behalf of his cousin, who, sensing the jeopardy he was in, remained silent.

"What is it exactly you are saying he did not mean to do," Stanton pressed, "spread terror or invent law? Mr. Merian is a sizable landowner here. The Merians have always paid their taxes and performed what was required of them in civic matters. Now you have sent out a highwayman, masquerading as a tax collector, who carts him off to jail for not having proof of his freedom? Why, John, what proof have you of yours, any more than he of his?"

"None," the other admitted, "but it's not the same thing."

"It isn't? The only thing I want to know is how the legitimate law intends to stand behind Mr. Merian in protecting his rights."

"But Rudolph," the magistrate protested, trying to find suitable terms to make the matter go away, "he's kin to me. You can't mean for me to jail him."

"Then what do you propose?" asked Stanton, who thought children should always be given the chance to choose their own punishment.

Magnus had not dared to speak all the while this was going on. He knew his father had been held in esteem by his neighbors, but his own contact with them had been so scant he was genuinely surprised to see another man stand up and defend him. Watching Mr. Stanton and the magistrate, it seemed to him they were two great men involved in private discussions of very weighty matters and affairs affecting the whole county, until he remembered he was the reason for the day's proceedings. So when the magistrate said he would fire his cousin from his post, and Rudolph Stanton added that the man should first issue him a written apology, it took a very long time for Magnus to make his own request.

"Begging pardon, Mr. Stanton, but how can I know the next tax collector won't try to do the exact same thing?"

"Indeed. How will he have confidence of that?" Stanton asked the magistrate, raising one of his large bushy eyebrows.

The magistrate looked at the papers before him, including the letter Content had written, which was now in the book of evidence. "I suppose I could notarize this," he offered tentatively, "but it would be highly unusual."

"You must do so then, in order that my neighbor here has peace of mind again on his lands," Stanton said. Then, as if continuing a previous conversation with the magistrate, he added, "John, the law must be strong but blind. That is the true test of it."

The magistrate took Magnus's old forged papers and embossed them with the great seal of the House of Burgesses. Magnus felt a heavy stone lifted up from him when he saw the official seal of the colony on his freedom. After that, according to all accounts, he was at ease as he had never been before. Not only because he was finally free as other men— he had been that in fact for a long time already and, no matter the outcome of his trial, knew he was not going to be returned to his previous condition—but because he knew the law now stood solidly behind him. He was altogether different after that in the way he encountered and moved through the world. Immeasurably so.

The roads around Berkeley had grown chaotic with activity from the universe outside its boundaries, though, and things did not turn out so fortunately for everyone that year. On the last Sunday in September, Bastian Johnson went out to Turner's Creek with Caleum and Julius, whose Sabbaths were of his own employ, to fish for walleyes and catfish. Of the three, Bastian was most successful that particular day and was overweaning in his pride of the fact.

After they hauled in their catch, which included several speckled rainbow trout as well, the boys built a fire and cleaned some of the fish, then roasted them over the embers. As they ate and relived the adventure of how the fish came to be in their fire, all praising Bastian's skill, he himself ladled out fishing advice. "Walleyes don't like no bait too fast. You need patience if you gone catch em. Now, trout is the opposite." The anglers all reclined on the bluff above to the pool and debated the merits of various bait and techniques for the different fish, such as is common among trawlers and fisherfolk everywhere, regardless of age, language, or particular liking for fish.

As it grew late, Julius, tiring of Bastian, asked whether either of them had heard the tale of Witch Mary from Canary. When they told him they had not, he gave the others the story of how there lived a well-known witch on the African coast who, many years previous, had lost a son of sixteen. "Once a month, every month, she get on her broom and fly over the whole wide world looking for her boy. If she can't find him, then she snatch another black boy of about his age and take him back with her. They say her son used to brag on hisself and so she always go for a loud talker. Say she keep her victim for about three weeks, but once she start to remember what her son looked like, she kill the one she brought back. They say the last thing he hear before she get him, and right before she kill, is three real loud knocks."

They were all quiet in the purplish evening light as he told the story, and when he finished all said he had made it up. "That's just another fish tale," Bastian cried, waving him off. As they stamped out the fire, though, Julius told them to be quiet and listen. Sure enough, they could hear a sound in the trees like a hammer banging against the bark. When they heard it a second time they began to move closer to each other, uncertain what to do.

"We better go see what it is," Julius said.

"I don't think we ought to mess with whatever it is," Bastian warned, not wanting to venture any deeper into the woods. "It's getting late out here."

Finally Julius and Caleum convinced him he was only being scary, and the three set out into the nearby forest. "Keep quiet, though," Julius whispered, "Cause, if it is Mary, they say she always go for noisiness."

As they walked on a small path in the direction from which the sound had emanated, they heard it again, then a third time in rapid succession. After the last there was a loud scream right afterward, as Caleum and Bastian both jumped back, startled. As they stood there afright, Julius began to laugh at them. He then pulled his hand through the air in a wide arc, after which there was a loud knock. He moved his hand again and laughed as Bastian and Caleum drew close enough to him to see he was holding a length of fishing twine. At the other end he had affixed a branch, which he could pull through a contraption he had rigged and knock it against a tree. He pulled it once more and laughed at them.

Finally, they laughed at the joke as well, as the three friends parted for the week, each taking with him some of the leftover fish. "Y'all be careful of Mary from Canary on the way home," Julius called good-naturedly, as he went off to feed his master and mistress.

On his way back to Stonehouses, Caleum was in good spirits, thinking Julius very clever and Bastian in need of the lesson. Indeed, Bastian himself was in a fine mood and did not hold it against his friends for showing him up after he had bragged so much on himself. Still, he remained on edge from his earlier fright as he moved through the forests, and even the slightest sounds made him flinch. Even though he had walked through the woods around Berkeley his entire life, he was glad to be out of them when he reached the main road and breathed altogether easier. When he saw a coach coming down the lane he relaxed completely, no longer being alone on the evening road.

When the coach was even with him it slowed down, and he moved out of the way to allow it to pass. The wagon proceeded on a few paces, then came to a stop. Bastian continued walking in the gulch of weeds on the roadside, wondering briefly what had caused the wagon to stop but being otherwise unconcerned.

Once he was spotted, a man he didn't know called down to him to ask what he was doing out at that hour. "I'm just comin' in from Turner's Creek, sir," he answered.

"Looks like you had some luck," the man called back.

"Ah, just a little," Bastian returned.

"Say, can you tell me how to get to the wheelwright's place? I think I bent a spoke back there," the man said.

"You just keep headed straight around that bend," Bastian answered. "Ain't but two roads through town."

"Why don't you hop up?" the man said. "You might as well ride as walk."

Bastian thought it odd that a strange white man should offer him a ride and declined, not knowing what sort of fellow he might be and not wanting to fall into the wrong hands.

"All the same," the man replied, flicking lightly at his reins, until his horses started to gallop. The wagon went on until it disappeared around the bend ahead, and Bastian gained the main road again and continued on, already planning the week before him.

When he reached the bend, though, he found the wagon stopped and the man inside waiting for him with his pistol drawn. "Here, put these on," the man commanded, throwing him a pair of iron brace-lets.

"No, sir," Bastian said. "My people expecting me."

"Well, I don't imagine they'll be seeing you this evening," the man told him, busting the side of his head with the pistol butt. Bastian blacked out and fell to the ground.

He woke up in the back of the wagon and, it seemed, as far from Berkeley as he had ever been his entire life. He could not tell by look-ing out of the tarp where they were, or even whether Berkeley was north, south, east, or west of his position. Through the top of the wagon he could see the sky, and it looked to him the same as the one he was used to, but he knew it was not. The only other thing he knew for certain was that it was deep into the nighttime and he was unlikely to make it home that evening.

Nor had he any sense of bearing until the next afternoon, when they stopped for lunch. The man, whose name he had not yet learned, came into the back of the wagon and gave him a tin plate of hominy that had a tiny piece of hog's fat in it. "It won't be so bad," the man said. "You'll see, one master is just like any other." Bastian did not say anything in acknowledgment of this statement, and the man picked up a round stick, which was leaned against a barrel in the wagon, and slammed it into the soles of his feet, so that his knees buckled and he nearly lost the plate from his lap. "You answer when I say something to you," he said.

After he left, the wagon set off again, and, late that night came into a town. As it moved through the streets Bastian felt a great heart's sickness when he began to recognize where he was. They were in Bertie County, in Knowleston, which is where he and his family had lived before settling in Berkeley.

When they stopped at the other end of the town it was fully night, and his kidnapper left him in the wagon as he went to negotiate terms in the rooming house. When he came back, he led Bastian into a barn with the horses and tied him to a railing, first making sure he had a blanket and straw for a pallet. "Wouldn't do for you to catch cold," the man said, before leaving.

About an hour after he was fastened to the rail, a boy of twelve or so came out with a plate of scraps for him to eat. As he refused the plate, Bastian asked the boy whether he knew Goodwin Johnson's place.

The boy said he did, and that it was about five miles from where they were.

"That's my uncle. You got to go tell him what happened to me," Bastian said, recounting his sad adventure.

The boy was terrified when he heard it but promised he would figure out a way to get word out to Goodwin's place.

Bastian Johnson did not sleep through that night but lay awake in the foul stench of horse sweat and urine, stirring at the first sound as he awaited rescue. The barn door did not open again until morning, and, when it did, it was Harris, his kidnapper, who entered.

"Wake up," the man barked. "It'll never do to be a lazy slave."

Bastian sat up as commanded, and Harris handed him a bar of soap and a pair of trousers. "You clean up and put these on," he instructed.

"I can't take you to market like this. Make sure you wash the mess from your face too. The market subtracts for every defect."

When he saw the bewildered look on Bastian's face, he sat down next to him on an overturned pail. "You and me going to the Exchange here today, and I need you to be at your best. If you act up, though, I will kill you. I would rather make no profit than get cheated out of fair value. Now, what do you suppose you might be worth?"

Bastian stayed silent.

"I told you about ignoring me," the man warned.

"I don't know," Bastian answered. "I ain't never been for sale and don't imagine how you can put a price on a person, though I know some people do."

"On the contrary," the man answered, directing him toward a pail of water to wash in. "It is not people who do, but the market. People ain't smart enough. But the market is brilliant, and it can price anything—that horse, you, me, the pail—it makes no difference; the market will tell you exactly what everything is worth and will not lie or cheat you. If you bring to her what she deems valuable, she will lavish you with reward. If you bring her something worthless or not to her wanting, she will taunt you and make you suffer as sure as getting beaten with a stick for squandering her time.

"You she wants, and knows exactly what a healthy seventeen-year-old Negro is worth. Tell me now if you have any skills that should be considered, because, like I said, I hate to be cheated. Besides, I think every man should have a clear idea what he is naturally worth."

Perhaps it was from youthful pride, or perhaps he had fallen under that man's brainwash, but Bastian answered him. "I was born free and am skilled at gunmaking."

The kidnapper sucked his teeth. "Do you make shaky Negro guns or the good kind?"

"Me and my papa make the truest guns in three colonies. You can ask anybody that know guns."

"Yessir," his abductor said delightedly. "The market will know what you're worth. Now me, I am only bold, and many men are that, but you are skilled at something there is need for, so I daresay you will go at a premium. You should be proud to be worth something. Tell me, what do they call the guns your daddy make?"

"They go by his name, Bastian Johnson," the boy answered. "Same as mine."

Upon hearing this the man whistled. "You are valuable indeed," he said, taking his own pistol from its holster and showing it.

"I see you ain't mean as you look," Bastian replied brazenly, when he saw the pistol, as he put on his new clothes and followed his abductor out of the barn. They hitched the wagon again, then drove to the courthouse steps, where twice a month an auction was conducted.

When his turn came to go upon the block, Bastian was rigid with fear as the man who had taken him from his home announced his skills. "He is a seventeen-year-old Negro boy of fine build and exceptional skill. Owing to his good character he has never been touched by the lash, and he is a master gunmaker already, a skill he learned from the renowned Bastian Johnson."

A murmur went through the crowd when the auctioneer mentioned this, and the bidding for him did indeed open with a frenzy, until a voice from the crowd called out, "That child is free and has been stolen from his family." It was his Uncle Goodwin, out of breath as he came into the square.

Bastian had never been so happy as he was then to see his uncle, who had come to save him, and nearly cried like a child.

"You watch what you say," Harris cautioned, pulling his gun from his waistband and pointing it at Goodwin. "His father owed money and sold the boy to pay his debt."

"That is a bald lie," Goodwin said, walking toward Harris.

Harris cocked his pistol, daring Goodwin to come any nearer.

"On what grounds are you calling this man a liar?" Someone challenged from the crowd.

"Because his father is my brother Bastian, who many of you know, and he would never do such a thing. First of all he has never had debt in his life, and secondly that's the last way he would try to pay it."

Now many of the men knew both Johnson brothers, and they began to discuss vigorously how everything should be allowed to play out.

"Do you have a bill of sale?" The auctioneer called to Harris.

Harris, who had long practiced his thievery, produced a forged document, which the auctioneer took and examined.

"It looks authentic to me," the man announced. "The sale will proceed, Mr. Johnson."

Goodwin, along with several members of the crowd, was outraged, but he had no choice. When the auction resumed, he joined in the bidding against the others for his nephew, torn between looking at the boy to comfort him, and not wanting to upset either of their emotions.

Goodwin, like his brother, was a trained craftsman, who made a decent living for any man, and he had ready enough cash. After those who were not serious about buying fell away, his chief rival in the competition for his nephew proved to be a colonel from the Royal Army. Against him Goodwin bid all he was worth, and all his brother was worth. When the man did not drop out of the auction, Goodwin kept bidding what he thought they might reasonably borrow from friends. After that he bet what was unreasonable, but the colonel was unmoved. He had entered into the contest to buy the boy and he intended to have him no matter the price. As Goodwin neared emotional exhaustion, the colonel looked at him coolly and could tell he was beyond his limit. He added then a thousand pounds to Goodwin's last price.

It was exorbitant, and a murmur of shocked disbelief spread across the crowd's lips, but it was the final price set fair by the market. Goodwin was defeated.

He looked at his nephew and began to weep on the courthouse steps.

The kidnapper Harris gloated perversely and said to his former property, "I told you you was worth more than me, boy."

As the auctioneer swung his gavel down, Goodwin Johnson pushed his way through the crowd toward Bastian, and everyone parted to make way for him. When he emerged from the throng, though, instead of going to his nephew he charged at Harris, his fists ready for a fight. Unfortunately for the poor man, he was dealing with a rough sort who knew the use of a pistol better than he. He was outmatched again, and for the last time among his days. Harris, when he saw him coming, fired but once from the pistol. It was true and Goodwin fell to the ground.

Amidst all this, the colonel paid the bursar of the court, and the sum he turned over that day was the second highest ever recorded for a slave in that colony.

The highest price was the one Rudolph Stanton's father had paid for his mother, who everyone said was a countess abducted from the court of the Ottomans, or else the consort of a pirate king from the Barbary Coast, or, more outlandishly, even the queen of Dahomey herself.

That she was noble was as certain as that she was a slave, and later she refused to reveal her origin from shame that her house could not redeem her.

Wherever she was from, she was queenly haughty and even the block could not steal that from her, and when the elder Stanton paid it was with a suitcase that required two men to lift it up, inside of which was naught but pure gold.

For Bastian a lesser sum was required, but the purchaser was no less pleased with his prize as they left the market.

three

The day after Mr. Johnson discovered what happened to his son it seemed the entire Negro population, free and enslaved, learned the boy's fate at the very same time, and all began to descend on the Johnson house as if a call had gone out.

The Johnsons were not surprised when their nearest neighbors showed up, or when Bastian's friends came to grieve his absence. And when the Darsons and the Merians arrived it was only slightly out of the ordinary, as both of them had boys Bastian's age. However, when people began to arrive from as far away as Chase, and then from towns at the far edge of the county, they were caught completely unawares, but sensed something extraordinary was occurring. By that night their relatives from as far away as Knowleston had arrived as well, and the house overflowed with people, including a few who came only to see the scene of such misery.

All were welcomed there regardless of why they came, and there was a great gathering then of all in one place, such as had never before occurred. Mr. Johnson's house was not large, but it was able to accommodate everyone who streamed in from the shops of the town and the surrounding farms that week, as they heard Bastian's story. They came with gifts of food, pots of liquor, and instruments of music making such as those who played them thought appropriate.

As the adults congregated inside, the young people gathered in a yard outside the house, where Caleum and Julius sat at the center of the group telling the story again of their last afternoon with Bastian. "He was here headed home one minute, just like the two of us, but never made it," Caleum said, for the tenth time that afternoon.

All of the young men then began bragging about what they would have done had it been them, while the young ladies thought Caleum and Julius must have done something very clever or brave to have made it home. Caleum and Julius knew, though, it could have been either of them just as easily, but for chance.

In the midst of all the attention, Caleum saw a young woman he found especially pretty, before realizing he had met her before when they still attended Miss Boutencourt's school together. She had grown very much since then, and it was difficult for him to keep from noticing her too obviously, but he forced himself to tear his attention away as soon as he realized it was George and Eli's sister, Libbie Darson.

The girl knew of the fight her brothers had had with Caleum, and their hatred of him, but as she listened to him that afternoon, and watched him move among the other guests, she forgot about loyalty to her family. Whenever Caleum said something she agreed with, or that agreed with her, she made her approval known with an open smile, and when food was served she conspired to be the one who brought him his plate.

Caleum was disarmed by this gesture and even lowered his shield enough to return her smile. After that, and throughout the meal, he allowed himself to gaze at her openly. She had hazel eyes larger than any he had ever seen, and her skin was the hue of a chestnut's inner husk, though smooth as polished walnut. She was the tallest of all the girls gathered, but her height did not detract from the well-balanced pro-portions of her shape. When they stood next to each other after supper, he found himself looking directly into her eyes. When he did, as the other young people gathered round the musicians, Libbie turned her head away in embarrassment, being unaccustomed to the feelings he provoked in her.

He was not used to them either, but he knew them for what they were and did not shy away. "Meet me tomorrow on the north side of the square," he said, when no one else was within earshot, although all could see them in conversation.

Before she could answer, her brother Eli came and took her by the elbow, neither looking at Caleum nor avoiding him, simply leading his sister away without another word. Libbie did not resist, but she felt a sink-ing in her breast as she moved away, like a jewel falling to the bottom of the ocean. Caleum felt this loss as well, when she left their conversation, but his was twinged by renewed anger at her brothers.

That evening, when all the guests finally left the Johnson home, he was still in turmoil as he headed back to Stonehouses with Magnus and Adelia.

Seeing him still out of sorts the next day, Magnus tried to comfort the young man.

Adelia, however, could tell immediately what else was bothering him. "I don't think it's just Bastian that has him feeling so," she said. Magnus was about to ask what she meant when the statement made itself clear in his head. He laughed slightly and shook his head. He was going to tell Caleum not to go falling for the first girl he met but thought better of intervening.

"Who is she?" Magnus asked.

"Libbie Darson," Caleum answered quietly.

"I thought you had strife with the brothers," Magnus reminded him.

"The brothers ain't the sister," he answered.

"All the same. Are you old enough to court, in any case?" Magnus asked next, giving Caleum the chance to think about the question.

"It doesn't all have to happen all at once," Caleum answered. "We can take our time about it."

"Do you want to court her then?" Magnus wanted to know, trying to determine in his head the advantages and minuses that particular union might make.

"I need to think about it some more. I will let you know what I de-cide, if you trust me to," Caleum said, being both straightforward and mature with his uncle, to the relief of Magnus and Adelia. "I understand what is involved."

He was not so moody in love as his uncle and father had been, but forward and direct as his grandfather. He did, however, wonder to him-self, even as he rode into town to meet her the next day, whether he ought not turn back and seek someone more prudent to give his affection to, or perhaps wait until a later time to do so.

Their meeting, when it occurred, was exceedingly short and formal and without hesitations. They met at the northeastern corner of the square and began a conversation of pleasantries, followed by Caleum telling her that his parents had left him as a child in the care of his uncle and grandfather, that his ambition in life was only to increase the success of Stonehouses, that he liked fishing to relax, and his favorite meal was spring rack of lamb.

She responded that she was learned in reading and writing, as he knew; she was also a good sewer and needleworker, and that her mother already let her have a sizable hand in running their house. She was bright in her disposition, as he always remembered her being, and if she had any pressing concerns she did not let on.

By the time they arrived in front of old Content's place, on the southwest corner of the square, they concluded their conversation, and Caleum went home afterward to tell his uncle he did indeed wish to enter a courtship with Libbie Darson.

When Magnus received the news he was very worried and not at all approving as Caleum had hoped. In fact he told his nephew he thought it foolish. No matter how mature Caleum was in many ways, seventeen was uncommonly young to begin a courtship, and he did not want his nephew to live to regret a youthful decision, made in haste, about something so important as who he shared his heart and home with. Out of respect for the young man, however, in the end he concluded that it would be best if they both considered it overnight and reconvened in the morning.

Adelia, being more romantic about such things, claimed it was possible that Caleum, young as he was, simply knew his mind in that way already. "Or would you rather he go about it as you and your brother did?" she asked her husband pointedly, as they lay in bed that night.

"I think you should better hold your tongue now," Magnus said in reply, being unusually harsh with her, especially as theirs was a relationship in which love, when it was finally allowed to flow between then, did so without cease.

All the same, trusting her judgment, he found himself swayed by the argument, and not unrelieved the next morning when Caleum said his mind had not shifted during the night. After breakfast, then Magnus saddled his horse and went alone to call on Solomon Darson, Libbie's father.

Mr. Darson was not much in touch with the domestic goings-on of his house and was surprised when Magnus announced his purpose. Still, it was a pleasant shock, and he was happy to receive the visit, for his daughter was at a suitable age and Stonehouses was quite a desirable place. Magnus then offered terms, should the courtship end in marriage, and named the dowry he expected in return. He could not help adding a premium to the amount, both because of Caleum's tender age as well as the size of his eventual inheritance. Mr. Darson, who was normally quite garrulous and loved nothing so much as to argue and bargain, grew quiet when he heard the price but agreed quickly, if not enthusiastically— because he understood in the end how he was benefiting. He also delighted in his ability to pay such a fee.

Magnus concluded by telling Solomon Darson he thought a long courtship might be best, as Caleum was still young. Mr. Darson, who was more than a little obsequious toward Magnus, agreed that the courtship should be as long as he said, and offered his guest a drink in celebration, which Magnus declined.

His terms settled, Magnus stood to leave without ceremony, but confident in his position as the stronger party in the negotiations, and asked for his horse to be brought out from the stable. Before he left, however, not wanting to give offense, he thought to make a bow to Mrs. Darson and shake hands with her husband in front of her, warmly enough that they seemed like old friends who had just finished dinner instead of a business deal.

When he returned home Magnus called Caleum into the parlor and told him he was free to begin courting Libbie. Caleum, when he heard, sat up in his seat very straight. Instead of fear, which Magnus had been half expecting and half hoping to see on his face, the young man seemed self-assured and smiled at his uncle as he thanked him. "I know you don't think I'm ready yet, sir, but I am."

"I still think you would be better served to take your time with all of it. If she has your heart, it won't go anywhere."

"I'm not anxious about that," Caleum said precociously.

Looking at him in that moment Magnus saw the same confidence Purchase had always carried with himself and was proud of his nephew that he had inherited that quality.

"All the same, it's my business to shepherd your affairs, and I would be failing you in that if I advised otherwise."

Caleum, ever dutiful, could see then how much his uncle had worked to be a good guardian and felt himself lucky to have such a parent in place of his own, who had abandoned him. Still, he knew his own mind and thought himself well prepared for the next phase of shepherding and guarding himself as well as a wife.

He called on Libbie at the end of the week, riding his horse through the tumult of autumn colors as first frost descended into the valley from higher up. When he came up the narrow way to their house, Libbie, who was in the parlor, saw him and left in an excited rush to prepare herself. It was no coincidence she was at the window, which had no glass, only wooden shutters, and still stood open at just that time. She had been lurking about there the entire four days since Mr. Merian had come to see her father.

When Caleum knocked at the front door, Mr. Darson himself opened it and welcomed the young man into the house. The two of them entered the parlor together, and the entire family was there. Caleum greeted each in turn, even Eli and George, though more distantly.

Similarly, George and Eli were forced to defer to Caleum when they saw their father treated him like a grown man and equal while he still treated them like boys. It did not sit well with them, but they were without power to affect the situation for the time being.

"Libbie, why don't you show Caleum your embroidery," Mrs. Darson recommended, after he had sat down. "Libbie is very accomplished at needlecraft and sewing."

The girl, suddenly shy, smiled downward and sat without moving for a moment, before gathering herself to go off and fetch the things her mother suggested. She returned with a square piece of cloth she had decorated for a pillow.

When Caleum saw it, he thought it was artful indeed and complimented her on it. "It is so pretty," he said, looking her in the face until she turned her head downward again. "It's going to make the prettiest pillow in the whole county." He looked at her for a response, as she continued to smile into her own lap for embarrassment of looking at him directly.

"Why don't we all leave them so they can talk together a spell," Mr. Darson told his sons, standing from his own seat.

Caleum stood until the family had left the room. When he and Libbie were alone, he sat down again closer to her. "How did you learn to embroider so well?" he asked, grown more awkward when they were left alone.

"It only comes to me," she answered. "For each piece of fabric, I think what it most reminds of, then try to fashion that."

"Well, it sure is something," Caleum told her. "I could never do such a thing myself."

"You yourself must make something, though," she replied modestly. "Everybody makes something."

"No, not me. I don't have the eye for it."

"Well, I bet you'll make a good planter," she said. "That is something that requires knowing a great deal. Maybe not everyone's talent after all is to create, but that some people have a talent for shepherding, which is just as necessary."

"Perhaps," Caleum replied, impressed with her good sense. "I think the two together must complement each other handsomely."

Libbie could not help but turn away again.

When she did so, Caleum reached out and briefly took her hand. She turned her attention directly to him after that, and they stared straight into each other's eyes, until Mrs. Darson returned to the room. Caleum quickly stood up again when he saw her in the doorway.

"It has been very nice visiting with you, Mr. Merian," she said, coming into the middle of the room, where she stood like an immovable pillar.

"Yes, I must get back now. May I return next week?"

"Please do," Libbie said, then quickly looked to her mother.

"Yes, we would enjoy that," Mrs. Darson affirmed.

Caleum was happy then as both women wished him a pleasant ride back to Stonehouses. On the way he dreamed of the home he would create with Libbie, and all the comforts and security it would contain. That will be my great talent, he told himself, to make a home like Stonehouses for my own wife and children. As he thought this he began to think of his parents. He spurred his horse then into a fast gallop, wanting to burn away the memory of rejection.

It was over ten years since he had last seen them, and he could barely recall either in his own mind, except for the gossip he sometimes heard—

for the story of his parents had become notorious in those parts and was even known on the seas. He knew his love for Libbie was not like theirs but a thing patterned after itself that he was very glad for. Still, he was careful when he daydreamed of his intended that it was temperate, and not feverish as he knew devotion could sometimes be, when its heat consumed both self and host.

f o u r

Caleum and Libbie's courtship was not long, as the older people, excepting Mr. Darson, would have preferred, but barely a year in duration. The spring after he started wooing her Caleum persuaded Magnus that he was set to see things through to their formal conclusion. Magnus, wary but trusting his nephew to know his own mind by then, accepted the decision without debate and informed Solomon Darson he was free to publicize the engagement and ensuing marriage, which they agreed to have six weeks hence at the Darson place.

Magnus and Caleum spent the rest of that month taking long rides together, to survey the land and search out the best spot to put up a new house. Caleum in his heart had already set on a place about a mile from the main building, overlooking the valley, which he thought might keep Libbie from homesickness. Magnus overuled the idea, however, telling him it would not be good soil for his crops or good grazing for his animals. He led him instead around to a place on the southern side of the lake that sat up on a small rise, lower but almost identical to the one Stonehouses itself occupied.

"This is the second-best land," he said. "You take it and never worry for dependency, on the main house or anybody else."

"I don't fear that so much as being apart from it," Caleum answered, full of appreciation and gratitude for his uncle's gesture—for he knew it was the best land but would never have presumed to try and claim it.

Magnus was pleased then that he had been given a good son and proud that they had managed a bond between them that was not only filled with warmth but also with respect and mutual understanding.

"Your father would be very pleased for you," Magnus told him, putting onto his brother what he himself felt, as they rode back to the stable. Caleum was silent in response, and Magnus allowed him to remain so but only added, "You must never think ill of him. You cannot judge them."

"No, sir," Caleum replied.

In truth he sometimes thought his father the meanest man in the world, and at other times greater than everything else he knew, and both feelings made larger from their seed by his absence. No matter his thoughts, however, he never spoke ill of either his parents, neither when alone nor with others, as he would not dream of giving voice to such personal inner grievance.

They returned to the house at suppertime, to find Merian, who sometimes but very seldom still joined them for meals, at the table.

He spoke, when he did at all, in a garbled way, which those around him had learned to decipher, though not always accurately—so that one sentence might be taken to mean a certain thing by Adelia, another thing by Magnus, and yet something else entirely by Caleum. Despite this, they tried to keep him informed of all the goings-on in the family, not certain how much he took in or failed to but honoring his position there.

"Caleum and I have just chosen the spot for his house," Magnus said, as they sat down to table that evening.

Adelia, who was just about to bring a spoonful of warm mashed potatoes to Merian's mouth, paused to see whether or not he would answer.

It was clear that he understood the words and their meaning but was slow to formulate his response. When he did, he spoke extremely slowly. "Is he separating now?"

"Soon," Caleum hazarded to answer.

One side of Merian's mouth curled in an enigmatic smile when he heard this reply. He turned then to Magnus and asked, "What ground?"

"The southern side of the lake," Magnus said. "I thought it was the best after Stonehouses itself."

"It was hard husbanding."

No one knew what to make of this, and they all looked to one another for guidance until Adelia replied, "He will be a good husband."

Merian looked to his bowl for more food, which Adelia brought dutifully to his mouth. After he had swallowed, he looked at his grandson and asked, "The wife?"

"She will be good as well," Caleum said, looking directly at his ancient grandfather. "I am sure of it."

"Caleum has made a good match," Magnus vouched for him.

Merian tried to nod his head, as to say he agreed with marrying while young, but it had become a very difficult maneuver. Frustrated by his body's refusal to do as he would have it, he swiped at the bowl in front of him and sent it to the floor. As Adelia cleaned it up, he sat there sphinxlike, feeling prisoner to the decay that had claimed him, mind and body. No one knew then what it was he wished to communicate, as even his simplest gestures were not what they always seemed.

Caleum and Magnus both knew, however, better than to pity Merian, as his fate might be either of theirs. Rather, they continued to treat him as if he had never known dementia and was still as he had been in the major part of his life.

The morning of Caleum's wedding to Libbie Darson, a pale blue sky arched unblemished overhead like the ceiling of a godly cathedral. The air was also warm enough to go about with naught but a vest, and the day seemed soft and tremulous with possibility. Merian called his grandson to him in the parlor that morning, where he sat dressed very handsomely in an old-fashioned suit. When Caleum entered, Merian pointed over the mantel to the sword Purchase had crafted long ago and indicated for him to take it down. Caleum walked to the place where it stood and lifted it from its hooks, which made Merian smile from the side of his mouth that still cooperated with him. Caleum went then to embrace his grandfather, and when he did Merian pressed his carved wooden doll into his hand. "For young husbands," he said.

Besides his lands it was the most cherished of his possessions. The thing third most valuable to him was a golden pocket watch, which hung in his vest and was bequeathed in his will to Purchase, if he ever returned to their lands.

Caleum had long been curious about the wooden doll, which frightened Adelia and made Magnus none too happy. He was honored to have it, though, and placed it in his pocket before either his aunt or uncle could come into the room. "For luck at Caleum's house," Merian said again emphatically.

When Magnus came into the room old and young parted conspiratorially, Magnus looked suspiciously from one to the other but decided against asking what they were about. He only dusted away invisible lint from Caleum's vest, telling him it was time for them to set out and he should help him take Merian to the waiting carriage—whence they made their way to the Darson place for the ceremony.

When they entered the Darson house that morning everyone grew hushed to see Jasper Merian present, for he was the oldest man in the county after Content's death and had been one of the first to settle there. He was also said to be one of the richest, so an undeniable mystique attached to him.

They were careful about noticing his frail condition, however, and only the smallest children and boldest of the men came directly to greet him. He seemed very aloof to many of them and would barely speak to any save Mrs. Darson and Libbie, though he could not remember her name.

Jasper sat still as a mountain while everyone else moved around him and came to offer good wishes for the union. Mr. Darson was especially desirous of his attention, seeking to shake his arthritic hand several times, and deeply hurt when Merian failed to receive it.

"Did you feed my horses?" Merian asked, the final time Solomon Darson held his hand out to him, as if he were the stable boy instead of the bride's father.

Darson knew better than begrudge such an ancient soul, but he could not help feeling abused and thought again of the high price Magnus had set for the marriage contract, which is perhaps why he did not stop his sons later that morning.

Promptly at eleven of the clock Libbie came into the hall, glorious and radiant in her wedding dress, and Caleum took his place beside her. When the minister, who suffered from religious melancholy and was extremely dour, asked ceremonially whether any protested the union, Eli Darson and his brother, George, both stood to speak.

Mr. Darson was embarrassed that they might already be drunk and anxious of what mischief they were up to, especially in the instant he looked at his daughter and saw the mortification on her face. Still, he did nothing to intervene.

"On what grounds do you object?" the minister asked them impatiently, as the time for such matters was during the engagement period.

When the preacher asked this, everyone, including George and Eli themselves, could see the childishness of what they had done, for they had no serious grounds but only a general dislike of the groom. Both of them jogged nervously from foot to foot, trying to think of something to redeem themselves, as the guests waited with horror upon their faces.

"If there is no objection," the minister then went on, seeing it was only boys being churlish.

"On grounds," Eli Darson spat out at last, "that neither his religion nor his origin is generally known."

The preacher was very annoyed at their shenanigans, but when Eli said the groom's religion was not known he paused amid the babble that had overtaken the room to ask Caleum whether he was Christian and had renounced Satan and all his works.

Caleum answered in the affirmative, as Magnus shot daggers from his eyes at Mr. Darson and Libbie began crying. Everyone present was made exceptionally uncomfortable and thought the Darson boys either nefarious or simple. Having started, though, they refused to give up. "Ask him about his father," George said, grown bold with foolishness. "He is not decent people."

"Why not ask him yourself?" a man's voice asked from back of the room, after the Darson boy had finished his speech.

When the couple and their guests turned around to see who had spoken, all in the house went quiet.

A formidably tall man stood up then, his head nearly scraping the ceiling where its wooden beams met the wall. He was wearing a blue brocade vest, silken breeches of a mauve color, and a black waistcoat, also of silk. A starched white shirt and embroidered cravat were visible on his upper body, embroidered stockings on his legs, and all was topped with a three-cocked camel's-hair hat, which was the first of its fashion ever to be seen in Berkeley. His light eyes seemed to dance, though his face was otherwise filled with a gravity and character that comes only from ceaseless care, or thought and study of human nature at close range. His hair was gone stark white, and he was considerably older than when last they knew him, but everyone could tell, not only from his face and his words but even from the feeling that emanated from his person, that it was Purchase Merian.

How he had gone unnoticed until then none could say, though most who had not seen him for ages were greatly pleased to do so again. Others, who had only heard his legend, were excited to put flesh to lore. Still others bore him grudges decades old. The two Darson boys, though, when they saw the man standing in the back of the room, both found the seats nearest to them and sat themselves down, deciding there was no need of pressing further, such was his natural presence and authority.

At the altar, Caleum felt pulled toward the stranger from the moment that he spoke, but averted his eyes, and returned them to his bride. He nodded for the preacher to carry on with the ceremony. The minister looked at Magnus, who gave his assent as well, and began to read the marriage oath.

After they had at last sworn themselves to each other, and the ceremony was successfully concluded, Purchase strode to the front of the room where the marriage party was standing. When he reached the front row he stopped first to approach his father and kissed the old man warmly, not having known before whether he was alive or dead. Jasper looked up at him, and when he spoke it was the first time he had recognized anybody in a very long time, saying only, "Purchase."

"Yes, Papa. It's me."

"You were on time," Merian said.

"I suppose," Purchase answered him. "You could argue it both ways."

When he greeted Magnus, the two gave each other a hug of great fraternal affection, old enough to know and rejoice that many paths in life are crossed again.

Magnus next introduced his wife, Adelia, whom Purchase knew from when she worked at Stonehouses, and they were happy to be reacquainted as well.

The next person he greeted was Libbie, who found him charming as women invariably did, even though he was old enough to be her father and, by law, now in fact was.

He came then to Caleum. Upon his first approach Caleum held himself back, refusing to look directly at his father. When he did, he felt a huge pressure against his chest and forehead that made it feel as if he were about to come out of his skin. He did not recognize the man from the image he carried in his memory's eye, but he knew him for who he was with an instinct beneath the illumination of words. He knew the two of them were part of a single whole, however reluctantly. His emotions then were divided, but he held out his hand formally when at last he responded to Purchase's greeting. "Father."

The man was sensitive not to cause the boy any further discomfort and held out his own hand in turn, neither drawing any nearer in familiarity nor pulling away from offended feelings. "Congratulations," he said solemnly. "May you two know nothing together but shared happiness."

Before Caleum could reply Purchase pulled from his coat a leather satchel, which he handed to the bridegroom. Everyone standing around pressed close to see what it contained. Mr. Darson leaned especially hard against his son-in-law's shoulder while Caleum thanked his father and opened the parcel. Inside the worn pouch was a multitude of golden coins, shaped larger than any he was used to seeing. Upon closer inspection he saw that one side of each seemed very familiar, though he could not tell exactly why, while the other side bore the image of a young couple on their wedding day, who were uncannily similar to himself and Libbie.

Mr. Darson, when he saw the coins, tried to calculate what each was worth and exactly how many the purse contained, but even without an exact number he felt vindicated, as he could tell at a glance it was far more than the price Magnus had demanded from him.

Had they merely been gold coins, Caleum might have returned them as a bribe against his affections, but these bore all the beauty and artistry that had won Purchase Merian unrivaled fame—even before the notoriety of his affair with Mary Josepha—and it was impossible for him not to feel moved. He could see immediately they had been crafted for him and his bride, and that the tale they told had been with his father for a long time indeed, though he knew not how. More ancient perhaps than he himself was. Certainly, though, it was very old.

Caleum closed the purse and gave it to Magnus for safekeeping, as he and Libbie adjourned to the lawn for the wedding feast, where they presided over the banquet table. Family and friends came then to lavish gifts on them throughout the afternoon, but none more impressive or valuable than Purchase's.

After eating, the slave Julius led the celebration by pulling out his panpipes and beginning a serenade of the wedding couple. Other musicians joined with him to create a ravishing improvised song of love for the newlyweds. There was also much dancing and playing of cards, as everyone celebrated the new union.

Only the Darson brothers, Eli and George, withheld from the toasting, for they had disgraced themselves and knew better than show their faces. Caleum and Libbie danced, though, full of lightheartedness.

No matter how contented he was with the morning, Caleum knew he must eventually speak full on to his father, but he put it off as long as possible, first filling himself on punch—which was a near calamity as he was not used to its strength—then dancing yet another round.

At the tables Purchase sat with Magnus, Adelia, Mr. and Mrs. Darson, and his own father, Jasper, who did not drink or dine. Their feelings at seeing Purchase again all ran a range, but none of them were as complicated as Caleum's, even though Magnus knew perhaps better than the others what must be going through his thoughts at that moment.

"It might take a while for him to want to speak to you," Magnus said to his brother, at one point during the conversation. "His feelings are probably powerful mixed."

"So they must be," Purchase agreed. "What about your own?"

"Will you stay on?" he asked. "Are you back at Stonehouses now?"

"I'm back as long as I am here," Purchase said testily.

"Well, we are happy for that," Magnus told him. "All of us."

Purchase thanked Magnus, then turned to seek out his father's attention. Merian placed his hand on Purchase's arm and rubbed it very tenderly. "Stay," he said, the word very slow to form and exit his mouth.

Purchase clasped his fingers. "In my heart I am always here," he answered, "but we cannot, all of us, always be where our heart is."

"But where we should," Merian said, and he was very clear and lucid then.

Purchase loved his father and owed him honor so did not want to argue with him, but he was full grown a long time already and his life was as much his own as any man's could be said to be—he needed neither father nor brother nor even offspring to define that—and he was learned enough in his life to know what its purpose was: His was the fate of the lover. He argued neither with men nor with God that it should be different.

His time there was a holiday for him from the tribulations of that life, and he wanted to treat it as such, so when the music began again, he was among the first to the dance, going first with Libbie, then Mrs. Darson. To Mrs. Darson he seemed imposing and unreadable, like no man she had known before. When Libbie danced with him, though, she felt a soothing comfort that, while she had never yet felt it in such a way, she knew immediately to be profoundly masculine. There was sadness in it, but while she danced with him she feared nothing and wanted nothing else.

"Will you be a good wife for my son?" he asked her.

"I will do my utmost best," she answered, and he knew that she would.

"He is a very lucky man in that case, and I could wish nothing more for him," Purchase told his daughter-in-law.

Just as he knew the boy would be safe when he sent him to live at Stonehouses, he sensed he would be well off with Libbie, especially as— and this he could divine by looking at him—his son's life would be full of its own trials.

As their dance ended Libbie could scarcely believe the rumors they said about her father-in-law and his wife. What woman, she wondered, would deny such a husband? She hoped, as she went back to her new groom, he might become such a man as his father one day. And it pleased her to think what this future version of Caleum might be like.

Caleum himself was still engaged with distractions and did not muster the resolve to confront his father until it was near eventide. Purchase amused himself in the meantime by watching Julius and Cato gamble at cards. No longer having the desire for that particular vice himself, he watched only in the manner of one who is advanced at chess watching precocious children play at checkers: with interest in the players and how each approached the board and formed his strategy, but little care for the game itself, being able to see the result far in advance.

When his son finally came to him, he knew there were but few possibilities on the board, and what each move was most likely to produce for an endgame.

"How did you know about the wedding?" Caleum asked first, staring at Purchase in the amber light of a setting sun that seemed to burnish everything around them. "Or was it only happenstance that you arrived today?"

"It was published," Purchase answered him. "When I read it, I knew I must attend."

"And my mother?" the young man pressed.

"It was her I was looking for when I read the announcement," Purchase answered him without elaboration.

All Caleum knew of his father was what he had been told by his relatives, or else the gossip of those who were not necessarily friends. Some saw his state as a sickness that could not be purged. To others he was renowned for his boldness and courage. His son tried to divine between these poles. Standing before him he still could not tell, and it took all of his courage to look his father in the eye and ask, "Is it true what they say of you?"

Purchase looked on Caleum with sympathy. "I cannot tell you that because I do not know either who *they* are or the words from their lips. What men believe is according to each his own needs, but what are facts are well known and I would never deny them to you."

"Did you come here to mock me with riddles?" Caleum asked.

"The opposite of mocking. I came to celebrate you and your bride and your love for each other," Purchase said. "I will answer whatever you ask of me, but for what is in other men's minds I do not know and do not concern myself with. Nor should you so much."

"The schooling years have passed for me already."

"May they never."

"Teach me this then, Father," Caleum said, looking him steady in the eye. "Where is my mother?"

"I have not seen her for a year," Purchase answered. "If she knew of your wedding, I am certain she would be happy for you, as I am."

"If you cannot answer that, what about this?" Caleum looked away at his guests, enjoying themselves on the lawn, and tried to find voice for what was truly on his mind, as it caused him more pain than the fear of his father's wrath. It was fear of rejection being replayed, but he stoppered that and asked anyway, "Why did you disown me?"

Purchase followed the boy's gaze out toward the celebration and, beyond that, to the precipice where the Darson property fell off and the rough valleys of that country resumed. "They are disowned—fatherless, motherless—who arrive here every day. Is that what I did?" Purchase asked. "Or did I give you a parenting other than my own? Perhaps it was so you did not have my failures or ambitions to cloud your judgment, or pin your failures upon, and could be your own man. Or do you fear that?"

"All my fears were consumed by the ocean when I traveled upon it as a boy. I have had no fear since then," Caleum said, drawing up proudly.

"You will be afraid again yet," Purchase reproached him, "unless you will be a fool. But just as fathers cannot always fathom the minds of their sons, sons do not always know the hearts of their fathers. Cannot feel empathy for their fates. You were only differently fathered, Caleum, such as happens every day and has happened at Stonehouses since my father first cultivated it."

"Aye, and which one will stay?" Caleum asked, feeling an onrush of emotion for his old father, whom he could admire in many ways but did not understand, any better than when he was only a memory carried from boyhood.

"I don't know how long I will stay," Purchase said. "My only home is with your mother, and I hear she is on the other lip of the ocean."

What maze the two of them had traveled no one outside that relationship could know, but that it had been a complex dance of love and heartbreak and strange devotion was plain for anyone to see. Caleum looked at his sire and was afraid—not that his own marriage might turn out so but that they were part of a scheme larger than themselves he had yet to grasp, and that such quantum weight might be given him to bear. For his mother, he did not know whether she loved his father or not— or what she thought of her son, for that matter—but he felt sadness for both his parents.

"I hope the two of you figure out a way that brings you peace," he said at last. He knew then, the moment he felt empathy for his father, that his own fate would be otherwise, and the point and purpose of his life would be different. "I hope you find a way home." He left

Purchase and returned to seek out his wife, who would give him untold joy and a life far apart from the other generations at Stonehouses.
Of this he was sure.

That evening, when the wedding was over and the newlyweds made
their way off to start their life together, Purchase Merian picked up again
his own permanent burden and set out in search of his wife. The purpose
of his road was to find her, and he still imagined that if the two of them
could only unite in lasting happiness it would be very glorious. He would
not have rest before this and knew that as well. He was glad indeed his
son was at Stonehouses and protected from knowing too much at too
young an age, even if he was proving very precocious.

five

⟋

Libbie had always heard about the generosity of those at Stonehouses to friends and strangers alike, especially when Jasper Merian was still in his prime. The winter she first made a home there, however, was the coldest time she had so far known in her remembered life. She was not in the main house, of course, but the new place Caleum had put up with Magnus's help on the southern side of the lake, and she could not imagine a place of greater desolation and distance from life's comforts.

She knew her husband had built their home with her in mind, and it moved her to see all he had done to make it pleasant for her; still, she could not help but notice what was absent. For instance, when he showed her the glassed-in windows that framed the parlor, with a view out to the blue-green waters of the lake—gathering both the eastern and western light of the sun as it passed through the day—instead of thinking herself lucky to have such a fine picture window, she wondered only how she would endure not looking out on the vista she was used to from her parents' house. She always reprimanded herself after such a thought, but the glass in the window seemed hard and forbidding to her, as opposed to the warm wooden shutters with which she had grown up. Furthermore, the distance from Magnus and Adelia in the main house, to say nothing of the next nearest neighbor, seemed to her so great that they might as well have been at the other edge of creation.

The building itself was the same size as her parents' home, but, because it was occupied by only the two of them, it felt massive and empty. At night it was especially barren, and there was an echo that reverberated through the halls, which reminded her that she no longer heard her mother's voice in the morning, or even her brothers fighting with each other at all hours of the day.

"I have built it for us to fill together," said Caleum, who had spent the entire summer with his uncle and two hired men building for them a small replica of the main building, and he could not believe she did not find it agreeable, as he himself felt very rich when he finished putting it up. "The parlor will be warm when you have made curtains of your own design for the windows. The empty sounds will be padded by the paper you hang on the walls. The echoing rooms will fill with our children."

She listened to him attentively, and was soothed by his words, until she heard his voice say *children*. Children? She knew certainly it was part of what was expected of her; however, she had not thought what it meant until she heard it from his mouth. When he said the word so assuredly she felt a crisis of fear, as its reality was brought home to her. She did not know if she was brave enough to face the danger she knew birth to be. She started then to weep.

Her mother had lectured her on what she might expect during her first days and weeks of marriage. Even if it had been for the most part a pleasant picture, and she had entered married life optimistically, Libbie could not divorce it from the stories she had heard since her girlhood of women who died during their labors. So when her husband came into their bedroom that first night, despite all her excitement about their new marriage, and even the physical spark that had passed between them early in their courtship, she was afraid to be with him as his wife.

Caleum was mystified by her tears but tried nonetheless to console her. "You are only being homesick," he reasoned thoughtfully, unaware of her growing panic. "You will get used to it here."

She tried to stop her tears. "Yes, you are right," she said. "I know we will have a successful marriage and life together."

When she finally recovered from crying, he drew nearer to her. He was at first patient, thinking her reluctance was like her tears, and that it would pass just as soon as she became accustomed to him and her new surroundings. When his patience was not rewarded, though, he grew angry and became increasingly hostile in his entreaties.

This did not have the intended effect, however, so that in the end he backed down and drew to one side of their new bed. She stayed on her side, as each stared out separately into the first night of their life together.

"I don't mean to be rough with you," he told her from his side.

"Nor do I mean to keep myself from you," she answered.

"We are married now."

"For what it means."

"It is supposed to mean we are bound up with each other for the duration of things."

"What is it we will have to endure?"

"That I do not know, but I don't mean to be rough with you either."

"Nor do I mean to keep myself from you."

Having reached an understanding in principle, they both relaxed slightly in the darkened room. They did not have a long history together that they could call upon, or even a fight before this one to use as trail mark, but they tried to find their way back to one another nonetheless.

"How will you decorate the house?" he asked her eventually.

"I don't know. I've never had anything so big or empty to try and fill."

"I will help you in it."

"You mean you will help me with the sewing and choosing fabric for curtains?" She laughed.

"No, not the curtains, but I might have something to say about the tableware," he replied lightly, making her giggle even more. "I knew from the very first that you should be my wife and all that means," he said then, catching her unaware with tenderness.

"As did I," she answered him, finding herself grown less afraid.

He ventured then to approach nearer to her and reach out with his fingers for hers under the covers. She seized on them violently, and he could tell by this pressure what it was the matter.

"Are you afraid?"

"Mm-hm."

He could not truthfully tell her not to be, because he was amateur as she and not so experienced as to give advice. However, he took care to show her every consideration after that, so when he moved closer beside her, she did not startle but simply closed her eyes. She knew it was part of her duty and was also anxious to have it be over, and as he inched closer to her she felt herself on the edge of some radiant mystery, which she understood to be general knowledge among her sex, but nonetheless seemed colossal as she lay at its gateway.

221

As she relaxed, Caleum's thoughts and actions juggled between giving attention to her, his own nervousness, and the sheer excitement he felt at being upon his marriage bed. Under his touch her anxiousness began to pass and her senses awaken. They kissed passionately after that for a great long time, and began to explore each other as they had not before. Try as they might, though, neither of them could quite get used to the fact that their actions were not illicit. Because of this there was not any great freedom their first night together, but general awkwardness, and they were both happy to keep the covers pulled up as they explored and found their way beneath them. Their lovemaking then was clumsy and awkward as birds taking flight for the first time.

When it was over, their early embarrassment returned to them and they could only hope that, in time, it would do so less and less.

Nor was Libbie so afraid of her new husband anymore, or so fearful of the idea of babies, and in the days that followed they stayed near each other until they began to grow quite comfortable around each other's nakedness.

The new surroundings were another matter. When Caleum left during the day to go work on the land, Libbie felt utterly deserted out there on the far side of the lake. She would busy herself with cleaning in the morning, but, the place lacking furniture, she was soon done. She would then plan the meals for midday and evening, but as there were only the two of them it was no great affair. Afternoons were spent in the chores of the farm and those did not vary, so she was soon bored by the ones in her own house as she had been in her parents'.

Her only respite from this tedium would come when she thought of some excuse to walk the half mile to the main house for a visit. Sensing how alone she felt on these occasions, Adelia would also come over and visit out there when she could. The main topic of their discussion then was how the rooms should best be finished. As the weather worsened, though, neither of them could make the trip as easily or as frequently. When winter fastened its grip, Adelia encouraged Libbie to throw herself into this work, as the only way she would ever feel at home in her new place. "You have to make it your own," she admonished, with a mixture of sympathy and firmness. "It is your only home now."

Libbie took this advice perhaps too much to heart that first winter. The wallpaper she decorated the living room with was an almost exact match from her mother's house, the only difference being a graduation of color from straw yellow to gold. The furniture she ordered was the same as well, so much so that when the cabinetmaker was uncertain of something she had described he would go by the Darson house to reexamine the original. The only thing she made exception for was the fabric she used to decorate the windows, bedclothes, and cushions. "Each of these has its own character," she claimed, examining the material."It's own thing it needs to be to bring the house lively."

It was as she set about trying to create the house dressings and furniture that she began to find the character of her new rooms. A blue that was originally intended to upholster the sofa might instead become curtains for the windows. The eggshell-colored material meant to be used for the curtains then become the bed sham, and the burgundy she had intended to use as a simple design for pillows turned into a footstool for Caleum.

Her husband was happy she had found something to apply her attention to, and he was not in the least bothered by some of the bolder choices she had made, finding the house both more comfortable and more an expression of his wife's personality instead of merely a miniature version of the place where she had grown up. As her work progressed the bare rooms became a welcome retreat for them when that cold winter stretched on longer than usual.

In the morning Caleum would leave before daybreak to attend to the winter work of the farm. During the morning hours, if she had no other substantial chores, Libbie would sit by the window, doing her sewing or embroidering, staring out at the white blanket of snow spread over the hill country. She was by herself all day and all those long hours, surrounded by the still whiteness of the landscape and her own work inside.

She began slowly to grow used to it and, though she had not forgotten her childhood home, was even able to imagine a future for herself there. When the holiday season arrived, though, she began to grow terribly sick after Caleum had gone. She wanted nothing more then than to return to her father's house, where she knew she would be well cared for. Instead, she took to her bed.

When Caleum returned in late afternoon and she finally stood again, she was still light-headed as nausea gripped her entire body. Alarmed by this, Caleum did the only thing he could think of, which was to go to the main house for help.

When she heard Libbie was sick Adelia took immediate charge, telling Rebecca, her maid, to pack a basket with salts, medicinal roots, and certain herbs that she pointed out in one of the cupboards in the kitchen. When the parcel was prepared, they set out for the other house.

They found Libbie lying in bed, shaking and terrified, as she was so often that first year. Adelia began by asking her when it all started and the exact nature of her symptoms, as Caleum sat helpless and very still at her side.

As Adelia slowly began to hone in on the exact nature of her complaint, she asked Rebecca and Caleum to leave the room so she might have privacy with Libbie. The two of them then spent about twenty minutes talking alone together. Adelia, when she had finished her interview, left the bedroom and mixed a potion of ginger and wild yam root, which she said would make the nausea go away, and told Rebecca to take it to Libbie in her room. She then gave instructions for Caleum to go out and dig up a pound of choice clay.

"What is the clay for?" he asked.

"Just go, dear," Adelia answered. "I will tell you everything when you return."

Caleum went off, annoyed that he was being treated like a child again. Nevertheless he took a shovel from the barn and walked half a mile out to the hillside, where they always dug the best clay for firing bricks. After throwing off the snow that had accumulated on top of the ground he attacked the frozen earth with an edge of the shovel, until he had carved the outline of a square. He then stood on top of the shovel with all his weight trying to break this portion free of the ground around it.

The clay, which was beige in summer, was dark with frost and coldness, and it took him the better part of an hour to remove enough to satisfy Adelia's demand. Once he had, he hastened back across the frozen fields to the house, so Libbie's pain might be eased and to learn what was the matter with his wife that she needed dirt.

When he reentered the warm house, he found Libbie sitting up without discomfort for the first time that day, for which he was already thankful to his aunt. Adelia was not done with her cure, however, but took a small piece of the clay he had brought back and fed it to Libbie.

"Take the same amount every morning," Adelia instructed, after Libbie had swallowed the medicine. "You'll see you feel better directly."

"What is the matter with her?" Caleum asked, no longer able to remain patient and beginning to fear he had married a sickly woman.

"Why, she is pregnant," Adelia replied.

Libbie looked at him and smiled weakly. He smiled back at her. She did not seem as afraid as she had been when he first brought her there to Stonehouses. The same, though, could not be said of Caleum himself.

"What do you suppose of that?" he asked, of no one in particular.

"I suppose it means you're going to have a child," Adelia answered, with a tone that struck him as slightly mocking.

"Thank you," Caleum retorted. "Whatever would I do without such sound advice?"

Seeing that he was not happy as would be expected but nervous about Libbie's new state, Adelia was softer with him. "You should be thankful," she said. "It has been a long time since Stonehouses was blessed with the sound of a baby's crying and laughter."

"Of course, Aunt Adelia," Caleum said, "I am very glad for it. It is just that I am anxious to do everything properly."

"You will, husband," Libbie said to him, knowing how important that was to him. "It isn't, after all, like I am first ever to have a child."

In the days that followed, though, both Caleum and Libbie were nervous about even the smallest things, so that instead of simply taking a pinch of clay with her fingers to eat each morning, Caleum and Libbie took a balance and weighed the exact amount so it should never fluctuate from what Adelia prescribed.

When Magnus saw how worried his nephew had become over his wife's health, he decided to help relieve his burden by hiring a maid to help them. At first he thought to send Rebecca over to the other house, but Adelia told him medicine was specialized knowledge, and Rebecca would probably cause more harm than help. He then cast about among the other women on the place to see if any were knowledgeable about midwifery and general medicine. When he failed to find any on his own land, he put word out among his neighbors that he was in need of a nursemaid for his daughter-in-law.

Eventually a small brown woman with red-colored hair and the scars of pox on her skin turned up at the door, announcing herself as Claudia and saying she had come about the midwife job. She was the slave Julius's older sister, and like her brother she was hired out at whatever tasks were available, to earn an income for her master as well as her own keep.

When Magnus interviewed her he was at first happy, thinking she would be perfect, as she was not too much older than Libbie and so could serve as a companion as well. When he thought about Caleum's friendship with her brother, though, he was made wary she might take it as license to overstep her bounds. When he considered she was a slave on top of this, he was struck with further uncertainty, as there had never been anyone working at Stonehouses who was not free to command their own time and labor.

"It isn't as if we would be holding her in bondage," Adelia argued that night in bed, as they tried to decide whether they should hire Claudia or not. "We are giving her work and paying her a wage for it."

"It's not Claudia we are paying but her master," Magnus countered. "She will have to give him whatever she earns."

"Then we can pay her something just for her, perhaps," Adelia said, wanting the matter settled quickly. "You'll be doing well by both of them."

Magnus's mind was still undecided when he woke up the next morning, and sought out Caleum to see what the younger man thought about the idea, thinking to give him final say, as it was after all his roof and not Magnus's she would be housed under.

Caleum, uncertain of the future and wanting whatever support he could have, was of the same opinion as his Aunt Adelia, telling Magnus that they would be doing Claudia a great favor. "Now she has to find work week to week with no guarantee of anything but that she will be hungry again," he reasoned logically. "Here she will have steady employ and steady meals. She is after all the person most suited. Perhaps we might even try to acquire her outright from her master, and let her use her salary to repay us."

Magnus was set against the last part of Caleum's scheme, as it would violate all Jasper Merian stood for, even if it would benefit everyone concerned. He looked at the younger man a long time when he said it, thinking Caleum must eventually decide the affairs of his own house.

* * *

Magnus hired Claudia to the position that next afternoon, sending money to her owner in advance for the first six months of her services, so as not to have regular dealings with him.

It was a happy arrangement for all in the end, and Libbie's pregnancy proceeded smoothly, until one day—when Claudia was at the original house with Adelia and Libbie, who was then in her seventh month of pregnancy—Jasper Merian asked who she was.

He was blind as an oracle by then and shriveled as a date in a jar at the bottom of the sea. According to the birthday he had given himself when he emerged from captivity, he was eighty years old, and Magnus had long since stopped consulting him in day-to-day decisions, he being no longer able to discern right from wrong, sense from nonsense—or so it seemed.

When Claudia answered, "I belong to Mr. Barrett and come from his place to help Libbie with her baby," Merian grew so agitated he started to shake in his seat. Everyone watching was terrified for his health, thinking he was having a convulsive seizure. When it became clear, however, that it was anger that vibrated so through him, they grew even more afraid.

Alas, he could not voice what was in his heart to say. He ended up slurring the beginning of a single word, which was all he could manage, before losing completely the power of speech. Everyone present tried then to decipher what he had attempted to tell them.

He had little formal religion, aside from being once baptized, and he had done as much that was worldly as any man who ever lived, but what they all thought he said was *shame,* or else it was *sin.* It was hard for Magnus, who was sitting closest to him, to know which, but that it was one of them—perhaps even both—he had little doubt. He began to cast about then for some way to remedy the problem, for if he had heard correctly it was very serious business for them all.

"Do you want me to send her away?" Magnus Merian asked his old father in quiet tones, drawing nearer to hear what he would say. Merian shook, and sounded out no, and Magnus comprehended that the thing was done and sending her away would only compound it.

Jasper Merian sat up in his high-backed chair and pounded his fist weakly on the table, until his anger subsided. He had toiled there near half a century without resorting to either imprisoned or indentured hands to win a livelihood. He had given the same edict to each of his sons as he himself had lived by, hoping they would hold it as dear as he did. For the two, son and grandson, who walked on his dirt every morning and evening, it should have been obvious what free hands could do, and never miss anything for their lack of knowing chains. God had blessed them out there on that land, without ever showing too much the stronger force of His love. He saw doom now before himself.

Magnus tried to explain the logic that had brought the girl there. Seeing Merian still unsatisfied, he offered again to send her away. Merian only shook. And there could be no other word in the matter.

Jasper was exhausted from emotion and the effort required to communicate with his family. Where only a minute earlier he had seemed furious as an angel, he looked now again like a feeble old man and soon began to sleep where he sat, like a child too long awake. However, they could not dismiss his anger. On the contrary, everyone took it gravely and tried whatever they could to reverse its course and cause.

While they usually had a country preacher who came to the house every Sunday to give a sermon—as he did for all the estates with population enough—that week Adelia had everyone dress for church in town.

The four of them—Magnus, Adelia, Caleum, and Libbie—all shared a single cab and were silent on the way, none daring look at the others or mention what had happened out there. It was the middle of winter and the going was slow, but when they arrived they had been silent a long time and were happy to be in the fresh air again.

All their friends were glad to see them as well and congratulated Libbie and Caleum on their pending child. The family's mood remained solemn. Magnus, in accordance with the plan Adelia had devised, paid the preacher to have the congregation pray for them at Stonehouses. In Adelia's thinking it would wash away whatever ill any of their other decisions might have brought and bring forgiveness.

Too ashamed to tell the real need for absolution, what Magnus said, as Adelia had instructed him, was that his old father was very ill and he would like everyone to send prayers to heaven for him to recover and for his soul if he did not. The parishioners were all touched and only too eager to comply with this request, as Jasper Merian had lived so long and been there so long with them.

Nor was this ruse merely a deception: Jasper was mortally ill. He had lost as well, it seemed, the will to go on. While everyone around thought he might live to be a hundred, he had no desire in him to do so. Even before he lost the power of speech, he often claimed he had only stayed around as long as he had in order to gain back the years lost to servitude near the beginning of his life. So when Magnus and Adelia asked that everyone pray for their father, all understood they were seeking for him a final blessing.

Jasper Merian himself might have argued that the care of neither one's soul nor other properties could be left to others. As he faced his death, though, locked in a state of inarticulation, he sent one day for Caleum. When Caleum came to him Merian labored with all his breath to say what it was he wished of the young man. The syllables as they left his mouth were all disconnected, but Caleum was able to puzzle them back together. His grandfather was instructing him about the care of his home and children, and even how he should name his own.

Caleum was always eager for his grandfather's advice, but this particular instruction seemed strange, and at the time he did not fully understand it. He swore nonetheless he would abide by it. For Merian it was part of his final reckoning, as he counted out the successes and failures of his life and worried for the last time over the survival of all at Stonehouses.

Had he had voice, he might have enumerated his two natural sons, a like number of wives, and half that for grandchildren, so far as he knew; over fifty years of freedom, a quarter century, or thereabouts, in bondage at Sorel's Hundred. His own parents he never knew, but how he came to Columbia had been for a while a famous story in the watery parts of the world. He counted both, the legend it engendered and the fate he had escaped, as among his worthy possessions and achievements.

His original father, it is said, was a seaman—though his origins before or beyond that are unknown to any record—who took a wife on the African coast. When he returned to her after an adventure that took him all the way to the South China Sea, he found she had taken another man in his place. To punish her and the son she had borne, he sold both to a merchant vessel. Such was the fate of the infant Merian and his mother.

On shipboard his mother suffered from a severe illness, succumbing to fever that swept the vessel two days out. When she died they brought her infant abovedecks, where it was taken to the captain's quarters for instruction on whether it should join the mother at the bottom of the ocean, as was the custom. The captain, a man in his forties who had already made enough money to retire and was in fact plowing this route through the world for the final time, looked at the wrinkled creature they had brought to him, and for the first time on his journeys let show some small sympathy, some tiny, infinitesimal human heart. Instead of putting it where the mother was, he took the child and kept it with him for the rest of the journey, feeding it with milk from an onboard she-goat that had been intended for slaughter.

He took it ashore with him when he disembarked in Liverpool, and when he and his wife moved to the new colony some years later he took the boy with him there as well, having grown as attached to the creature as a familiar. When he cleared land for a farm the boy was with him still, and he called him little Columbian, as he seemed to take to this new place naturally. So Merian counted for himself four parents but no proper home, until he built Stonehouses with his own hands.

It was this he worried over at the end of his days when he gave his final instructions to Magnus. Their congress that afternoon was the last time Merian worried about earthly things.

When Jasper Merian finally died, the shadow on the sundial in his front garden stood exactly at noon, and all the hours of the day afterward were plunged in sadness for the residents of Stonehouses. Work on the land came to a halt. Neither the hired men nor the beasts they drove would work again before Merian's body was lowered into the earth.

Magnus was at one end of the fields when he heard, and Caleum at another, and both made their way home to the center of the land, where the women were already dressing and preparing the body.

Merian, like his sons, had been a behemoth in life, and everyone remembered him as one of the tallest men they had ever seen. But when Magnus Merian saw his naked father that afternoon he could scarcely believe how small he was, like the tiniest of babies. When he called the carpenter to take measurements for a coffin and the man confirmed his actual measurement, he told him to build the box larger than they needed, because it also needed to encase his spirit, and that was giant-sized still.

At the funeral the next day Merian would have hardly recognized a soul, as most of his peers had passed on before him. All the neighbors came out, though, and from town the daughters of Content with their husbands. Both the Methodist and Baptist preachers wanted to give the sermon, and argued among themselves about who should have the privilege. In the end both men spoke, each competing to outdo the other in oratory.

Rudolph Stanton sent over a full kitchen staff, so that no one at Stonehouses should have to work that day, as well as a group of musicians to entertain, such as was their custom, and they celebrated Merian's life until the end of the week, each man according to his fashion. It is said the main of these festivities were divided between those that were African and those that were Christian, but others spoke of strange going-ons that belonged to customs no one had ever heard of. They spoke of seeing lights, and spectral phenomena, and claimed to feel such magic as they never had before, as the ice on the lake groaned like the world coming apart.

When things finally returned to normal and work again resumed on the land, Caleum came in from the fields one evening and, without knowing what prompted him, took down the sword that hung over his mantel. There he saw the strangest thing of all. On the blade he would swear, as he stood there afright, was his grandfather, at the prow of a ship headed on a voyage of shades.

His eyes were sharp and he stood again a full head and a half taller than other men, and the boat went where he commanded. Whether in search of Ruth or Sanne or his father and mother, or even a trip more mysterious, the writings fail to say. But that Jasper Merian was a giant as great as Columbia had ever seen is well agreed upon. And that he is gone from here. Aye that is carved in steel.

s i x

Libbie Merian felt the pain of labor for the first time in mid-July that year—as if one soul had first to cross over before the other could begin its outward journey. She was sitting in the front parlor, knitting a blanket for the expected child, when her waters burst without warning. She felt her former fear descend upon her but was calm as she called Claudia, to come help her.

Claudia, who had delivered countless young, was perfectly poised as she came to her mistress's side. "It will most likely be awhile yet," she said, leading Libbie to the room they had prepared for her to give birth in when the time came. None of them could have known, though, how that time would reach and stretch—until it had taken up near two days and consumed all their hopes and fears—before putting them down to rest again.

Libbie sweated through the night, cursing all she could think of, and all who crossed her path, so unbearable was her torment and tribulation. Caleum had decamped to Stonehouses for the duration of the labor, and Adelia had in turn gone over to the new building to aid with the birth and comforting of the mother.

At Stonehouses Magnus sat up with Caleum until late in the evening, speaking of how long it had been since there were children on the land. Magnus next told stories of what Caleum was like as a boy and laid wager as to what the new arrival's character would be like. They also noted things, such as who was tallest in the family and who was strongest, and bet about the child's height and strength. When the two men went to sleep that night, each abundantly happy at the prospect of the new birth, both were certain the ordeal would be over before they awoke.

In the morning one of the women who worked on the place told them the women were still at the new building and the baby had not yet come into the world. Magnus and Caleum took the news in stride, as they went to work inspecting the fields, thinking they would be summoned before midday.

They came home that noon unbidden, as they had yet to receive word about the delivery and were grown anxious from this lack of news. In their concern they decided to go over to the other house to see what the matter was, even if it was not their place to do so.

When they arrived they were told nothing was wrong; it was only proving an extraordinarily long labor, and they should perhaps better return to the other place. Libbie, flush-faced and exhausted, was in the throes of the greatest pain, and when Caleum peeked into the room where she was, he could see this, and became filled with apprehension. "You are very brave," he said to her.

When she saw his doting face, Libbie cursed him for being there and added further obscenities, ending with, "It was an evil hour I met thee."

At nine o'clock that evening her torment finally ceased. The child who was so long in coming into the world decided at last to join it, and Caleum was called back to the birthing house. When Claudia came to summon him, though, instead of joy he felt a passing second of dread, like a fast-moving cloud that plunged him temporarily into shadow. He found himself hoping nothing was the matter with his wife, but, as he walked through the crowd of women in his house and approached the room where his wife was, he heard a loud, wailing cry that filled him with sadness and hope.

Caleum's fears all left him then and he was overjoyed, as he could not have imagined just hours earlier. When he held the child he had no sight for anything else. It was a feeling unlike any he had known, as he looked on the boy's shriveled new face, like a bud on a vine that had yet to fully open. The child was so small Caleum could fit him in one of his outstretched hands, though he was careful not to do so for danger of dropping him.

At last he turned to Libbie and stroked her face as she recovered from the long labor. "How are you feeling?" he asked, looking at her where she rested.

He could tell how much her ordeal had taken from her, but her dread at least had lifted and she was no longer afraid. Too tired to speak, she merely smiled at her husband.

As they gazed at the child together, what sprang first to Caleum's mind was that, coming so close after Merian's death, the boy must somehow be blessed by the departed. To honor the connection, he suggested they name him accordingly.

Libbie nodded in assent when he told her. "I think Jasper is fitting. But I also had in mind John."

"That is also a good name." Caleum negotiated, wanting to give her what she wanted. "We can give him both."

So they named their first child together John Jasper, and Magnus and Adelia were nearly as pleased as the parents to be made grandparents, or granduncle and grandaunt, such as it was. To give thanks, Magnus declared the next day a holiday for all of Stonehouses, so they might celebrate Libbie's motherhood.

How long he stayed with them though, or, rather, how short a while, was soon the cause of great desolation. The child for whom it had been so difficult to gain life only held on to it until the end of his first week, when they found him dead atop his mother's breast.

"He seemed perfectly healthy," Adelia said with despair, coming over from the other house after she learned the boy had passed away, "but God strikes and snatches what He will."

"It is true," Claudia agreed, as she tried to coax the child from its mother's arms. "And for all His own reasons He did not give the boy this day as He did the ones before it." She had seen so many little ones whisked back away in her work, she knew whereof she spoke.

Libbie, though, shunned Claudia's hands, refusing to let go or relinquish the boy's lifeless body. She went on holding her baby in her arms the rest of that day.

Caleum had the opposite response. Pretending a coarseness that had known greater suffering than was in his history, he refused to look on the corpse at all, saying there was no reason to glance back.

He sent word over to the carpenter to come make a box for the body and instructed one of the overseers to dig a grave in the far valley, which was their graveyard at Stonehouses.

So its ranks swelled, from two who were very old—and one very old for its kind—to three, and their average age fell considerably.

Everyone was pained to witness such misfortune befall a couple so young, but Magnus, in his grief, thought it to be more than just bad luck. "Somebody cursed us," he said, speaking roughly. "I seen it among the slaves in Virginia. Somebody is trying to punish Stonehouses."

In his mind no one was above suspicion, and he soon began to sow his dark fears all around, so that everyone began to regard the others nearby with distrust. Each listed the possible culprits in his head, and, though no one had real grievance, any could have been envious of them at Stonehouses.

Understanding he would never sort out one person, but that ultimately nothing less than their future safety depended on acting swiftly, Magnus did something very rash immediately after the funeral.

On the other side of the valley was a slave called Sam Day—who was married to Effie, a free woman who worked as a maid in the barns of Stonehouses—and who was rumored to be very powerful with roots and the like. He served not only the other slaves but, through intermediaries, much of the free population as well—either when something happened that the doctor could not cure or when they were taken with superstition because of something no one could explain and turned to him. When the child died, although it was not uncommon for such to happen, it was him Magnus sent for in his grief.

When Sam heard from Magnus's messenger what had happened at Stonehouses, he sent word back, first with questions and finally with the prognosis that the new house had not been properly blessed when they built it. It was easy enough to remedy, he said, but the ritual must be performed by him in person.

"Well, where is he?" Magnus asked the boy he had sent on the errand.

"They don't allow him to leave his master's place," the boy answered.

Desperate, Magnus resolved to find a solution. The next day he left Stonehouses early in the morning, saying only that he had business beyond its gates. Where he went then was to see Sam Day's master, a man named Michael Smith.

Smith, being Christian, detested Sam's practice of magic, and when Magnus showed up, saying he had come to see him about his slave Sam, Smith grew irritable just to hear the man's name.

"I would sell that troublemaker Sam Day for the next hundred pounds I saw," he said.

"I just wanted to see if it was possible to hire him from you for the season."

"Hire him? For what?" Smith asked. "You could find better workers among your womenfolk."

"That may be so, but I'm short of hands this season, Mr. Smith, and they say he is a strong-bodied worker. Plus his woman is at Stonehouses, which I figured would make it an easy adjustment for him. I have ready cash."

"If I hired him out to you, Magnus, I'd never know the end of it," Smith said. "He would run, I swear to you he would. For a hundred pounds, though, I would sell him clean and free of any claims."

A hundred pounds was a very good price for a man in his prime, and Magnus looked at Smith to see whether he was only talking idly. When he saw Smith meant what he said, Magnus made a counterproposal. Though it was never his intention to do so, the low price coupled with his own need overtook him and all his higher principles almost before he knew it. "I can give you seventy for him," he said, although he knew it was less than any man was worth.

"A hundred is my price," Smith repeated. "You say you need a man and have ready cash. You'll never get a better price than that on a slave good as Sam."

"It seems like he causes you a lot of trouble, Mr. Smith. You should just let me take him off your hands," reasoned Magnus, who had grown expert at bartering in the marketplace each year. When Smith moved down ten, he offered to close the deal. "Since we're only that far apart let's just split the difference."

"It is done," said Smith, though he did not shake. He only rang a bell and instructed the servant who appeared to go fetch Sam Day from out his indigo fields.

* * *

236

Sam had been taking a much-needed break from work, resting his head on a cool rock in a little gully that hid him from sight, when he heard footsteps approaching his resting place. He stood up and looked around to see Smith's boy from the house, calling his name.

"What you want with me?" Sam asked, taking up his work so it seemed he had never ceased. He was immediately tired out again, though, and took out his annoyance on the boy.

"Master Smith want you to come round right now," the boy told him.

"Well, what he want with me, boy?" Sam asked with irritation. "You too thick to know that?"

"He sold you, Sam!" the boy cried. "He sending you away!"

"Boy, stop meddling with me and get from out of here," Sam barked, raising one of his hands, which was permanent black from the indigo, to shoo the boy off. When the boy left, he went back to the spot where he had been resting and took back up his pillowstone.

No sooner had he laid down again than he heard one of the overseers call out his name.

"I'm coming right there, sir," Sam answered, wondering for the first time whether what the boy had said was true.

He was on the verge of panic as he approached the overseer, fearing he might be at the start of a trip to another unknown place, where no one knew him and he was only currency in a transaction that satisfied everyone except him.

"What you need, Mr. Paul?" he asked, looking at the overseer.

"It finally happened." The man whistled. "He finally sold your arse, Sam. Go on up to the house now and meet your new master." Never an admirer of Sam's, the other man showed just the hint of laughter at the edges of his mouth, like tiny shards of glass, as he turned and walked away.

The spores of panic in Sam's head continued to grow, as he began to wish for an alternate fate. "Can I go round and say my good-byes to everybody first?" he called after him. "He can't just lift me up like that and move me on."

"Mr. Smith wants you at the house now," Paul told him again. "Seems to me, if I had a master and he called, I wouldn't try to do nothing but go find out what he wanted."

Sam cursed under his breath and glowered as he went up to the back door of the house and announced himself—not that his arrival could have gone unnoticed. Throughout the plantation the news had spread, and eyes watched him from every corner of the land as he mounted the stairs.

Mr. Smith came around about ten minutes later with a tall Negro man, ten years or so older than Day. "Sam, I want you to meet your new owner, Magnus Merian."

Sam looked at both men standing in front of him, as he comprehended what had transpired. "Oh, good goddamn Jesus why is y'all doing this to me again?" he asked aloud.

Smith hit Sam before he knew it, knocking him flat into the dirt. As he lay sprawled there, Sam knew better than to get up too fast. When he did rise, though, he heard Magnus Merian telling Master Smith, "Thank you, Mr. Smith, but I can manage my own men." Sam allowed himself to think he might have lucked and found a better master when he heard that, until Magnus approached him.

"Get your ass up and apologize to Mr. Smith," he said.

He could not believe what was happening and was no longer sure which of the two had actually clapped him. It was as if the entire world had reversed itself, until he could not tell the black man from the white one. It wasn't surprise at a black master, but that he was used to being deferred to by Negroes because of his powers, and never thought another one would make him bend his head without the use of force. When he looked at Magnus, though, who still had the long memory of slavery and how a certain type was handled in Virginia, he saw something fearful there and made haste to do as he had been commanded.

"I'm sorry, Smith," Sam said, looking his old owner square in the face. He turned to Magnus and added, "I apologize to you too, Master Merian."

Looking at Sam then, contrite and confused, Smith was half tempted to offer Magnus his money back. In the end, however, something told him Sam was putting him on somehow, and he was relieved to be rid of the worrisome slave. "It has been a pleasure conducting business with you, Magnus," he said. "If there is ever anything I can help you with further, please do not hesitate to let me know."

"Thank you," Magnus answered. "I imagine everything will go just fine from here."

Sam had, of course, heard about the Merians long before he left with Magnus that afternoon, but he had little idea of what they were truly like or, more important, how they treated their men. He had never seen a Negro act with a white man as Magnus had with Smith, and he was uncertain and afraid he might do something to upset this new master and get clapped again, so when they left, he followed at a respectful distance until they reached the wagon.

"You climb in and ride back there," Magnus said, motioning to the bed of the vehicle.

Sam pulled himself up into the wagon and waited for the chains to be secured around him, as they had been the first time he was sold. When Magnus continued on to the front of the wagon and took up the reins, Sam could not hold his tongue. "Master Merian, ain't you gone chain me?" he asked.

"I hadn't figured to," Magnus replied. "You planning on running?"

"No," Sam said, then added with a hesitant pride, "but I could."

"As long as it stay at speculation, Sam, we'll be just fine," Magnus answered.

Master and slave then began the journey back to Stonehouses.

As they drove through the hill country Magnus was fired by guilt. He wanted to tell Sam that he had not intended to come and tear him from his known life and meant even less to cause him harm. He only wanted to hire his services as an herbman, because his own house had been cursed. As he drove, though, he knew he had miscalculated and could no longer ask for the the man's help. He owned him now, and if he was going to keep Sam from running over him he would have to be absolute, which, in his position, meant not explaining more than the other needed to know.

"You will like it at Stonehouses," Magnus said. "Of course, it is only a temporary situation for you."

"What do you mean by temporary, Master Merian?" Sam asked, in fearful confusion.

"I mean that I intend to make you free after the season," Magnus said, as he could not force the kind of work he needed from Sam or otherwise coerce the spirit.

"What happen to me after that?" Sam asked. "Where I'm supposed to go, Master Merian?"

Magnus had not reflected on it before, but he knew it would never do for him to set the likes of Sam Day free in Berkeley. The rest of the town, black and white, would surely turn on him. "Well, we'll figure something out, Sam," Magnus said, "soon as the harvest is over."

Each man then was flax-hearted and silent, as they made their way through the country, each wondering what he had gotten into, and what would become of him.

Lord, what have I done? Magnus thought to himself, knowing he had purchased another soul and now owned him and all his burden. There was, he knew, no way to alleviate the consequences of that.

What happen next? Sam wondered as the wagon rolled through the unknown countryside, reminding him of his original trip there, the only time before he had been anywhere other than his natural home.

When they arrived back at Stonehouses, Magnus drove up next to the barn and stopped the wagon. "This is it," he announced. "This is where you'll be staying." For he still could not admit to himself it was the man's new home.

If Sam had been impressed by Magnus before he was even more so now, as he could see plainly his new master was wealthier than his old one.

"Where I'm supposed to sleep, Master Merian?" Sam asked, inspecting the barn, then looking deep into the country for the slave cabins.

"Down with the rest of the hired men," Magnus said, calling for a boy to show Sam where that was. "I'll send for you later," Magnus told him, as he himself turned to go into the house.

Inside, the first person he saw was Effie, whom he hurried past, making his way upstairs. He did something then that he had not done since his very first days at Stonehouses; he went into his bedroom and drew the curtains until it was dark and fell asleep during the middle of the day.

He woke up to find Adelia sitting next to him.

"Are you all right?" she wanted to know.

"Adelia, I bought a man today," he told her, sitting up and looking her in the eyes.

"So I hear," she answered, stroking his forehead. "What happened?"

"It was not on purpose. I will let him loose, just as soon as I figure out how to do it."

"You'll figure out something," Adelia said.

"Where is he now?" Magnus asked.

"I think Caleum put him to work already."

Magnus was thankful at least to hear the younger man had done so sensible a thing. That evening at dinner he tried to conceal his own thoughts as he asked his nephew how the day had gone with the harvest. Caleum, sensing his uncle's true concern, replied that no other healthy body lazed about while the sun was up, so he saw no reason why Sam Day should be allowed to either. "Slave or no slave, he has to put in an honest day's work."

It was impeccable logic, but Magnus knew he had done something gravely wrong, and they had not yet seen the end of suffering for that year.

"I'm going to turn that man free, just as soon as I lay a plan for what to do with him," he said to his family. No one at the table objected to his words, though no one else thought it was quite so dire as he.

seven

When the harvest months arrived Magnus began estimating the yield from his lands, and it looked to be slightly more than the year before, which had been a good season all around, and this pleased him despite the earlier events in the summer.

Sam Day watched the harvest process with disbelief, as the men all arrived in the morning of their own accord, and only very few had disappeared from the fields by the time the sun reached midday. There was no lash and no prison for idlers either. When he asked one of the other men about it, he was told they were paid for their work according to how much they gathered, and besides this wage there was also a prize at the end of the season for the man who had pulled in the most. "It is a solid gold coin, Sam, worth I couldn't say how much, but, if it's yours, I doubt you would have to work the whole next year."

Sam Day had never touched money before in his life. He was paid for his farm work not at all, and for his root work in kind—mostly favors of food and cloth so that he never went lacking for what he needed, especially as old Master Smith had been on the stingy side with both cornmeal and shoe leather. Sam, though, had managed to live like the priest of a well-devoted temple, and he carried himself in accordance with this authority of position whenever he was called on as a healer. In his other labors, by contrast, he was more humble, even to the point of being lazy, as he resented having to do anything other than his born calling.

When he heard about that gold coin for the man who was best at harvesting the fields, though, he could not help but daydream about it. He thought, if he won it, he would first get something for Effie; then, if there was any money beyond that, he imagined to himself he might use it to have a great party that would last the better part of a week. He got himself so worked up with the idea that he showed up on time next morning, without having to be sent for after the others went out into the fields.

Having never worked in earnest before, though, he was not so quick as the other men and could barely walk on his tender feet by the end of the day, as they were burned and bleeding from use against the thorny weeds and hot ground. Being so unused to physical exertion, he could not help but comment on his condition that night when the workers gathered for supper. "How much you think that gold coin could be worth to get all of us killing ourselves for it?"

"It isn't just the money, Sam, but the sport as well," one of them answered him.

"I see," he replied, without being convinced of anything other than his own pain at that particular moment.

When he went to sleep that night, his joints were still aflame from the day's work and he thought he would rather be paid in kind for divining than gold for physical labor. In his dreams that night, which were wild and deep, he was dressed all in finery, and people came from far and wide to seek him out and ask his favor. He was seated throughout on a claw-footed chair, and whenever anyone approached he would listen from a distance to what they had to say but not allow them to come any nearer to him.

"I dreamed I was a king last night," he told any who would listen, as they ate breakfast early the next morning. "I was sitting on a throne in the middle of my country, passing out solid gold coins to all my subjects."

They all laughed at him. "What did you call your kingdom, Sam?"

"Laugh all you want," he said. "I just wanted to let you know fair that I had a vision about winning that coin, so the rest of y'all can stop trying for it."

The men were still filled with mirth as they returned to the tobacco, but Sam was a proud man, and his dream had infected his imagination. Their laughter only raised his cholera and determination to win.

When Sam returned to the fields the next day he put himself back into his labors as if his life was at stake. No one was laughing at him by the time the sun went down on that day. In a week they had all legitimate respect for him, as he stripped stack after stack of the broad green leaves, and by the end of the month they allowed he might even have a fair chance at the coin.

The only man among them who begrudged these efforts was one called Angus Carson, who had won the prize the year before, and was counting on winning the money again to see his family through the winter. "He'll win it over my dead body," Carson said, once he saw the threat from Sam Day was real. "It will be the same day he takes food from my little ones' mouths."

As they went into the final week of harvest, which according to the ledger Magnus kept was a fortnight earlier than the year before, the other men around them had all chosen sides and laid wagers as to which of these two headstrong men would win the prize. At supper each night that week the contestants would occupy opposite ends of the table, with his followers seated beside him, attending to his needs. In the middle of the bench were two empty chairs to keep distance between the two camps, and they hectored each other from across the divide.

At his end of the table Angus sat bare-chested, drinking bock and otherwise silent as his men boasted of his exploits.

"Angus Carson is the strongest man in all His Majesty's realm," they taunted. "He's also the fastest and will never lose, especially not to the likes of one like you. It's folly, Sam Day—nay, madness's mischief, if not the thing itself—to think ye can compete against him."

Sam Day governed the other end of the board, looking to all like a leader among his men, but he too was silent, allowing them to speak their minds on his behalf.

"Sam Day has been blessed with the gift of fore prophecy and can see well into the future," they called and countered. "What he saw there last time he looked was Angus Carson coming to borrow a shilling."

Thus were all the men in good spirits as the autumn rain started to come in and they hurried to draw the harvest to a close. Each could look forward then not only to his pay but also his profit from betting, as none imagined losing what he had wagered, and they boasted of it each chance they got.

Such was not the case for the chief adversaries, who eyed each other stealthily around camp, each trying to measure his opponent. Angus, at first, had thought Sam Day all blowhard and nothing hale about him, due to the slightness of his physique. Then he saw the work the man did and thought perhaps he was aided by the harpies and demons it was said he could conjure at his beckon and call.

Sam Day, on his end, had seen men bigger than Angus Carson, and he would even bet half the men in the barracks of Stonehouses were stronger than his foe, but he had never seen a man want something so bad as Carson seemed to when his fingers reached out to harvest the plants. Even his own friends said of him, "He's stubborn as he is mean, and the only thing that loves him, besides his wife and children, seems to be tobaccy leaves." For no sooner had he fingered one than it seemed to be in his stack, as he moved down the rows like a drowning man who had figured out a way to harvest air.

Despite their different styles, the two men were dead even in the counting when they rose the last morning of the harvest.

It was an hour ahead of the sun when they came to the communal table, where all the men ate before heading into the fields. That morning, in place of hominy, the table was piled high with bacon and biscuits for each of them to take and eat his fill, but instead of feeding their own gnawing hunger all the others held back and let Sam and Angus in front of them—even the men who herded the cattle or worked the rice deferred.

Magnus and Caleum, who always ate with the men on the final day of the cropping, were the only others seated at the table besides the two contestants.

"I looked at the ledger this morning," said Magnus, who always loved being among the men in the fields at that time of year. "This looks to be the best reaping we had all decade, if we gather just a bit more."

"How far short are we?" asked Caleum.

"Only a couple hundred pounds off four years ago."

"I remember that year. It would be something to outdo."

"It sure would, and if it happens I think I might just make the harvest prize double," Magnus went on, looking at Caleum but speaking so all could hear. "What would you think of that, Sam?"

From his side of the table Sam stopped chewing and looked toward Magnus. If he had heard the same thing only a month before he would have thought Magnus was funning him, but now he thought only of the gold and let another coin settle beside the first in his mind's eye. "I think we better get to reaping."

Dawn had broken by then and stood rosy and mysterious at the edge of the horizon. As it spread, it grew bright and golden, touching everything at Stonehouses evenly and portending well for the final gathering of the year.

After breakfast the men all stood from where they sat and looked out at the neat, even rows of plants, which were nearly bare from earlier pickings—except the tender leaves at their tips that are always last to ripen.

Angus Carson looked out over the rows, thought of the new prize, and said to one of his men, "It's not so much a doubling the old one as it is that I'm going to whup his arse twice now."

The two rivals then started at opposite sides of a single row; they could have looked each other in the eyes over the tops of the plants, if they had so chosen. Each man's hand went out and each retrieved a leaf, being careful not to harm it, then stacked it in a cart that went alongside each of them to keep the new leaf from getting bruised; nor did they look up from their work.

By the time they were halfway down the row, both men were covered with sweat and each forgot about the other. They concentrated on the bright green plants and thought about the weight of gold that would rest in his hand at the end of the day.

Nor did they stop to eat at lunchtime, but merely called to have water brought out to them. By three in the afternoon the heat of August was unbearable, and no one would have been surprised to see them both fall down from exhaustion. They kept at their work, though, determined to have both prize and the honor that would go with it.

At six o'clock everyone else came in from the fields, and the plants themselves stood bare—save the final two rows, which were still divided between the two, but no longer evenly as before. While Angus Carson started at the top of one, Sam Day was already midway down the other.

Angus, drenched in sweat, saw him in the far distance and began to quicken his pace, though where he found the energy and stamina no one could tell, but as he looked at Sam's back he hated all he saw and worked as if moving through the plants quickly would bring him closer to annihilating the object of his ire. As he worked his rage grew, until he found himself inventing new categories of it to indulge his intemperate passion. I hate the African, he began. I have always hated his tongue, his dress, his manner. Nay, he has no manners. I detest men who eat their corn in rows instead of columns, he added, until he could truthfully say the problem with the world was Africans who ate their corn lengthwise instead of going all the way round as was proper.

Sam in his row could sense Angus gaining, but from pride refused to turn around and look. Nor did he have the energy to spare. He willed his hands to keep moving, though they were already cut and bleeding from his efforts.

A gold coin for Sam Day, he said to himself to heal the pain, and the other I'll spend just on Effie.

He could see the last tobacco leaf at the end of the row and willed himself to keep moving. He thought of the freedom he would gain with it—to be master and overlord of his self unbound. He thought of the land he would buy and the house he would put up there. He thought of the crops he would grow, one field just for the herbs he used in the practice of his religion and medicine. He thought of the first home he lost and what it would be never to stand in danger of losing so again.

When he reached the last plant he heard a great cry go up as he put his black hand out to clasp it. He broke the stem and lifted the wide leaf, feeling victorious and expansive. As he turned to stack it with the others, though, he saw Angus Carson there, smiling in the periphery of his vision. The cheers belonged all to Angus's men and those of Sam's who had turned their sentiments toward the winner of the race—as some men inevitably do after a contest has been decided—but it was false noise as the winner was he who harvested the most weight, not who was fastest.

As he sat down and rested, his woman, Effie, came over and kissed him on the cheek, proud that he had done so well. Sam, feeling only his defeat, brushed her kisses away.

The curers came round then to collect the last of the leaf, weighing it, and working quickly to string it all onto poles. On the giant scale the leaves crested and ebbed, before finally coming to rest as the balance groaned, then settled. The results were impossible to tell beforehand, for everyone except Angus and Sam themselves, as the contest was nearly dead even according to the scales. Both men had gathered near twelve stones in weight, but Angus had pulled a dozen and one.

Sam sat down on his haunches in the dirt and took a long drink of water from a dipper. As he looked up, he saw a shadow looming over him. It was Angus Carson, and he moved quickly, lest Carson kick him where he sat.

"You're a hell of a man for one who never did this work before," was all Angus said, extending his big maw of a hand.

Sam did not want to accept his defeat again, but he shook anyway, though he did not speak.

By then the evening sun had all but disappeared from the horizon, and there was little left of its light except the last red-golden rays. The men added to this the light of bonfires, which they had set up all around the camp to mark the end of their taskwork. Magnus watched it all from astride his favorite horse, who was called Annabel, as he had watched the harvest all day long. He dismounted then when the results were settled and called for silence as he reached in his pocket for the coins.

"Angus, you proved yourself once again to be the best worker of all my men and, I would wager, equal to any in the entire colony."

He gave him his prize, which Angus measured in his palm with relief and satisfaction before slipping one into each of his pockets for safety.

"The contest this year was better than any other, though, and it would be a shame if that went unacknowledged," Magnus went on, going into his purse again. "Sam, this is yours," he concluded, "for making a show that in any other year, or on any other farm, would have won you two." He then handed Sam a single glittering gold coin, which seemed to him as he received it to slip through the light like a fish through a stream of water.

He held it in his palm for a good long time, examining all the strange letters and markings embossed upon it, which were all indecipherable to him except the image of a crown. At last he closed his fingers around the warm metal. He thought how much he had done to get it, and how it had excited and divided all the men in the barracks.

"What do you suppose it be worth?" he asked Effie, finally putting it away and turning to his woman.

"Why, Sam, it be worth a whole lot," she said. "A whole lot."

The men all congratulated him on his great showing as the night wore on, but the excitement had faded from the air, and to rekindle it someone had started up a series of games. First there were to be foot races, then wrestling, and someone else suggested boxing, but Magnus vetoed that idea, knowing it would surely get too far out of hand.

When they began the wrestling, Caleum ached to join in the trial, as he had with his friends when he was younger, knowing he could defeat any other man there, but Magnus also put a halt to that notion, claiming the reason for his decision should be self-evident. Caleum accepted his uncle's authority but only reluctantly, because he loved few things so much as a contest and knew no one could beat him.

"If you did win, you would rob the men of a prize, and if you didn't win it would just never do," Magnus said to him, as he watched the two final contestants circle each other inside the ring of men.

Magnus then left that circle and made his way through the bonfires and the music to seek out his slave Sam Day. When he found him, at the edge of the gathering, where he was drinking rum punch, he drew him away from the crowd, saying only that he would like a moment of his time. It pleased Sam to be spoken to this way, and, though he was much absorbed in the other games, he went willingly with Magnus to hear what his master had to say to him.

They walked together away from the others, and Magnus was not commanding and aloof as usual but waited so that Sam was at his side and stayed there as they made their way across the cow-shorn grass of the home meadow.

"Sam, I should never have taken you from the home you knew," Magnus said, without looking at him, as they rested at the top of a rise. "I had a problem, and I let that get the better of what I knew to be right, so we have some business to settle between us."

Sam listened without saying anything, but he was surprised to hear Magnus admit his fault, as that was not usual to hear from men who owned other men.

"I told you when I brought you here you could go at the end of the season," Magnus reminded him, as they surveyed the land out to the edge of their sight and the darkness beyond that. "I didn't know how to do it sooner, on account of not knowing what the town would think of me buying slaves just to turn them loose. You'll have your wages, though, Sam, same as everyone else; then you can set up on your own. I suppose somewhere out here on my land."

"You would give me a part of your land?" Sam asked incredulously.

"Not give, Sam," Magnus corrected him. "Sell."

"Master Merian," Sam said, looking his owner in the eye, "I know what kind of problems plagued you before, and I don't blame you too much for what you did. We both know, though, that if people think you buying slaves just to turn em free, they run both of us out from Berkeley."

"I thought about it, Sam," Magnus interrupted him, "and I think it's what's best. I can grapple with the consequences. The only other thing is for you to head out with the caravans at the end of the month, and that's still a hard road."

Sam looked at Magnus and understood what he meant. "I know ain't nothing free to a certain way of thinking," Sam said. "How much you think a plot of land cost me?"

"I'll think of something fair," Magnus answered him. The two of them then stood looking out over the country. "There's a place out that way that might suit you just fine," Magnus went on. "Good land too if you got a mind to do a little work, which I know you do."

When he was Sam Day's age Magnus had already been free for more than a decade, and he had been free now almost as long as he was captive. He did not know if Sam could learn everything he needed so late in life, and to manage his own place instead of just taking on itinerant work. The thought of him and Effie out there by themselves gave him pause, as he knew how difficult it would be, but he was willing to do it because he knew he had to restore the balance he had upset. "Tell you what, Sam, I'll give it to you for your wages from this season," Magnus said. "Then you'll still have enough to start out with, and you can do some work around Stonehouses during the fall to earn a little extra."

"Let me weigh it over, Master Merian," Sam said, reckoning the prospect of turning into a farmer. "It's not something I ever had a notion of before, so I need some time to wrap my mind about it and talk to Effie."

"It's good terms," Magnus said, without telling him the only thing he himself had ever got such good terms for was Sam Day himself.

"I never thought getting sold away would work out like this," Sam said to him.

"You know, I was once a slave, Sam," Magnus said to him, trying to express what he felt just then.

"Couldn't nobody never have told me that."

"Well, I was."

When Sam looked at Magnus at that moment, his master was a mystery to him: that a man who had been a slave could take one for himself. He did understand, though, why he was being set free.

"I'ma put a blessing on this place for you, to keep anything wrong from ever happening to it again," he promised, having learned by then the original reason he was called there in the first place. It was his word, not as one grateful returning a favor, but as a doctor and expert in the workings of complex roots and hidden phenomena.

eight

~~

It started raining the first of September that year, and rain was still descending violently two weeks later when the western caravans set out from Berkeley. Three-quarters of the way back in the train, Sam Day and Effie drove a used wagon he had bought cheap from the wheelwright, because it tilted a little more to one side than the other and there was no way of fixing the condition. It was drawn by two piebald hinnies he had also gotten a deal on, who were the strangest animals he thought he had ever seen. They pulled his wagon without complaint, though, and he held the reins, guiding them westward with all the provisions he had bought for what he hoped would be his best chance in life. Nor did he have illusions it would be anything but difficult. He knew as well there was no real place for him anywhere else anymore, except that he might make one in a new country. Effie would go wherever her man did, but she was powerful afraid to be giving up Berkeley and Stonehouses, and she had heard many frightening tales about the western lands.

She knew in the end that her husband would never be satisfied to live as a near fugitive in Berkeley, and there could be no other life, and but few opportunities, for them there, with everyone knowing them from before, no matter his new status as a freedman.

Before they left, Sam gave Caleum a bag filled with a powerful concoction of plants and animal bones, with which to soothe the ground his house was set upon. "Every time you break the earth or otherwise interrupt the natural world, you have to heal it again," Sam had said, walking around the house until he found the spot he was looking for.

"You bury this right here, and things will be back to how they're sup-posed to be." In truth he had felt very strong energies coming from the land there from the moment he arrived and was not sure his craft was powerful enough to placate it. But he knew they had always had good fortune there at Stonehouses, and eventually whatever had been upset would be restored, as things always go back to being in the right bal-ance. Still, he wished sincerely his charm would speed that process along for them, for he truly wanted nothing but blessing for the people of Stonehouses.

Whether it was only bad luck or a curse placed upon them, Caleum and Libbie's problems did not end with Sam's interdiction—but they weighed a bit less heavily upon them that entire autumn and winter, and the rift that had developed since the death of their child, keeping man from wife and vice versa, began at last to abate. The good spirits of the harvest, along with the shift in seasons themselves, made them feel closer again, and they began to spend the still temperate nights sitting out-of-doors together on a bench that looked out over the lake, talking until the cool hours of early night.

They went to bed on these nights very much enchanted with each other, as they had been when they were newlyweds. "We will have another child," Caleum said to her that fall, after the caravans departed but before winter had set in. "You will see. We will have a whole house full of them."

"We will have what it pleases God to allow us," Libbie said solemnly.

In her heart she wanted the same thing he did and felt great affec-tion for him when he spoke so boldly, wanting for their house to be filled. She dared not say so, though. She was no longer fearful of birth, as she had been on her wedding day, but she had new apprehensions about motherhood, including that it was possible she would never know its particular satisfactions, and so began to treat everything to do with chil-dren with superstition. So much so that when she first suspected she might be pregnant again she kept the news to herself for as long as pos-sible, which was a great many weeks. At last, as they cleaned the kitchen one day, Claudia turned to her mistress without further remark and said, "You pregnant, Miss Libbie. You might better sit down."

Libbie wondered then how long Claudia had known of her condi-tion, or whether she had only just figured it out. Whichever the case, she knew her state would soon betray itself and thought it best to tell Caleum before it did, lest he accuse her of ill intent.

When she revealed her pregnancy in their bedchamber that night, Caleum was elated and showed none of her caution. "You see, it's just as I said it would be," he said. "And so close to Christmas!"

"Please, husband, don't blaspheme," was her hushed answer to his unchecked joy.

Adelia and Magnus were also reserved in their expression of emotion, having been cut down before by tragedy. "Perhaps Libbie should take to bed," Adelia suggested to Claudia, when the winter holidays drew near. "She must be careful not to overexert herself."

Claudia herself was of the opinion that hard work in the months before led to an easy labor, but in the end she acquiesced and Libbie was confined to her bed as the holiday preparations took place all around her. At first she protested against her idleness, but soon grew content being waited on by Claudia; as the smells of baking reached her, she began to feel as she had as a little girl in her parents' house before Christmas.

This bred in turn its own nostalgia and melancholy, and in order to keep it at bay she began to embroider a scene of the first Christmas she could remember. She was a little girl and her brother Eli had just been born. Her young parents were filled with merriment; in her mind's eye she saw them both smiling broadly. It was mild that year and she remembered everything being green on Christmas Day—not only the tree in their yard but also the landscape all around them. She received for gifts that Christmas a doll with a lovely dress and a small, bright round ball of a kind she had never seen before. When she held it before her face its smell tickled her nose, making her shriek. "Papa what is it?" she asked excitedly.

He told her it was called an orange, and that she was supposed to eat it.

She laughed gaily at this. It was so lovely she was drawn to taste it, but she could not imagine ruining such a wonderful gift. Instead, she carried it around with her doll, until eventually her mother remarked that her father had gone to great bother to get it for her, and if she didn't eat it soon it would rot, leaving her neither toy nor fruit.

She sat down dutifully and, after her mother started the process, finished peeling the rind from the flesh. She was then careful to remove all the fuzzy white strings and divided the sections evenly. When she brought one of them to her mouth and bit into it, the thing was like a secret in her mouth. She could not believe she had carried it around with her for so long without knowing what it truly was. As if to make up for being such a slow learner she devoured the first six sections hungrily, as if she had never eaten before. With the last four slices, though—there were ten in all she remembered, for she had counted carefully—she became miserly again. She lined them all in a row on the kitchen table and allowed herself one every thirty minutes, so they lasted her almost until suppertime. The last hardened slice, though, she shared with her doll, thinking to be generous with her new treasure.

When she was done she went and thanked her father again for the orange. "It was the best thing I ever ate," she told him. He smiled at her and reached into his pocket, from which he pulled out another.

"I was saving this, but since you like them so much why don't you have it," he offered. She could not believe her good fortune but took the orange from him and ran around the room, laughing in happiness.

This was the scene she tried to embroider as she lay in bed: a family at the holidays and a little girl eating an orange. It was very difficult, as the orange always seemed too big and the girl too small, but when Caleum saw it he proclaimed her work so well done he could smell the fruit itself on the fabric. He always loved her creations and found they put him in whatever mood she had hoped to invoke.

"You're the best wife a man could have," he said, sitting down beside the bed. "All will be safe."

She smiled at him, as she thought how one day she must create a scene that was not only from her own head but from their life together there at Stonehouses. Alas, it would not be one from that winter.

With the exception of Christmas Day itself, she stayed in bed through the holidays until the first of the New Year—though she counted it bad luck to be idle on New Year's Day. She ate the food Claudia prepared for her in the kitchen, and took her medicine as well. When Adelia visited she said she thought the girl looked in far better health than she had that time last year, and left thinking it only required patience before all was over and well.

Caleum, living with her every day, was more anxious by then but careful not to let his wife see his growing worry. There was, after all, nothing that had triggered his concern except her own, and his wanting everything to turn out as it should. As late as the third week of the year he could still hope this would be the case—things turning out as they should. However, he entered the house one day, after a morning spent out in the barns and curing sheds, to hear his wife's diminishing sobs and Claudia saying, "There there, mistress."

It seemed to him then he could hear a woman crying in each earthly direction outside the window, and her maid with her, replying with the same consolation. "There, there, mistress."

He went to his wife's room, where he found her no longer in bed but seated in a chair next to it. "What happened, my Libbie?" he asked. "What has gone wrong?"

Claudia looked between the two of them, then hurried from the room. Caleum looked after her retreating form and felt an unpleasantness in the bowels of his stomach.

"The baby," Libbie said. Her tears had dwindled by now, so there was scarcely any emotion on her face. "I have lost another child."

When she was finished speaking Caleum heard echoing in his ears again Claudia's words from when he first entered the house. "There, there, mistress." His first gesture was to give his wife a solacing embrace. His mind, however, immediately began to race with suspicions. "It is not your fault," he consoled. "Only bad luck."

When she heard him say this, she knew that was not the case either; it had nothing to do with luck at all. "It is simply a woman's lot," she retorted. "Just as it is sometimes her lot to have children, she sometimes must lose them."

Caleum had never heard his wife speak so hard before, and his impulse was to try to shield her from her own words; to say she did not mean what she had said. However, looking at her withdrawn face, which was like some ancient stone mask, he thought it better to hold his tongue for the time being, deferring to her in the matter. "Is there anything you need?" he asked.

"No," she answered, looking at him tenderly for the first time during that conversation. "Let me rest now. Everything will be as it is supposed to be."

He took comfort in her words as he left the room, thinking she certainly knew best, and if it was what she thought then all would indeed be as it was supposed to be. As he sat alone in the darkened parlor, though, drinking a glass of rum, which for him was very rare since his days as a schoolboy, his comfort began to leave him and his mind to grow cold. In each direction he turned then, he heard again his wife's cry.

When Claudia came to ask what he wished to eat for supper, he looked at her distantly and the machine of his fears began to whir and hum. He was not a hard-hearted man, but felt very passionately for what had befallen his wife, and that passion found then a place to alight—before he even knew that it was searching. "It's a shame about your mistress," he said.

"Yes, sir," Claudia answered him. "But it ain't no more than she can bear."

He looked at the woman narrowly and knew he could see her guilt. He thought then only of punishing her. "Claudia, I think I'll have supper over at the main house," he informed her. "I must attend to something I forgot about before. Please look after Libbie."

He was so cold as he answered her that Claudia knew instantly she had somehow misspoken. "I'm sorry if I said something out of turn," she offered, not knowing why she apologized. His reply, though, was all equanimity.

"You didn't say anything but what was on your mind, Claudia. There couldn't be anything evil in that."

He was conciliatory when he spoke, but when he left the room she felt herself to be in gravest danger, though, of course, she did not imagine for one moment the cause.

Caleum walked the half mile through the frigid evening to the main house, thinking the entire time about revenge for the wrong he had suffered. When he entered the room where his uncle and aunt were sitting down to dinner, he tried to calm himself. Adelia invited him to join them at table and called Rebecca to make another setting. When he sat down in his customary place, he felt a great weight lift up from his shoulders and was soon enveloped in the comfort of familiarity and security.

His aunt had prepared roast beef, which was cooked pink as he liked it, and he took a slice from the serving platter and placed it on his plate.

He cut into it and ate silently for a while, with his head bent down, looking neither at Adelia nor Magnus.

"Caleum, what has happened?" Adelia asked, after she thought he had enjoyed sufficient time to warm up from the cold.

"Why do you ask me what has happened?" he asked. "Can't I only come by for a visit?"

"And to that you are always welcome, but something has happened to upset you," Adelia answered, not seeing any reason to argue or to explain how she knew this to be true.

"Aunt Adelia, Libbie has lost our baby," he answered, sitting up straight, only to slink back down in his seat. A caul seemed to descend on the room when he said this, and they were all silent where they sat.

"How is she now?" Adelia asked finally.

"Resting," said Caleum. "She is out there with the witch who poisoned her. I would not have left, but I don't see what further harm she can do to her now."

"Caleum, what are you talking about?" Magnus asked.

"Claudia," he said, looking at his uncle directly. "She is a witch who has poisoned my wife."

"Did Libbie tell you that?" Adelia asked.

"No," Caleum replied.

"Then what do you have against her to sustain your charge?"

"She walks at night in the fields, or else the woods. I have seen her."

"Is that all of it?"

"She cannot look me straight on, and not because of modesty, but from her guilt."

"What does Libbie say?"

"That it is her burden, and all will be fine. I think she is still under Claudia's spell."

"I thought her brother was a great friend of yours?"

"He was a friend of my youth, Uncle Magnus."

"Aye."

"My father warned me about taking her on."

Caleum understood at last that Claudia was the reason they had seen so much misfortune.

"What do you plan to do?" Magnus asked the younger man. "You have no proof she has done anything."

"I have the proof of what she has wrought," he answered.

"Caleum, you know sometimes life by itself brings misfortune, and we can only live with it."

"Why are you taking her side, Aunt Adelia?" he asked. "She poisoned my wife."

"You should ask Libbie and see what she says."

Caleum then felt there was some great conspiracy against him that even his family was party to. Was his wife as well? The thought was enough to make him mad, and he stood from the table in a barely controlled fit of anger. "I think I should go see how Libbie is," he said. "As for Claudia, I don't think there can be any more debate about her. Do I have your support or not?"

"Well, what do you want to do?" Magnus asked.

Adelia looked at him as he stood from the table, and there was a coolness in her gaze he had not appreciated before when she replied. "That depends," she said. "How will you run your house?"

He looked at his uncle for support, but Magnus nodded in consent with Adelia.

"No one is against you," his uncle continued. "Only there is not always a convenient place for us to lay down blame for our miseries."

Adelia was pleased to see her husband with her, instead of joining Caleum in his witch hunt, but she was concerned Caleum would not see things that way, and still do something rash.

"Good night," he said.

Magnus and Adelia looked back and forth between each other, and Adelia stepped forth to say something to Caleum, but Magnus checked her. "Good night, Caleum. Give Libbie our heartfelt regards."

As he left the room Adelia took his hand and squeezed it.

How will you run your house?

When Caleum descended the front stairs back into the frigid evening, a gust of wind swept the tails of his banian, and he could feel a chill that reached through his clothing to embrace him with its icy fingers. He wished then he had ridden over, and thought briefly about going to the stable for a horse. Instead, he took the wind as part of that design counter to his well-being, and pulled the fabric close to his neck as he trudged along, hugging the shore of the lake on the path that had been worn between Stonehouses and his own house.

What have I done to be treated so? he asked, of no one in particular. He felt then the entire world arranged against him in a unified mocking he was powerless to affect, nor could he escape it. It was a torture for him, as he walked on under a crisp, low moon and heard again the sound of his wife crying. I had only this one wish, he thought to himself.

He became convinced as he went that his aunt and uncle had sided against him only because they had never had children of their own and were jealous. No sooner had he thought this, though, than he realized he did not know the reason for their childlessness.

Because his mind was well-formed and rational, he was forced to admit as he continued on that there were those whose wishes were daily denied them, and he was only unused to it—having been granted far more than was withheld. He knew then there was no pact against him, only bitter circumstance; not two-faced plot-making.

I shall still throw her out, he thought to himself, with some small satisfaction. If he could not prosecute her criminality he could at least expel her presence and give himself peace of mind. A stab of guilt shot through him no sooner had he formed the thought, though, and he admitted to himself it was only wicked fantasizing. Still, to accept what had happened to him meekly was not the way he was used to being. He had been raised to think he could achieve whatever he wished with the strength of his body and will and his mind's cunning. He was now defeated, however, and the barb was all the more jagged because it was with something that came so easily to others. He felt crushed as one upon whom a monumental boulder has fallen. It was with this admission that he opened the door on his house.

Inside he smelled smoke and was at first worried that, on top of his other burdens, fire had broken out in his absence. Only slowly did he realize it was not the house on fire but the smell of lit tobacco. He followed the scent out to the kitchen, where he found Libbie and Claudia sitting on stools at the table, puffing away on little pipes. He had never known Libbie to smoke before and was stupefied to see her engaged in it now. He held his tongue, though, not knowing whether he should chastise her or let the grievance pass. He was certain Claudia had introduced her to this as well.

When the women saw him they were at pains to extinguish their little smokes, fanning the air as if he had not already seen their misdeed. "Libbie, how are you?" Caleum asked, feeling a deep weariness that seemed to the others a kind of patience.

"I am fine," Libbie answered, as Claudia withdrew. "How are Uncle Magnus and Aunt Adelia?"

"They are well," he said. His earlier suspicions still had not left him entirely, but now came to rest upon Libbie herself, and he wondered whether if, fearing as she had, she had been the one to enlist Claudia in her aid. Nevertheless he pressed ahead in his original inquiry. "Libbie, I want to ask you something," he said, seeing no reason to be mysterious about it. "How trustworthy do you find Claudia?"

Libbie felt a pain when she realized the jealous suspicions that were unleashed in her husband's mind. "Completely," she answered.

"You do not think she could have a hand in any of our misfortunes?"

"No," Libbie answered, afraid of where she knew it might lead. "I told you it was only misfortune."

"Very well," Caleum concluded, with the same patience he displayed before, leaving his wife there in the kitchen as he went to the parlor to be alone. He sat down on a sofa that allowed him to look out on the lake beyond the window. He was not fully satisfied there was no pact against him, or that his wife's misfortunes were only what she said. He had no evidence, however, of any foul deed, and no course to act, so tried to find a position of calm and stillness within himself.

How will you run your house? When he thought of his aunt's question from earlier that evening it seemed a very different thing in this light, and he was shaken again with self-facing grief that he knew he must undo.

After a long hour of staring at the lake and listening to the frigid wind as it whistled through the trees and even seemed to move the house a tiny fraction, he finally went to bed with no answer and no true satisfaction; no peace at all save a mature, abiding grief.

n i n e

❦

The spring rains were as relentless as the ones of the preceding autumn, storming down cold and hard from late February until the middle of March nearly without intermission, until the landscape began to show shadings of green that put all in mind of new beginnings: new hopes and chances in all their struggles, great and small. When the rains finally did ease, the stench of manure and winter decay mingled on the air, announcing the start of the new season. Caleum was happy that he could once again spend the better part of his days out-of-doors instead of inside the barns or his house, and he began to walk his land, like one who had been doing so many years, to assess its state and plan its future.

Of cloven-hoofed beasts there were four cows in calf that spring, and six ewes ready to lamb. The hogs rooted in the blood-red mud, searching out mushrooms, the occasional nut, and other treasures, after having tasted nothing but dry grain for so many months. One of the sows had birthed at the beginning of the month, and her sucklings fought for dominance and who should be first to feast and fatten from her milk. The hens sat their eggs patiently in the musty gloom of a coop that still retained its winter heat and darkness.

Caleum and Magnus toured each district of the larger farm, glad to see the bright green shoots in the pasturelands as the grasses bloomed again; debating how soon to let the animals out to graze, or wait for the higher pastures to open. When they saw stalks of the same grass in the rice and tobacco fields, though, they were made anxious, and discussed the best method of weeding it out so that it would not reappear. It was the same conversation they had this time every year, and it never failed to soothe both of them, no matter what their other worries— to know spring had arrived and the certainty and rhythm of life at Stonehouses was reached anew.

Libbie was with child again as well, but Caleum did not wish to dwell on the subject—it would turn out for good or ill, and there was nothing he could do—so he stayed focused on what he had some sway over: when the crops went in the ground and the animals were let out to pasture— though not how much that planting or shepherding would increase and yield.

When they finished their tour, Magnus, who had not been into Berkeley since the fall markets, suggested they go to Content's place for a pint, as the sun was not yet set and there would be light out for still another two hours.

As they took the road into town, Caleum gave his horse a loose rein, letting the animal exercise its powerful legs on the open expanse of road after being confined all winter. Magnus had never been one for flashy riding, but the perfume of the air and the vigor of the new season inspired him to let his animal open up as well. The beast he sat was the mare Annabel, and he knew her stride as well as he did his own and trusted her as much to carry him where he wished to go. As she gathered speed, though, he felt a violent jerk in his arms and thought she had lost her footing in the mud. He looked for a place to jump clear in case she went down, but soon after the initial pain he realized the hot sensation he felt was not the mare losing her hold on the ground but his own arm losing hold of the horse. His entire right side clenched up then and froze against him, and no matter how he tried he could not move. As both the animal and his own body flew away from his control he knew something grave was the matter.

Caleum was still within calling distance, but even in this state Magnus would have felt foolish to call for help, so suffered his agony alone as Caleum moved farther away and Annabel stormed on under her own guidance. Slowly the pain that moved through his arm began to identify itself to him, and he realized what was wrong. When he did he was glad indeed he had not called out. His arm had frozen not from paralysis or stroke but from age and the same rheumatic condition his father had suffered. As it thawed, and he was able to resume a light hold on the reins with that arm, he cursed his body for betraying him so but was satisfied he had not lost dignity in front of his nephew. Still, he felt frail and small, as he could scarcely remember feeling before, and was swept by a wave of self-sorrow that he could be so exposed. How long, he thought, with a different kind of anguish, before his body did fail him in some serious way he could not prevent or control?

He remembered his father, Jasper, during those long last years of his life—when he had asked himself what went on in the man's head when his body would no longer obey him, and his weakness was laid bare for any who cared to behold it.

Well, it is as it will be, he thought, but if I am to be made a fool I will not aid in it. He pulled at the reins with his other hand and Annabel slowed her gait, turning to look at him in the saddle. "You sensed something different and wanted to know what it was, didn't you, girl?" he asked the mare, stroking the gray fur at the base of her neck. If he were another type of man he would claim she had gazed on him with sympathy, but he was not one to attribute to animals what belonged only to humans. Still, he was pleased he had chosen that particular mount to carry him that day.

By the time Magnus made it to the tavern, Caleum had already fastened his horse to a post and was standing in the road waiting. "Sorry, I shouldn't ride like that," Caleum said, thinking he had been inconsiderate of Magnus for going at such a pace.

"No," Magnus answered, "I shouldn't ride like that, but like a man my own age."

Caleum saw then that his uncle was in pain, and hastened to take the reins of his horse as he dismounted. Magnus did not object as he normally would have, but accepted this kindness and came out of the last stirrup with a little cringe. When he saw this, Caluem grew afraid. He had never known Magnus to be sick his entire life and grew worried it was more serious than the other man let on.

"I am fine," Magnus said, seeing Caleum's face, and trying at first to hide his frailty. "It is only arthritis," he explained, "such as might plague you one day." Caleum's face registered relief as they walked into Content's together, and Magnus was glad he had told him. Still, it ached like the devil.

Once inside they claimed a table near the window, and John Barnaby, Content's son-in-law, came and waited on them. "What brings you

round today, Magnus Merian?" John asked, surprised to see him there
before the summer season, as he usually only came during the productive months.

"It was good weather today, and Caleum here thought we'd do well
to breathe a little air."

"Well, I'm always happy to see you," John said warmly, for the two
families were still familiar with each other, even if they did not see one
another so often. Magnus was pleased to have come out and asked John
after his business and family, and they traded news until he had to return to work.

Caleum and Magnus then sat silently nursing their drinks, until a man
neither of them knew sat at their table, begging excuse as he did so.

"Help yourself," Caleum said to him, though there were many places
free in the rest of the tavern.

"You see I have lost my way," the man said, in a matter-of-fact tone,
after he had sat.

"I beg your pardon?" Magnus asked.

"I used to be a teacher in Great Philadelphia, but I lost my way. Now
I support myself with this," the man explained.

"What is it you do?"

"I'm a pamphleteer," the man answered, opening a leather folder.
"For a shilling I will sell you a pamphlet on any subject you like. How
about fertilizers and the care of the soil for my country friends?"

"No." Caleum cut him off. "Thank you."

"Suit yourself," the man answered, not taking offense. "But you
should take better care. You see there is a fissure happening, and much
will likely be lost."

"Pardon?"

"It says so right here in one of my pamphlets."

Caleum smiled. At first he had though the man simple. It dawned on
him then, though, that there were certain men, like his own father, who
were sentenced—he would not go so far as condemned—to wander the
earth. He reached into his pocket and retrieved a coin, which he slid across
the table to the man. The pamphleteer gave him in return a small tract
called "On Civil Government," and reached into his own pocket to
make change. He gave Caleum at the end of that transaction two coins
of silver mint, both of which had eyes embossed on their nether sides,

encompassing the entire surface of the metal. When he saw it, Caleum thought he recognized the design as similar to Purchase's in style, although it was a different motif than the ones his father had minted. Still, he had spent long hours studying them, and they were very reminiscent.

"It is true silver," the pamphleteer vouched.

"Indeed," said Caleum. "I have seen the likes of it before."

"Have you?"

"Not the pattern, but the style."

"They were given me by a woman in Philadelphia."

"Before or after you had lost your way?"

"Surely it was before, though not long."

"Then you will stay your course," Caleum said, feeling then as if he belonged to some secret fraternity. It was only silver specie, though, and not some secret union.

"Which side are you on?" the stranger asked him.

"Pardon?"

"The divide."

"None but our own," Magnus intervened, not wanting a political argument with the man. He shifted his concern back to Caleum. "I think we must sow in the next three days."

Seeing himself locked out of the conversation, the stranger got up to leave.

"Deny what you want," he said as he departed, "but it is surely happening."

"I will believe it when I see it."

"There are men who look but never see."

"Aye. Women as well."

After the man had left, though, they thought about what he said and the events that were swirling everywhere about them but seemed so ethereal that, for when and where they alighted, there was nothing but speculation. Their attention had been so focused on their own fortunes that they had not yet joined in the general debate about the looming prospect of war, which was more and more all anyone spoke of. Magnus, being cautious and having his own profitability to keep him occupied, hoped there would be no disturbance of the status quo, as he had never been upset in his doings other than the unpleasant business with the tax assessor. In his mind that is what it was by then, "that unpleasant business with the judge's man." Other than that he did not look at it in his memory. Of liberty he had what he required and saw no need to change who he paid taxes to, and certainly no need of arguing it with strangers.

Though he had come to know more of its shape, Caleum still tended to be idealistic about the world in general and claimed everyone should be master of his own house, reaping as he planted.

After finishing their drinks they shunted aside political matters and rode back to Stonehouses, satisfied with the evening and the start of the new growing season. If there was a drawback to the day's adventure it was only this: Magnus had not ridden so far in many months, and the saddle did take its toll on him—so that when he returned home he wished only for his supper and to retire for the evening.

This first desire was granted in full when Adelia served the last winter ham from their stores for dinner, along with pickled beets and potatoes. Caleum and Libbie joined them that evening as well, such as had not happened in a long time outside of Sunday, so Magnus Merian was much satisfied: able to forget the day's politics and his own physical complaints.

Adelia, pleased to have her family's full company, delighted in spoiling Caleum with extra helpings and the promise of a rice pudding for dessert, and spoke of a bonnet she thought Libbie must have before she went home. Her love of their visits was matched only by her crossness whenever it was time for them to go, so that when she mentioned dessert Caleum knew to steel himself, as it was usually around this time that her bad mood would descend.

"Aunt Adelia, have you started your garden yet?" he asked, steering conversation toward a topic sure to please her.

"Yes," she answered, "but I'm already afraid it won't be as nice as last year. There was a frost the last two nights running, which in likelihood ruined half of it, and if not the frost then the birds."

There had been no frost, of course, and the birds were no worse than any other year. Magnus looked at Caleum with a wry smile, as if to say he should have known better.

"It doesn't matter anyway," she went on. "No one appreciates the garden anymore. I remember the first time I saw it. I thought it was the most beautiful place I had ever seen, and it was a privilege when your grandmother Sanne invited me to help her with the planting and weeding of it."

"We all love your garden," Libbie interjected. "I think it is the most beautiful I've seen."

"Thank you," Adelia answered, pleased but not satisfied.

From the time he noticed it, Caleum was amazed that older people could be so sensitive, or else vain, and especially his aunt. He thought it was something one should naturally shed with age, like a first skin. In time he had come to find it reassuring, as a promise that certain things in life, and one's character especially, never change after a certain point. Because of this he was happy to see his wife fawn over his aunt's garden, or else little things that gave her pleasure or that inflamed her pride, much as she delighted in treating him at times like a boy. It made him feel the world was stable and unflagging in some things, no matter what happened around them. "I will come round Saturday and help with planting, Auntie," he told her then, "and I will bring bell jars in case of another frost."

"I will get the rice pudding," she said, smiling as she left the table. "There are raisins in it, Caleum."

He smiled at her in turn but suppressed the greater part of his joy at this dessert, from embarrassment that something so simple always brought him such pleasure but also from feeling he had been coerced.

It was as Magnus and Caleum waited for Adelia and Libbie, who had gotten up to help, to return from the kitchen that the knocker at the front door sounded. It was a very deep and assured rapping that startled them, because no one ever used the instrument, and in time they had come to think of it as purely ornamental. Caleum rose to go to answer the insistent visitor, not knowing who on earth could be out there on the other side.

When he returned he announced their neighbor, Rudolph Stanton, had come to pay a visit. Everyone was taken by surprise that the mighty man should come down from his place at Acre to see them, instead of sending a messenger as was his usual custom no matter what the business, let alone at such an advanced hour.

"Is it really so unusual?" Magnus asked, as he went to the door, relishing the honor. "He's a man just like I am, and he isn't so far above us after all for all his fancy titles and what not."

When he greeted Mr. Stanton he recalled in his mind the great turn his neighbor had once done him all those years back, and there was a real warmth he felt for him, though of course he did not dare express it in familiar terms. "Good evening, Mr. Stanton," he said, when he entered the parlor where the other was waiting. "What an honor to have you here."

"I did not mean to interrupt your dinner," Stanton replied. "I didn't mean that at all, but I figured better your leisure time than working hours."

"It is nothing to think of. Can I offer you anything?"

"Whatever you're having," Stanton answered.

Magnus was a bit astounded to have Stanton accept his hospitality, and worried he hadn't anything suitable for the man. His father, Merian, would have produced something rare and exquisite that was the best of its kind, but he himself had never been one for entertaining visitors or all that kind of indulgence. "Well, we were just having a rice pudding my wife made."

"Then I will join you in that," Stanton said. "If it is not too much a bother."

Caleum stood up at once when Stanton came to the table, and the women looked at each other, uncertain what to do, for in that part of the world he was grand as a duke, maybe even a prince, and was in fact directly related to one of each.

"Please pardon my intrusion," Stanton said, as he sat down, "but Magnus has been bragging on your rice pudding all over the county, Mrs. Merian, and I was wondering whether it is everything he has said."

Adelia beamed broadly and nearly giggled aloud. "Stop," she said. Libbie smiled into her napkin as Adelia took up a bowl, which was not fancy and silver laid, as in some homes, but plain. She then served Mr. Stanton a generous portion, feeling like a girl as he tucked into it.

Their guest still had not announced his business, and as he ate Magnus wondered whether the man's mind had not gone off wandering, or whether he was not perhaps just sad over in that great big hall by himself, and perhaps really had come over only to share in a spot of pudding.

"It is the best I have ever tasted, Adelia," Stanton said, as he finished the bowl. "May I call you Adelia? There wouldn't happen to be any more, would there?"

Libbie served him this time, watching him smile from the corner of her eye. He was perhaps ten years older than Magnus but looked nothing like his age, being a bachelor and having no doubt access to such potions as only men of his station did to maintain themselves.

"You have a fine place here, Magnus Merian. You have truly done well," he said, reclining in his seat with such ease one would have thought he dined there every evening. "It is too seldom that I visit with my neighbors, I'm afraid."

"I suspect, Mr. Stanton," Magnus said, "that you are far too busy with your time for much visiting."

"True," Stanton answered, pleased that someone acknowledged how hard he labored and how scarce his time was. "Between my farm and the business of the Legislature, I don't always know where an entire day has gotten off to when it's over and done."

If before his presence there seemed unreal, it began to seem perfectly normal to all of them as he tucked into his second helping of rice pudding and indulged in the counting of his time—such as had always been a great pastime there at Stonehouses.

"As I rode up I noticed a very handsome sundial out front. Do you mind if ask where you acquired it?"

"My father built it," Magnus answered with pride.

"He was a quite a man, Jasper Merian," Stanton said. "I always wished I had known him better. And how is your father, young lady?"

Libbie sat up straight as she could. "He is well, sir. Thank you for your thoughtful inquiry."

Stanton smiled. "What a fine family you have, Magnus. Do you mind if I call you that?"

"Not at all, sir," Merian said, flattered by such familiarity.

"And how is your holding?" he asked, turning to Caleum, for it was really him he had come to see.

Caleum had not spoken at all other than to greet their guest, and, if the others had forgotten, he still wondered what he wanted there, as ever since Stanton entered the hall he knew it must be very serious news that he was only delaying in delivering.

"I cannot complain. I have been blessed with good soil, and I imagine I'll start putting out seeds in a day or so."

"So soon? I was thinking of waiting until next week myself. Do you think I am making a mistake?"

"No, sir," Caleum answered with equanimity, not betraying any surprise that such a man should seek his opinion, nor showing any bashfulness in tendering it. "Acre sits up on a hill, and the way the winds come in this time of year I imagine another week of frost for you in the main field."

"Just as I have always maintained," Stanton answered, impressed with the younger man's reasoning and observation. "That is very sharp of you, Caleum. Then they say around Miss Boutencourt's that you are a bright young man."

Caleum did not think to ask how Stanton knew this, or why he should go seeking it, as it seemed natural that Rudolph Stanton would know everything that went on in Berkeley.

"Tell me now, what do you think of the disagreement with our friends in London?"

"What in particular?" Caleum asked.

"Do you think in the main it is time to separate out from them?"

"I don't know about time," Caleum answered, "but it seems headed that way. As to which side I would choose I have no doubt."

"No, nor I," Stanton said.

It was unclear whether they meant the same thing, and Libbie and Adelia were concerned then to know why Stanton had shown up in the middle of the night to begin a discussion of politics. Magnus, however, had his suspicions and looked at Adelia, and she at Libbie, and the two of them withdrew.

"I imagine Caleum sees things much as you do," Magnus interjected, not wanting to leave him alone on such uncertain ground.

"Does he?" Stanton asked, giving Magnus his full attention. "How do I see things?"

"Well, Mr. Stanton, neither of us would presume to know your thoughts," Magnus said, uncomfortable with what he feared was a trap. "But if I had to guess, based on my dealings with you from the past, I would say you thought people was pretty much the same and deserved to be treated fair and that whatever side you take would be for the best reasons."

"Is that what I think, Caleum?" Stanton asked.

"Equal," Caleum answered. "Not all the same, but yes, in the main, equal."

Stanton was pleased, and nodded.

"Do you think as well that men are all born as blank slates and that only experience makes them what they are?" Caleum asked then, grown a little bold.

Stanton smiled at him. "Indeed, boy," he said, "I do. Is it what you think?"

"In principle," Caleum said. "I think, though, some men might be born inclined more toward one thing than others, and what they experience might only bring it out in them."

"Well, it is a ticklish business." Stanton smiled. "You know then why I have come here?"

Caleum and Magnus both admitted that they did not, as Stanton took his pipe from his vest and began to smoke, much at home in the Merian house and happy with Caleum's natural good sense. "I have been charged with organizing a militia," he confessed, "and I wanted to know whether you might have any interest in it."

When Stanton said *charged,* it was clear he was in with other powerful people, and by *interest* he meant Caleum's loyalty.

"Are you expecting troubles?" Magnus asked, concerned only for Caleum's well-being.

"What is on the horizon I cannot say, but I plan on Berkeley being prepared and all our properties protected, whatever occurs."

Both men looked at Caleum, who took in everything before him but did nothing to betray his thoughts.

"He'll answer you tomorrow then, Mr. Stanton, unless of course you need an answer right this moment," Magnus said, knowing they would be granted what he had requested. It was not that he thought Caleum a child and unable to decide properly, but only that he wanted to protect his boy's interest and well-being as he was used to doing, even if he was a man by now. In this case time would best achieve that.

"I'll join," Caleum said abruptly, defying his uncle and grown tired of the game with Stanton.

"I think you had better think about it," Magnus reprimanded him. "Mr. Stanton, you know we've always tried to do whatever we could in support of Berkeley, but this is serious and needs to be thought about seriously."

"Yes, you should think about it," Stanton said to Caleum.

Caleum agreed to think it over for the night.

He did not wish to trade the harmony of his life for the lawlessness of war, but he already knew what he would do. It was less a matter of political belief than the fact that his neighbor had asked him, and he felt he had a debt of honor to repay and would not fail his responsibility.

His natural beliefs, they were not far behind, though they still needed time before they would be fully developed.

t e n

Caleum joined Stanton's militia in October, and they began immediately to prepare for battle. Stanton himself drilled the troops in the beginning, having experience of warfare from the French and Indian campaigns. However, as the seriousness of the political situation grew, he had recourse to hire a seasoned colonel to give the men greater discipline and lead them like conscripts in a full army. Each Saturday they could be seen out on the town square practicing maneuvers, as the colonel lectured them on various theories of warfare. These discourses were sometimes formal, as when he spoke about the use of mobile artillery, and other times they were ribald tirades on the privation of war, or else dissertations on the rights of the colonists. No matter the conversation, though, it inevitably spilled over and continued at Content's tavern afterward, where the men argued the day's lesson and often made merry.

To assemble his army, Stanton had gone through all the families in the valley and hill country and picked those he thought were best fit to serve. Caleum knew many of the other men in the militia by name or reputation, but he could not claim friendship with any of them, as they were from so far and wide, and he seldom associated beyond his small circle. Because they had been individually selected by Stanton, though, it was considered quite an honor to serve, and they bonded over their position as the ablest young men in the county.

They were also envied by those men who had not been asked to join, a thing that turned to jealousy whenever womenfolk mentioned the militia with approval. "I don't think those British would dare show themselves in Berkeley with Stanton's militia guarding us."

They were a fine assembly, who feared very little of the sacrifice they were being asked to make and, though young, heeded Stanton's admonishment to be farsighted enough to ask what their colony and country should be after the strife of war had passed and gone.

At Stonehouses this looming reality still yet to settle, and everything seemed to move and progress as normal for that time of year. In June the corn was high as a yearling, and in July they prepared for the harvest that would soon be upon them. Libbie's pregnancy was well advanced, and though Caleum urged her to stay off her feet, she was defiant about it—helping with the summer chores as any other maid of the country. Adelia worked her garden, and was trying that year to introduce orange trees from seeds Magnus got for her after they saw Libbie's embroidered picture. Magnus, as he went to work that season, thought for the first time in years of his past humiliations, first at Sorel's Hundred, then at the hands of the tax assessor—and also those little assaults that are too small and diffuse to be given name in memory but only stored away. Through this reminiscence he managed eventually to convince himself in the rhetoric and need for war, and that what came after it would outlive what had been before, as everything would be equal in it, and none captive to the major part against his will. It was not something he shared with anyone, but whenever he saw Caleum ride into the stable in his militia uniform his own heart was made very proud, though of course not vengeful or thirsty for blood.

Whenever she saw her boy in his uniform and considered the news that reached them out there that summer, Adelia too had no doubt but that there would soon be a war of some kind. She remembered when Caleum first showed up there on the land with his guardian, Rennton, and how fearless he seemed, as only a small child can be. It was the same confidence that seemed to reawaken in him during that summer, and where before it had worried her to no end, now she allowed it to dispel her natural fears for his safety. She had thought from the moment he came there and became her son that he would always be with her. Now she realized she was foolish as any mother to have ever harbored such hope. She wept in private like an old woman, as it dawned in her mind that he was leaving.

Libbie was even less certain what shape the events unfolding would take and still had hope they might reverse their seeming course. She began in secret nonetheless to make her own war preparations and to craft for her husband a new suit of clothes for the winter months, including a hunting shirt and a greatcoat, the inside of which was decorated with a scene from Stonehouses, with everyone who lived there represented. There was but one face she could not weave in yet, as she had never seen it, but left a space for it to be filled in later.

Caleum himself worked all day long, as if nothing were out of the ordinary, even though there was a weighty congress taking place in Philadelphia that summer, which would determine the future of the colonies. At night, though, heeding Stanton's suggestion, he would read books borrowed from the library at Acre, which made his positions better reasoned, as he considered what his own future, and that of Stonehouses, should be. He struck on many plans in those days, each of them fired by a sense of new possibilities and in its own way utopic.

Because Stanton approved of his young intellect, Caleum had complete access to the books at Acre and was free to go and borrow a volume even when Stanton himself was not home. Caleum was at first intimidated by the big airy rooms. He had thought when he finished at Miss Boutencourt's that he was educated, and he had always carried himself as such. In the library at Acre for the first time, though, he felt his immense ignorance hit him like a storm wave slapping an untested vessel. It took all his self-control then to keep from showing untoward emotion, for his first instinct was to cry.

He threw himself at the books with zeal then, so he should be as strong in mind as in body. However, even in his enthusiasm, he took care not to go softheaded with their pleasures and also not to become like some men, who read only part of a book or, worse yet, learned only its reputation, then prattled on as if they had read the entire volume.

He moved slowly through the shelves, letting one book lead him to the next by way of suggestion, so that this folio would take him to that folio and in turn to such and such octavo; from there it was on to a certain quarto or duodecimo, then back to the original folio, and so on. When he could not find a clear answer to something using this method, he was scrupulous in questioning Stanton, especially about Greek or Latin terms.

"Mr. Stanton, what is the difference between *a priori* and *a posteriori* knowledge?" he might ask in those early days.

Stanton always answered these questions with the utmost patience and care, so that if the young man was led astray in his thinking it would not be because he had been provided faulty maps and teaching but because he had sought to go wandering in too curious a place.

One day while returning a philosophy text, a slim leather book with gilt lettering caught his eye because of its great beauty. When he removed it from its shelf, he realized it bore the name—Antigone—his grandfather had once told him to give his daughter should he ever be so blessed. Although he was not usually one for made-up stories, he opened the little book, intending to read it. As he gazed at the first line, however, he felt he was doing something wrong. "I have heard this story," he reasoned to himself. "What if the second telling changes its original meaning?"

Although it was contrary to his usual discipline with books and their information, he had read enough by then to know stories that have been heard or otherwise interrupted were often very different than those seen with one's own eyes and mind. In this case he preferred Jasper Merian's rendering, with whatever faults of interpretation and possible misinterpretation, so chose but once ignorance over knowledge.

Once was a powerful king, whom the gods did favor.

Not that one needed books to receive a political education that summer. Everywhere people debated what was happening at Philadelphia, even as they prepared for the seasonal harvest. Slaves, hired men, landowners, and governors all argued among themselves, and sometimes with each other, whether they should break from the mother country and chart a separate course or hold to the path they were on. All men then were expert on the subject, and each held either that war was anathema to their interests or else the only way to secure their rights and rightful consideration.

The debate raged on even after the Congress voted for independence in midsummer. After the harvest games that year, which had become tradition, Caleum and Magnus drove into town to buy such winter supplies as they could not produce themselves on their farm.

What he paid that year incensed Magnus, as there was a tax on nearly everything he needed, which cut deeply into his cash profits. After loading the cart with wares, though, they headed to Content's, to forget the labors they had just completed, as well as the sting of giving money for nothing in return. The tavern was emptier than was usual for that time of the year, and the two of them sat looking out on the square in reflective silence for quite some time, before Magnus said to Caleum at last. "You know I will die some day."

Caleum was at first taken aback by this pronouncement and wondered whether something was the matter. "Are you ill, Uncle Magnus?" he asked, with gravest concern.

"No," Magnus replied evenly, drinking from his mug. "But I will die one day all the same."

Caleum thought about it for some time again before answering. "I understand." They continued drinking their beers in silence for a while, before Caleum asked, "Do you think they will rebel?"

"I don't know. You?"

"I suspect."

Magnus was thoughtful and withdrawn into himself then, reflecting on all the change he had seen and the change he knew he would not see. It was true that he was not ill, at least not in any immediate manner, but he had been aware since that spring of his mortality in a new way, and the mortality of their way of life as well. He wanted to impart some sense to Caleum of how it was, how it had been for him and his father—and Caleum's own father as well—when they were all there on the land together, and what Stonehouses was for all of them. He settled instead on asking, "Do you think the eastern field is getting overworked?"

"It would not hurt to rest it," Caleum answered. "But it is still good land and only needs fertilizing and a rest."

"It was always the most productive field."

He asked next after Libbie and her condition.

"She will not stay off her feet, though she is otherwise well and good," Caleum replied. "She says she isn't due until September, and might as well do now what she won't be able to then."

"Well, I suppose you have to trust she knows best in this."

"I suppose so."

At last he put forth his question about the militia, very casually.

"There is nothing new to report," Caleum answered, "but Stanton has us drilling in secret now, so I think he knows something we do not."

"He is always first with news."

They returned to the discussion of the past harvest, then finished their beers and went outside to claim the wagon. Magnus mounted on one side of the vehicle very carefully, and Caleum took the reins on the other, neither of them self-conscious or apologetic about his age, yet both enjoying where they were in life at that moment. They rode leisurely then, back to the country, stopping to enjoy the great swells of greenery and lushness and the fields all under cultivation. When they arrived home, each of them went to his own place feeling somehow they had had a very meaningful conversation that settled something of great import that day. As each ate dinner with his wife and discussed his plans, both knew that the future would arrive only after a rupture with the past. That is the understanding that had blossomed between them, that they were in the final moment of that shared past, and as for the other part—what the future would be—that would be decided only in time. For what it was, though, and what they themselves believed in, they were very clear on that.

When Libbie gave birth in November it was a daughter, and Caleum was finally able to honor his promise to his grandfather by giving to her the name he had asked him to. Libbie, however, when Caleum told her the story of where the name came from, insisted they give her another as well, "Because we don't wish for her too many sorrows either."

She suggested at first that they call the girl Lucky, but Caleum, being superstitious in such matters, thought that was too tempting of fate. Instead they agreed together on Rose, which was the name she was known by the length of her days.

In the weeks immediately after her birth they did not have the kind of celebration they had before on such an occasion, but at Thanksgiving that year mother and child were foremost in everyone's prayers. The other great topic, which was now ever-present before them, was the fighting that had broken out in Massachusetts between the colonists there and the Royal Army.

Caleum and Magnus were both ardent supporters by then not only of Berkeley, but also of independence in general, and Caleum continued to drill with the militia that winter in anticipation of being called to serve. It was then that he remembered the sword his grandfather had given him. When he went off to battle it was this weapon that would serve him best. He would also wear the coat Libbie had made for him, with the scene of Stonehouses on its interior, and that was complete now with the birth of young Rose.

He would sleep nights in the future with it wrapped around him, swearing it to be warmer than any three blankets combined and that he never knew coldness when it was upon him.

The day he left Stonehouses was late in winter, and Magnus Merian had already turned his attention to the coming season. But Caleum Merian was not to be there as they tilled the earth that year and planted their hopes on another spring.

The two men had just mended a hole in the fence of the western pasture together and returned home for dinner in the main house. They were all seated, and had complimented Adelia on the meal, as Libbie nursed young Rose, and Caleum carved the roast. It was as he doled out the food that they heard the sounding of the knocker on the front door. When the great clacker sounded again, they knew it could only be one person in all of Berkeley.

Caleum went and answered Stanton's knock, and their neighbor entered the hall all in a flush. "We are sending a regiment up to join the Continental Army," he said. "Naturally, I have volunteered the Berkeley militia to be among it."

Looking at his face then, it was clear to all that what he was announcing had been a lifelong wish, which he kept secret until that moment. During the hours when he debated other men and seemed to take their opinions into consideration, it was just they themselves he considered, as his own opinion was etched already and he waited only for its soundness to become obvious to others. It was clear as well that all else in the world was present in his mind only to serve this one great purpose.

He could not stay for dinner, he said, having much else to do that night. He gave instructions to Caleum as to when the militia would assemble and depart, leaving him with his family until that time. Caleum went back to the table and delivered the news.

All in the hall were feverish with the excitement and uncertainties it induced. These they did not speak of aloud, because they did not want to burden Caleum with worry. Instead they tried to turn dinner that evening into a proper feast, eating and conversing until late at night and sparing nothing for Caleum's pleasure.

He was happy for these comforts of home, as he dined with his wife and child and the uncle and aunt who had reared him as their own. In his mind, however, he was already preparing himself to live without them.

He did not wish for bloodshed, but he could barely wait for the next day, when he would leave with the army. His impatience was only partly due to confidence; the other part was the fact that one night while practicing with his sword he looked at the metal and saw there a picture of himself, which enveloped both sides of the blade. He stood with the weapon in a position of conquering, and all around him men fought in battle. He was larger than the rest and cut through a great many of his enemy.

He startled when he first saw this, having never noticed such an engraving on the sword before, but he knew, when he did, that this was perhaps his own great purpose and duty to fulfill. That he did not fail in his responsibility was a thing as meaningful to him as Stonehouses itself.

His life made sense to him then, as he mounted his favorite horse the next morning and flew to join the battle, and the morning sun lit up and reflected off of Stonehouses as he sped away.

IV
lamentations

one

He is strong as any man in the thirteen states and his arms have grown thick as oak boughs from wielding his sword to hold them. To see him you would think he was born to martial life and never did know the country fields or hearth of family. It is these he misses most, however, on his long war campaign, which has stretched far beyond what he or anyone else ever imagined when he first left home.

He knows now how seldom victory comes swiftly; that it is always hard-won and bloody. As he waits for the battle to be joined again at Saratoga, the farmland reminds him of his home, which was called Stonehouses, and he wants nothing more than to return to his family and take up his plow again. He will be moored permanent to his land then—instead of in brief respites such as he enjoyed winters during these three years of fighting—and no more leave it for any reason. Yet deep within himself, he knows there is also another possibility: that movement is in his blood now, and nothing can suppress what it has taught, and even homecoming will not alleviate it. It is the privation of having been apart from everything dear to him with no certainty of returning. Some knowledge, he thinks, is never lost, nor the cost of acquiring it forgotten. It has made his brow heavy and wise seeming, but it is sadness he feels when he stretches out for the night.

It is something other in the morning—a hotness—as he anticipates the next battle.

In the early months, when the colonists first faced the Great War Machine, they tried to match it gear for gear. However, they quickly found their enemy was all levers of warmongering and cogs of empire-making, and they were mowed down incessantly beneath it—or else humiliated by what they did not know. It was only when they learned to separate and attack individually that the spirit flowing between them had room to reveal itself, like a massive inevitable net, and they had any chance of winning.

As they sat around camp in early autumn, with the cooking fires aroar between them, the men took stock of their supplies and cleaned their equipment after the long days of silence, during which time the pastures of Saratoga had not known blood but only waiting. Lunch that noon was a thin soup provided by the farmer who hosted them on his land, augmented by a few wild hares some of the men had snared that morning. He sat under the cool October sun to share in the meager repast before the time when fighting would start up again. John Corbin, a freemason out of Burlington, who had fought so gallantly at Long Island and Brooklyn Heights, sat on his left. Herman Van Vecten, who had spent his twenty-fifth birthday in that camp and looked at least a decade older, was at his right. Carl Schuyler, who was commended for bravery at Trenton by their commander in chief, sat in front of him, slopping soup. There was also one called Ajax, a slave out of Maryland who had proved his worth at Brandywine. His other companions were a freedman called Mace, who took rather too much glee in the doings of battle, and a man called Polonius from Delaware, who had been promised his freedom for fighting and had surely won that already, snatching it from death again and again during the spring campaign just passed. The slave Julius, whom Caleum knew from youth, had also been enlisted by his master in the third year of the war, after he found out what the bounty was. For the fight he gave, though, one could not have paid enough, and the others soon forgot his status.

Among them all none ranked higher in the esteem of his compatriots than Caleum Merian himself, whose exploits were known through New England and the southern sphere alike. Even among those tempered and hardened soldiers, he was most skilled in killing.

As they ate their meal, a sentry came into camp and had words with the general in charge. When he left, the officers could all be seen gathering hastily in the center of camp for a war college. After a brief conference they sent out instructions among the men, who all knew by then that a fight was in the offing. They were ordered to ready themselves and form battle lines, as the British and Hessians were advancing toward their left flank in ambush even as they ate.

A panic spread through the newest recruits, who were fresh plucked from the farms of the country and still knew only what they had heard about the might and invincibility of England's army.

Caleum and his fellows finished their own meal as if nothing unusual were afoot, took up packs and muskets, and assumed their positions in the column that was forming out in the open meadow. They were the center of the formation and its pillar, as they were the most seasoned and would be hardest to break.

When the bugle sounded they marched out toward the enemy line obdurate as Spartans, prepared either to die or seize victory from those fields of death.

At three o'clock that afternoon, they finally met the enemy across a distance of some fifty yards.

As the mountains rose and stretched in the distance like a great stone spine, the British and the Hessians raised their muskets at the patriots, taking slow and careful aim. A volley of thunder rang out then, deafening all around, as the report from fifteen hundred guns sounded a testimony of certain slaughter.

The unseasoned Americans scattered in every which direction when the volley sounded, as mounted officers tried to whip them back into formation. When the gun smoke cleared, only Caleum and his men were still standing in their original formation, with none yet wounded—and no one yet dead.

They raised the muskets on their side then, for the first countercharge of the morning, keeping their nerve and aim steady amidst the chaos. Each fired in unison, releasing their own noise to answer the enemy's— a report of Continental will. The sulfur rose like steam as the British and Hessians fell from the lead that rained upon them.

What happened next, no one was prepared for, as it had happened so seldom before in history. The British line broke.

As the patriots rushed forth, it scattered here and yon without the collective discipline or thought that struck awe and terror in all who had gone against it, and the Continental Army began cutting them down in a frenzy as they fled. The farm boys, who had not seen battle before, grew over bold in this melee and rushed forth ahead of the rest of the line, looking for glory. They almost knew it, too, but were soon turned back on their heels, as the Englishmen regained the advantage and formed their line again.

The redcoats next gave chase with their bayonets drawn, having not time to reload their muskets as the Americans flew before them. The newer troops melted away again, like so much wax before a match, so the British met Caleum and his men instead, at the center of the American column. They too were without ready muskets, except Carl Schyuler, who could reload faster than any other man in their army. He fired on the advancing line, and one of the Hessian mercenaries fell onto a spot that was still green with grass.

The remainder of the center kept charging until the two lines crossed, point for point, and steel for steel. Instead of his bayonet, Caleum met them with his sword drawn, and he cut many men down that afternoon. One after another they fell under the steel's swift working. As they died each felt a great heat when their spirits departed their bodies—even those whose destination was the cool rooms of Heaven. They felt the heat alike who had lived in right correctness and who had lived in profitable sin, for the sword was indiscriminate in this and knew only fore from aft, foe from author and master.

Not that the fight was all one-sided that day. The British and Germans eventually rallied again, pushing the Americans back and taking from their ranks such souls as they managed to reach with their own war metals. They claimed lives that day from Massachusetts to Georgia, reaping seasoned soldiers along with the farmers, who fought with more spirit than skill. They made widows of the wives of officers and infantrymen alike, tangling with all the ferocity they were renowned for.

The tide of battle reversed itself again only when General Arnold, who had been stalking his prey all morning, gave his marksman the order to fire and General Simon, his British adversary, fell from his mount in a heap of flesh. With their leader lost, Arnold led a charge into the British center, which gave way before him and began to withdraw.

Caleum gave chase with the others all the way to Berryman's Redoubt, where Arnold was finally checked, nearly losing his life. The fighting continued, though, even without generals but with a will of its own. The soldiers kept falling on both sides all morning, but native love of native land was favored over Albion greatness by the end of that afternoon, and Fortune exchanged one for the other in her bosom.

Caleum pushed forth in the midst of this possessed of the spirit as the rest of them, but he stood a full head above the next tallest man on the battlefield and was almost as high as their standard, so when he let out a great bellow it seemed to proclaim the strength and intent of the entire army as it fought to stave off defeat.

He was magnificent that day, as he fought against the best Great Britain could muster. And when the redcoats heard his cry and saw the glint of his blade, even they were stirred with respect for their enemy. As darkness fell the fighting began to end at last, but for Caleum there was still one more contest in the day.

The Hessians had fallen back to their earthworks and were well dug in, firing cannon from inside that hailed down on the other army as a detachment defended the walls from without. Behind the line their commander of artillery, who had replaced his uniform of common wool with blue velvet and was dressed in it from head to foot, walked back and forth, making adjustments here and there to the cannon. After each walk down the line, he always returned to the center, where another figure, dressed all in red velvet, sat on a field stool, whispering advice to the commander from time to time, though they looked like two figures from Gin Lane. The man was their munitions expert, but Caleum recognized him immediately as Bastian Johnson, once of Berkeley.

He could not tell what the two men were discussing, but it was gravely serious, as it was only these guns that kept Caleum and the others from annihilating their side completely, and the cannon fire did not cease and was unerring in its accuracy.

As they drew up for one final assay before darkness drew its final veil, a figure lumbered out of the gray quarter light toward Caleum Merian. He alone of the men on the field that day was as tall as Caleum, and everyone in his path knew immediately who offered the fight. He was called Jupiter and came down originally from Mashpee. He had won his first fame on Bunker Hill, though it was a losing day for his side. He fought first for his freedom, as many men did during that campaign, and then he fought on for the love of it.

When Jupiter saw Caleum, each knew whom he was meant to face that day. And as they moved closer to striking, each was worthy. Both their hearts were enflamed with want to vanquish his rival, because each knew the other to be the strongest from his side, and each had it in him to test his mettle, steel against steel, not flint and ball from afar.

When they stood inside three yards, each drew his sword for killing. When they were nearly close enough to touch, their blades clashed in the air with a ringing that seemed as if it could be heard for miles around, as if the entire war had come down to only this battle between the two of them.

Unlike many who had faced him, Jupiter's sword did not give way immediately but took the shock of Caleum's blow when it struck his own. Nor was the man himself overwhelmed. He simply drew back and attacked again.

As they fought, Caleum felt for the first time he was fighting his only natural equal. In another time they might have been friends, and one side against all others, having some shared understanding. Here they were enemies. Each wielded his strength and skill for his cause and each fought superbly—as they came at each other again like Titans in the bitter mouth of chaos—and neither yielded from fear nor lack of stamina or tactic.

In contests of giants, though, there is never a deadlock but always the annihilation of the weaker ego, as fate lashes out with cruelty. In the course of seeking out advantage, one side must give so victory can progress, one over the other, no matter how tremendous a fight has been waged or the goodness in each warrior's heart. So it was for the two of them.

Here it was Jupiter who first felt the heat of steel pierce his flesh, making his blood run purple then red into the dirt of Saratoga.

He grew enraged after that, as he started to drink from death's cup just handed him. In a flight of madness he let go all caution and training to rush in toward Caleum's blade, either to kill his opponent then and there or else speed the course of his own blood's flowing.

Caleum moved to dodge this blow, and was almost safely beyond reach, when Jupiter's blade found his leg and dug in very deeply, teaching him well the agony of metal conquering flesh.

Wounded, they fought on from strength of will, long past when other men would have expired. Each was inspired by the other's resolve, and each was determined to leave the field of battle with another victory, another day of life.

Jupiter's wound was to his vital section, though, and he soon sucked and gasped for breath.

Caleum was also hobbled and fought with his weight pressing down on what was no longer a sound limb. And, as they drew up for one last thrust and parry, their eyes met. They lunged again; Jupiter fell upon Caleum's sword. When Caleum withdrew it, the other man lay dead before him.

The rest of the British had already abandoned the field to nightfall, leaving their dead and wounded all around. When Caleum killed mighty Jupiter, he knew the man deserved to be delivered back to his home at Mashpee, or at least deep into the silent earth there, but such was not possible. He barely left that field himself, as a pair of friends led him off to the medical tent so his leg might be attended to—if there was still hope left to save it.

Although the pain was unbearable, he insisted on leaving the field under his own power, limping slowly with a wince round his eyes each time the afflicted limb touched the ground. It took toward an hour, but they finally gained the doctor's attention. The scene all around that place was ghoulish and filled with moans as night thickened. Men of all ranks lay willy-nilly, nursing their injuries from the fight. Some were only modestly hurt, while others were too far on death's journey ever to be brought back and died in the afterglow of victory instead of on the field of battle. They themselves could scarce tell the difference, except that on the battlefield someone might have given them a friendly blow of mercy, while here they died slowly.

Several camp followers came round, bringing water to the men or administering rum to those who were about to have surgery. Between those who had only suffered shallow wounds and those whose death was certain, Caleum waited his turn for treatment.

His comrades who had brought him bandaged his wound themselves with rags they found in the infirmary. They then left to report back to duty—as there was more fighting to be done the next day—leaving Caleum among those other war claimed. He felt fatigue creep through his entire being then, although the pain in his leg kept him from sleeping, as it did almost that whole night through.

As he listened to his fellow soldiers' moans the only thing that gave him solace was to remove his coat, which was cold with sweat, and stare at the scene of Stonehouses his wife had embroidered into its lining long ago. It comforted him as he saw his uncle and aunt, then wife and child, although all were older in life than in the picture. It was a magical thing Libbie had made, even if her craft could not hold up against the movement of time. Young Rose was five already, and conversing about all she saw around her, and they already had another who was no longer so small. Why their father was gone was hardest for them, but they understood he did something very important and was any day going to return. Staring then at all of them from Stonehouses, even from so long ago, he was filled with all the universe of love. It was this alone that gave him comfort in his pain and allowed him to suffer through that night without succumbing to the well of grief that claimed those who were injured and did not hold on so strongly as he. Through all the hell of that night, it was the only tether that kept him fastened to the world.

He suffered there in the medical hall for four days, as the surgeon let Nature work upon his wound. Each one was a greater agony for Caleum than the one before, and he dreamed feverishly during this time of all manner of things. By the fourth day of the ordeal he could bear it no longer, as his wound had begun to fester and the pain tossed his mind like some small play toy. He saw himself in a dark cavern that last night, descending endlessly.

When he finally reached the end of his descent, Jasper Merian was waiting for his grandson before a massive gate. He took from Caleum his old sword, which the living was at first hesitant to relinquish, and handed him a carved stick to help him walk. He bid Caleum to follow, and led the way through the entrance. They emerged in one of the gigantic rooms of that place, and soon after reached an open field. When they came into the field, there was a great swarm of people, some in the most tortured positions and others very content. Jasper Merian pointed out each group and explained all the men and beasts there to his grandson as the two of them walked along the bank of a river that flowed through the field, dividing it in half. One of the demi-spheres was hung with dark clouds, while sunshine and abundance ruled over the other. It looked to Caleum like one of the scenes from his sword, and he strained to see all he could, and to understand it.

On an island in the center of the river was a great assembly, and Jasper pointed at those gathered there, as they looked back at Caleum with keen interest and longing. His own curiosity was unbearable, and he wanted nothing more than to hear what each had to say, but Jasper would not let him cross over, although from where he stood their voices were just beyond comprehension. Among them were two who needed no explaining, as they looked at Caleum and he at them for a very long time—all wanting speech and communion: Purchase Merian, his father, and beside him his wife, who Caleum knew to be his own mother, though he had not seen her since he was a tiny boy. Each of the others was also either an ancestor or descendant of Caleum himself; Merian explained who each one was who came before him but said little about those who would come after, except to point out how many of them there were and to say some would achieve great things in their day.

How he craved to cross the water then, but Jasper Merian still held him back and began to lead him away from the shores of that river and out of that meadow.

When they reached the gates again, Jasper concluded his conversation with his grandson and bid good-bye to him until it was his time to join them there, and was instantly gone from his side. Caleum, who had been warned to take care, stood straight and marched back through that tableau of misery, until he reached the cavern he had first come down. He began to climb endlessly against those sharp walls, until he was finally back in the air and light of the earth.

He sought to stand then, thinking he had some mission to accomplish, but a brace of men stood over him, holding him down. It took all of them there to keep him from moving, for the agony he felt next filled him with inhuman strength, as the physician began cutting at his fetid wound.

He had felt pain before in his life, but nothing had prepared him for the anguish of that day. He struggled at first against the hands holding him down, but soon had no choice but to relent and bite down upon the musket ball the surgeon placed in his mouth, as he continued cutting away the skin and flesh that had gone bad. When he finished with that, the real pain started, as he took a saw and began to cut through the bone.

After the surgery was done the doctor covered the wound with flour and lint, then wrapped it in cloth to keep it dry, and moved on to the next man down the line. The hands that had been holding him came off; there was no fear of his standing anymore—for that he had not strength to do, or means by which to do so.

He lay upon his cot, with his greatcoat pulled close beneath his chin, but shivered nonetheless, as he could neither find comfort nor stop the coldness that clung to him that night. When he looked at the picture inside his coat he turned his head away, not wanting to see, for sorrow he might glimpse himself from before.

For two weeks he stayed there, healing from the surgery. When they changed the dressing over his stump, at the end of the first week, he was told it was going nicely. He no longer cared. He only wanted to be able to move around again under his own power, and he longed to go away from that place.

By early November he was able to stand at last, and they gave him a pair of crutches to hold himself up with. He wrapped his coat around his shoulders and moved himself out of the tent—for how he did it he no longer considered to be walking.

It was three years since he had first signed up, and his natural term of enlistment would soon be over. He himself counted it done, and that he had fulfilled his terms of service. The tide of war had turned with that fight at Saratoga, and the army had moved on, and he was alone in the world again.

There was one place on earth he belonged to and ought go, and his mind was locked hard upon it. He had in his possession money enough, and this he used now to hire a coach to carry him down to New York City, where he might get a fast boat back to Stonehouses.

t w o

~

It was late in the evening when his hired coach finally reached town.
The streets were all deserted, and he took his trunk from the driver in
the darkened lane, uncertain where he would sleep the night. The coach-
man had suggested the hotel they were standing in front of, but, looking up at the shabby building, he knew it was not a place for him. He
hoisted his trunk over his shoulder, with a rope tied to both ends, and
started up Pearl Street on his crutches in the failing light. The weight
of the trunk and the unevenness of the paving threatened several times
to steal his balance, but he held fast and at last came to an elegant building with a small plaque on its door that seemed suitable. He turned the
brass handle, entered the foyer, where a small desk stood on top of an
Oriental carpet, and approached the man sitting behind it to request a
room. When the proprietor asked how long he would be staying, he answered that he did not know. He only knew it would be until he had
concluded his business there in the city. "A week seems right."

The clerk stared at him, as if trying to make some determination.
Caleum looked straight ahead, reached into his purse, and retrieved two
gold pieces, which he slid across the counter. When he saw them the
man seemed to decide quickly and stood to show the new visitor to a
room.

As he clambered up the stairs, Caleum was filled by a small burst of
rage each time he lifted his stump upward. What point did any of it
serve? he asked himself, in this mood. Although it was being claimed
that Saratoga had changed the momentum of the war, he could only
curse the master of the dead that so much toil and suffering should gain

so little—other than the fulfillment of its own form. This much blood shall be let and this much death meted out, because these are the terms.

When they reached his room, the clerk put his trunk down and asked whether he required anything else for his comfort. He did. He asked the man who the best carpenter in the city was and how one might find him.

"Jacob Miles," the clerk answered, without hesitation. "He is a shipwright by trade, but there's been little building since the British occupied the city."

"Send around for him first thing tomorrow," Caleum instructed.

The man lit a lantern for his new guest, nodded, and withdrew, leaving him alone in his rented chamber. Caleum stood looking at himself in the glass over the washbasin after the clerk left, and could see plainly how much his bearded face showed the strain of the last several years. He had also lost weight during his time in hospital and found that he barely recognized himself. He was grown old, and looked what seemed to him to be half possessed in the lantern light.

He washed the dust of travel from his body in the basin, put on a clean shirt, and donned his fraying greatcoat, before leaving to go find dinner. As he made his way through the streets of the town, he was still not completely used to moving himself with his arms instead of his legs and sometimes took too ambitious a piece of ground with the crutches. He had to pause then, as if before a jump, to make certain he ended up even with his arms again and not on his backside. He propelled himself down Broadway in this fashion until he came to an inn emitting a glow that seemed to him warmer than the others on the street, and so chose to venture inside.

The room was filled with the sound of men laughing and the smell of pipe smoke, both of which he found welcoming and familiar, and he was shown to a table near a latticed window facing outside. He ordered pot roast from the menu and sat looking out on the streets of the island as he ate. It was the first satisfying meal he could remember in many months, and when he finished he was one of only a few customers remaining. Still, he was not yet ready to go and wished for the first time in his life that he smoked a pipe, so he might sit in that room a while longer, looking out on the city. However, without an excuse to linger, he paid his bill, stopping on his way out to tell the owner, a smallish Negro in a gray waistcoat, how much he had enjoyed his dinner.

"Well, you must join us again, sir," the man replied cordially. "I will save a place for you."

"Thank you," Caleum said, smiling and content with the hospitality that had been extended to him. "I might do just that." He walked back into the cold air and made his way slowly up Pearl to his hotel.

He slept well that night for the first time since his surgery and was embarrassed to be found still asleep when one of the hotel staff knocked on his door the next morning.

"Mr. Merian, Mr. Miles is here to see you," the man announced, when Caleum at last opened the door.

He struggled to recognize the name, but then remembered his conversation from the previous evening and informed the attendant that he would be downstairs presently. He dressed quickly and took up his crutches to go meet the carpenter.

When he went downstairs, the proprietor of the hotel directed him to a room he had provided for their meeting. By the time he entered the buoyancy of the previous evening had left him entirely, and he sat down very gloomily.

"How long have you been at your craft, sir?" he asked Mr. Miles first off, wanting to know to whom he was entrusting himself but also simply to master the man and let him know what type of service he intended to have.

"Twenty years, sir," Mr. Miles answered, although he looked to be the same age as Caleum.

"And where did you learn your trade?"

"Here in New Amsterdam. I started first as apprentice to a ship's joiner."

"Have you ever crafted a human leg before?" Caleum asked him, getting to the point.

"I daresay I have," the carpenter answered. "It's not so uncommon as you would think. I'll only need your measurements."

"I didn't ask how common it was but how often you had done it."

"Please, sir, your measurement."

Something in the man's voice was reassuring to Caleum and he stood up, allowing Mr. Miles to take his measure with a length of cord he took from his pocket and marked expertly with a piece of charcoal.

"What sort of wood would you like it to be crafted of?" he asked when he finished.

"What is the best and strongest you have?' Caleum demanded.

"For strength, it is probably lignum vitae. To my mind it is harder than iron. If you don't mind me saying, though, it's very dear, sir."

"Are you paying from your purse?" Caleum asked, before giving the man a gold piece weightier than any Mr. Miles had held before. "Will that be enough?"

The carpenter nodded like a mandarin. "You'll be very pleased, sir."

"I'll be all the more pleased the better it fits and the sooner I have it."

"For fit I can promise you will be satisfied. For the time it takes, sir, I make no promise, it being a leg, after all, and more art than handiwork. I will let you know as soon as it is done."

Upon hearing that the man could not give him an estimate of how long he would have to wait, Caleum grew more irate but tried his best not to be rough with him.

"You'll do your best, I'm sure of it," was all he said.

"Yes, sir," Miles answered, feeling pity for his customer. "Nothing leaves my workshop, Mr. Merian, before it reaches the highest standards."

"Which standards are those?"

"My own, sir."

"Good day, Mr. Miles."

"Good day, Mr. Merian."

The carpenter left, and soon after a lad of twelve appeared. "My father wishes to know, would you care for something to eat?" the boy asked.

It was nearing noon, and Caleum had not eaten since the night before but had little appetite. "Just a bowl of porridge," he answered.

"Yes, sir," the boy replied crisply, running off to tell the kitchen. He returned a short time later in a great rush, and Caleum was amazed at the gracefulness with which he managed to lay the table before withdrawing.

When he was finally left alone, Caleum ate his meal faster than was his custom, wanting to get out into the fresh air before he lost too much more of the day. He finished, put his spoon down on the tray, took up his crutches, and set out on a path of no particular choosing into the city.

After maneuvering his way first through a group of businessmen, then a brace of soldiers, he found himself on a wide bustling street, which was crowded with gentlemen leaving their offices for the midday meal. He moved himself against the onslaught of people and continued on to the foot of the street, where he came to the market, which was on the waterfront and guarded by its own cannon. Along the pier he paused and looked out over the East River to Long Island, staring down to the farthest visible reaches of its shore.

The last time he was here he had seen only the opposite view, the island floating on the other side of Brooklyn, unattainable to them as they tried to defend their position on the heights. After they were routed, he watched the cannons and smoke rise over the river as they retreated through the forest, so that it appeared the whole city was on fire. If it were any other town, everyone knew, they would have burned it long ago themselves instead of leaving it to the British. Instead, they had strict orders to preserve it at all costs, and so relinquished the place to the enemy. It being more important than the outcome of the war, as it was so vital to the commerce of the entire world—just as the river mingled universally with all the waters of the ocean, carrying whatever flowed on it out into that same ocean as lapped the shores of Europe and Africa.

That night it had seemed the city would burn nonetheless, and when he woke the next day he was amazed to see it still standing. It was indestructible, he thought then. It was an opinion Stanton had later confirmed, during one of his last conversations with him.

"Wheresoever there are coffeehouses that serve the brew of Speculation, and men gather to buy at one price, hoping to sell at another or else turn Information into Profit, or Time into Assets, or are in any way otherwise engaged in the Free Trade of Goods and Ideas, they are doing the business of that town, and it is useless to try to stop them in that, because it is how Free Men everywhere have conducted their affairs since the rise of civilization. None but a Tyrant would seek to suppress it or think to slow its march. If anyone ever attempted to burn it, however— a thing that must be preserved from happening at all costs—what one would find very quickly is that there is another New York beneath the first, and another beneath that. And so on. Further, beneath the very last New York is a City that floats not on water but on the very air and it is indestructible, being the inheritor of all Free Cities before it and all their inspirited dreams. And so with great Boston. And so with Philadelphia."

Now that he had the chance to see it up close, he could only look out the other way, though, as the ducks also swam against the current on the dark water, and the reflection of the clouds made it appear that ice had already formed here and there.

In his free-floating state he could think of no place else he should be at that moment other than the city that would not burn. He thought how, because of that, the Brits had been spared as well from swelling with so many more dead.

He could also think of no other place, with the exception of Philadelphia, where men from so many nations gathered for so many different purposes that one would not know they were at war with each other at all, except for the blockades locking the harbor waters shut to the vessels that normally plied them—and even many of these still managed to get past the inconvenience of war and on with their business.

Strange that he should share a sidewalk with those he had only recently engaged in combat. Yet even when he had passed British patrols walking through the city, he did not feel they were at war against one another but merely men on separate errands. That strangeness turned to bitterness, though, as he turned from the river and leaned on his crutches again.

He had been told in the beginning, and was inclined to believe for a time, that he was fighting for some noble spirit in his country, or else in nature itself, and some inalienable right of that spirit. Now he saw he had fought only so the colonists might better control their own wealth. As for liberty and the rest, he thought, they were freer all before. What liberty could be claimed here in the market but the freedom of traders to collect profit no matter who ruled? Or, better still, the liberty for them to rule themselves, according to their needs alone, and collect as vast a profit as could be gotten from nature? He turned and walked back up Wall toward the North River.

When he reached Broadway, the street began to slope downward and he grew tired before he knew it, being unused to navigating different types of terrain with his crutches. He changed his intended route and turned south instead, until he was on a narrow street with many pubs lining its sides and thought to go into one in order to relax and take a proper meal.

All along that way a stream of men from every walk of the city flowed, and each broke off like a little tributary through that doorway best suited to men such as himself—either because of religious affiliation, station, mother language, or trade. Caleum stood watching awhile until he discovered a doorway that seemed less a cohesive whole than a collection of those who did not belong to the other tributaries. Into this he himself went, following with the general current and certain that even if he was not as comfortable as he could possibly be, neither would he be uncomfortable.

He was proved correct when he crossed the threshold, as the clientele of that place could be described as neither rich nor poor, nor was it old or young, or even British or American, but just what it had seemed from outside.

Behind the counter a tall dark man served beer and conversed with his customers. It was not refined as the inn where he was sojourning, but it was far more convivial for that sea of company, where no man could claim to be lost. He took a table by the window, so he might look out onto the street, and waited to be attended.

After a short while the serving girl came round and asked what he wished for.

"What do you have today?"

"Same as every day," she answered. "But if I was you I'd take the shepherd's pie."

The only time he had ever eaten that before was in the army, when they would cover horse's meat with a layer of thin dough. He entrusted himself to her suggestion, though, and nodded. "Then shepherd's pie it will be."

He was surprised when she returned from the kitchen with a plate piled high with a thick dish that gave off steam as she carried it through the room to his table. When he cut into the shell it was flaky, and filled with succulent meat and vegetables that had not yet lost their bite. The food warmed him as he stared out on the street or else took in his immediate surroundings. The room was loud with conversation by then, but not so loud so as to intrude on his own thoughts, and Caleum took pleasure in hearing pieces of these conversations from time to time without having to listen until they became wearisome, as he would in company. There were also quite a few others who sat by themselves, either reading or daydreaming or else still engaged in their work.

He was glad he had chosen that establishment over the others, and when he finished his meal, took out a pipe and pouch of tobacco he had acquired on his walk. As he smoked and thought about the events of the last months, the crowd slowly disappeared, until he found he was the only person left in the room. When he realized this he grew slightly embarrassed, thinking he might give the impression of being an idler, which he had never been. It was only that his particular business at the moment was only to wait.

When he saw the girl pass, he caught her attention and asked her to bring his check.

"Leaving so soon?" she asked.

He only nodded and smiled at her.

To his surprise she smiled back, and he allowed himself to notice how beautiful she was. He wondered whether it was only a courtesy of her profession or whether her attention was meant for him, or if it was the habit of all young women in the city to always be so friendly.

"You should come back tomorrow," she said. "Mother always makes something special at the end of the week."

Again he could not read her intention, but to have an invitation at all made him feel thankful and welcome. He could grow accustomed to such. At least it might give him the comfort of having a routine.

"If my business allows it," he said, "I will."

With that he pulled himself up and balanced to put on his coat. When he reached for his crutches, though, he found them missing. He looked around until he saw the serving girl standing on his other side, thoughtfully holding them for him.

"Thank you," he said, accepting the kindness of her gesture without protest.

As he walked back to his inn he wondered again what her interest in him was. Perhaps it was exactly as it appeared, he told himself. He had not known such affection in a long time and was heartened, thinking for the first time that perhaps his new condition was not so disastrous as he had thought in the beginning.

He was glad then for his respite in the city, but he knew there was only one place for him and he must get back to Stonehouses soon. As the sun disappeared, casting the island in shadow, he pulled his coat up at the throat to keep out the cold air and carried himself just a bit faster, wondering if perhaps the carpenter had called while he was out.

three

$\backsim$

Nothing. When he returned to the inn there was no message for him from Mr. Miles, and none the following day either. As he sat in his room the third day, waiting for the man to contact him, he began to grow angry at the time it was taking. Whenever he heard someone on the stairs his breath would catch for a small expectant moment, until the footsteps inevitably passed by his door, like good fortune. No one came at all, and, as he knew no one in town other than casual acquaintances, the days seemed to stretch on with an endless bleakness.

The city beyond his windows was nothing but shadows when he looked out that evening near the close of shop hours, and the room itself was reflected back at him in the leaded glass. He could hear now and again the sound of travelers making their way home, but little else that had immediate meaning for him. He let his mind drift toward his own family, whom he was increasingly anxious to see. In this mood of longing he went to his closet, where he took his coat from its hanger to look once more at the scene on its inner lining that he had gazed at so often. To his surprise he found it had faded even further and looked crude to him. He had not noticed this wear before and peered at certain places where the stitching was frayed, attempting to make out already-lost details. What would they think when they saw him again? Had he faded as much from their memory's care? he wondered, until the thought became suffocating.

He did not remember falling asleep, but when he awoke it was already well into night. He roused himself from bed to go for his evening meal, if one could still be had, but instead of leaving immediately he

wanted first to put on a clean shirt, as had always been his custom before the war. He was surprised when he looked in the trunk to see he
had none left, and was aware for the first time that all his clothing was
in great disrepair. He was not a vain man, but he did not wish to give
the wrong impression about himself either, such as might lead someone to mistake him for other than who he was and what his station was.
He decided then to have his dinner that night in the hotel, and went
down to the dining room tentatively on his crutches. Once there, he was
pleased to find they were serving rack of lamb, his favorite dish, though
he had never had it on any day outside of the Sabbath. It seemed a great
decadence to him, but one he was happy to indulge.

As he ate, he felt his earlier sense of contentment return, drawing a
satisfaction from his stomach that seemed otherwise to elude him. When
he finished his meal he took out his new pipe and began smoking. He
did not, however, enjoy the pipe as he had before and was about to extinguish it when the proprietor's boy came over to the table with a small
pouch.

"My father said to offer this to you. It's hard to get decent tobacco in
the city now."

When Caleum filled his pipe with the proprietor's offering he could
scarcely believe the difference between the new tobacco and the smoke
he had purchased earlier, even though it had cost him dearly. He had
thought when he first tried it that it was simply a vile custom, but this
new tobacco made clear to him the pleasure of the habit. He luxuriated
in the rich aroma of smoke and ordered another cordial, for the boy came
round to check on him with an attentiveness he had not observed anywhere else. He thought then there was nothing unavailable to a man in
that town and delighted in the satisfactions of the table.

After finishing the cordial and pipe, he went upstairs, well contented
with both himself and the city and beginning to feel rejuvenated. When
he lay down that night he fell directly asleep and enjoyed a deep restful
slumber.

The next morning he rose early and went down to the dining room,
where instead of porridge, which had been his usual breakfast for as long
as he could remember, he had a plate of eggs with bacon and sausage,
thinking he might as well enjoy himself fully while he was able, such
leisure being unavailable to him ever before, and it coming after such

sacrifice. When he finished his meal, he asked at the front desk where he might find a good tailor, as his clothes were in a state such as he could no longer bear.

The proprietor was quick with a suggestion and pointed out the way to get there from the hotel. As he walked up Broadway through all the bustle of the business day, Caleum felt as if he were on holiday instead of merely performing much-needed chores, and this in turn livened his mood. When he arrived at the tailor he chose the fabrics he liked best, then instructed the man to make him four complete suits of clothes and ten good shirts, as he was unlikely ever to be in the city again.

When the tailor asked whether he would also require a new greatcoat, Caleum thought it over for a very long time before answering in the affirmative. His old coat was much worn, and it had besides been a coat meant for war, not civilized life, and he was now again a gentleman of peace. He paid out his gold and asked where he might find a good barber.

"The best Negro barber in the city is said to be John Paige, up by the Collect," the tailor answered promptly, writing down the address. Caleum thanked him and left.

It was still before midday when he reached the street again. He thought about hiring a coach but decided on walking, as he had grown quite used to his crutches, so much so that he had begun to move about on his three legs as well as other men on two. He went up Broadway lightly, until he came to Chambers Street, where the bare trees lining the road allowed the sunshine to fall unimpeded across the wide sidewalk. It was a bright if brisk day, and the warm light felt good to his skin as he turned east toward his destination.

He was immediately overcome by an unbearable stench, though, and saw that he had entered a precinct of tanneries. The odor of animal skins and lye strangled the air, as dirty reddish water ran over the sidewalk and into the gutters. Here and there, he could see large clay vats filled with different-colored dyes, all very rich, and skins stretched out for drying. Bits of hair, or wool tumbled down the street, which he was careful to step around, not wanting to trick his balance.

When he finally passed those stinking streets he was in a small lane filled with breweries. He was reminded then of the serving girl who had brought him his lunch the day before. Perhaps he would eat there again, he thought, looking down to check the address of the barber on a slip of paper the tailor had given him. When at last he found the place he also found himself weary, having walked farther than he had reckoned on its being, and searched out a place to sit down. All the clients inside the little shop were Negroes such as himself, but of every caste of life, from the African who spoke but little English to the stern faces that seemed to him more Dutch than Negro. Still, he was comfortable, as he was in a good mood in general, and reclined amiably in his seat.

When he finally sat in the barber's chair, he requested a full shave and haircut. The barber was a tall dark man who looked gruff, but when he began working he was very ginger and methodical. It soothed Caleum to feel so well cared for, which he could not remember being since he was a boy, and the shave was the best he could remember. When it was done he looked as though he had shed five years off his age, and he left the chair feeling like his better self again. More than that: He felt he had shed a carapace that had grown up around him in place of his normal skin.

He set about then to find the pub from the day before. He walked back the way he came, past the breweries and through the tannery district, at which point he was too tired to continue and decided to hire a coach.

By the time he found the pub the lunch crowd had all left, and the room was nearly empty. The same waitress who had attended him before was working again, though, and when she came to show him to his table there was the same enticing openness about her.

"You're a bit late, aren't you?" she asked, as if their meeting had been previously arranged.

He did not answer, not knowing how one was supposed to deal with such directness. He wondered whether she would take offense if he were to give his own tongue such free rein. He had not made an advance toward a woman in that way since his marriage to Libbie, and then it was according to the rules of proper engagement, while here in this city he could not tell what rules governed the different interactions between the sexes.

"I see you've had a haircut?" she went on, not seeming to mind that her last question had gone unanswered.

"I did," he answered, taking the same seat he had previously occupied.

"Well, it looks very smart," she continued.

"Thank you," he told her. "What do they call you?"

"Elissa," she answered him. "And who might you be?"

"Caleum Merian." He introduced himself with both his names, even though that did not seem always to be the custom of the island.

"Well, it is very nice to see you again, Mr. Merian," she replied. "I think the chowder is good today."

He simply nodded, allowing the woman to chose his meal for him. When she brought it around, she had the same smile as before, which prompted him to wonder again how she would respond if he made an advance. Emboldened by the fact that he had no reputation in that city, he decided he would do just that when she next came by the table.

"Would you care to meet me this weekend?" he asked, when he saw his opportunity.

"And just where is it you want me to meet you?"

"At Bowling Green," he answered, trying to think of a place that would not seem too intimate.

"It'll be freezing there," she said. "But I'll be at Mary Hamlet's on Saturday, around eight, if you should happen by." She smiled at him again.

"Where is that?" he asked.

"You're not from here?" she teased him. "It's over on Mulberry. Everyone knows it if you have any trouble."

It wasn't until he left that he realized the implication of what he had just done, and it occurred to him that he knew nothing about the woman. He worried he had made a bad decision and told himself he was not bound to go there, as she knew little about him and would never find him again if he chose not to go. As he remembered her smile, though, he knew he would venture to meet her. There was something about her he found exhilarating in a way he could not remember having encountered before, and he allowed himself to trust this instinct.

He remained hesitant, though, as he was very strict with himself in such matters. What he argued then was that it was only lack of feminine company for so long that made him feel as he did. The line of thought turned on him, however, and he found himself arguing that this was a perfectly good reason why he should enjoy her company the coming weekend. He told himself to let his boldness have its way and see how far it would get him. Despite his efforts to quell it, he found this inner arguing and turmoil delicious in and of itself, both as its own pleasure and as an intimation of larger ones to come.

He reached the inn with the same lightness he had felt the day before, knowing he would accept her invitation, from curiosity if not the growing loneliness he felt there in those days.

He hoisted himself up the few stairs that led to the door and entered the hotel, hoping his new suits might be ready before the weekend. As he continued on to his room, he heard his name called. He was delighted indeed when he turned around to see Mr. Miles waiting.

"Mr. Miles," he said, greeting the other man. "Have you been here long?"

"No, sir," Mr. Miles answered. "Only just ahead of you. I have your order ready, and have brought it around so you can try it for fit." Caleum nodded, and indicated that Mr. Miles should follow him up to his room. When he closed the door, Mr. Miles opened the large box he was carrying and removed from it the most beautiful piece of wood Caleum had ever beheld.

He peered at it a long while, then stretched out his hand and let his fingers touch the new limb, and it looked exactly like a leg, so much so that but for its texture and shading he would be hard pressed to tell it from his other. It felt cold and ungiving, such that no one would ever mistake it for the living thing, but it was no less accomplished because of that and even seemed alive in its way.

"Do you wish to try it?"

He nodded, and Mr. Miles approached and began explaining the fastening mechanism he had crafted, so that the binding of wood and flesh would be absolute and dependable.

"It takes a bit getting used to," he went on, as Caleum sat down and allowed the man to affix the wood to his gnarled stump with greater care than any doctor he ever encountered. When he stood, Mr. Miles handed to him a cane made of the same wood as the leg, and it was just as well-fashioned and polished.

"You might want to keep with the crutches for a while, but in time this will give you a little better mobility," he explained, while Caleum walked from one end of the room to the other.

"I have seldom seen such craftsmanship, Mr. Miles," he told the other man, moved to joy by what he had made. "It is not so heavy as it seemed in the box and feels very strong."

"Aye, your coins are the same mint, but for this, Mr. Merian, even steel could not cut it."

"Aye, Mr. Miles, I knew the blade that could," Caleum said, casting his eyes at his visitor, who then looked at the still living stump of Caleum's leg above the wood, before averting his gaze.

Caleum went back and forth across the room several more times, growing used to the new appendage, until he thought he could feel not only the impact of the wood with the floor, but that he also sensed when anything was near the wood as well, even though he knew this to be an impossibility. When he was satisfied, he sat down.

"Thank you for such a fine job, Mr. Miles," he said.

"I tried to give it my best, sir," the man answered. "If you need anything else at all, please don't hesitate to send for me at my workshop."

With that he stood and began to withdraw. Caleum lifted himself again to see his visitor to the door. When the other man had gone, he went back and forth across the room again, before putting on his old coat and going out to try his new leg in the street.

Once he exited the hotel, however, he felt an immediate self-consciousness. To see a man without a leg did not seem so strange, but to see one upon a wooden leg he worried would be odd. Nevertheless, he began walking toward Bowling Green with as much confidence as he could muster, trusting this new leg beneath him would be faithful.

By the time he reached the great lawn he could feel the weight of the wood and found himself tired from carrying this new burden. He found a bench to rest upon and sat there, looking out toward the Sound as the autumn wind blew north. As he watched the sails moving out in the harbor, through the barren branches, he wondered which of these vessels might take him home if he went down to the dock at that moment to book passage. If he went that very day he might even make it in time for Rose's birthday.

He knew, though, he would not go that day. He needed at least another week to finish his business there, and to recuperate, before taking up the burden of travel again, to say nothing of husbandry.

He thought again about the shock it would be for them at home, when they saw him, and wondered how he would be able to fit into his former life again. Although every year he had seen those conscripted go from being farmers to soldiers and others going back again the other way, he did not see how it could be so simple a movement and knew the first one was easier than the other. It takes awhile to relearn one's former self, he thought to himself, as he looked toward the ocean, if ever it is possible again.

He wrapped his arms around his shoulders, pressing the embroidery inside his coat against his body. I will make it there in time for Thanksgiving, he promised himself, and he was satisfied as evening fell and he walked back to the inn for supper.

four

~

He arrived at the hall, on a narrow, slanting street off the main way, promptly at eight o'clock, only to find it still deserted. He went to the bar and ordered a glass of rum, which he took to a table off on one side of the room and sat alone, nursing it. By nine o'clock the hall had grown half full with people, but he still did not see Elissa. He told himself it had been the remotest of possibilities to begin with, and that she had never promised him her company. Perhaps she had been teasing, and it was only her way. He tried to decide then whether he should leave to find other amusement or stay on in any case, to see what else might unfold there that night. He felt foolish, though, and had decided to leave when he saw two faces appear at the entrance whom he recognized from his past.

The first to enter was Carl Schuyler, from the army, and just behind him was the slave Julius from Berkeley. When they saw him they immediately came over to his table, and he stood up to shake each of their hands, glad to be reacquainted and, beyond that, elated to see familiar faces.

Julius, who had known him longer, was first to speak. "The last time I saw you, they was leading you from the battlefield, and we all thought for sure you'd died."

"I did not," Caleum answered, signaling to the waiter for more drinks. "But I came powerful close. Has your own tour ended?" he asked next, changing the subject from his own fortunes.

"No, but the fighting has stopped for the winter, so we were given a leave."

"We can travel on to Berkeley together, then," Caleum said to Julius. "It is good to have company on the road."

"Any other time I would, but I'm not headed back that way."

"That's where your sister Claudia and the rest of your people are," Caleum said. "They'll want to see you."

"Unless I want to be always and ever somebody's slave," Julius answered, "there is no place for me there anymore."

Caleum could only nod at this. "Where will you go instead?"

"I don't know yet, but not back to bondage," he said defiantly. "Not under my own power, at least."

"Then we must make the most of our meeting," Caleum proclaimed. He had never been one for rich meals and lavish wines, but he ordered as well as they could from the menu offered in the hall that night. Their table was laid with the best fruits of the harvest, and the choicest meats, and they dined sumptuously, reminiscing and telling feats of past bravery and wishing one another only good fortune for the future, especially for Julius in his new plans.

He had all but forgotten how he originally learned of that place called Mary's Hamlet—and was lost completely in nostalgia and boasts with his old acquaintances—when he saw Elissa standing at the end of their table. He offered her a seat among them but did not stand.

"I've come with friends," she answered, but his own friends were well supplied with drink by then and eager to have women's company. They told her there was more than room enough for all of them at their table.

When the places were filled, and everyone had been introduced, the laughter and fellow feeling reminded Caleum of those festive days as a boy when his grandfather entertained in the great hall at Stonehouses. Although he was not among kin, he felt as cheerful as he had then, enjoying the pleasures of sharing his board with friends.

Elissa sat at his side, and each time she laughed she leaned toward him and brushed lightly against his arm. It had been years since he felt a woman so close, and each time she touched against him he wondered what it meant, but also why he had held himself so chastely and apart from feminine company. He thought then of his family and children. And was reminded in general of all those things the heart will not relinquish. Julius and Carl were both surprised to see him so casual that night, as he was always rigid with dutifulness since each had known him.

Now he relaxed, letting the evening expand unchecked and allowing whatever suggestions it might make to hold and seduce him.

He watched the girl Elissa as she interacted with his friends, and, though some might think her beneath the women he was accustomed to, especially Libbie, she had a way of making those around her feel relaxed, as all mingled freely according to whim and will and not as was dictated by usual social customs. Caleum also held Julius in the light of friendship again, as he had not done since they were boys and all equal.

"Did you notice anything strange at Saratoga?" he asked, taking Julius by the shoulder, when they had exhausted their talk of battle and everyone they both knew from Berkeley.

"Everything was strange at Saratoga, and all of it too familiar."

"Did you see anyone you knew from other days?"

Julius nodded in recognition. "You saw him too?"

They both shuddered with sadness. "To see him there, you would think he had never known any other life," Caleum remarked.

"I'm afraid he doesn't know any life at all anymore," Julius said, going on to report how Bastian had been mortally injured at that battle, as he oversaw the artillery with his lord. "When he was shot, the Blue Colonel was on the other side of the field, and they say he would not let anyone else touch him, calling them all commoners who tried."

"How far some men seem to travel from their origins," said one of the ladies, who was deeply affected by the story of Bastian Johnson, when Julius had finished relating it.

"Aye," they all uttered at different volumes, then paused to lift their glasses in a toast of remembrance. As Elissa placed her glass back on the table she touched Caleum's arm again, and in that moment he felt a doorway back from the isolation that had gripped him for so long.

It is not good always to eat alone, he thought, placing his hand upon hers, very briefly, without looking at her.

"Would you like to dance?" Julius asked the woman next to him, who was called Sally, as the table grew quiet. She took his hand gladly, and they stood to make their way to the ballroom floor.

"Let's all dance," Carl suggested, at which everyone at the table stood up eagerly except Caleum and Elissa.

They all looked to him, to make certain he was not offended, but Caleum only looked back, then pushed his chair from the table slowly and stood to his full height. He held his cane in one hand and offered the other to Elissa. She took hold of it and followed him to the dance floor, smiling but nervous for his safety.

In the middle of the room, Caleum placed one arm around Elissa's waist and held her hand with the other, grasping his cane simultaneously in case he should lose his balance.

He did not, and when they moved over the floor it was as if wood had great respect for wood, and while he was not perfect in his movements, he was more graceful than any would have expected. They danced through two songs and made their way back to the table only when he was well tired out.

After they sat down the waiter brought over another bottle of cordial, and the two lounged in comfortable weariness. They were easy with each other then, as they had not been earlier in the night, and spoke tenderly in whispers as the rest of the room went about its affairs.

Eventually the others returned to the table as well, but by then the rest of the crowd was thinning and it was time for all to go home, or wherever they were passing the night. Caleum made arrangements to meet with Julius and Carl later in the week, when they announced their departure, but he and Elissa stayed on in the hall, reclining and talking softly. At last the music ended and they could stay there no longer, so walked out into the freezing night air together.

Under the white light of the gas lamps Caleum was bold indeed when he invited her to return with him to his room, but she declined, saying it would not do. There was, however, another inn, known as a place where lovers carried on surreptitious affairs in secret warrens, and he assented to this and let her lead him there through the frigid streets, until at last they reached the place and climbed the stairs and could be alone—as they were anxious to be.

They were still ensconced there two weeks later on Thanksgiving Day. Despite Elissa's desire to cook for him from her own pots and serve him off her own table, they could not go where she lived, for fear of scorn and disapproval. Instead, Caleum took her to an inn he had heard of, which had the reputation of serving the best food in the city.

Julius and Carl had both left the island already, Carl to visit with his family in Boston and Julius to see a woman he had met at Mary's Hamlet from New Jersey, but Caleum had only moved from one hotel to another, being enchanted by Elissa as their affections for each other seemed to grow and grow. He would not—and perhaps it was only guilt that held him from it—term what passed between them love, but it was a rapturous thing all the same and he thought it a worthy rival to domestic contentment, though whether it could last he dare not ask himself.

At the inn they were seated at a good table by the owner, and all through the room were elegantly dressed men and women, many with children, enjoying themselves as the waiters brought a sumptuous feast to every table. When their own table was laid, Caleum gave prayer and named all his thankfulness for that year.

Elissa testified after him, and, although she had been made nervous when he mentioned his children, she told first how glad she was for the gift of his affection—claiming to have never known any before it.

They feasted then on a meal that made clear how the place had earned its good name. Such fine food, such good drink, such merry company—however, all that could not stop Caleum from wondering to himself what was happening that day at Stonehouses. If he had been wearing his old army coat he might have gazed at its interior scene then, but that garment was on the bottom of his trunk, and he wore his new clothes, which neither comforted nor burdened him with any memories.

As she watched him, Elissa began to grow cross and asked where his thoughts were. She was in a hard position, and knew she could not make too many demands on him or even ask him to stay on beyond what he wanted, even if it was her deepest wish. She was relieved therefore when he answered her duplicitously—claiming only to be thinking of old acquaintances—satisfied that he did not say outright he was thinking of his family or else that he wished he had left already to be with them.

"This is the best Thanksgiving I have ever known," she said, touching him on the arm and holding him fast.

"It is one of my best," he said truthfully, thinking first on that list was the year he was first blessed with Rose.

Their joy with each other had not traveled its full course, but Elissa was afraid then it was running out, and throughout the meal she kept asking her lover for reassurances. This in turn soured Caleum's mood, as he felt he was being pinned down.

"Let us have another cordial," he said, "and enjoy our meal. I am as happy as I have ever been here. You must not worry so much about me leaving you." She was serene when she heard his words, secure for the moment that his heart and devotion were with her.

Nor was what he said merely a deceit to put her off pestering him with questions. He was as happy with her that day as he could remember. It was merely a different sort of happiness than what he was used to, and the knowledge that pleasure itself could be pursued in the same way he had gone after his wife, or his yearly production, was a small unsettling revelation to him. He had thought before that stable marital harmony was the only dependable kind there was, but now he knew it was only one of many and not better than those others, merely a different formulation. It dizzied him to think of it, as he saw how arbitrary one way of life might be over another.

When he first found himself thinking this he feared it was devil's logic; however, he did not know how to resist it, for he could find nothing sound on the other side that satisfied the question of why one form of life was better than another, or even why going after what was strenuous and correct was better than going after what delivered the greatest joy.

He knew men learned in religion would reproach him sharply and make clear with moral reasoning what was unavailable to his intellect alone—but that he loved a woman who was not his wife, even the most pious of them could not argue away, or tell him why he should not believe in its existence.

His heart then had its own method of philosophizing and reckoning, which did not square with the others at all, asking his conscious mind whether, if a man's sin is that he is not an angel, might he still not be a worthy man.

"Will we spend Christmas together?" Elissa asked him in the midst of all this, for she was equally in love with him and saw in his eyes that she had gained ascendancy in his mind.

"Yes," he answered her, smiling. "We will."

She was made happy by this, but for her position to be truly impregnable she knew there was only one way to achieve that goal. For a woman she could compete with, no matter how fancy she was, but his children would always tug on his bosom, unless he had others with her. It was not a cold calculation on her part, only a reasonable one, as matters of the heart often need aids of reason to sort out their arcs and realize themselves.

When they finished with dinner, she was especially affectionate with her man and, rather than seek out other amusement for the evening, insisted that they go back to their little hotel, where they might pass the rest of the evening together in bliss.

That night as they lay again in their secret chamber, she thought how the spell of love alone could not last indefinitely, and asked him again to tell her his love for her. He answered with sweet words and knew there was much truth to them.

When he married it had been from compatibility and a sense of duty, as he was very young and feared all those other footpaths the heart might follow. With her his duty was to his heart's happiness and his desires. He could be content with that for a very long time, he knew, perhaps even so far as the end of his days.

"My heart did not know it's true deepness before I met you," he said, holding her naked breast. Their affection for each other had actually startled him, when he realized how simple and pure it was, but also when he recognized the profundity of that weightlessness.

She was exuberant when she heard this, for she had spared herself no sacrifice in order to take care of him and increase his gladness. Although she tried to be discreet, she knew it had already cost her her reputation, for everyone spoke of her as a dishonored woman. If love be dishonor, though, she was happy to be infamous, as they shared in that room on Catherine Street an ecstasy whose heat consumed all other fuel.

"Will you stay with me?" she asked him again.

"Yes," he said. "I will."

"How long?" she begged, for she wanted him to be clear about what she offered him and what she needed.

"As long as can be told on all the clocks in heaven," he answered. He fell back into her arms after that, until he began to forget about all else outside that room.

"And I will always be devoted to you," she promised. "If you left me now I know I could not live."

He was possessed then by her touch as she was by his words, and the two of them fell upon each other in lovemaking.

They were still awake late into that night, long after most of the city had already retired and was dreaming. Under the twilight that ebbed through the windows, they held each other still.

"Do you know what would please me more than anything else?" she asked him sleepily, as he held her about the waist.

"No, but I want to know nothing more."

"I cannot ask it."

"Tell me."

"It is to have a house and children with you," she said, telling him next how tired she was of living like a fugitive in their rented room, and promising how much happier she could make him if only they had a home of their own to be in together.

Caleum did not need to think about it very long before telling her that he would find her a house where they could be together. For he also missed having a home and knew that making one with her would bring him no end of pleasure. "I will buy you a house," he promised.

He did not know about children, but he knew that after taking up with him for so long it would be impossible for her to go back to her people without disgrace, and he did not wish to see that ever happen to her—or that she should go wanting for anything, or beg favor of any-one else, even if he could not make her his wife. His honor required at least this much. He would give her a house.

He did not think then what it would mean for his intention of re-turning to his own home, as that place had grown very distant from his mind's eye. He only thought about Christmas with Elissa, and what he should do for an income if he stayed on in that city—as his purse was not as full as it used to be and would be taxed very definitely by the purchase of a home.

five

He searched the city continuously during the weeks leading up to the holiday, until he found a place he thought would be suitable for the two of them. It was a respectable merchant's house though not grand, built in the Dutch manner with a little store on the bottom floor and living quarters above it. When he presented it to her Christmas morning, she was overjoyed as she went through the rooms, planning out in her mind the function each would serve and how best to make them happy there.

When they moved in, he found everything in the house had been arranged around his needs and satisfaction, so that he never had to think of anything disagreeable while he was there and, in fact, marveled at how constantly pleasant his new house was and how untroubled he felt in its rooms.

For income, Caleum Merian set up a small concern in the shop on the first floor, selling wares that were much coveted but difficult to come by during the war. It proved very popular with the people of that city, as it was filled with delicacies, and on weekends he would share with Elissa those things he had hoarded for the two of them alone. Having scoured the wharfs for smuggled goods, there might be fine Irish lace or hats in the latest fashion from France, one of which he might present to her, reveling in the happiness it brought her. He also received things such as sets of silver from colonists whose means were stretched by the occupation, or even items in gold from the better families on the island, which always reached him by way of intermediaries, and he was always understanding and discreet.

He found himself becoming a true citizen of that town as his business grew, until he thought very little of wanting to be anywhere else in his life again. He was near thirty years old and found the new rhythm of his days quite agreeable, and the material pleasures of this life were such as he had not known existed before. Something had changed within him, but, however different he had become, he was at peace from his former self. Dear Elissa, who did not know him before, embraced the man he was instead of remarking on the changes that had taken place, as any from his old life surely would have. This was a liberation for him, and he always felt free with her to say whatever he thought and do as he wanted, with no burdens of any other sort to support.

Elissa was finally confident in their home together, and although her own family worried for her that she was not married but living with a man who was, they accepted it as a better situation than her being merely some passing soldier's fancy. To her, though, there was no difference than if they had exchanged vows in church, because, she thought, marriage is sanctified first in the heart above all other places.

When he stopped speaking of his farm and his children, she knew he was with her completely and intended to remain. No one could fault her that another woman had gotten to him first, but the two of them were together now and that was also meant to be. Nor could anyone reproach her treatment of him, it being such as any man would desire and covet in life.

All of this fortunate domestic routine was at last interrupted one day when an ancient sailor came into Caleum's shop with a set of finest china, which he offered for sale. As Caleum examined the wares, his customer looked at the name stenciled on the glass window and again at Caleum behind his counter.

"Strange name, Merian," he said casually. "I once knew a fellow called that. Aye, I knew his entire family."

"I would comment on your name too, friend," Caleum remarked coolly, "but I do not know ye, so keep my mind and tongue to myself."

"The son would have been around your age," the stranger continued on, undaunted by the rebuke. "They lived near the quays in Providence, but were originally from a place called Stonehouses it was that I did visit on a journey once."

"I will give ten shillings for the china," Caleum offered, ignoring the rest the old man said and walking to his strongbox to get the money. As he went across the room, the sound of his wooden leg striking the floor resonated through the shop and was the only thing that could be heard, as the other man watched him silently. A curious thing about his leg: Either because of it or his growing status in the commercial life of the city, whenever men looked on it, even white men, they deferred to him almost instinctually. If it was a man of very high station, he would always make a little nod of the head, as if wishing to bow but being forbidden that ritual due to caste. In time Caleum had grown used to all this, until he seemed indifferent to anyone else's regard entirely, and they in turn lent him wide berth. Not so the stranger, who let the money remain on the counter and resumed speaking, looking Caleum directly in the eye and not allowing him respite or quarter from his old gaze.

"The man's given name was Purchase, and he was quite a fellow in his day, though I don't think anyone would much recognize it now. He stood near tall as that doorframe, and there wasn't a woman who ever met him who didn't fall squarely in love. Since the first time he knew her, he only had eyes for one, and it was she he gave his whole life to, though happiness was elusive for them.

"They had a little boy, whose name escapes me just now, and the father one day asked that I deliver the boy to his family's place down the coast. As he was my true friend, I obliged him.

"On the way there a storm met us off one of the capes, and I've never seen anything like the boy's lack of fear during that gale. Every man on board was white or gray, depending on his original self, but the boy stood at the edge of the railing staring right out into it. Someone said he spied a ghost ship, which were known to run off that coast, though no one I knew had ever seen one. Whatever the case, when he left the railing the storm abated and we reached land safely.

"He was just as impervious to fear when we set out overland to his people's house, which, when we reached it, was one of the most comfortable places on this earth I ever laid down my head.

"Purchase had a brother, called Magnus, who was almost as tall as he, and their father, who stood somewhere between the two. He was named Jasper Merian, I remember, he was a man in the old style and paid me in gold for delivering his son's boy safely to their door. All of them had the same habit of paying for whatever they got in ready cash, and rarely an argument about the price.

"The other brother had a wife, Adelia, if my mind is still sound, and she was the kindest maid of the country I ever met. She doted on the boy, and I remember thinking, though I was only there a short while, his life was something blessed that he should be so loved by so many people, as I myself had none by then but my wife who loved me—and she died not long after that trip. In any case, those were the Merians I knew in my day. You would not happen to have heard of any of them?"

With each word the old man said and everything he described, Caleum felt a peeling away of the hardened membrane around his memory and recalled a little bit more with each word, until he could recognize the man before him. Rennton had changed very little since then, having turned gray and a bit more wrinkled, but otherwise being obviously the same— as some boys do not metamorphose so much from youth to manhood, so some men receive their true face early in life, which deviates very little from then until their last days.

Looking at him, Caleum remembered that journey they made together with a clarity that illuminated his interior mind like a fire, and he felt then like Adam the first time God called and he refused to answer his Maker, knowing himself finally to be naked.

"Aye. The man was called Rennton who carried me home."

"I did not think you cared to remember," Rennton said.

"How should I ever forget?" Caleum asked, regretful of his earlier arrogance toward the man. "Please, you must be my guest at dinner tonight," he said. "It would be an honor for me."

"Aye," Rennton agreed, remembering the hospitality and good fellowship he had known from Merians in the past and extending to the son the bond of friendship and alliance he had shared with the father.

Caleum wanted to embrace the man who had saved him from orphanage and certain death as a boy, but fearing this would be too familiar, he took Rennton's hands in both of his and pumped them warmly. "We live above the shop here," he told him. "Dinner will be at six, if that suits you."

"I will be there promptly," Rennton answered.

After he left, Caleum closed the shop and went upstairs to tell Elissa they would be having a guest for dinner, which for them was a rarity. In his good mood he also suggested that she invite who she wanted, as they had not entertained a proper party since moving into their home together.

"Maybe your sister would like to come," he said, knowing how her family shunned her since she began living with him.

"I do not think so, but I will send word to her," she replied. "I had better hurry now before the markets close, if we are to make a dinner for so many." She was elated as she left the house then, for she saw how jubilant he was and was in her turn glad to open their home to friends.

When Rennton arrived that evening, he saw Caleum had spared no expense on the meal and had even gone so far as to hire a group of musicians to entertain them. He thought then how much like the father the son had become. He was also was very stirred when Caleum stood to toast him, giving him credit for saving his life.

The house that evening was filled with Caleum's acquaintances from the city, who were all curious to ask questions about Caleum's life before, for it seemed he had just showed up among them with no ties to any place before that one. Elissa at first did not want to hear about Stonehouses and Caleum's family, and she herself was always careful not to wake the memory in him, but she was certain about their life together by then and let her curiosity draw her near to listen.

Rennton for his part was happy to answer what questions he could, but he was also curious to hear what had happened to Purchase's son since he last knew him.

"Tell me how you ended up here?" he asked finally, when the two of them were alone, sharing a glass of port in Caleum's study. "If I had a place like yours I would never venture forth from it, although your father did the same."

"He was drawn out by love," Caleum answered. "I left for duty and the war."

"But you chose to stay here instead of returning?" Rennton asked.

"That is what happened," Caleum said, for he could suddenly no longer remember his reason for staying. He looked across the room just then, and saw Elissa in the doorway, and knew again why he had remained so long. When he first came to her he was broken. Only he did not think he could tell Rennton such.

As Elissa watched him talking to his old friend, she saw both how much she did not know about him and that he was very far away in his thoughts. She went over to him and tried with her touch to bring his mind back to where it had been before.

Caleum felt like a stranger in the house that evening, and everything around him seemed foreign. Although he knew the rooms and the things in them to be his own, he could only think how they were not the rooms he had grown up in or shared with Libbie and their children. How he was not at Stonehouses. He longed profoundly in that moment to be there. When she stroked his arm, he reciprocated her touch, but only lightly on the hand.

When Elissa turned and left, to attend to their other guests, Caleum asked Rennton when he was sailing out and what port he was calling on next.

"I am leaving in the morning, but I'm headed eastward," the old mariner said to him, "but there is a frigate, called the *Enki,* docked off Wall, sailing for southernmost waters at the end of the week. If you are set on going there, the captain is a friend of mine, and he will get you to your home port safely. He is a peculiar man, though, and you must be careful not to upset him."

Rennton had once made the same offer to Caleum's father, on an occasion when his wife had left him and he was despondent over it.

He could see the same sadness settled over Caleum now. It was not for him to say where a man belonged or not, but only in his power of friendship to help him get to where he wished to be.

They feasted throughout that night, and it felt to many like a wedding banquet, as it kept expanding until it encompassed the whole house, and the mood among the guests was merry. Elissa alone worried that it seemed like a good-bye feast.

She tried to block this from her thoughts, and when he came to her in bed that night she made no mention of her worries. He was as loving as he had ever been with her. Nor did he mention any other home, or a desire to go away—until she became calm again and no longer heeded her first fears.

He had determined to leave at the end of the week, however, and told himself that it would be best to spare her feelings, not wishing to draw out or increase her sadness. It was the best of noble reasons; however, as sometimes happens, the opposite is what occurred.

He harbored his intentions secret in his breast the entire week, going about as if all were normal. When the day of the ship's sailing finally arrived, he woke up before sunrise, before Elissa had stirred, to leave from out the house undetected. He did not take anything of his life in that town with him, and nothing to remember her by or otherwise knot his memory. He carried instead the same little trunk he had hauled around with him for the last four years. Nor did he wear his fine clothes, but took from a corner in the bottom of the trunk his old coat with Libbie's embroidery inside.

The picture was faded almost entirely and the coat looked even shabbier than he remembered, but it is what he covered himself with as he set out for the docks, leaving all else behind, no matter how precious. His sword he had not seen since he left the battlefield at Saratoga, nor did he miss it, but he carried its memory still, as it was carved deep. And this was all he had in the world, but what was at Stonehouses.

It was still dark when he arrived on the wharf, and fog covered the entire southern tip of the island. He had forgotten the ship's berth and was forced to ask around for the *Enki* until he discovered her and made his way aboard.

"So you made it," said the captain, when he saw him arrive.

Caleum, who had booked his passage earlier in the week, was the only one still missing from the passenger list, and the captain, having been so long in port, was anxious to sail. He had the second mate show Caleum to a tiny cabin and told his crew to be ready as soon as the fog lifted.

Caleum was guilty and heavy-hearted as he waited belowdecks for the ship to begin its journey. When it began to grow light out, he went up above to see why they had not yet sailed. The city was still shrouded in a ghost-white fog, and the captain, a very powerful-looking man with a face like a gigantic angry baby, refused to set out. He looked perturbed, and everyone hastened to get out of his way as he paced the deck.

Remembering what Rennton had told him, Caleum went to the other side of the ship, lest he raise the man's ire. It was about six in the morning, and he knew Elissa would awaken soon and discover his absence.

He hoped the gift of the house would ease her hurt and make her feel less poorly used. Though he knew he had caused her pain, but it was never his intent. It was only that God, He had other plans for him.

At seven o'clock they still had not left port, and Caleum knew Elissa was awake and about by then. He knew as well she would think he had only gone out on errands, or else for a morning constitutional. Still, he feared she might somehow find him there and thwart his journey, and so hid himself below like a smuggler.

An hour later, as they continued to wait, he began to have second thoughts and wished profoundly that he could see Elissa one last time.

At eleven that morning the low cloud over the water finally burned away, and the captain weighed anchor. When they finally set out, all the passengers crowded to the railing, and looked either backward toward Manhattan—and what they were leaving behind—or else forward toward the open sea and the place they was going. Caleum looked first to one and then the other. Toward Elissa, who had loved him so dearly, and then to the destination he had been trying to reach for so long.

Elissa awoke with a start and sensed immediately that Caleum was not in bed where he was supposed to be. Although the emptiness of their room was the first thing she noticed, she did not make much of it. Instead, she dressed, then went down to the kitchen to prepare breakfast, thinking he had been called out early on business and was certain to have an appetite when he returned.

When he did not show up, she left his breakfast warming for him in the stove until about eleven o'clock, after which she threw it out behind the house for the stray dog that sometimes wandered in the alley back there. She knew it bothered Caleum that she sometimes fed it, but even a stray dog deserved not to starve in the streets.

When he was not back for the midday meal, she began looking around to see if he had left any sign to tell her where he had gone. By evening she was worried enough that she swallowed her pride and went to her sister's house, not knowing where else to turn.

Her sister counseled her to be patient, though in her own mind she wondered whether a man who had appeared so suddenly out of nowhere wasn't bound to be off just as quickly.

To pass the time she stayed on and had dinner with her sister's family and, when she left, told herself Caleum would be there with a good explanation when she opened the door, and all would be well.

He was not, though, for the first time in the year they had been together. She went to bed early that night—but stayed awake until it was

almost dawn, listening for his footfall on the stairs. When she awoke
and felt the cold space around her again she grew angry, which was very
rare for her. It was the first night he had spent away from home since
they became a couple, and she grew wrathful at how he had hurt her.
Still, he did not come. When she got up from bed and checked his closet
she saw his trunk was missing. Her anger then began to dissipate and
was replaced again by worry, until she became miserable again. She ate
alone that night and, when her sister knocked on the door, she pretended
to be out, not wanting visitors.

Nor did she want to leave the house the next day but was forced to in
order to buy groceries at the market. As she walked through the stalls,
she did her best to avoid coming into contact with anyone she knew. At
the produce stand, though, Mr. Miller called out to her and came to her
side. "It is so good to see you, ma'am," he said. "I have some winter
squash today at a good price, I think you might be interested in." She
was in no mood to haggle, but took two medium-sized vegetables from
him all the same.

"By the way"—he chatted on, as was his nature—"if you don't mind
my asking, where was Mr. Merian going off to the other morning?"

"What do you mean?" she asked thinly.

"Early Friday he was down at the wharf and boarded a ship that left
going south."

"He is only off to visit relatives. Is that a crime?" she answered curtly,
then began walking away as fast as she could, forgetting the gourds. Her
heart pounded in her chest and she could feel its beat in her throat, as
the taste of blood was brought to her mouth, and she hurried to get
home.

Her breathing was going rapidly, and she tried her best to control it,
but when she arrived back at her house she was drawing in air faster
than she could exhale it. She locked the door soundlessly and stood in
the hall a long time trying to regain control of her breath. Once she had
managed this, she went out to the kitchen and made a cup of tea for
herself. She drank it down quickly and was soothed by its warmth.

"So he has gone away," she said to herself. And no matter what other
reasoning she tried to give herself, she knew he would not be back.

When she finished the tea she washed the porcelain cup out in the
sink and put it away. She then took a lamp from the cupboard and lit it

at the stove. She placed a handful of long wooden kitchen matches in her apron, and set out through the house.

In the living room she torched the curtains, taking a match and holding it steadily, until they began to burn. As they went up in flames she walked to the dining room, then each of the other rooms of the house, setting them all alight. When at last she reached the bedroom she had shared with Caleum, she lay down on the mattress and folded her arms, waiting for the fire to reach and consume her. Nor did she regret it at all, being determined in her plan. She had been cast aside and was without any way to return to her family or anything she had known before. He had left her an exile from his affections and all others as well.

The flames came under the door slowly at first, burning copper and specked with a red the color of old wine. After the door gave way it came for her mercifully swift, and she was waiting for it. Outside the house, though, and as far away as the next three blocks, her cries could be heard—whether from the pain of death or heartbreak or hotness of love no one ever knew. But all who heard her that morning felt an immense sympathy, and any who could have saved her from that fate would have done so, for it was unbearable to hear.

In the street in front of the house the neighbors all gathered, but it was impossible to enter the building. They could only hope to keep the ones around it from burning as well.

When her cries finally died away it was after twelve o'clock and all was silent in that street for a very long time, outside the sound of a dog's barking, as the building continued to burn well into the day.

Finally they tore themselves away and returned to their lives, taking care to avoid that place as best they could in the days afterward. Those who did walk that street in the days following, and indeed far into the future, claimed to hear the sound of a woman wailing, and it did strike them cold for a moment before they could continue their journeys. The one who caused it, however, never knew any of it, or her final agony, as she lived on in his memory the way he had known her, long into the future and even till his own final days.

six

⁓

Winter in the country around Berkeley was unusually dry that year, with no sign nor hint of snow or rain for weeks on end, until everything was desiccated and brittle as ancient parchment. The woodland creatures all burrowed deeper in their earthen hollows, to search out the soil's hidden moisture, or else moved higher up into the mountains—where the underground streams that usually fed the lakes of the valley still flowed a short distance before disappearing. There was also one summit, remote in the impenetrable wilderness, where water was always plentiful, and those migrating animals that knew of it passed the dry months. The people in their houses were careful to keep well water on hand to extinguish errant sparks from their cooking fires or tobacco pipes and so protect their farms and freeholdings, but all else it was at the mercy of Heaven.

When snow did begin to fall, the week after Christmas, all were happy for it and rejoiced, thinking it would relieve the parched valley and replenish the streams high up above. However, no one counted on what moved in with the snow clouds. Great, measureless branches of lightning cleaved the sky like a celestial Nile as the storm moved over the hill country, illuminating the entire valley each time one of them exploded—brilliant as a harvest moon or star shower. There was nothing passive, though, about its radiance, and when it finally subsided, little fires could be seen burning. Wherever it had touched the earth—either the stubbled ground itself or else massive oaks and pines high in their upper reaches—all was set ablaze.

At Stonehouses, Libbie gathered Rose and the smaller one, called Lucky, around her in the kitchen, and they watched through the small back window as the world outside was made bright by the pale blue light, moving closer and closer toward them. Libbie worried briefly for Magnus and Adelia over in the main house, but there was no way to reach them, and then it was they had all weathered out storms before.

The next time the sky lit up, though, it was not by one of the massive jolts of lightning but three prodigious balls of it, which seemed to sit directly on top of Stonehouses. The entire farm took on a spectral pink and white glow, and when it died away the hill where Stonehouses itself sat looked to be aflame—as did two of the barns on the shore between the original structure and Caleum and Libbie's place.

Her first instinct was to go over to check on Magnus and Adelia, but she feared leaving her children alone, and it was impossible to tell in which direction the ground fire was moving. Nor did she want to chance being struck by lightning or getting otherwise caught in the path of the blaze. She sat there with her children as the crackling of the clouds continued, knowing that if anything happened while she was there with them she had at least a passing chance of keeping them from harm.

When the onslaught from the tempest died down and all seemed quiet again, she bundled the children off to bed, put her coat on, and went over to check that nothing had happened to Magnus and Adelia at the main house.

As she walked along the path hugging the lake, she could see fire burning in the distance, though from two different directions. The first was off on her left-hand side, about a hundred yards from where she stood. The wind was blowing it away from a barn that had burned down already, and the fire in grasses around it were moving out toward the barren fields, where they would wither away from lack of anything to feed upon. The other blaze came still from the direction of Stonehouses. It was not until she rounded the lake that she could see the house itself was alight with flame. She quickened her pace after that but tried not to panic as she ran on toward it.

When she arrived, she found Adelia and Magnus standing out there in the storm, looking at their home as it burned to the ground.

"Isn't there anything more we can do to save it besides just standing here?" Libbie demanded, looking first at them then again at Stonehouses as it cackled and crumbled in the still-falling snow.

Magnus shook his head stoically. "The lightning was right on top of us, and the whole place seemed like it went up at once. It will have to burn out now or not."

They looked ghostly and faded standing there in the snow, wrapped in blankets and watching the house burn from the inside out. Libbie felt pity when she looked at the two old people, saying only that all of them should all better get in out of the storm before they caught chill on top of everything else. Reluctantly, then, they began to follow her back to the other place, filled with sorrows for all that departed that day.

As they made their way down the path, however, Libbie could see the winds were shifting, and the fire that had been burning toward the meadow was moving instead toward her house, where her children were. All at once she started to run, trying to outrace the flames that were feasting so swiftly, and cursing herself for leaving them there alone; promising to never do so again if they were still safe.

When she arrived at the other building, fire was already licking at the back wall, and she had to rush round to the front to get in, where she ran up the stairs through a thicket of black smoke that had filled the room. Mercifully the two girls were unharmed, though both had stayed there and were deathly afraid when she reached them. Rose, the older one, knew exactly what was happening, and what fire was and the danger they were in, but Lucky had hidden under the bed, and Rose had been unable to coax her out. Nor could she leave without her sister.

"Mother, the house is burning," she said, pleading.

"Come with me," Libbie told her sharply, bundling them up and hurrying outside.

Behind the house, Magnus and Adelia were carrying buckets of water from the well, which they struggled to throw onto the flames. Libbie joined in, running back and forth with water buckets, as Magnus battled against the fire with all the strength in his old body, knowing that, if they failed, all was lost, and what had taken so long to make would be snatched away in a single day.

They fought out there for hours, and even Lucky and Rose tried to help, carrying a single bucket between the two of them to give to Magnus, with barely a word passing between them all, until, as darkness fell at last, they began to gain the better of the fire. It was finally extinguished around seven that evening, but the exact time was impossible to reckon.

Much of the house was still standing and useful, and they went inside what remained of it to rest, all shivering from wetness and exposure to the freezing air.

Libbie put on a pot of water for tea, and brought the first ready cup to Magnus, who aside from the coldness had grown stiff in his joints from the diseases of age. He was still covered in gray ash from head to foot and coughed violently from time to time due to the smoke he had breathed in. The smell of burning still clung to him, as it hung in the air in general, but in greater concentration. Still, he wanted to go out and inspect the damage the fire had done to his lands. Libbie and Adelia, though, prevailed on him to rest awhile longer. He seemed then to all of them to have grown ancient, and he felt as much in his own mind, as it was true.

"It is nothing to worry about," he said, trying to speak to their collective worries and console them, even as they looked after him. "We will rebuild everything just as soon as Caleum returns. It only took four of us a summer to put the majority of this place up, and I don't imagine it will take half that to fix." The main house he was less certain of, whether there was need to rebuild, or whether they could on that scale again. During the time he drank his tea, he tried to recall what Stonehouses had looked like the first time he laid eyes on it. Certainly it was bigger now than it had been then, and rooms had been added not from a plan but according to where and when they were needed and the purpose they were to be put to, so that he was not even certain he could draw a plan of the place from memory, even though he had been in each of its rooms a thousand times and could walk through each of them in his sleep at night.

When Magnus mentioned Caleum's name, Libbie was silent, as was Adelia. Having all expected him home so long, there was no evidence now that he was anything other than dead. Magnus had counseled them steadily against assuming anything until there was ready proof of it— such as the army usually sent back to fallen soldiers' families. However, as the weeks and months passed with no word from him, Libbie had all but given up hope of ever laying eyes on her husband again.

"I had better see what the damage is to the house," she said, not wanting to speak out loud what was uppermost in her heart.

When Magnus offered to help her, though, she declined.

"You should rest, Uncle, and get back your strength," she urged him. "Besides, I know better how everything out here was before."

"Then I'll walk around to the main house to see what is left of it."

"Are you rested enough?" Adelia asked her husband.

"It's just to have a look around," he answered. "You stay here and tend to Libbie and the girls."

Magnus left the women, then, and walked back to his house, surveying his lands as he went and the damage done to them. At the same time, Libbie went off to assess her house and how much of it was still sound.

What she saw was that the kitchen was in far worse shape than it had seemed before, and the upper portion of the house was burned very badly, so that those rooms were all open to the outside. She had also lost many of her household effects, but on the whole it was stable enough that they could live there until spring.

At Magnus and Adelia's house, fire had taken a far higher toll. Besides the barn and an acre of trees around the lake, most of the main house was gone entirely along with everything it had held, except for the fieldstone outer shell. The fireplace and chimney was all that remained of the kitchen, and a few of the rooms that had been added over the years sat exposed to the elements, like something children had built and left in the woods. The original structure could be discerned for the first time in decades, so that Magnus could see, as he had not before, that for all its grandness Stonehouses was really two cabins, identical to the ones he had known at Sorel's Hundred, built side by side. Being used to the completed house, this foundation seemed unimaginably small to him, as the house was already four times its original size when he came to live there, and it had grown four times that again. In his sadness, when he returned to Libbie and Caleum's place, he told Adelia that the house was destroyed completely. "It claimed the whole thing, except some scraps you can have at if you want."

He agreed with Libbie that it would be best for all of them to live in her and Caleum's house until spring, when they could decide how best to go on—and either build that one out or else restore the original.

"Once Caleum gets back we can figure the best way to go at it. It doesn't make sense to start before." It cost him great effort to admit this, thinking how proud his father had been of that house, as well as the rooms he himself had added. However, he knew he could not build

anymore by himself, and Caleum would have to decide what he preferred for the future.

When he said Caleum's name again, though, Libbie turned silent and
moved away from the rest of them.

"Libbie, what's wrong with you?" Adelia asked, seeing that the
younger woman was upset.

"Aunt Adelia, Caleum isn't coming back," Libbie said coldly, forgetting Lucky and Rose were still there. "Maybe we can get help from the
neighbors or hire hands to help us build, but if we wait for Caleum we
will be living out in the woods come next winter."

Her words wounded Adelia to the core, and tears began to fall from
the old woman's eyes, seeming to trace each wrinkle of her face. "That is
not so," she said, but then spoke no more, being consumed with crying.

"Stop your tears," Magnus told his wife crossly. "She doesn't know
what she's talking about, and you know better than listen to her." For
he had been at Stonehouses longest of all, and they had never given up
on their people. "Libbie, we've always buried our people when they died,
but not before that," he told the younger woman, gently but with a fi-
nality that did not allow for argument.

Libbie felt very ashamed of herself then, and apologized for what she
had said. "It has been a difficult day," she tried to explain, turning her
head low. "I did not mean it to sound hateful."

"I know, dear," Magnus answered, not wanting more strife to befall
the house than already had.

"I will cook something for us to have for dinner," Adelia interrupted,
standing to go out to the exposed kitchen. When Libbie volunteered to
help her, Adelia accepted gladly, and the two went off, leaving the girls
and Magnus alone by themselves.

Magnus slumped down in his chair and closed his eyes, thinking to
rest before he ate. However, Rose and Lucky, who were normally very
shy with him, came and sat near his feet and looked up at him as he
nodded.

Magnus felt their eyes upon him and sat up again in his chair. "We
had a great setback today," he said, looking down to them, "but we will
get beyond it. Just as everything outside that window used to be wild
until your great-grandfather, Jasper Merian, came here. He tamed the
land, and built the house over across the lake from nothing but his own

will. Maybe, though, it is not enough to only build once, but you must improve on what you have done, and sometimes build it over, if God wants you to prove yourself again. This is our place, though, and as long as we don't do anything to foul that up it will always be so, and we will always be blessed."

The girls let his words wash over them, not certain what he was telling them, or even that he was talking to them at all, but pleased to have his attention and warm mood. He in his turn spoke as he could only to the two of them, as they were after all his blood and his future.

"When will our papa come back?" Rose asked, worrying for the first time that he had not been there since her third birthday, when there was a break in the fighting.

"I don't know, rightfully," Magnus said, "but you must believe that he will."

When Adelia and Libbie came in from the kitchen, bundled in their coats and carrying pots for the evening meal, Magnus and the two girls both went to offer to help with the table. The five of them then said grace and sat down to supper.

They finished late that evening, then began to search for bedding for all to stay warm through the night. After that they dispersed through the two undamaged rooms of the house, Magnus and Adelia downstairs in the parlor and Libbie upstairs with the girls on the other mattress left to them.

The air still smelled of smoke from the fire that had burned through their lives that day, and all were spent from the ordeal. When Rose and Lucky tried to ask their mother questions she quieted them and fell hard asleep, thinking of what all she had to do the next day, if they were to get on properly the rest of the week and, beyond that, the winter.

Downstairs Adelia could see the toll battling the fire had taken on her husband and fed him a glass of warm milk to help soothe his nerves. She listened then as he tried to get comfortable but was unable to because of the aches that racked his body. Whenever he found a position that seemed conducive to sleep, he would soon feel a pain he had not felt before and shift to avoid aggravating it. She rubbed his shoulders to ease his mind at least, but he was unable to find slumber and rest, so neither could she.

The two of them lay awake staring at the ceiling in the dark room, as they had occasionally done through the earliest days of their marriage but most memorably before they were wed. "We have been with each other a long time," Magnus reminisced, without looking at her. "Through more than I ever thought we would survive."

"Longer than I dared hope," Adelia, who was always modest about such matters, answered. "But not longer than I wanted."

"You have been a good wife to me," Magnus said then. "Just as you will continue to be good to all of them when I am gone."

She hated to hear her husband speak this way and usually tried to quiet him when he started down such a line. However, they were both very old and she could see he was feeling each of his years that night— those that weighed heavily on him as well as those that were light and sweet to his memory as spun sugar. She allowed him to say his piece, knowing there might not be very many more opportunities such as this one to count blessings and, though they had suffered a blow, give thanks.

"If I have been a good wife, it is because I had a good man, and it was easy," she answered.

Magnus laughed softly at this, knowing she bent the truth for the sake of sentiment. They were like young lovers then for a moment, though in his limbs he still felt the accumulation of all his years. "It will be easier on you after he returns," Magnus said. For he knew that, since he first became theirs to raise, Caleum had supplanted him in her affection. He had long ceased to be bothered by this, as he knew it to be a different emotion than that between man and wife. "Though I fear it might not be easy for him."

"Do you think Libbie will be able to support him as he needs to be," Adelia asked, "or might she be overwhelmed?"

"They will have to reckon with that," Magnus replied. "Everybody figures out how to be with their troubles. But they are both grown now and will just have to figure it out. All I know is I myself was lucky with who I had for a wife."

When she touched him he shifted himself again and took her in his arms tightly. "Not every man has a home."

He was still holding her in the morning when she awoke, although he himself did not move. She turned, trying to get free of his grasp without waking him, so that she could go out to the kitchen and make his breakfast, as she had done every morning of their marriage. When his arms did not give way immediately she reached to pry his fingers one by one from the opposite forearm.

She knew as soon as she touched him that he felt no more pain. She took each finger in hers very gently then and coaxed it open. When they were removed from their final grasp, she squeezed his hand, and smoothed it tenderly, then withdrew from his embrace. She stood, and finished arranging his body, then went out to the kitchen, where she lit the stove.

She prepared that morning eggs, the last bacon from their larder, biscuits and wildberry preserves, then poured out a large glass of milk, which she set on the table beside his place at the table. Upstairs Libbie rose as soon as she smelled cooking coming from her kitchen and came downstairs to help.

When she entered the room, though, Adelia brushed her aside, telling her to sit down and stay out of the way of her work. Libbie, on the verge of protesting, saw something in Adelia's face that bade her refrain. "What is wrong, Aunt Adelia?" she asked, concerned for the old woman.

"There is nothing wrong," Adelia answered her. "It is only that I am cooking for my husband for the last time."

He died without the chance to count and reckon his days or accomplishments, but were they ever to be laid down, the list would surely include his roughly eleven thousand days of bondage—though it was hard to know the true figure—and thirteen thousand his own man. Untold acres planted and a like number reaped, as he had been lucky in his day and increased his till. He grew rich as well—at least far beyond what he had dared to dream.

When he passed he left behind a wife whom time did teach him to love and a boy who, though not his, was his brother's and he raised him like a son. He was mostly fortunate as well in whom he saw buried during his lifetime: both parents—one in old age and one very old. He had also a brother, whose body they could not put in the ground at Stonehouses but who was known to have had peace at the end.

He was a solitary man, but he had still a few whom he called friends and brethren, and all these were present in the lower southern meadow of Stonehouses when they added his body to the rank of those buried there, although it was bitter cold that day.

Many others came out as well, but it was a more intimate affair than some funerals they had had there. The ground was still frozen, and it had taken a long time to dig the grave, so no one wanted much to stand out in the cold any longer by the end of the sermonizing for him.

When it was over, entertaining the guests was made difficult by the fact that they no longer had the space they once did, but crowded all into the room at the front of the newer house. Those there did not stay long, though it had been very moving, and they were truly saddened by Magnus Merian's passing away.

When they left at the end of the funeral feast, however, many were tempered in their grief by fear of the sounds that seemed to emanate from the woods around the house when they reached the road.

Inside, the women all went to bed as soon as the guests had gone and they were done with burying Ware, called Magnus. That night each of them heard strange sounds as well that they could not describe, and knew not what they were nor how to respond to them.

seven

~

As the *Enki* plowed the winter Atlantic, Caleum fell into low spirits, watching the city recede from view. One of the few things he found that helped was walking the deck in the early morning, when it was nearly deserted. Every day near sunrise, he would pace the left side of the ship, stopping at the railing for a spell, reflecting silently as he looked to the eastern sky, until the sun had grown too bright to look at—although it did not warm the air.

The only other people about at that hour were the lookout in his nest, the captain—who always stood at the ship's prow—and another passenger, who paced in shadow on the starboard side of the boat and whom Caleum had never seen at any other hour aboard the craft.

The three men would acknowledge each other from afar with a nod of the head each morning, but never spoke until the third morning out, when all arrived on deck to find the sky too overcast to see the horizon. The captain then stopped both his passengers in conversation, which was a first for Caleum since the day he boarded the ship.

"You are an acquaintance of Rennton's from Providence then?" he asked.

"Yes," Caleum answered. "He was a friend to my father."

"Aye," the captain said, seeming to want to say something else. "How is it on land lately then?"

"About what it always is, I suppose," Caleum answered, not entirely certain of the man's question. "Sir, you would know the answer at least as well as I."

"Nay. It is a long time since I've been ashore."

340

"Since how long?" he asked, having never heard of such a thing. "How is that possible?"

"My thirteenth year. The sea is a thing complete and no need ever to leave it, if it's your element. It is my element."

"How is it you met Rennton then?"

"We ply the same route on occasion," the old man answered. "There are not so many sails in some waters that you can't learn them all."

Caleum was at an age then when he and the world had begun to make way for each other, or he might otherwise have gone on questioning the man, whom he found fascinating, but the captain was not talkative, so let him speak or remain silent as he chose.

"He is an apt sailor."

As the two of them stood there in the early fog, the other passenger paced his side until the captain caught his eye and hailed him.

"Morning, Toombley," the old man called in greeting.

"G'morning, brothers," the new arrival said to the others. He was very clearly a man of the cloth, being dressed like an old-fashioned monk, and although Caleum did not wish to nose into anyone else's business, he thought it permissible to ask where the man was headed.

"Down to San Juan," the other answered him. "I go there to pray."

"Why there?" Caleum asked. "It is very far."

"They have a statue there of the Revelator, standing in the ocean at the mouth of their river Alph, which has been said to work miracles."

"It is a sea altar," said the captain approvingly. "What miracles has it made?"

"Well, it is told that it caused a sightless man to see all the world, and all it is made of, both the gross things and the extremely fine ones."

"Was the man blind his whole life before that?" Caleum asked the pilgrim, as the captain nodded in understanding.

"Nay, he was never blind before."

They were silent a moment then, until the captain, who was not known to be social, invited both of them to share his table later for supper. He also pointed out that they were making good time to their destinations, before withdrawing to his own quarters to amend his log.

"Where is it you're headed?" Toombley asked Caleum, when they stood alone upon the deck.

"I am going home," Caleum said to him, all at once much contented with the idea, as he was then beyond the midpoint of their voyage. "To where I belong."

"Aye. From the war?" Toombley guessed.

"Since four years."

"They say this is a special time in the eras of history."

"They do say it."

"That we are lucky to live in it."

"Aye, and to die, I suppose."

The pilgrim nodded at him, and the two men took the rail together, looking out at the gray passing sea. Perhaps it was a special era, Caleum thought, wasn't that what Stanton had tried to have him believe? Who could not want to be part of such a thing? he asked himself, beginning to reach terms of peace with everything that had happened to him. If it was truly in the service of something besides capital, he told himself, he could embrace that as well—as he had when he was a younger man. His own belief by then was in himself alone, though, and beyond that in Stone-houses, where he was his own lord overseer. For anything farther than its boundaries he would lay even odds only.

He had no other example but what he knew from his own time, and so would follow that, returning to Stonehouses as an army of one, as Jasper Merian had first arrived there, but without the need to start from oblivion, because the place was known to him and waiting to receive him back. If there was one overstructure of rule that permitted it prosperity better than others he would cast a vote in it, but, for faith in structures themselves, he had little stock but in the governance of himself and his lands and would ever be wary of all else, power being a finite thing.

The sea was unusually calm that morning, and the ship made little movement upon the water, so that the only motions seemed to be those of his own mind within him. Looking over the side he thought he could remember his first time upon the ocean, though he suspected it was only false memory of him knowing he had been there before. He tried to remember when he was first at Stonehouses as well, but it was a useless effort, for everything he thought he remembered he knew he was matching to some received tale or present need, and so was hesitant of the tricks he knew one's mind could play. When he looked out upon the water and saw a great squall coming toward them, however, he knew it was not only his mind's imagining of the past but a true and present storm. He did not leave the rail but continued to look out, mesmerized, onto the ocean as it began to rise in the distance.

A call rang out from the crow's nest at the same time Caleum pointed out the swells of water in the distance to Toombley. The other man, being cautious and fearful, went immediately belowdecks, but Caleum, remembering his last journey on these seas, stayed pressed against the rail.

When the winds came in, the ship began to toss violently and the captain called for all sails to be lowered, realizing he would not be able to outrun the squall. He yelled angrily for Caleum to get below, as even his hardiest sailors did not want to be out in that storm. Just as he said this, however, the ship pitched to the side, as a giant wave caught them and swept over the vessel. When the boat righted itself again, the captain saw his passenger was no longer at the railing but snatched away by the ocean.

"Man overboard!" sailors yelled out from each corner of the ship simultaneously, throwing life preservers into the ocean.

In the fierceness of the storm, though, it was impossible for them to see more than a few feet in any direction, and they could not tell where Caleum had fallen, let alone whether he had emerged from the water.

Beneath the waves, Caleum struggled against the current, which felt like a massive hand around his midsection, pulling him down, until he managed to wrench his body free to the surface. The water tried again to submerge him, but he was able to get back to the open quickly and breathe air again. When he did he inhaled very deeply and tried first off to espy the *Enki*.

He could see nothing but a deep velvet darkness, as if night had fallen over the entire world. When he had finally caught his breath and began to relax, floating on the choppy sea, another wave crashed overhead, pushing him down again. He was just barely able to take in and hold a lungful of air before disappearing back under the waves.

It was as black below the water as above it, and he could not tell which medium he was in as he tried to swim toward what he took to be an island of dry land. It was a mirage, though, and, when he tried to breathe, he inhaled nothing but sharp salty water. He thought he could hear the sound of perfect voices singing clearly then, and their song was very beguiling to him, until he struck out with one of his hands and it was free.

He reemerged in another spot altogether, and he no longer thought of finding the ship but only of keeping air inside his body instead of brine. He battled the ocean like this for another hour, as the sea kept crashing down on his small ebbing form in the midst of its own immense providence, until he was worn out and could fight no longer.

After a wave the size of a hillock had fallen over him, Caleum sank under the waters and did not give thought to rising again. His wooden leg had grown heavy and water-logged, but he could not remove it, for it was so well fastened, and his other limbs were stiff and lethargic.

His death seemed certain when he went below, then bobbed up this last time, and he was spared that fate only because he rose next to one of the buoys the *Enki* had thrown out earlier. He threw himself around it and clung to the contraption as best he could with his raw hands. There were no thoughts in his head by then, nor desires in him beyond this. He was in a contest for his life, and it took all his strength and courage to wage the battle.

He had been swept from the side of the ship around seven in the morning, and at midday he was still out in the water. The storm was past by then, and the water still as the desert floor, as the sun beat high overhead, casting a reflection on the water that made everything to the horizon stark white. He was blinded by it and longed for the thing to pass on overhead, as it gave but little warmth and no solace but only robbed him of sight.

Unable to withstand the assault on his eyes, he was forced to close them as he floated in that cold firmament. He was disoriented entirely but managed to think then of all that had happened to him with clarity for the first time. He envisioned his home as well, and the faces of all he loved, and after that where each field at Stonehouses was and each barn. He counted in his mind the panes in every window, and the animals in their stalls. He thought of the coming planting season and longed to be in his fields again, as he longed for his old bed.

Of all the things on land he wished for, little could compete with how he missed children, for they made him feel connected to the world in a way nothing else did. As for Libbie, he had made her a promise long ago, and he still had not fulfilled it. When he could no longer bear to think of what was good and comfortable, he tried to still his mind again, until it was completely blank and without desire but to endure his present ordeal.

When he chanced to open his eyes the sun was still unrelenting, but it had passed on a few degrees, so he could see what was at the horizon. He saw there a ship, moving parallel to him in the distance, and began to yell to it. The boat did not seem to hear or notice him, as it did not alter its course. But when it was nearly on top of him, he could see a man standing at the prow whom he would swear was Magnus Merian.

The man did nod to him but was otherwise mute, as though they were on a leisurely walk and what they had to say had already been settled. Caleum kept calling out desperately for help, until eventually several men came to the starboard side of the ship. "We can come no closer," one of them called. "Godspeed thee."

He looked at their faces as they moved past him, and in the center of all them was the captain of the vessel, who looked to be the image of Rennton. He recalled then the ship he had been on before, and thought he remembered that boat as well from when he was a child upon these waters. His mind was panicked and chaotic, and he closed his eyes trying to calm it. When he next looked, turning to follow the progress of the ship, it had disappeared in the hard glare of the ocean.

He wailed to be left alone there and despaired of ever reaching safety. He had faced suffering before without protesting, but dying alone in that watery nothingness, divorced from everything he held dear and all he called his own in the world, took away his remaining strength and courage. He bawled like a child.

There was no further sign of the ship, nor any other form of life, as he clung there, only an immense silence, as if he had left the world and was cast into some colossal antechamber of death. He hung fast to the little buoy as his hands bled without feeling, hoping only that the sea would not churn up again.

The ocean did remain calm, as the sun began its long descent, but the temperature was still well below what he could bear, and he felt himself falling into a druggish stupor as he floated out there in the silent void.

Nay there was something. It was his angst and fear, though none would call him coward for it, but he struggled against them until he was spent.

He had been out on the water almost six hours, and the only thing he had to look forward to was night, when the sea would be cast into complete darkness again—unrelieved by anything save the distant stars, if the clouds did not blanket over them. Thinking of his prospects, he started not only to lose but to give up on the fight and began to fall from consciousness.

When a lantern appeared in the distance through the clouded horizon he could not even muster the strength of voice to call it, having no speech left in him, nor energy even to save himself with. The lantern came from a ship, which had nearly run past him before the pilot spotted his small shape on the water.

"Ahoy!" the pilot cried out, but his call was echoed by silence. "Ahoy, if thee be alive," the man yelled again.

Beneath the hulking ship Caleum called out very weakly. "Aye," he said, before being seized by a coughing fit, as the salt water washed over his face and into his lungs.

The bottom was too rocky and dangerous for the ship to come to him, but they did drop a boat, manned by two sailors, who piloted it to where he was and lifted him out of the cold. When they pulled him up he was completely gray and shriveled, and could feel nothing at all as they tucked their arms beneath him and hoisted him into the boat. When the boat reached the ship, they had to lower a sling to lift him up by, as he was unable to grasp hold of the rope they put over the side for the men to climb.

They pulled the harness onto the deck of the *Meredith,* as the ship was called, and unfastened him—then covered him quickly with a blanket, before offering him hot rum to get warm by.

"It is miraculous you survived out there," the ship's mate said, as they led him across the planks of the vessel. "Not one man in a thousand who goes down on this coast lives, and I bet not one in a million in this storm. You are lucky too that we weren't another kind of ship." Caleum could only nod at everything the man said, for he was exhausted beyond all knowing.

They moved him to a bunk belowdecks, covering him with another blanket, then added another very carefully every hour after that, as they were superstitious and it was a good omen for them to save a man from the ocean.

No matter how many blankets he was given, though, Caleum Merian could not get warm and began shivering there in his bed. The sailors, who came from Nova Scotia and had seen men suffer exposure before, took it as a good sign that he responded at all, and kept adding more blankets, ministering warmth by degrees so that he was not shocked by the difference. When he could feel his hands again, late that night, his body finally carried him off to sleep.

He awoke the next morning to find he had been moved to the ship's galley during the night, although he could not remember it. He startled when he looked around, not understanding how he came to be in that place, or indeed where he was at all. The cook, when he saw him stir, shoved a bowl of hot soup at him, without comment, which he took up and began to eat.

He was comforted as he brought the hot fish to his mouth, for he had not eaten in more than a day, and quickly finished the bowl. When he was done he was given another, which he ate at a more leisurely pace, still not slow as was usual for him when sitting at table, but at least like one who had sat at table before.

When the ship's mate, a man called Silas, came in and saw him, he began to beam broadly, much pleased that Caleum had made it through that night. "I see you have an appetite too," he continued, though he was usually very strict with rations for his sailors. "That is good."

"Thank you," Caleum answered. He could think of nothing else to say, for he was humbled by their hospitality and their having saved him. "I cannot thank you enough."

"It was not us but Providence who made it possible," Silas replied. "This voyage is surely blessed by Him."

Caleum was not pious as some men, but he had been near to death and was now eating cod chowder so he could not argue without offending his host. But he did allow himself to comment on the man's sentiment. "I did not think men who made their living on the ocean were so believing."

"On the contrary," said Silas. "I'm afraid we believe too many things. Now tell me, friend, where you were headed when the storm caught you, so we can deliver you there safely."

When Caleum answered, Silas said they were very near there, and would reach that port well before the end of the day. The ship continued on under a fair wind, and it was hard for Caleum to believe that it was the same ocean that had treated him so roughly the previous day.

When they docked, not long after noon, Caleum wished again he had some better way of thanking his rescuers, as he tried to make them know how grateful he was.

"We may all need to be fished from the ocean yet." Silas waved him off, refusing all thanks, and telling how it was custom with them not to remind a man of a favor, lest he come to resent it.

"We have a legend Down East of a man who saved his neighbor from certain starvation one winter by giving him a firkin of smoked cod. All that spring he kept harkening back to it, and all the next spring, never growing tired of reminding the man or of letting their other neighbors know what a good turn he had done for his luckless friend.

"When winter next fell, and there was nobody else on the road that passed by their part of the world, the man who had been saved murdered the one who saved him, unable to bear his gloating any longer. That following spring, when it all came to light, the neighbors were sympathetic toward him, and did not prosecute the crime half so harshly as you might expect."

Still Caleum was humbled that the *Meredith* had stopped again, just to let him ashore, but, as he went on land he was even more grateful to be back in the stable world.

When he touched dry earth again it was a strange sensation, and he needed quite a few moments to grow used to it. He vowed then he would never go again upon the water, but he would not think of seafarers at all the way he used to. He turned then to see the boat that had saved him one last time and wave to the crew, but search as he might he could not catch sight of it anywhere.

When he finally had his bearings, he began to look around the port where he had disembarked. It was not so busy as Manhattan, but its business was much the same, and he was careful as he waded his way through the lanes of traffic. Once he had come into the town proper, he inquired about where he might find a horse, not wanting to waste any more time but to get on to where he lived.

He had but a few coins left in the little purse that was sewed to the inside of his pants. However, he was able to secure a decent colt and furnishings for the trip, but it was almost his last money.

When he set out from the coast then, it was already the middle of the afternoon, and he hoped to cover much ground still before night fell.

e i g h t

◄━

After the death of Magnus Merian they tried to put their grief behind them at Stonehouses, telling themselves and one another everything would still manage to right itself by spring. The winter was hard that year—stretching on for weeks longer than it should have—until they had eaten their stores so far down there was little left to them but seed grain. Finally the weather looked as if it was going to relent, and they had a whole week that was warm enough for the lake to begin thawing, which was always the first real sign of the new season. However, by the time warm days should have been upon them, they were besieged again with bad weather.

Several animals had already died from cold during the last storm, and Adelia tethered a lamb that had lost its ewe in a bower behind the house, intending to slaughter it as soon as she decided how best to preserve the meat from spoiling. The old woman was used to hardship from her childhood, when they were first settling that part of the country, and could work as well as any man, so never despaired before her task, as there was little on a farm she had not done before. The girls had also adjusted to this new way of life, following Adelia about as she carried on all the farm chores she knew from her first days at Stonehouses and even made games around all the rigors of their new existence.

Libbie proved less adaptable though, having always accepted farm life, but never needing to engage its most difficult labors, so that, as soon as Magnus's death sank in, she began to despair of how they would manage out there on their own and even at the funeral had let it be known to her brother Eli how she feared for their future.

Eli Darson assured his sister that as governess of Stonehouses, fire or none, she need never worry. He set about then, from the next day onward, spreading word in respectable circles how his widow sister was prepared to marry again and that she brought with her a handsome dowry for the right suitor.

She was not the only mistress of Stonehouses, however, and, when she learned of her brother's plan she worried greatly what Adelia would say once she found out. Out of prudence she tried to hide his doings from the other woman for as long as possible.

By the time the second storm had closed in on them, though, she was grown feverish from being cooped up indoors with no way to leave and openly looked forward to being courted, no longer caring for anyone else's opinion. "I don't want to live like a half wild woman," she said to Adelia. "Perhaps we should just sell what's left here and move into town."

Adelia heard this as sacrilege and said as much. "You would sell my boy's land from under him, wouldn't you?" she asked, not disguising the note of hardness that crept into her voice. "Well, it is not yours to decide." She left the house to go slaughter the lamb, which she had finally determined that day to kill, and smoke its meat.

When the old woman left, Libbie went to find her daughters, who were playing in the small room upstairs that they all shared. She sat down on the bed next to them and watched their play silently for a while before saying anything. "When I was your age," she began at last, stopping their game, "I did not know anything in our lives could ever go wrong. Now you poor innocent darlings must suffer because your father went off to war. I just want you to know everything will be right again."

The girls were very quiet, never certain how to speak to their mother when her mood turned to the past. Unable to take up their game again, they watched Libbie as she went over to the trunk at the end of the bed and picked up the cushion that lay upon it.

"This is what life was like for us when I was a girl," she said, holding the pillow out for the two of them to inspect. They were delighted by her embroidery but were usually not allowed to touch it, so it was a great treat for them indeed, and they strained forward to feel the material.

"Papa will come back," said Rose, turning away from the pillow, even though it cost her great self-control not to go on looking at it.

"Dear, sweet girl," Libbie said tenderly, "you are right to love your father. He was a great man in his way, but I am afraid he is not coming back." While the main part of her words were compassionate and filled with understanding, her tongue stood very rigid at the word *not,* reducing everything else before it.

Rose was quiet through all this. When she thought it safe to do so, she simply left the room and went back downstairs, where she sat on the sofa perturbed, looking out the window toward the lake.

When she saw a pair of riders coming toward the house, though, she ran back upstairs, calling to her mother as she went. Her first thought was that it was her father returning, even if she dare not allow herself to say it, or even hope for it too much, but that is who she wanted it to be.

When the riders drew closer, she was glad she had not said anything, as she could see then it was not Caleum Merian but her uncle Eli and another man she did not recognize. Libbie, though, did not seem to be surprised by their visit when she came to answer the door, having changed into one of her old but still elegant dresses.

When Eli and his guest entered, the adults sat down. Rose could see immediately how happy her mother was, as Uncle Eli introduced his friend as a Mr. Paul Waylon from Chase. Libbie was always made happy to see her brother, but she was surprisingly demure toward the other man, especially as she usually held herself aloof from strangers.

After a pass of conversation that left all the adults laughing, Rose, who had been listening to them from a corner of the room and surmised they were plotting something against her father, went to the strange man and stood directly next to him, glaring coldly.

When he turned to her and remarked what a sweet child she was, then asked her name, she was seized by defiance and replied very evenly, "You are sitting in my father's chair."

"War is so difficult for young people." Mr. Waylon smiled, looking at Eli and Libbie but unmoved by the girl's outburst. "There is so much they cannot understand."

"Rose, go upstairs this second," Libbie told her daughter. "She is usually such a well-behaved child."

"You mustn't apologize," Paul Waylon countered, continuing to smile indulgently. "It is all very natural." He then turned to Eli. "I'm afraid I should be heading back now. I must attend to some business in town before the shops all close."

"Well, it has been very nice visiting, Mr. Waylon," Libbie told him pleasantly, though within she was seething at Rose for ruining the afternoon.

Instead of going on to the bedroom as she had been told, Rose hid on the stairs out of sight from the adults and continued to eavesdrop on their conversation.

"Paul, you wouldn't mind if I let you ride back alone, would you? My sister is a fine cook, and I think I'll stay here for dinner."

"Not at all. I will contact you tomorrow."

"I look forward to it."

"Well, thank you for coming all this way. It was really a pleasure."

"It was that, but entirely mine."

The man could be heard taking his leave, and Eli and Libbie were left alone in the living room.

"He is from the best family of any Negro in the colony," Eli said, pouring himself a drink from a decanter on a shelf, which had not been touched since Caleum Merian last opened it to offer spirits to his guests. "He can prove his blood too."

"My husband was one of the finest men I ever knew—of any color," Libbie countered, letting her feelings for Caleum show for the first time in many months.

"Yes, of course, Libbie, but please don't behave like the rest of them in this house. You need a man to manage this place properly, and look after yours and your children's interest. Mr. Waylon will do that, and he is also a gentleman, as you saw when the child behaved so hideously toward him. I think it would be a very successful match."

"I know what's in my interest, Eli," she said. "That doesn't mean you can sit there and insult my husband."

"I did not mean to. I only meant Waylon is worthy of you, dear sister."

At this Libbie softened again. "If he is interested, I will consider it seriously. Do you think it is too soon, though? That I shouldn't wait longer?"

"The crops have to go in the ground every year, and every year be brought out. Your house has burned down and will not rebuild itself."

"You are right, dear brother," she asserted. "I suppose there are widows made every day."

"You have suffered so much," Eli said then, making a great show of his sympathy for what she had been through. "You deserve to be happy. You always deserved that."

"I have been that before, Eli, but thank you," Libbie answered. In the past she had thought her hardships only the wages for living, but she saw her brother might be right, and there was no need for her to suffer unduly or veil herself in black for the rest of her life. "You will let me know when you have a response from him."

"I will," Eli promised. "I cannot imagine it would be anything other than yes, though. After all, what man would not have you?"

On the upper stairs Rose took in all their conversation and grew scared. She strained not to betray herself. However, it was impossible for her to stop, and she flew from the stairwell, screaming, "My father, Caleum Merian, will be back soon!"

Even before her mother punished her, Rose knew she was powerless against what was happening. She went on in the face of their authority nonetheless, if only because she could not bear being silent with what it made her feel, or not defending herself as she had always been taught to do.

Libbie tried not to be angry at the child, knowing how she loved her own father, and how she herself had felt in the beginning. Even after Caleum enlisted for a second and longer tour after the first, she told herself it was in the service of something greater than they were and was an honor for all of them. She received him on breaks during the fighting with open arms and never mentioned the petty worries of her day-to-day life, reckoning that eventually all would be restored and better than before.

"We must master our destinies, all of us who can," he said to her, before leaving the final time two years earlier. She wanted to believe him but soon knew better, as she came to feel her own destiny was being mastered by his needs and those of the war.

When he finally wrote to say he had decided not to enlist for a third term, she knew it must have weighed heavily on him, as he had taken to army life so well and risen to the point that he had distinguished himself beyond anyone else from Berkeley, and indeed to the point that his name was known beyond their own colony; and might even be known to history. It will be difficult for him to trade that for farm life again, she told herself, but we will make it through all the same.

She had not heard from him since that letter, however, and it was long past the time he should have returned. The last anyone could confirm was that his regiment had been at a battle in New York State, just before his enlistment was to end. Beyond that there were no reports. She waited daily for news and hoped each horse or wagon that came down their lane was her husband. Her heart would set to beating faster in her breast, until she could hear it in her ears as the rider approached—and showed himself to be other than Caleum. At night as well, those first weeks, she heard horse's hooves beating toward Stonehouses that later proved to be phantom apparitions. Three months? Six? How many days of this before she admitted to herself she was widowed? How many more should be expected of her? The crops indeed did have to go in the ground soon, or else they would starve and the question answer itself.

Libbie looked at Rose, whose punishment she had yet to pronounce, and thought Adelia could hold out as long as she wanted. She had lived to see her husband die at home of old age and had nothing left to fear. Not one in ten other women could claim the same. Of course, she thought, there was still hope. She knew Rose did not mean to aggravate her already uneasy heart but was only showing loyalty to her father, as indeed she should. But the child needed to learn to behave in all matters, and not only those she chose for herself.

"You were very rude today," Libbie said to the girl, who stood before her, still looking angry. "As punishment, you will go without your supper tonight," she finished. "You may go now."

The girl glared at her mother with more outrage at the gross unfairness of all around her and began to march off.

"Rose," Libbie called after her purposefully, "you may miss your father. You may not defy your mother."

Rose continued up the stairs with a haughty look on her face, certain of her rights in that house as a magistrate in his own court. She had not

intended to hold one parent above the other, but if that is what it meant
to keep Mr. Waylon from sitting where he was not supposed to she was
prepared to pay that price.

As she sat on the floor in the bedroom sulking, she heard Adelia
downstairs, returning from her chores. She wanted to run and tell her
what had happened, but knew she would only get into more trouble.
Instead she strained to listen as they began preparing dinner.

At table that night Adelia asked where Rose had gotten off to, and
Libbie told her the girl was being punished. When pressed why, Libbie
was reluctant to answer at first, but finally put down her fork—it could
be heard clinking against the plate—and replied defiantly, "Aunt
Adelia, I am thinking of marrying again."

Adelia did not speak but continued with her meal in silence. "That
is not right," she said, long minutes later, after it seemed she would let
it pass without comment.

"It is what will happen."

"But it is not right."

"It is my intention."

"That is what you punished your daughter over?"

"It is what will happen."

The three of them finished dinner, without speaking another word
to one another. Adelia had never thought she would live to see such a
day, but she was powerless to make the younger woman do anything
she did not wish. She only knew she herself would not live there with
them if it should come to pass. She would rather live alone in the shell
of the old house or even in one of the barns.

Lucky was too young to understand all the rancor that was festering
in the house, but felt the tension and tried to hide herself like a garden
snail under a leaf.

"Who will you marry?" Adelia demanded to know at last, breaking
the tension in the room.

"I am considering Mr. Waylon," Libbie answered.

Adelia did not know the man and was tempted to ask about him, but
she decided to remain quiet and let things reveal themselves—which
in the course of time they did.

*   *   *

Eli Darson rode to the house again the next day to see his sister and tell her of Waylon's interest in the marriage. When he entered the parlor, he was surprised to find the old woman there as well and so saw no possibility of a private conversation.

"Perhaps I should return another day," he proposed to his sister.

"No," Libbie told him, for she had more backbone than her brother. "There is no shame in what I am doing that I need to hide it from my children and relatives."

"Very well," Eli went on officiously. "In that case he has suggested, as both of you are well known and reputable—and there stands no obstacle in the way—that you should begin a formal courtship, followed by a timely marriage, with the understanding, of course, that the bridegroom, who does not bring the same resources to the union the bride does, will have certain protections, much as if the scales were reversed. All of which seems reasonable, and as your brother I would counsel you to accept."

Libbie cast around the room until she caught hold of Adelia's eye before answering. "It does seem very reasonable, all of it."

Adelia did not say anything, but Rose, still unrepentant from the day before, said again with perfect evenness, "my father will not like that when he comes home."

"It is fine," Adelia said to the girl, before she could get into trouble with her mother. "Everything will work out as it is supposed to, no matter what that might be."

Eli and Libbie looked at each other. "We can discuss the exact terms when the occasion nears, but I will tell him he is free to call on you," Eli said with self-satisfaction. He then turned to his niece. "Don't worry, Rose, you will see that Mr. Waylon is a good man."

Rose looked at Adelia and held her tongue.

"Your Uncle Eli is talking to you, Rose," Libbie said, grown furious with the girl.

"It is understandable," Eli said. "She will come round. I am only glad this is all concluded favorably." He stood to leave.

Once he had gone, the two women sat there a long spell, looking at each other and thinking about their fate out there, until snow began to fall again on the farm beyond the window. Adelia was slowly resigning herself to the fact that another age had passed there at Stonehouses and that Libbie would eventually have her own way no matter what. She only thought how she herself might best preserve that portion of the land and its memory that was her own, separate from the rest, and keep it out of Waylon's possession.

As they sat down to supper that evening, the snow was still falling and they were silent, neither speaking to each other nor crossing paths but only sharing the same table. Libbie was decided on her course of action and that it was best for the future.

Rose, for she was old enough to have a will and full conscience of her own, sensed it was inevitable and already began to wish for the day when she would be independent and free of them. She knew the time must come, only she did not know when.

They sat there eating from yesterday's meat and plotting each her own course, separate from the rest but compatible with her own view of the world and her place in it, and all was silent and blanketed by the snow.

As they finished their meal and began to prepare for bed, though, an awful sound such as none of them had heard before filled the room, sending shivers through each of them and making everything seem stiller than it was before.

The two youngest were afraid, and Libbie knew it was not a natural thing she had heard. Adelia alone had any idea what was happening, although she had never witnessed it but only heard of it, back before in ancient days when her own mistress, Sanne, was alive. She knew then that all was lost and beyond saving.

"It is called Ould Lowe." She answered their unasked question. "It is an unvanquishable demon." So say the legends.

n i n e

Beneath the icy surface of the lake the monster battled against his chains, as he had every day since they were first fastened around him—never ceasing to try and free himself in all the years he had been held captive by the links of iron. Rust had finally softened the shackles enough that he was able to snap one of them, like an enemy's bones, before swimming to the surface of the water. But he was not yet free. Ice encased the top of the lake, holding him yet in his watery penitentiary. Five nights he did pound against it—and all the length of the days that circled round them—his rage increasing with each desperate knock. As he dwelled then in the refracted light of his aquarium, his memory of the years before began to be restored, like some fearsome returned king, and he knew again his former life and how he had lost his lands and came to be chained. He pushed against the ice in another fit of rage, wanting nothing more than vengeance against those who bound him there.

In the house the women heard the noise the monster made and each day grew a little less certain of what it all meant, trying to tell themselves and each other it was only the ice melting. When strangers came to the house, though, the beast was gravely silent, as if his ire was some private thing meant for them alone.

Rose had her own understanding of his bellow and was least afraid, though, she knew not what he wanted, or how to defeat him, but felt the sound was less separate from the right world than she was first told, when they claimed he was evil refined.

How information passed to the creature itself is more mysterious, but he knew of all that had happened on the land in the time he had been away, and who all everyone was. When at last his raw hand escaped the ice—pulling the rest of his massive frame after it—he was as bold and knowledgeable as he had been when he ruled there before them. He sat on the shore of the lake then, and his only thoughts were to conquer all that had displaced him from his station.

He came forth in the afternoon, letting the sun warm his cold form, and every living thing scattered from that precinct before him. When night fell he was strong again and stood to begin his haunting, letting free oaths as he went that were all the more baleful for having been unheard so long. At sunrise his second day he began a demented singing, which was a wild murderous ode of all he would do in his new reign and all the reasons to fear him.

He grew hungry after that, and spent the morning scavenging for something to fill his cravings. He was all pain and all want. The forest of his former prowling, though, was little more than a tame garden now, and the game he was used to was no longer to be found, forcing him to roam wide on the chase before he hunted down nourishment for his needs. Sated, he went back to wait on the one called Merian.

When his nemesis did not show himself by evening, Lowe grew impatient and went to go look for him, first at the old house, which was destroyed but not yet abandoned, then at the new place, where Adelia, Libbie, and the two little girls were.

Adelia had hung the place with amulets, which Lowe laughed at, but she also left a plate, which he did consume, and it was enough to satisfy him for another day. Soon, though, all his hungers would be filled but one.

He slept that night not in his bed under the lake but out in the open beneath the stars, where he dreamed and cursed in his sleep all through the night, like some wayward handmaiden of creation.

The next day he rose again, and walked the grounds again, swearing without pause. His memory was bitter long and it filled him with rage, until he began a bellowing that lasted half the morning. When it was done there was nothing living in the county that did not know Ould Lowe was returned, and intended to have back his place in the cosmos there, which the man had tried to overthrow. He had never done harm to anyone who left him undisturbed, but all who tangled with him learned ultimately to know defeat and isolation—which is the feeling men were said to have before Lowe stopped their knowing anything else at all—and he longed to bring such knowing loss to the man.

He stood outside and began to call out the man's name, which was all of their name as well.

It was only when Waylon came for a visit that he gave them a moment of peace that day. But when Waylon left in the late afternoon he was also accosted by the beast, who knew then his intent and called him after that everything but man, driving him off in such a violent manner that he knew it was better not to return, no matter what else it might be worth to him. Libbie suggested then that they leave Stonehouses and move to town but Adelia refused, and despite whatever rancor was between them Libbie was fearful of making the journey with the girls alone.

He now had focus for all his wicked intents and walked by the door of the house constantly, hoping they might venture out, but neither they nor the man showed themselves.

On the fifth day of his resurgence Lowe started to grow desperate for his purpose. What he did then was surprising, but it was to cry tears hot with self-pity—for he wanted only one thing and it was denied him. The sound that emanated from him, however, was such that no one would have thought it crying, yet another verse of his foul hell song.

The next day the cattle began to fall down dead, certain as if pestilence had been unleashed among them. In the same manner they had taken over all that was his, he reasoned, surrounding his name and memory with silence, brought on by guilt fastened around their tongues when they thought of him.

He walked the shores of the lake and he named out all their names in the valley and hill country to show how intimately he knew them, but they too hid themselves from him, like Adam, instead of being as all the ones who would be lord before that who did say, naked and baldly, "I usurp Thee."

"What have we done?" Rose asked behind the door, thinking it punishment for some crime.

"We have done nothing," Adelia answered her. "The monster Lowe claims all and does its evil work, as it is wont."

"My father will kill it," Rose reasoned calmly.

Adelia smiled at her, and was eased a little in her worries by the girl's ignorant words. If man could face it she knew Caleum would, but he was not there and it was known the fiend he could not be defeated. The demon himself was first to know of the man's return, smelling him when he was still far off from Berkeley and did not yet know what had happened to his home. To give him fair warning, or because it was his nature and he could not control it, he started singing his hell song again, which curdled the blood of everyone in the country but especially those few with memory old enough to remember it from other days.

Caleum heard the noise from a distance and it did not frighten him, as he had heard sorrow songs before, belonging half to this world and half to other realms. Nor did he know where it was coming from, but only that something was different in the land he was traveling toward. That had been his lot for many years, however, as he rode toward the sundering of one thing from another, until he held very few illusions about anything anymore.

He reached instinctually for his sword, but it was not there, and he tried to remember where he last held it, but could not recall having it since his injury, though his hands themselves remembered wielding it. He felt a surge in his blood's pulse and asked the colt for more speed to return him home to Stonehouses. He did not fear the thing, whatever it was. On the contrary he felt pulled toward it. If it was his last labor before walking his own land and seeing his family again, he wanted it to arrive as soon as possible, so he might vanquish it and rest awhile. Nay, he did not know what it was.

The beast felt the man's progress and was placid. He was prepared for him long ago and would no more fall for his tricks and deception but rout him, as he should have before. He would have satisfaction and rest again in his rightful home.

When Caleum turned onto the road leading to Stonehouses his heart was buoyant and radiant, but he felt the cut of sadness as he approached the main house and saw it reduced by fire. He walked around and looked in the cold ashes, wondering what had happened there, before getting back on his mount and heading to his and Libbie's place.

On the path on the shore of the lake his blood came to a dead stop as he saw the most fearsome and cruel giant he ever beheld in all his journeys and all his days. He remembered when he was younger and had been told the legend of the monster buried in the lake. Whether it was called Ould Lowe or else Old Love he could not properly remember, but it was only legend, and this thing before him was howling real and intent solely on his destruction. He stopped his horse and tried to think of how he would battle it, when the beast saw him and called.

t e n

A blanket of densest snow covered the hills, and fog filled the valley that morning like smoke blown into a goblet of water. Miniature islands of ice floated out in the center of the springtime lake, cresting and ebbing with whatever wind was passing, like a ragtag army on the march to a new battle. All below him the people were still in their houses sleeping, without knowledge of the disturbance beyond their doors, so there was no witness to what passed that morning—and nothing but lore as it has come down, to tell of that struggle.

The man was still weary from his journey, and as the beast stood before him he looked out over his lands, down into the valley, and back at the path he had taken and thought how there was no road and no nation there at all when his ancestor first arrived, but a confederacy of valley and hills, and permanence in that place was only a freelance idea. Nor was there law or commerce, but an untouched and perfect peace such as would never exist again. There was little in the country that had not changed since the Titans' age, but what he wanted was much the same, and he would fight again to have it.

Ould Lowe stood balanced on his one leg and stared down at the man with godlike scorn. He did not need legs or arms or even fists to do his work in the world. He possessed the instrument of unyielding will, which made him permanent there.

"What is your business with me?" the man asked, looking back at him with much the same gaze.

The monster laughed and drew nearer, until he had taken hold of the horse's bridle. "It is for you to get down from your mount and square things."

Caleum nodded and stepped out of the stirrups, slowly leading the beast away from the horse, as he tried to remember all he had ever heard or read about the fiend.

"He was bigger, the first one," pronounced Lowe, who loomed two full heads above the man, after measuring him. "This will be easy work."

"Let us have at it," Caleum answered.

"You cannot overcome me," Lowe declared. "I am your history and religion."

"There are two views of the thing," the man answered him.

"Nay. There is a third."

"It is false."

"Who is to say but me?"

"There is much falseness that is believed."

"I am your master."

"Aye? Then there is much we must debate."

They fell upon each other then like two great khans, only one of whom could have ascendency there and no other arrangement possible.

The man did not know how strong the fiend truly was until it was upon him, and when the monster's hands reached him he knew at once it was stronger than anything he had known before.

The beast arched and circled like a snake, and began squeezing life from him with all the slowness of a game he was destined to win. He would let him breathe, then tighten his grip and begin withdrawing his breath again, wanting to relish his victory, wanting to feel all the man's strength leave him, until he cursed his days and that he ever walked the earth. He was like some primordial antecedent, demanding tribute that day, or else some taunting sphinx showing himself, then falling away, as the man struggled to understand what had been.

When Lowe let him draw breath again, he felt a surge of strength and was able finally to grasp hold of the beast and wrestle him to the ground in a great tangle of violence as they battled on in the snow.

The monster learned from that moment Caleum was no plaything but game for a contest, and each then directed his blows with all the more force, knowing he had no more room for error.

When the creature's anger fell on him again, the man felt each hard punch with a great clarity of pain that made him wince and nearly cry out. When he was able at last to retaliate he put an equal energy into the blows he delivered, which made the ogre grimace and recoil, but it would not release him.

Thus did they keep up their brawl through all the morning hours, before full light had come to fall on and wake the world. They were forming or else untying something there that could only be made in blood and darkness, and they were engaged in their terrible, boundless brawl through all those still early hours.

The man fought to keep what was his and already won and leave what was behind in the past. The beast fought for what was once its own, like an illimitable ancient passion.

He, the man, was not learned in magic, nor was he a giant, but he fought as he had to for his home, which was burned down, and the dwelling place of many accumulated sorrows now—but no less loved because of that—for it was not destructible. Neither by fire nor flood, or fissure in the earth, but existed in the spirit, and only the death of that could make him fall to the beast. As they clasped there, though, there came a time when all his strength did leave him. Sensing the nearness of his victory at last, Lowe picked him up, and threw him five full feet, so that Caleum was left flat on his back, unable to move.

Lowe was triumphant and came to finish him. However, as he knelt down to the man a strange gleam on the snow caught his attention, and he could not resist lifting it from the white field where it shone dazzling in the sun. He turned it over endlessly in his hand, mesmerized, wondering what sort of strange new food it was.

It was only when he was caught in this state that the man was able to recover and encircle the monster with a length of chain he took from his traveling trunk.

Lowe, when he felt himself bound again, let out a long morbid call that distressed all who were still sleeping, as they felt a mute unutterable sadness in their dreams.

The man opened his purse and took out another of the coins and threw it into the center of the lake. The fiend Lowe struggled to go after it, forgetting about the man momentarily. The man then fastened a rock from the shore of the lake to the beast's new chain and dragged him down into the water, where he was able to do with Lowe as he pleased. When he dove below the final time, he secured Lowe to another stone on the bottom of the lake bed and lifted another over him. He let Lowe keep his spoils.

He resurfaced after a very long time spent submerged in the beast's den, empty and trembling from what had passed, feeling as though he had journeyed through all the halls of the dead. It seemed like some strange dream as he made his way around the lake after that and continued on toward his home. It was no dream, but the wages he paid that morning to reach his front door.

Inside he saw Libbie and Rose curled up on the couch, where they had fallen asleep the night before. On the floor in front of them was a piece of fabric Libbie had been sewing, and when he knelt to pick it up he could not tell what she was making, as part of the thread had been pulled out, leading to a bundle under the sofa, and only the outline of what she was creating remained.

He touched both of them gently without waking either, then went and sat on the other side of the room, waiting until the house stirred from slumber of its own accord.

Adelia woke first, and, as she moved through the rooms, she let out a great sound of joy. She was grown very old and frail, and Caleum was careful when he embraced her that he should not be as forceful as he wanted, though he was transported to see her and held her fast, as if sensing she was all that remained of his ancient past.

Their reunion stirred the rest of the house, and soon the others were all awake and standing near him. No one commented on his injury then, or on the turmoil the house had been cast into, but he could tell there must be much to relate.

When he asked after his Uncle Magnus, Adelia only answered that he was in the far field where they would all end up some day.

"Yes we will," he said, with a feeling of only slightly tarnished happiness. "All of us."

He asked next how their stores had held up, for he could see it had been another hard winter for them there on the land. Libbie answered, saying they had lost much, and that it had been terrible indeed not knowing whether he would return or not, but that he was there now and they could bid farewell to strife.

The others they did not say anything, but waited for him to answer. "Well, it is spring soon, and as long as there is a single mule left to us we'll rebuild it all even greater than before."

"It has been an awful winter," Libbie said again, pressing close to him. "But we did not despair too much."

"I knew you would come," Rose said, not able to constrain herself anymore, as Lucky only played around his feet.

"Aye. I wanted to be here sooner," he said, then looked again to her to whom he first pledged his love and to whom it belonged.

He had not yet surveyed all his lands but knew there would be much to be attended to as soon as the weather allowed him. As for his leg, it would be more difficult but not impossible—or even so hard as other springs had been out there—and he knew that as long as he did not fall into self-sorrow he would be able to face it. That was the way life was with them out there, and he knew he could either accept his rightful challenge or else let the wilderness reclaim everything. Though that was not an option for him or any of them at Stonehouses that morning, because the maidens of that country, as has long been told, were famous as wives, and the men of that land were all worthy, if sometimes fallible, husbands.

What kept them all pushing up against that wilderness year after year, other than an oxlike fortitude of the heart, he could not say. It was not fear of annihilation, or even any longer that there was no other place for them. He knew by then there were many others, but for Stonehouses there was only one such place in all America.

He did not know whether he could be bold in his time of leading it, as Jasper Merian had been, or shrewd as Magnus Merian, but he would take his challenge as it was given him, because it was his now and he had no fear of that. They would begin rebuilding as soon as the weather gave way and he had mourned his father who had died.

"See how peaceful it looks," he said to Rose and Lucky, looking outside the window at the snow still falling down in the valley, feeling that the world was fixed again and knowable. "If we keep faith in what it is and who we are, it will never demand of us more than we can bear." It is what he had always been told, and he saw now he had no choice but to believe that, because he had wandered through the world and knew that morning, as all his battles began to recede into memory, that these were his blessings and what he had fought for, and they were glorious. And this was the only home he had, and it was the only one he would ever have and the only one he ever wanted. It was morning then in the world, and it was the morning of his life. In his own country.

The girls stood there with him looking out the window, across the hills, on the other side of the lake, and Libbie came and touched a hand to his shoulder, as Adelia went out to prepare breakfast. They were together again as was always meant to be.

Beneath the surface of the lake Old Lowe, if that be his true name, wailed with grief in his den and began working anew at his chains, but he was fastened tight to the bottom on the lake bed. In time he would stop all protestation—knowing he had been vanquished again in fair contest.

He would rest then, near silent, almost a hundred years.